BY WAY OF DECEPTION

Center Point
Large Print

Also by Amir Tsarfati and available from Center Point Large Print:

Operation Joktan

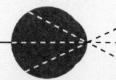

This Large Print Book carries the Seal of Approval of N.A.V.H.

BY WAY OF DECEPTION

—A NIR TAVOR MOSSAD THRILLER—

AMIR TSARFATI
AND STEVE YOHN

CENTER POINT LARGE PRINT
THORNDIKE, MAINE

AMIR DEDICATES THIS BOOK TO . . .

God, all-powerful and ever-present. This past year You have shown me that no matter the trial, You are always there.

My father-in-law, Hanan Lokes, a pastor, a father, a friend, and a brother. You were a true patriarch who led this family in our pursuit of God's truth. You read online with Mike and me the verse from Psalm 116, "Precious in the sight of the LORD is the death of His saints" (verse 15). Two days later, you passed into the arms of the Savior. You are loved and you are missed, and we anticipate the day we will reunite with you in the presence of our God. For now, we hold tight to the hopeful assurance of Romans 8:28 that "all things work together for good to those who love God, to those who are the called according to His purpose."

STEVE DEDICATES THIS BOOK TO . . .

The Almighty Creator and Sustainer of all things. Your beauty, creativity, truth, and humor are the muses that feed my passion to put words to paper.

Madeline, your joy at life lifts me, your beauty overwhelms me, your passion to educate challenges me, your laser wit ensures that I never get away with anything. You are the greatest gift God has given to your mother and me. You are my light, my Liora.

ACKNOWLEDGMENTS

God, You are faithful. You have taken this idea for a fiction series to places we never imagined it would go. We are humbled and grateful.

Amir thanks his wife, Miriam; his four children; and his daughter-in-law. Steve thanks his wife, Nancy, and his daughter. You are what gives us strength to fulfill the calling God has placed upon us. Thank you for your many sacrifices.

Thank you so much to the Behold Israel team— Mike, H.T. and Tara, Gale and Florene, Donalee, Joanne, Nick and Tina, Jason, Abigail, and Kayo. It is your tireless work that ensures that the gears of Behold Israel keep turning. We are so blessed to have you serving alongside us.

Thanks to Salina Kimberly Etrusco for your artistic wisdom. Thank you to Jason Elam Jr. and Ryan Miller for your military and weapons expertise. Big thanks to Maayan Tsarfati for her assistance with Hebrew slang. Thank you, Jean Kavich Bloom, for your editing work. Finally, we are so grateful to Bob Hawkins Jr., Kim Moore, Steve and Becky Miller, and the whole Harvest House team. You have become part of our family, and we are thankful to be partnered with you.

"If the man constitutes a capability that endangers the citizens of Israel, he must stop existing."

**YOSSI COHEN,
FORMER HEAD OF THE MOSSAD
(2006–2021)**

"The dirtiest actions should be carried out by the most honest men."

**MEIR DAGAN,
FORMER HEAD OF THE MOSSAD (2002–2011)**

בתחבולות תעשה לך מלחמה
"By way of deception, Thou shalt do war."

**FORMER MOSSAD MOTTO
(PROVERBS 24:6)**

CHARACTER LIST

ISRAELIS

Zakai Abelman – Kidon team leader
Dima "Drago" Aronov – Kidon agent
Omer Azoulai – head of Shayetet 13 team
Lavie Bensoussan – Kidon team leader
Malka Bieler – ramsad's executive assistant
Efraim Cohen – assistant deputy director of
    Caesarea
Ravid Efrat – Kidon team leader
Irin Ehrlich – Kidon team leader
Yaron Eisenbach – Kidon agent
Karin Friedman – assistant deputy director of
    Mossad
Oren Geller – prime minister
Yossi Hirschfield – Mossad analyst
Ira Katz – ramsad (head of Mossad)
Doron Mizrahi – Kidon agent
Avigdor Neeman – former Kidon agent
Asher Porush – deputy director of Mossad
Liora Regev – Mossad analyst
Dafna Ronen – Mossad analyst
Lahav Tabib – Mossad analyst
Nir Tavor – Kidon team leader
Yoram Tzadik – Mossad agent-in-charge of
    Operation Deep Sleep
Imri Zaid – Kidon agent

SOUTH AFRICAN

Nicole le Roux – Mossad agent

SAUDI

Ali Kamal – member of Saudi royal family
Saad Salim – owner/CEO of ASEnergy

AZERBAIJANI

Elnur Isayev – former assistant deputy head of
the Azerbaijani Foreign Intelligence Service

IRANIAN

Lieutenant Asadi – member NAJA
Dr. Mohsen Fakhrizadeh – head of the
Organization of Defensive Innovation and
Research (S.P.N.D.) and "Father of the
Iranian Bomb"
Dr. Ghasemi – IRGC specialist
Officer Kazemi – member of the Traffic
Police of the General Command of the Law
Enforcement of the Islamic Republic of Iran
(NAJA)
General Arash Mousavi – head of the
Intelligence Division of the Quds Force
of the Islamic Revolutionary Guard Corps
(IRGC)

AMERICAN

First Lieutenant Caitlin Bader – USMC
helicopter pilot

Lily Cohen – Tommy Cohen's daughter
Tomaso "Tommy" Cohen – security guard
Alicia Marcos – artist
Captain J.J. Marks – USMC helicopter pilot

BELGIAN

Mila Wooters – executive assistant at Yael
 Diamonds

GERMAN

Dr. Horst Lindner – nuclear physicist

FEBRUARY 2018

CHAPTER 1

MOSSAD SAFE HOUSE, ASTARA, AZERBAIJAN— FEBRUARY 1, 2018—06:40 / 6:40 A.M. AST

Y ou look like someone stole your wife, Tavor," Elnur Isayev said in his stilted English. "Are you not pleased with the progress?"

Only a thin line separates pessimism from realism, which is particularly true for the Jews. Life had made a habit of unexpectedly rising and punching them in the mouth. And that was why, Nir realized, he was preparing for a taste of life's fist even though Operation Deep Sleep had thus far advanced remarkably well.

Without looking at the former assistant deputy head of the Azerbaijani Foreign Intelligence Service, Nir replied, "She's not safe yet." Then catching his slip, "We still have a lot of sheep out there among the wolves."

"Ah, but it seems you are most concerned over one little lamb."

Nir turned to see a grin beneath the man's thick gray mustache. He wanted to poke back at the jab, but Isayev was absolutely right. He was anxious about the safety of each of the 20 players out on this operation's pitch, but worry about the fate of a particular one kept him pacing the cement floor of this safe house.

And why should Isayev's detecting his concern for Nicole stop him from what he wanted to do next?

"Call up Julia," he said to one of the four Mossad techs sitting in front of a computer station in the center of the open, low-ceilinged room. The man glanced at Yoram Tzadik, the agent in charge of the operation. Tzadik nodded his approval. Then after a series of keystrokes, a headset was handed to Nir, and he slid it on.

He leaned forward on his fists, resting them on the table in front of him, and waited.

"Julia," said a smoky, South African-accented voice, using one of the legend names for this operation. That one word was all it took for Nir to breathe a sigh of relief. Although Nicole le Roux was only 400 kilometers away, that distance was entirely in the Islamic Republic of Iran. She might as well have been on the other side of the world.

"Julia, Matt. Checking in."

"So far, so good. Looking forward to a nice hot bath and a good stiff drink."

"I'm guessing you'll have better luck with the first than the second. Take care of yourself. Out."

Nir pulled off the headset and handed it back to the tech, giving the young man a grateful tap on the back as he did so. Then with a twist of his wrist, he calculated the time difference between what he read on his G-Shock watch and Nicole's

16

probable ETA at the pickup point. At least her safety was now measured in hours rather than days.

For the first time that morning, he sat down.

Although he and Nicole lived in two different European countries, each leading a busy life, they found time to connect. Sometimes she visited him in Belgium. Often, he found an excuse to carry out business for his Antwerp-based diamond company near one of her photo-shoot locales. Or he'd visit her in Milan, her home when she could be there. Somehow their eight-year relationship seemed to be working—though on paper, it shouldn't be.

He was even starting to wonder if this South African, full-time model and part-time Mossad computer hacker could be "the one."

And that was why he hadn't wanted her to be part of this operation. It was too dangerous. Nicole wasn't an operative. She'd never even shot a gun outside of a firing range. The closest she'd ever come to any sort of danger was as a target in a gun battle in South Africa before she was even part of the Mossad. Putting her in-country like this without any kind of ops experience could get her imprisoned or even killed. He had tried to persuade Tzadik to remove her from the operation. When that didn't work, he'd yelled and cursed at the man. Finally, his superior had thrown him out of his office, threatening to pull him from the operation if he couldn't control himself.

Besides, he'd kept running up against the wall that told him Nicole's being a part of their team made perfect sense. She wasn't an Israeli, and her tech skills were essential for the success of the plan. But she was in Iran, the den filled with the most vicious of lions. There were so many what-ifs, and each one led to an even nastier conclusion than the last. As it turned out, though, his fears had been unfounded—so far.

Realizing his only caloric intake since last night had been a cup of sweetened coffee now and then, Nir reached into one of his cargo pants pockets and pulled out a PowerBar. Although it was 11 degrees Celsius and rainy outside—and not all that warm in the safe house either—the bar was soft from his body heat. He took a bite, closed his eyes, and breathed deeply.

Twenty minutes later, any serenity he'd achieved disappeared in an instant. Life had indeed swung its fist and delivered a direct hit.

CHAPTER 2

EIGHT HOURS EARLIER
TEHRAN, IRAN—JANUARY 31, 2018—
22:15 / 10:15 P.M. IRST

Nicole shivered as she slipped the gloves off her hands. It was below freezing outside, and the van's metal shell wasn't doing much to keep out the cold. Unfortunately, running the engine for the heater would draw undue attention, so she had to depend on layers of clothing and body fat to keep her core temperature up. She was wearing plenty of the former, but she was sorely lacking in the latter.

Holding her bare hands against the bay of computers in front of her, she soaked in the meager warmth they emitted.

Three others sat in the van—the driver and two techs, all men. One tech oversaw communications. The second, the only other English-speaker in the vehicle, monitored the picture from a small camera placed across the street from the target warehouse. A fifth member of their team in this secluded location was standing in the shadows outside, making sure no one happened to stumble over the thin wires that connected the van to the security system of the building next to them.

Their target's alarm system wouldn't be difficult for her to hack, but because it was connected into a closed system, it couldn't be accessed from the outside. The internet was no use, nor were phone lines. The only way to get control was to go to the building itself or to one of the four other government-owned structures that were part of the same security loop. And it was for this reason that Nicole found herself in an Iran Khodro Diesel van icebox with these three Azerbaijani Mossad agents in the suburbs of Tehran.

"Okay, Julia, roll the dice."

Immediately upon hearing Tzadik's order over her headset, Nicole began typing on her keyboard. This was her cue to shut down the alarm to the warehouse. Her fingers ached from the cold, but they warmed as they flew.

"Seven," she called when the job was done. Although the alarm was now disengaged, to anyone monitoring the system, it would appear fully armed—as normal.

"Okay. Gather your chips," Tzadik said.

With a few more keystrokes, Nicole tapped into the warehouse's internal cameras and began recording. As she watched her monitors, she once again shook her head at the audaciousness of what the Mossad was about to attempt. Only the Israelis would try to pull off a heist this daring. But when Nir explained the purpose of the operation to her, it made perfect sense.

She'd been home in Milan when he called to tell her he was coming to discuss Mossad business. That was unusual. Normally, her contacts from the Mossad came through encrypted emails, and only rarely did she and Nir work together—at least on this kind of business. He arrived with a bottle of wine and a bag of fresh prawns. Then later that evening, with their stomachs full and the wine bottle empty, the two leaned back on her plush linen sectional, Nicole tucking herself under Nir's arm.

"So what brings you here, Agent?"

"Your beauty drew me like honey draws a bee," Nir said with a stunningly poor French accent.

Nicole laughed and slapped his chest. "That was awful."

"Yeah, not my best."

Turning her body toward him and looking up, she said, "What best? There is no best. I've told you before—you have absolutely no game."

Nir took the moment to kiss her forehead. "You are one hundred percent correct. I am utterly gameless."

Nicole slipped back into Nir's side. "What does that say about me? I got won over by a gameless man."

It was Nir's turn to laugh. "Desperate people do desperate things. But seriously, you're right. I am here as Agent Tavor."

"What's my next mission should I choose to accept it, Agent Tavor?"

Nir sighed deeply and then remained quiet for a few moments. Nicole remembered running her hand up and down the contours and ridges of his arm as she waited.

Finally, he'd said, "First, you should know I fought against your being part of this operation. I understand why the team leader—Tzadik— wants you. You're just too darn good. But I don't like the risk." He sighed. "I made my case. He disagreed. I'm here."

"I don't need your protection, Nir Tavor," Nicole said with an edge in her voice.

"I know, I know. Duly noted. Just hear me out before you get too angry."

"Okay, go on. I'm intrigued."

"Okay," he began. "Here's the background. In 2015, Iran signed the JCPOA nuclear deal, opening them up to various inspections. The problem for them? They'd been secretly working on their nuclear program for years."

"Probably the worst-kept secret ever."

"True, but no one had the goods to nail them. Now if these inspectors discovered all the written materials documenting their work, our Persian friends would be in quite a *balagan*."

"A what?"

"Sorry. A mess. Their hands would be in the cookie jar, right? That's how you say it?"

"Close enough."

"So they decided to hide all the evidence."

"Makes sense. Shouldn't be too hard to do given the size of the country."

Nir had given a short laugh at that. "Agreed, but here's where it gets weird. Rather than dig a big hole for an underground vault out somewhere in East Camel Flop Province, they decided to use a regular warehouse in a commercial district in Tehran. They installed a bunch of vaults there, and then in early 2016 they started transferring load after load of their nuclear secrets into them. They thought they were being sneaky, but we've had cameras on this warehouse from the moment they first started moving it all in."

Nicole had tried to picture the scene in her head. "So what are we looking to do? The place has to be fortified like it's the national treasury. Walls, guards, state-of-the-art security system . . ."

Again, Nir laughed, and she could feel the movement of his head shaking. "That's the thing. It's not. It's like they thought they were so sly and tricky that nobody would have a clue that quite literally tons of nuclear secrets sit in that warehouse. They put in a good alarm system, and they have guards there during the day. But at nine o'clock at night, the guards shut everything down and go home, leaving the building one hundred percent unattended."

That's when Nicole sat up and scooted to the

next cushion so she could see Nir more clearly. "You have got to be joking."

"I know. It's mind-blowing." He feigned a small explosion from his forehead. "Your country's greatest secrets, and you walk away each night, saying, 'Oh, they'll be just fine.' "

"So is that the operation? Break in and photograph all the materials?" She'd crisscrossed her legs on the couch and tucked a small pillow onto her lap. She was starting to piece together what her role in the action might be.

"Not exactly. The Mossad head has been in the game for decades, and he knows the Iranians well. If we just took photos, Tehran would say we faked them, and the UN would undoubtedly jump to their side. So the *ramsad*—with the prime minister's approval, of course—has decided we'll break into the vaults, steal it all, and take it back to Israel. Hard to argue against hundreds of binders filled with Iranian secrets."

Nicole sat stunned. "They're going to steal it— all of it."

"Yep."

"And then haul it two thousand kilometers back to Israel."

Nir laughed. "I know." He'd leaned forward and tilted the wine bottle over Nicole's glass. But when nothing came out, he placed the bottle back on the coffee table in front of them and settled into the couch.

"It's called Operation Deep Sleep. At the end of January, we'll disable their alarm system, override their security cameras, and send a team in to steal the contents of thirty-two vaults, all in under seven hours."

Nir's mood changed, and he again let out a deep sigh. "Nicole, they want you to be the lead tech. That means going on the ground in Iran. They can't use any Israeli agents because it will be an international incident and a death sentence if we get caught. The team in-country will be made up of Azerbaijanis who live in Iran but work for us. They're loyal and good at what they do, but . . ."

"But none of them do what I do." A feeling in her stomach wavered between excitement and fear.

"I can't stress enough how important this mission is. Iran is racing toward a nuclear bomb. Once they get it, two things will happen. First, they'll have much more influence on the world stage. When you can dangle a nuke over people's heads, you're in a much stronger bargaining position. Second, the risk of Israel's annihilation increases exponentially."

"Do you think they would really use it if they had it?"

"Maybe, maybe not with this regime. But who knows who's coming in next? It's not like Iran has a track record of increasing sanity in their leadership. Besides, I'm more concerned with their putting a nuke into the hands of one of their proxy militias, like Hezbollah. With this solid information, though, we can prove to the world that despite their protests of innocence, Iran truly is racing toward possession of a nuclear bomb."

That dinner had been six weeks ago. Now here she was sitting in a freezing van with stage one of the operation complete—the alarm system disarmed. Stage two, the recording of video, was underway.

Nicole took a deep breath to tamp down her anxiety. It was times like this that she wished she had some god or higher power she could rely on. Just someone or something that would watch over her to make sure she was all right. But that wasn't the way she was raised. *Toughen up, girl. Between you and that guy on the other side of the border, you'll be okay.*

The more Nir had explained the plan to her that night, the more it reminded her of a movie she'd seen with her twin brother when they were kids—*Ocean's Eleven.* A group of con artists led by Danny Ocean, played by George Clooney, break into the vault of a Las Vegas casino. Nir hadn't seen the film, so they'd streamed it.

Nir loved the comparison, as had Tzadik when Nir passed it on. Soon it became the lexicon from which the operators drew their legend names and the planners identified the steps of the operation. Tzadik became George Clooney, and the team's number two man was Brad Pitt. Nir had to settle for Matt Damon's stuffy character for his *nom de guerre*. Technically, Nicole should have been Eddie Jemison after the *Ocean's Eleven* tech geek, but Tzadik had been kind enough to christen her Julia Roberts instead.

If all goes well in this *movie, Matt Damon's going to get the girl and George Clooney will go home alone,* Nicole thought with a smile as she monitored the static recording.

A voice broke through her musings. "Julia, George. Cash in your chips."

"Cashing in," she replied as she took her fingers away from her mouth. She'd been blowing on them. After just five seconds of keyboard work, the series of security feeds on her top monitor glitched almost imperceptibly. For the next six hours and 29 minutes, this video of an empty warehouse would loop every five minutes.

"Jackpot," she said into her microphone, confirming that her work was done. Suddenly, her coms were filled with a flurry of words she couldn't understand but knew were a mixture of Azeri and Farsi. Twisting open a thermos, Nicole poured herself some hot chai and settled in. For the rest of the night her job was twofold. First, to avoid freezing, and second, to ensure that all the activity about to take place in the live lower monitor didn't find its way into the looping video streams displayed in the monitor above.

CHAPTER 3

hy do the Iranians have to make everything so difficult? Nir thought as he watched the minutes count down.

Although the coastal town he was in sat northwest of Tehran, the time here was 30 minutes later. While everyone else in this global time zone slice added four hours to Greenwich Mean Time, the Persians had decided to add only three and a half. The way it was explained to him, long ago someone had noticed their nation was divided between two time zones and decided they'd split the difference.

It's a good thing they hadn't lived in Russia. Who knows what they would have done with that country's eleven time zones?

Overall, a lot more important reasons to dislike Iran were at play, but this one certainly was a pain when trying to plan an operation that had to be timed to the exact minute.

In the next room Nir had a team of six Kidon agents. He was confident that if he needed them in action, they would get the job done. In the hierarchy of lethality in Israeli intelligence, Nir knew that the Mossad is the spear. On the end of that spear is the sharp, iron head of Caesarea, and at the end of the spear's head is the nasty little tip of Kidon. The name itself meant "tip of the spear," and when a target needed to be eliminated or an operation had to be swiftly and silently executed, Kidon regularly got the call. But as ready as he and his team were for action, Nir hoped they would have a boring night.

First, as an Israeli, he had no interest in crossing the border into Iran. But second, if he and his team were called, that meant the operation was collapsing and Nicole was in serious danger.

Still, you hope for the best and plan for the worst. So before he'd walked into this main room, he'd checked all his weapons and gear. And he knew that even as the operation was progressing, his number two man, Yaron Eisenbach, would be rechecking everything just to make sure Nir hadn't missed anything.

A hush filled the room when the digital wall clock reached 22:59. The tension was heavy, and the anticipation was almost overwhelming. When the numbers transformed to 23:00, the room erupted in voices, most of them speaking Hebrew-accented Azeri into communications headsets. Nir pressed a button on his watch to start the timer.

On cue, a box truck appeared on the camera

feed of the warehouse's courtyard. The rear gate was gently dropped, and operators began to jump out. They were all dressed fully in black and wore odd-shaped helmets. While most of the men unloaded equipment, two of them ran to the large faded blue doors and started working on the lock. Nir tensed as he watched this part, hoping Nicole had been able to do her job with the alarm. A gap opened between the doors, and they were slid to the sides.

There was no panic, no running back to the truck. The alarm was off.

"She is good." Elnur Isayev pointed to the monitor, then lit the cigarette dangling from his mouth. It smelled of the strong, harsh tobacco that filled the coffee shops he'd visited in Turkey, and Nir held his breath for a moment.

I wonder how many years of smoke are trapped in that oversized mustache. His wife must have no sense of smell.

As the last of the men ran in with the equipment, the rear gate to the truck was closed, and it pulled away. According to the plan, the driver would park in a lot four blocks away to await the time for pickup.

Once again, Nir checked his watch. It had taken only four minutes to get the team inside. That was good, because this group of Persian-hating Azerbaijanis had only six hours and 29 minutes before they had to be loaded up and on the road.

The time 6:29 had become completely familiar to everyone who was part of this operation. It was drilled into the operators as they worked their dry runs, and every meeting had ended with each person present calling it out. Six hours and 30 minutes? Too dangerous. The team would be in danger of being caught. Six hours and 28 minutes? That would be a minute wasted when more materials could have been removed. As it was, they'd already determined that emptying all 32 vaults wouldn't happen in one night.

At 4:59 a.m. Tehran time, the trucks had to be rolling out of the gates. That would allow them two hours to get away, two hours' worth of highway to help disappear into anonymity. When the guards arrived back at the warehouse at 7:00 a.m., discovered the damaged front doors, and sounded the alarm, this Mossad version of Danny Ocean's team had to be well into the wind.

Now the team approached the doors to a long narrow room. The intel said the entrance to this structure within the structure had no separate alarm, a fact that once again amazed Nir. *These are your nuclear secrets! You might as well have left the front doors open with a plate of falafel next to a guest book and a sign reading "Feel free to help yourselves."*

One of the operatives tried to force the door open, but it didn't move. A second man worked on it while the first man checked the hinges. After a couple minutes of struggle, both men stepped back.

"The door is reinforced," came a voice speaking heavily accented English through the com system.

"Can you remove the hinges?" asked Tzadik.

The two men looked directly into the security camera mounted above the warehouse entrance. "Negative," one of them said. "They're fully enclosed in steel. We can torch it open, but it will cost us much time."

Tzadik cursed. The existence of a reinforced door had not been included in the intel.

"They've got to blow it," Nir told him. "They carried charges with them in case there was a problem."

"I was really hoping not to use those. Making that much noise is a huge risk."

Tzadik was right, but it was a risk they had to take.

"*Ha'mefaked*," the second operative said, "we could lose five or six vaults in the time it will take to torch open that door."

Tzadik repeated his earlier curse. "Yeah, I know. Okay, apply the charges and send someone out to the front gate to check the road. He needs to give you an all clear before you blow the door."

In a rush of activity, a couple of packs were opened and several lines of malleable explosive were attached to the door. Meanwhile, Nir watched one of the team sprint across the courtyard of the warehouse toward the gate.

When everything was ready and the man at the fence gave the all clear, the rest of the team tucked themselves away from the blast radius. Blinding light filled the screen, making Nir wish he'd thought to look away. Once he could see clearly again, the picture, now at a severe angle, showed an open path into the vault room.

Nir shifted his gaze to another camera view, and a light showing a long, tight room switched on. Against either wall was vault after vault— large, gray, Iranian-made, and each with a wide, black-numbered dial set into it.

It would take forever to try to crack the combinations, and they'd never had an ample supply of time. So they had decided to do away with subtle.

The team broke into seven pairs while, on Tzadik's order, the man at the fence remained in his position. The same inside source who'd told them about the non-alarmed door had diagrammed which vaults contained the most valuable information.

Each pair moved to their designated target, fired up a torch, and flipped down the front of the welding helmets perched on their heads. Although the torches burned at 2,000 degrees Celsius, the doors were thick enough that they

33

took a long time to cut through. The flares made the video feed difficult to watch, and Nir soon found his vision filled with blue dots of various sizes and intensity.

Walking away to give his eyes a break, he moved into the next room and gave his Kidon team a quick update. Then closing the door as he left, he decided to pour himself a cup of coffee. But the pot was empty, and the plate once filled with pastries now held only crumbs. Both thirsty and hungry, he returned to watch the monitors.

"We have headlights," whispered a voice through the coms.

Nir quickly turned toward the screens.

"Everybody, stop your work," Tzadik demanded.

Nir watched as all activity in the vault room halted and every torch was extinguished. Hopefully, someone just happened to be innocently driving by. But this could also be a police car with officers sent to check out the loud noise someone reported.

The view from the security camera across the street from the warehouse wasn't wide enough to show anything yet, and Nir caught himself holding his breath again.

Then an arc of light slowly spread into the picture, followed by the hood of a white car. The car's cab entered the screen next, including a bar of lights attached to its roof. Even though they were 400 kilometers away, no one in the safe house moved or said a word.

Finally, the red taillights passed the camera, and the car was gone.

Tzadik waited a full five minutes before he said, "Okay, back to work. You've got time to make up." Then to the man outside, "Keep your eyes open at the gate."

Because of the narrowness of the space, it would be impractical to empty contents as each vault was opened. So as soon as one was breached, that team moved on to the next on their list. The men were efficient and very good at what they did. Even though it was winter, Nir could only imagine how hot it must be in that narrow room.

It took more than five hours of the six hours and 29 minutes to breach all the selected vaults. Then the unloading began. Stack after stack of binders—most of them black—were piled on the floor near the front doors. Nearby, towers of CDs began to grow.

When the operation clock hit six hours, the box truck returned to the courtyard and backed up to the building, followed by two more. Four cars pulled into the carport on the right side of the property. The warehouse's metal doors slid open, and the loading began.

Nir's anxiety ticked up. They were out in the open, and all they needed to get caught was another policeman in a cruiser or soldiers in an IRGC jeep or just someone who worked in a neighboring warehouse to drive by and get suspicious.

"Matt," called Tzadik.

Nir turned to see his team lead pointing at him. He followed his finger and realized he'd been nervously tapping a pen on the table in front of him—a habit hard to break. Tossing the pen aside, he stepped back from the temptation.

The haul was divided between the three trucks, and then their cargo doors were shut tight and locked. One team member walked around to the passenger side of each truck and climbed in. After the warehouse doors were closed, the rest of the team hurried to the cars in the carport and loaded up. Then one by one, the vehicles left the courtyard.

When the final truck cleared the gate, Nir pressed a button on his watch to stop the timer—6:29.

Cheers erupted throughout the safe house. Nir spotted Yaron poking his head into the room, and he gave the man a thumbs-up. This had been an immaculate operation.

But the elation Nir felt was muted. Nicole was still out there. Tonight had gone well—yet maybe too well. A shoe could still drop, and he just hoped if it did, it wouldn't land on the woman he was pretty sure he loved.

CHAPTER 4

CHALUS ROAD/ROUTE 59, IRAN— FEBRUARY 1, 2018—07:25 / 7:25 A.M. IRST

Nicole heard the window roll down part way and inwardly groaned. Although her eyes were closed and her head was back, she knew exactly what was happening in the front seat. Sure enough, she heard the *click-click-click* of the driver's lighter—always three clicks. Then the smoke from his cigarette wafted into the back seat. The partially opened window did more to clear the man's conscience than it did to clear the air.

It's your own fault, she mentally chastised herself. *He asked if you minded the first time. This is what you get for being too polite.*

Opening her eyes, she glanced at her watch. They were two hours outside of Tehran. Picturing the map she'd memorized, she determined they should be coming up on Marzanabad soon. From there it would be another half hour to Chalus, where she'd become just another visitor to the coastal town, in-country for a few-days photo shoot.

The adrenaline had begun to dissipate about an hour after the Tehran skyline disappeared from the back window. Shurabad, the suburb where the warehouse was located, was in the southern part of the capital. This meant a long drive through the heart of Tehran before she and her driver finally exited the city limits to the north and began their ascent into the mountains. The man, who'd introduced himself as Yusif, had been kind enough to leave a wool blanket in the back, and she'd made use of it the entire trip.

She still couldn't believe they'd pulled off that heist. When word had reached the van that all was done and they needed to wrap up, it was all she could do not to cry out in joy. Quickly and carefully, she'd detached the digital video playback machine from the bank of equipment, then unplugged it from the power knowing it had enough battery to provide six hours of continuous use.

The tech next to her had asked, "Is it ready to go?"

"It is."

She gave the device to him, and he carried it to the van's side door and passed it to the fifth member of the team. In the dim light from the van, Nicole watched as the man walked it to the building, then set it on the ground, making sure the wires were still secure. Then he covered it with a ratty tarp and a torn bag of garbage. No need to worry about the rigged alarm. It would continue to show itself armed until someone discovered the tampering.

It was quiet as they drove off, the communications guy at the wheel. Despite the victory they'd just achieved, Nicole had found it unsettling to still be in the heart of the beast. After a ten-minute journey, they pulled into the parking lot of an empty office building. Three cars waited. As soon as she stepped out, Yusif waved to her and then hustled her to his car. She slipped into the back seat, and off they went.

Now, two hours later, Nicole closed her eyes again. It would be wonderful if she could sleep, but her nerves would never allow her to completely shut down. Once she reached Chalus, she could take a nap in her hotel room before her afternoon photo shoot. As much as she would like to bail out on the shoot, it was important to maintain her cover as a model. This gig got her into Iran, and if she suddenly disappeared after this major act of espionage, someone might get suspicious.

Well, maybe not this first time, but if it ever became a habit . . . Smart people out there could add two and two together and get Mossad.

For perhaps the thousandth time, she marveled over how she had ended up working for the Mossad. Yet the facts never changed. She'd been 20, her only modeling experience local to Cape Town. Tall, olive-skinned, and with dark curly hair, full lips, and ice-blue eyes, she'd determined to use her looks to get out of the hometown that held so many bad childhood memories.

That was when the Israeli intelligence agency came knocking on her door. They weren't there because they were eager for her to do a photo spread for them. Her other pastime had brought them all the way down to South Africa. Nicole smiled as she remembered how terrified she was when they confronted her about hacking into the legendarily unhackable computers of the Mossad. She'd been sure they were about to bury her at sea.

But then they surprised her by presenting to her an offer she couldn't refuse. *Come use your incredible computer skills to work for Israeli intelligence . . . or else.* It was hard to say no to a proposition like that.

Not long after that, the Israelis set her up with an international modeling agency and a flat in Milan. Every now and then, they would call on her to use what she labeled her keyboard artistry to hack her way into a place that needed hacking into. And while at times modeling gigs were arranged to give her an excuse for entering a certain country or for being at a certain event, this was the first time she'd been sent into a dangerous situation.

It gets the adrenaline going. But now that I think about it, if I have a choice, I'll choose digitally breaking into places from the comfort of my flat in Milan or a nice hotel room. Anything like a freezing cold van in the middle of Tehran? No thanks.

As she sat there hoping for sleep, her mind went to Nir, as it often did. Their off-and-on romance was very much in one of the "on" stages. In fact, she'd been picking up signs that he might be getting ready to take their relationship to the next level—whatever that next level might be.

It was so good hearing his voice when he called through coms. Just knowing he was watching over my progress—

As if on cue, her phone rang. Maybe it was Nir again.

"This is Julia," she answered, trying to calm the excitement in her voice.

"Julia, Matt. Just checking in again. Everything good?" His baritone was soft and soothing.

"It is. We're making good time. I never knew Iran is such a beautiful place. These mountains are amazing."

"I'll probably have to take your word for it. Enjoy your drive. What's your ETA to Chalus?"

Nicole checked her watch again. "We're almost at Marzanabad, so I'm guessing it's—"

A loud exclamation from Yusif interrupted her train of thought. She noticed his eyes in the rearview mirror and turned around. A white car was trailing close behind them, a bar of lights on its roof.

She'd pulled the phone away from her ear, but

41

she could still hear Nir. "What is it? Julia, what's going on?"

Every fear she'd had leading up to this operation—every dream that awakened her at night—came flooding back.

Lifting the phone back to her ear, she said, "Matt, NAJA is behind us."

As though a switch had been flipped, the softness of Nir's voice hardened into flint. "Can you see what branch of NAJA? Is it the Prevention Police? The Traffic Police? The Border Guard?"

"I don't know. But it looks like maybe the Traffic Police."

Nicole could hear Nir shouting orders, but his hand must have been covering the mouthpiece because she couldn't make out the muffled words. "Okay, I was just assured by the agency who hired your driver that he's very good at what he does. He wouldn't have been breaking any traffic laws. It's likely that they'll tail you for a while, but then—"

"Matt. They've turned on the lights. We're pulling over."

CHAPTER 5

Yusif opened his door and stepped out as three officers surrounded him. Just minutes ago, as he stared into his rearview mirror and tapped a rapid beat on the steering wheel, two more cars arrived along the side of the road. Nicole had asked the man what was going on, but his limited English vocabulary only allowed him to respond, "No worry. No worry."

His words and his attitude didn't mesh.

"Describe their uniforms to me," Nir said over the phone.

"Black leather jackets. Dark blue pants. Black berets."

After another muffled conversation on the other end of the line, Nir said, "They're Traffic Police. Maybe they're just looking for a bribe."

The conversation between Yusif and the officers was getting heated, and one of the uniformed men pointed to her in the back seat. Yusif shifted his body, putting himself protectively between her and the men.

"It's getting loud," she said, trying to keep the worry out of her voice.

She shook her head, clearing it a little. *Nicole,*

you're an agent of the Mossad. You are not going to panic over some ridiculous little traffic misunderstanding.

But it was well past seven o'clock, and the vaults would certainly have been discovered by now.

"Julia," Nir said, "so far we are sevens and elevens. You understand? Sevens and elevens." He spoke as though he'd read her thoughts.

The tension in Nicole's shoulders eased a bit. Nir's words told her there was no massive response to the heist so far. No BOLO orders had been issued. No roadblocks set. Maybe the Iranians were still trying to figure out exactly what had taken place. But no doubt calm would give way to storm soon enough. She'd hoped to be all the way to Chalus by the time it all broke loose, but this delay made that goal seem less likely every minute.

In a move so fast Nicole nearly missed its happening, one of the officers pulled his baton and drove it into Yusif's abdomen. The man doubled over. Then a second blow to the back of his knees dropped him to the ground.

"They're beating Yusif!" Nicole cried.

"Brown! Brown!" Nir called out. The code word triggered a transition in the cover operation. Nir was no longer Matt, and Nicole was no longer Julia. She'd become exactly who she really was—a model named Nicole le Roux hired

44

to do a photo shoot at Namakabrud Beach just west of Chalus. Nir was Giovanni Gualtieri, the Italian agent who had hired her for this layout in *Grazia* magazine.

"Tell me what's happening, Nicole," Nir said with an Italian accent that was so bad it would have been funny in any other circumstance.

After delivering several kicks to Yusif, two of the officers dragged his body toward their vehicles. He looked lifeless.

The remaining policeman stood at the front of the car, staring at her through the windshield.

"Yusif appears to be unconscious now. They've pulled him to their cars," she said, relieved to be herself again. Locking eyes with the policeman, she widened hers and increased her breathing. Her hope was to garner some sympathy from the man by letting terror show in her face. But his expression remained impassive, and his dead eyes never blinked.

She startled as the door next to her opened, and the phone dropped from her hand as she whipped her head to the right. *Stupid,* she thought. *You were so focused on the man in front of you that you ignored the others.*

Two uniformed men pinned her with menacing stares of their own. Nir must have heard her involuntary cry when the door opened, because his voice was yelling from the phone on the seat.

One of the policemen leaned in and spoke rapidly in Farsi.

"I'm sorry. I don't know your language," Nicole said, trying to force a scared smile despite the assault of his body odor and fish breath.

The officer leaned closer and spoke again, this time louder and slower.

Nicole managed a nervous laugh. "I don't understand. I'm so sorry. Do any of you speak English?"

Another officer walked up and tapped Nicole's interrogator on the shoulder. He was the one who'd dropped Yusif to the ground. As he took the place of the other officer, she noticed rank insignias on his shoulders.

He growled something in Farsi.

Raising her arms in a helpless posture, she answered, "I'm sorry, sir. But as I was telling the other officer, I don't understand your language."

He repeated himself, by his tone increasing his threat.

Stay in control, she told herself. *Fight the panic. Be productive.*

"I'm sorry"—she stole a look at his chest—"Officer Kazemi, but I can't—"

He slapped her face. The act was obviously designed to get her attention. Not strong enough to cause her mouth to bleed but hard enough to make her cheek sting.

Tears welled in Nicole's eyes. She wished she

could say they came because she was playing the part of a scared model, but in this moment, she was in fact a scared model. Nir's angry voice sounded through the phone, and she desperately wished he was here with her.

But then, as Kazemi yelled at her, a new thought struck her. *I don't need Nir here to save me. I don't need anyone to save me. If I could survive a heroin-addicted mother and a drunk grandmother, I can survive this.*

Nicole's fear transformed into anger. The officer must have seen the change in her eyes, because he slapped her again—harder this time, knocking her back into the cushions.

Now she could taste blood in her mouth. She turned, looked straight into his eyes, and swung a fist with all her strength. Kazemi, however, saw the blow coming and blocked most of its force. Still, she'd connected partially with his chin, drawing a little blood with the ring on her index finger.

"And that was with my left hand, you goat-loving camel herder," she hissed.

He grabbed a handful of her hair and started dragging her out of the car. As she kicked and flailed, the words that came out of her mouth made it clear what she thought of him and his family heritage. She was out of control—as angry as she'd ever been.

He pulled her through the open doorway, and

she could hear the two other officers laughing. This made her even angrier.

When she was on her feet, Kazemi spun her toward the car. Then leaning all his weight on her, he pressed her against the cold metal. The other two officers each took a hand and twisted her arms behind her back, making her cry out at the pain. Kazemi cuffed her, clamping the metal tight against her wrists. Then he kicked her legs wide and began to frisk her far more thoroughly than indicated in any police manual.

She squirmed and tried to move, but he was too heavy.

Kazemi made a comment in her ear as he pressed himself tighter against her body. The other officers laughed again and joined in what was obviously crude banter. Nicole whipped her head back, feeling it connect with soft cartilage and hard bone. Kazemi stumbled backward, and Nicole spun around. Blood poured down the officer's face.

Nicole had time for one more curse before the man's fist connected with the side of her head. Then everything went black.

CHAPTER 6

MOSSAD SAFE HOUSE, ASTARA, AZERBAIJAN— 08:15 / 8:15 A.M. AST

W hy are you in Iran?" said the Mossad inter-preter.

Nir had been communicating to Nicole through a headset, but once she'd said the lights on the police car were flashing, his conversation was switched to the speakers in the safe house's control room. He closed his eyes as he once again leaned forward on his fists—only this time the knuckles on his balled-up hands were white as he listened.

"I'm sorry, sir. But as I was telling the other officer, I don't understand your language."

"She's doing well," Isayev said calmly, a slight tremor of his cigarette the only sign of nerves.

"Why are you in Iran?" the translator repeated.

"I'm sorry . . . Officer Kazemi, but I can't—"

It took a moment for Nir to recognize the sound he'd just heard.

Furious—any trace of an Italian accent gone— he yelled, "He hit her! Nicole! Nicole! Can you hear me? Nicole, are you okay?"

Turning to Tzadik, he repeated, "He hit her!"

"I know! Shut up so I can talk." Then turning

49

to a tech, the agent in charge said, "His name is Officer Kazemi. Find out who he is, where he's stationed, what division he's in, who his superiors are—everything."

Nir paced as he shouted, "Nicole! Nicole, can you hear me?"

Another slap, this one much louder, sounded throughout the room, immediately followed by a female's cry of pain. Nir slammed his fists on the table in front of him, causing a coffee cup to go momentarily airborne.

Rage filled him as he gripped the table's edges. The woman he believed he was in love with was being beaten 400 kilometers away, and all he could do was helplessly stand here and listen to it happening.

"Nicole! Say something!"

When she spoke next, he almost didn't recognize her voice because there was so much venom in it. "And that was with my left hand, you goat-loving camel herder."

Isayev cried, "Ha! Yes!"

But then the sounds of a struggle began, and a hush filled the room. Nir had always known a fury lived deep down inside Nicole, but this was the first time he'd heard it vented. It was obvious she was being dragged out of the car and was putting up a fight—physically and verbally.

A thud sounded, and Nir was certain they were pushing her up against the side of the car. He threw his headset to the floor and strode toward the room that held his Kidon team. Yaron was standing in the doorway listening, and the other guys were gathered behind him. The same intense determination Nir was certain showed in his eyes showed in theirs as well.

"Prepare your kits," he called.

"Tavor, stop!"

Nir turned to see Tzadik marching toward him.

"What do you think you're doing?"

"I'm going—"

"Shut up, you idiot! That wasn't a question." Tzadik was at least four inches shorter than Nir, but his bearing was such that Nir felt he was looking upward at his superior. "Am I to assume you are going to invade Iran, break into a police station, rescue your girl, and then ride off into the sunset?"

"Yes, that sounds—"

"Did I ask you a question? Did I?"

Nir was pretty sure that was exactly what he'd done repeatedly. But he had the good sense to not answer. Still, he looked hard into the other man's eyes.

Another thud echoed in the room, causing both men to instinctively turn toward the speakers. Nir had no clue what that was, but it sounded violent.

Tzadik's hand came down on Nir's shoulder, causing him to turn. "Follow me," the man said, leading Nir away from his team. "Listen, Tavor, le Roux is an agent of the Israeli Mossad, and she is in enemy hands. Do we ever abandon our people?"

"No, *Ha'mefaked.*"

"Tell me about Jordan in 1997."

"I understand," Nir replied, knowing the exact incident his commander meant.

"Tell me about Jordan," Tzadik said, insistent.

"Botched targeted killing of Khaled Mashaal. Two Mossad agents posing as Canadians were arrested. First, the *ramsad* flew to Amman to see King Hussein, and when that wasn't enough, Netanyahu himself flew to apologize to Hussein and plea for the agents' release."

Tzadik was nodding. "Exactly. Both the head of the Mossad and the head of the country got involved. And who did we eventually trade to get just two agents back?"

"Twenty Hamas prisoners initially and dozens more later."

"Including . . ."

"Including Sheikh Ahmed Yassin, a founder of Hamas, who was serving a life sentence for conspiring to kidnap IDF soldiers."

Tzadik was right. These stories had been drilled into Nir from the time he started his training with the Mossad. There was nothing the government wouldn't do to rescue someone being held for protecting the State of Israel.

"Exactly. We will get her out, son. A time when

guns are needed may come, but right now our most powerful weapon is the telephone. So get in there with your men. Talk them off the cliff. Get your gear ready in case you're needed, and let me do my job."

"Yes, *Ha'mefaked,*" Nir answered, though reluctantly.

He turned toward his Kidon team, but Tzadik's voice stopped him.

"By the way, what did we do to Yassin in 2004?"

"Dropped a missile on his scraggly head."

"Israel never forgets."

Tzadik turned away, and Nir watched the man go. He was right. It didn't matter where Nicole was born or whether it was Jew or Gentile blood running through her veins. If she was risking her life for the State of Israel, then the State of Israel would move heaven and earth to safely bring her home.

That assurance was all well and good for when that time came. But at this particular moment, Nicole was in Iran being roughed up by a bunch of dirties—and there was nothing he could do about it.

When he entered the next room, his Kidon team was still gearing up. They all turned when he walked in. Tzadik was a strong leader, but these were Nir's men. *All they need is a helicopter, and they'll raid the Ayatollah's house if they need to.*

He looked at each of them, letting them see the gravity of the situation in his stare. "Stand down," he said, then walked out.

Cries of protest erupted behind him. He understood their frustration and appreciated their desire to save Nicole, but it wasn't time yet, and he didn't have the motivation to answer any of their questions.

"Yaron, fix it," he called back. Immediately, his second began barking out orders for the men to unpack their gear, recheck it, and then pack it again.

The coffeepot was now half full, so Nir poured himself a cup and dumped in a couple teaspoons of sugar for energy. He found a chair within eavesdropping distance of Tzadik and sat down, then took a sip of the sweet coffee, set the cup on the table, and promptly forgot all about it.

CHAPTER 7

POLICE STATION, MARZANABAD, IRAN—
08:05 / 8:05 A.M. IRST

Nicole woke. She shifted her body slightly, causing a metallic clatter. The first thing she noticed was the cold—bitter, permeating, reaching through flesh to touch her bones. Her shivering began immediately and increased in intensity until a hard exhalation involuntarily escaped her mouth in a thick cloud of condensation.

Taking a quick inventory, she realized her coat was gone, her boots were gone, and her socks were gone. Thankfully, they'd left her wearing her jeans and sweater. Looking at her hands, she saw that all her jewelry had been removed, including the ring that had put a little dent in Officer Kazemi's chin. Now she was sporting two shiny silver bracelets, each attached to a chain connected to the arms of the chair on which she sat. A quick movement of her bare feet let her know her body had four points of connection to her cold, metal perch.

Her head felt like someone with a wrench was torquing an invisible metal band around it. She probed the inside of her mouth with her tongue,

55

and the raw swelling let her know she would likely be chewing her food on the right side for the foreseeable future.

Your first in-country op in enemy territory, and what do you do? You assault a police officer.

But a part of her wasn't sorry for what she'd done. In modeling, you deal with a lot of piggy men—photographers, designers, and agents who let their hands "accidentally" brush or press or linger. So often, she'd wanted to do more than just stand there and take it. Several times she'd at least said something, angrily telling a guy what he could do with his wandering hands. But this was the first time she'd lashed out physically, and it felt good.

But now she'd pay for it.

Panic began to rise, but she quickly swallowed it. *Be smart. Be proactive. Know your surroundings.*

What would Nir do?

The room she was in was small, its only furnishings an old black metal chair with severely chipping paint and what she could only assume was a mate to her own. An unfruitful attempt to tip from side to side let her know the other chair had much more mobility than hers did.

She saw no windows, no mirrors, no cameras— only four walls desperately in need of a fresh coat of paint. But there was the cold. The room had plenty of that.

The door opened. Two officers walked in and took up positions in front of her, one in each corner of the room. A third uniformed man walked in behind them and closed the door. Even more than the stars on his shoulders, his attitude told Nicole he was the superior among the trio.

He stood behind the empty chair and stared at her. Nicole stared back until it became too awkward, then looked down at her hands. They were resting on her lap.

"My men and I are having a debate," he said, suddenly smiling.

Nicole quickly looked up again, surprised at hearing English.

"I say your name is pronounced le *Roo* like the French. They say it is le *Rucks*. But I believe that would be far too ugly a name for so beautiful a woman. I would be very grateful if you would settle the dispute."

"Your—" Her voice broke into a cough. She hadn't realized how dry her throat was. She continued hoarsely, "Your pronunciation is the correct one."

"Ha!" he cried. "Ignorant fools!" Turning to the other two, he spoke in Farsi. When she heard her name mentioned, the men scowled at her.

Returning his gaze to her, the man continued. "My name is Lieutenant Asadi, and I would like to thank you for increasing the contents of my wallet at the expense of my two officers. But

57

maybe you can help me more. We have another bet. We found some photographs of a Nicole le Roux on the internet. She looks a lot like you, but I say it can't be you. I can't believe someone who seems so modest in person could actually make her living dressing like a whore."

With that last word, everything in her mind shifted. All hope for a quick resolution was gone. This was bad, and it was only going to get worse. No one—not even Nir and his team of Kidon fighters—would be able to protect her from what was bound to come next. She didn't even know if they could save her at all.

Stepping forward, Asadi removed his phone from his pocket. He pressed several buttons, then held the screen in front of her. She recognized the photo immediately. It was from her modeling agency's portfolio. The bikini was quite spare, and the camera angle left little to the imagination. "Is this you, Miss le Roux?"

Nicole looked down once more and didn't answer.

Asadi's tone was firmer when he spoke again. "I asked you a question. Is this you?"

Without looking up, she nodded. "Yes."

"It is?" He looked at the screen for a moment, then turned and said something to the guards before swiping on his phone as he faced her again. "I must say I am surprised at you." He held up the phone again. "What about this one?"

The photo was from a lingerie shoot she'd done. She'd loved it because it had seemed so artsy. But now, seeing it on this man's screen, she felt dirty and ashamed.

"It's me."

Once again, Asadi said something to the guards, who both responded with obviously crude comments. "Tsk, tsk, tsk. Now I'm more than surprised at you, Miss le Roux. I'm shocked. I told my men it couldn't be you, but they were sure." He laughed. "I must say, they really love this picture. In fact, I think Officer Taheri over there has made it the new wallpaper on his own phone."

Nicole looked at Taheri, who leered back at her.

"I should be angry with you for causing me to lose my bet. But I figure it's just the money I won in the first wager. Besides, your body of work on the internet has simply given us all too much enjoyment for me to be mad," he said, emphasizing the word *body*. He seemed quite amused at his pun, because he immediately said something to the guards, who both laughed at his great wit.

Nicole fought to keep control. Adrenaline had warmed her, but now her shivering was from fear. She didn't know if she was about to be beaten, raped, imprisoned, or killed—or quite possibly all of the above.

The lieutenant sat on the chair opposite her.

"Okay, Miss le Roux, enough fun. It is time for business. Tell me why you are in Iran."

She knew this one. She'd practiced it over and over. "I'm here on a photo shoot. I have a session with a photographer this afternoon at Namakabrud Beach. I was in Tehran overnight because I wanted to see the city."

Asadi stared at her for a few moments, then said, "What a strange way of speaking. Almost as if you are reading from cue cards. Or maybe . . ." He leaned forward and put his hand on Nicole's knee. "Maybe it was rehearsed. Why would you rehearse what to say to me?"

He wasn't wrong. She had rattled off that little soliloquy like it was printed on a page.

"It is rehearsed," she said, admitting that part of the truth with a forced smile. "Honestly, I was so scared when we were pulled over that I practiced what I was going to say while I waited in the back seat."

"Ah, yes, we will certainly have to talk about when you were pulled over. But we'll do that in a minute. Right now, I want you to answer me truthfully. Why are you in Iran?" He squeezed her knee with the precise amount of tension to elevate the sensation from discomfort to pain.

"What are you doing?" She tried to move her leg, but he kept his grip.

"Answer my question."

"I did answer it. I'm doing a photo shoot at—"

"Liar! I have not been stationed here in the north for long, but even I know no one would travel to this country just to take photographs at Namakabrud Beach. I wouldn't even drive my family there on a weekend to take any. Now, why are you here?"

"I don't know what else to tell you," she answered, the volume of her voice rising. "What other reason would I be here? I'm a model. I have my picture taken for a living as you clearly saw on the internet. The magazine I was hired for is doing a series called Shore Line: Danger Line— photo spreads taken on beaches in dangerous countries. Yes, it's a stupid title, but it's a paying job. So I took it. I don't know what else to say."

Asadi released Nicole's knee and leaned back, then crossed his arms and watched her. She forced herself not to squirm under his stare.

After a long silence, he asked, "And do you think my country is a dangerous one?"

Nicole held up her hands and rattled the chains. "I didn't at first, but my mind is changing."

"Then let me tell you this, young lady. You haven't seen anything yet."

CHAPTER 8

08:25 / 8:25 A.M. IRST

The door opened again, and a man in an expensive, tailored suit walked in. Immediately, Asadi stood. Through the opening, Nicole could see another police officer just beyond the entrance to the room. Kazemi. His nose was packed with gauze, and his eyes were blackening. He was looking directly at her with violence in his stare. Then the man in the suit closed the door, shutting Kazemi outside.

Walking to the now-unoccupied chair, her new threat sat down and crossed his legs. He signaled for Asadi to lean toward him, and the lieutenant obliged. Nicole watched Asadi's face as the man whispered to him. Suddenly, the officer side-glanced toward Nicole with a surprised look.

Most likely busted, she started shivering again.

You can't give up now. You've got to make them doubt what they think they know. Remember what Nir told all his agents in case of capture. Fake it until you make it. Never admit anything. Every minute that passes is one the Mossad can use to gain your release.

Asadi straightened, and the new man turned his face toward her.

"*Lama at b'Iran*?"

Nicole recognized the Hebrew right away. Other than *Iran,* she didn't know what the words meant, but there was no mistaking the sound. This was a tactic Nir had warned them about. *The enemy will use Hebrew to try to get a reaction.*

Putting as much desperation into her voice as she could, she said, "I'm sorry. I don't speak your language. I wish I did." Looking up at Lieutenant Asadi, she said, "Will you please tell him I don't understand Iranian?"

"The language I speak is Farsi," said the man in the suit, sounding a little piqued. His accent made Nicole think of Patrick Stewart in the *X-Men* movies. "There is no such language as Iranian."

"I'm sorry," she said, this time looking toward the floor.

"The dumb, helpless model. Interesting cover. It might have worked if you hadn't caved in that officer's face."

She met his gaze, making sure her eyes displayed fear and regret, not fear and satisfaction. "He was assaulting me. I didn't think about what I was doing. I just defended myself."

The man sighed and tugged at the crease in his pant leg. "He is a fool, and now he'll be breathing through his mouth for the next three weeks. However, despite his being a moron of the highest caliber, he is still an officer in the Traffic

Police of the General Command of the Law Enforcement of the Islamic Republic of Iran. And you, my dear Nicole le Roux, have assaulted him. In my 'dangerous' country," he said, making air quotes with his fingers, "as I overheard you call my homeland, it seems you are the only one who could be categorized as dangerous. Do you know what the prison sentence is for assaulting a state officer? Take a guess."

"I wouldn't know," Nicole mumbled, looking down again.

"Twenty years minimum. Oh, and sometimes they also remove the offending hand. I wonder what the market is for middle-aged, one-handed swimsuit models whose bodies have endured twenty years in a foreign maximum-security prison. What do you think? You're the expert."

Nicole couldn't answer. She was too busy fighting her sudden nausea.

"I'll let you consider it," he said as he stood. "When you're ready to let me know what you're really doing in my country, simply call out. Someone will hear you." Then he stepped closer, leaned down, and whispered in her ear, "You just better hope it isn't Kazemi who answers your call. I don't think he likes you very much." He cupped her face in his hand. "Such a beautiful girl." Then he walked out with Asadi, and the two guards followed.

As soon as the door closed, Nicole blew out the

breath she'd been holding. She sucked in some fresh air, then quickly exhaled. But her breathing rate only increased, the breaths growing shorter and shorter until she was hyperventilating.

Slow down! Breathe. In through the nose, out through the mouth. Just like Christiaan taught you when we were kids and mom had one of her scary boyfriends over. Just breathe.

Slowly, she calmed down. How did she get herself in this situation? This was worse than anything she could have imagined. Twenty years as a Western female in an Iranian prison? Cutting off her hand? What kind of barbaric country was this?

God, I am not a praying person. I haven't talked to You since my brother, Christiaan, and I were kids. But, please, help me now. I'm as scared as I've ever been. Please, please help me.

CHAPTER 9

MOSSAD SAFE HOUSE, ASTARA, AZERBAIJAN— 10:20 / 10:20 A.M. AST

The fourth number on the digital wall clock switched from 0 to 1. Nir leaned his head back and tried to keep his emotions inside, but he was unsuccessful.

"It's been two hours—no, over two hours since she was arrested," he yelled into the room as he launched from his folding chair. "Do we know where Nicole is? Do we have a plan? What are we doing?"

The room was still as all eyes were on him.

A voice cut through the silence. "Tavor!" Tzadik said, his hand covering the mouthpiece of his phone. "Sit down and shut up. You're not helping."

"Of course I'm not helping! You won't let me help. My team is ready to mount up. A *Yanshuf* can get us there in two hours."

Tzadik said something into his phone, then turned his attention back to Nir. "So you can do what? Start a ground war with Iran? Cool it, cowboy, and wait for me. Five minutes, then I'll fill you in."

Tzadik turned away and began talking on his

phone again. Nir stared at his back for a few moments, then dropped onto the same metal chair. He wasn't used to feeling helpless. A man of action from as far back as he could remember, he'd learned to follow his impulses.

But sometimes following your impulses doesn't work out so well, he thought as he touched the long, faint scar by his left eye. It had come in a bar fight, courtesy of a member of the Fulger Battalion, a division of the Moldovan Special Forces. *At least he bought me a round when it was all over.*

But typically, his instincts were spot-on. That's what made him dangerous. That's what kept him and the teams he led safe. In this situation, though, he wondered whether he could trust himself. Maybe Tzadik was exactly right, saying he was acting like a cowboy. Still, it took everything he had to not put himself, his career, and even his men at risk by rotating up a helicopter and crossing the border.

"She really does mean something to you."

Nir turned to his left and saw Elnur Isayev. "The woman, Nicole le Roux. She's more than just a colleague."

Nir's first impulse was to tell this guy to mind his own business, but he realized this might be another time when his own instincts couldn't be trusted. "Yes, she is."

The man appeared to think for a moment,

then leaned forward, indicating that Nir should do the same. The smell of stale cigarettes was almost unbearable. "I am going to trust you with something, some information that needs to remain between you and me. Okay?"

"I can't fully give you my word. But if it's nothing I'm obligated by duty to share with my superiors, then it will remain between us."

Isayev chuckled. "Right out of the manual. Okay, that is good enough for me. You need to know that we have people already on their way to Marzanabad. If necessary, they will rescue her."

Nir nearly reacted to this news, but the thought that Tzadik could be watching him held him still. "He doesn't know this?" he asked, nodding toward his superior.

"He does not. We assist your Mossad, but we are our own people, and we will act according to what we think is right."

Nir was both happy and concerned. "Why are you telling me this? Why would you think I wouldn't go to Tzadik with this information?"

"Because I believe the safety of your woman is more important to you than following protocol. From what I can tell, a lot of things are more important to you than following protocol. That is why I trust you to do the right thing."

Nir smiled. "That's probably true. But why would your people do this? It's such high risk."

"Let me put it this way. If a gang of ruffians kept coming into your village, attacking the residents and destroying their property, you would try to stop them. But what if there were too many of them?"

"You would eat the elephant one bite at a time."

"Precisely. Every opportunity that presented itself, you would pick away at them. Shoot one man when he is off tending his horse. Gut another man when he is in the bushes relieving himself. Eventually, you would either kill them all or make life so miserable for them that they would leave on their own. Do you know how many who live in Iran are actually Persian?"

"I don't," Nir answered, thankful for the distraction.

"Less than two-thirds. So one in every three people in this country is a minority, and we are very much treated as minorities. Kurds, Baloch, Turkmen, Lurs, Arabs—this nation is filled with us. We Azeris are the largest of the minority groups with around sixteen percent of the population. And while we have no fight with most of the Persian people, who are good and decent, we passionately hate this evil regime running the country. Their Islamic Revolutionary Guard Corps are the ruffians who regularly attack our villages. While we would like nothing more than to kill the snake by cutting off its head, the ayatollahs are beyond our reach. So we will settle for shooting the man by the horses and gutting the man in the bushes."

Nir nodded, understanding the man's motivation. "So this is less about Nicole than about taking a shot at the regime."

"Certainly. But we would also enjoy the opportunity to rescue a damsel in distress," Isayev said with a wink.

Nir had been unsure about this man, but now he was seeing him in a different light. "Thank you. When you get the chance, please thank your people for me. However, for now, please make sure they stand down. I am the last person who should be saying this, but an armed assault is a last resort."

Isayev laughed. "The viper tells the dog not to bite. Don't worry, my friend. They are only gathering in case all the phone calls fail."

"Speaking of . . ." Nir said, nodding toward Tzadik. He was coming their way.

"Glad to see you're making friends, Tavor."

"Just arranging for karaoke tonight when this is all done. You in?"

"You bet. I do a mean Vegas Elvis."

Nir smiled. "Yeah, I want to get that picture out of my mind."

"Walk with me," Tzadik said. When they reached an isolated corner of the room, he spoke in a low tone. "Listen, I know this has been tough for you. Normally, I'd be telling you to go

70

join your men in the other room and sit on your thumbs. But since I know you've got a little more invested in this, I'm going to read you in."

"I appreciate that, *Ha'mefaked.*"

"But I'm not looking for approval or criticism. This is the plan, and this little meeting here is informational only. Understood?"

"Yes, *Ha'mefaked.*"

"We've got a chain of conversation going that will hopefully lead to the dirties releasing Nicole." Tzadik held up his phone as if to emphasize his point, then shoved it into his pocket. "I've talked directly to the *ramsad*, so this is being dealt with all the way at the top of the Mossad. He's contacting a deputy director of Italy's intelligence agency, AISE, who owes him a favor. He'll ask him to reach out to someone he trusts in one of the Milan fashion houses. The plan is for that person to contact Italy's state department to tell them they employ a South African model who has been arrested by the Iranian authorities."

"Why doesn't the Italian intelligence guy contact the state department directly?"

"We're trying to protect Nicole's cover for future operations. Think about it. If the AISE asks the state department for help directly, Nicole will be flagged in Italy and most other countries for the rest of her life."

Nir wasn't so sure Nicole's washing out of the

71

Mossad would be such a bad thing, but he said, "Makes sense."

"Protocol dictates that Italy's state will contact South Africa's state to tell them one of their citizens is being unjustly held in Iran and has been assaulted. South Africa and Iran have a very good relationship, and the Tehran regime won't want to risk that. We're hoping South Africa's state department will be able to leverage that to get Nicole out."

Nir's head was swimming. "That's a lot of steps, and every minute Nicole is in their custody puts her more at risk. Where are we in the process?"

"Bogged down in Italy's state department. It's only 7:30 a.m., and no one is taking calls until eight."

Incredulous, Nir took a step back. "You have got to be joking. Don't we have someone who can go wake somebody up?"

"Quiet, Tavor." Tzadik continued in a hushed voice. "This is informational, remember? We're working on it. I'll keep you up-to-date as more happens."

"Understood, *Ha'mefaked*. Thank you."

The commander nodded, then slipped his phone back out of his pocket as he moved on.

Nir returned to his chair, sitting down and lacing his fingers behind his head. It seemed like such a long shot, but right now it appeared to be the only shot they had—at least before Isayev's people would have to step in.

From across the room, Tzadik yelled into his phone, "Well, don't we have someone who can go wake somebody up?"

Go get them, boss, Nir thought as he stood to check the current status of the coffeepot.

CHAPTER 10

POLICE STATION, MARZANABAD, IRAN— 11:40 / 11:40 A.M. IRST

Lieutenant Asadi sat opposite Nicole. This was his fourth shot at interrogating her. His face, however, looked a little different this time. Despite the temperature in the room, which had not warmed with the progression of daylight hours, the officer had beads of sweat on his brow. An open file folder rested on his crossed legs, and he was riffling through a series of papers. He seemed aggravated, missing the calm superiority of his previous interrogation sessions.

This is not a good change, she thought. *He looks like he just got ripped apart by someone— probably the nameless man in the suit. Hold strong no matter what. Maybe the Mossad will come for you.*

But her belief in an impending rescue was growing less and less. In between the questionings—when it was just her, the cold, and her thoughts—she wondered. After all, she was just a *goy* analyst in the Israeli Mossad. How far would they really go to save her? She'd even begun doubting Nir's loyalty. Would he really risk his career, his freedom, even his life for her?

Besides, she'd assaulted a police officer. Even if they wanted to help her, what could they do?

She realized her childhood of neglect and mother's abandonment of her and her twin brother were likely feeding the flames of doubt. But the fact remained that she was hours into this ordeal and had heard absolutely nothing about anyone trying to at least negotiate her release.

Asadi abruptly tapped the papers on the folder to align their edges, then laid them down and closed the file. "Why are you here in Iran, Nicole?"

Exasperated, she said, "How many times are you—"

"Answer the question." He lifted the folder and waved it at her. "I have a file filled with evidence that everything you have said to me is an absolute lie. So I am going to ask you my questions one more time. And if you give me the same lies, then we will move to the next stage of our interrogation."

Nicole was pretty sure he was bluffing about the evidence in the file folder, but the "next stage" reference certainly caught her attention.

"Now, why were you in Tehran?"

"I don't know what else to tell you, except what I've already said two dozen times now." Her very real anger and frustration were evident in her tone. "I arrived in Tehran two days ago, then flew a charter plane to Noshahr Airport. But because

75

the flight had a mechanical delay, the light had gone by the time I arrived at Namakabrud Beach. We rescheduled for today, which left me with nothing to do. So I decided to return to Tehran and see some of its sights."

"What did you do in the capital city?" he asked with an aggravated sigh.

"Like I've said, I did tourist things. I visited Golestan Palace. I went to the Milad Tower. I shopped the Grand Bazaar. Isn't that what people do there?"

That's what preparation gets you, Nicole thought as she silently thanked the Azeris who had delivered to her last night's receipts from the palace and the tower and a bag full of souvenirs from the bazaar.

"And where did you stay last night?"

"As I'm sure your people have discovered, I was at the Parsian Azadi Hotel. Fourth floor. You'll have to forgive me for not remembering the exact room number." She did know the exact room number. She'd checked herself into it from the van by the warehouse. But it was those little details that made stories believable.

Asadi flipped through the papers. "Room 422."

"If you say so." Nicole knew very well that it was 418 and that he was trying to catch her in a lie.

Closing the file again, Asadi said, "What is interesting to me and what makes your story so implausible is that nobody remembers seeing you there. No one from the doors remembers seeing you walk in. No one at the front desk remembers checking you in. It is like you were a ghost."

Nicole lifted her eyebrows and gave him a *What do you want me to say?* look.

"Don't you find that odd?" he went on. "You must admit, you are fairly memorable, especially in a country where the modesty and devotion of so many of the women compels them to remain covered."

This was the one part of her tradecraft plan she'd been concerned about. Yes, she could check herself in from the van, make a room key, and have a local enter the room and make it appear that she'd slept there. But there'd been no way to get her face into that hotel.

"How can I be responsible for other people's lack of awareness?"

"Stop lying to me," he yelled, flinging the file at her. Its edge hit the bridge of her nose, but the folder had flown open, so the contact wasn't painful.

"I want to talk to my embassy," she said, making a demand of her own.

"Which one?"

"What do you mean? The one in Tehran."

A knowing smile spread across Asadi's face as he sat back in his chair. "No, I mean which one, the South African or the Israeli?"

Nicole masked her shock with laughter, praying that her sudden fear didn't show through. "The South African, of course. Why would I . . . Wait a second. You think I'm some Israeli spy?" Now she really started laughing, doing her best to play the part.

The mocking tone seemed to get to Asadi. "It is not a laughing matter, Miss le Roux. We have evidence—"

"That I'm an Israeli secret agent? I'm like a female Austin Powers but with a yarmulke? Nicole le Roux, woman of mystery. Supermodel by day, superspy by night."

"Stop laughing."

"Is that what this is all about? You've held me here for however many hours because you think I'm some undercover model spy? No wonder you've kept me chained. You're afraid I'll use my secret martial arts training against you."

"I said stop laughing." Asadi leaned forward and slapped her across the face.

Nicole froze. "I want to talk to the South African embassy."

Asadi had resumed his position in his chair, but she saw the rage on his face.

"What you fail to realize," he said, "is this. First, you are a long way from your embassy. And second, nobody knows you are here. That gives us options as we decide what to do with you."

It felt like a black hole had formed below her

chair and she was about to tip into it. "But I'm a South African citizen. I have a right to speak to my embassy."

Now the superiority was back in Asadi's voice, mixed with a little vengeance. "Oh my pretty little girl, have you still not realized? You have no rights here. Being white and beautiful may buy you the world in other places, but it gains you nothing here in the mountains of Iran. In fact, it's quite the opposite. Think about it. If we send you to prison, what once may have been your greatest assets will quickly become your greatest liabilities."

Nicole was angry with her weakness as tears ran down her cheeks.

Asadi smiled paternally, removed a handkerchief from his pocket, and dabbed her face. "Please don't worry too much. It may not come to that. We may decide to simply make you disappear." The lieutenant sat back and watched in silence as more tears formed in Nicole's eyes and traveled south.

Finally, he said, "If I ask you more questions, will you give me the same lies?"

"They aren't lies," she answered softly.

He watched her a few more moments, then stood. "Then I guess it is on to stage two of our interrogation. I'm afraid this part is not my specialty, so I must step out and invite in one of my colleagues. Goodbye, Nicole. I hope I will have the opportunity to speak to you again sometime soon."

As Asadi walked out the door, Nicole found her breathing once again speeding up. *Slow down. In through the nose, out through the mouth. In through the nose, out through the mouth.* Gradually, she gained control, but that did nothing to calm her fear.

Then the door opened, and her breathing stopped completely. Officer Kazemi walked in. His eyes were completely black now, and his nose was still packed with gauze. He spoke to himself as he circled behind her. Although she couldn't understand the words, his tone was enough to tell her all she needed to know about his intentions.

"God, if you are really there, please help me!"

Now Kazemi stood in front of her, staring down with hatred. With remarkable speed, his arm swung and connected with her abdomen. All the air expelled from her lungs as she doubled over, and then she retched as she gasped for air. The pain was like nothing she'd ever felt. Another blow landed, this one to the side of her head. Her vision grayed, and she continued trying to draw oxygen into her lungs.

A hand grabbed her hair and lifted her head. Kazemi's fist was poised to strike. But then the door flew open and slammed against the wall.

"Baseh digeh!"

Kazemi released Nicole's hair, and her chin dropped to her chest.

"*Baseh digeh!*" the voice repeated. "Enough!"

A harsh rasp accompanied every hard suck of air Nicole took. Digging deep, she found the strength to lift her head. Standing in the doorway was the man in the suit. He held a paper in one hand as he spoke rapidly to Kazemi, who quickly backed away from her.

The suit man looked back through the doorway and snapped his fingers, waving someone in. A fully veiled woman hustled inside carrying a large bowl in one hand and a white cloth in the other. Before Nicole could determine her intentions, her vision once again grayed, then went black.

APRIL
2018
[THREE MONTHS LATER]

CHAPTER 11

THREE MONTHS LATER
YAEL DIAMONDS, ANTWERP, BELGIUM—
APRIL 30, 2018—18:20 / 6:20 P.M. CEST

Nir kept the video stream on pause as Mila set two ceramic mugs on his glass-topped desk in his office. Around to his left, he'd dragged one of the two leather chairs that normally sat opposite him so she would have a view of his computer screen as well. As she sat, he prepared to click Play, but the aroma from the mugs caught his attention. He turned and saw a tower of whipped cream dusted with cocoa powder. A sprig of some sort of greenery gave a splash of color to the concoction.

"That is not the coffee I asked for."

"Oh, really?" Mila answered innocently, never taking her eyes from the screen. She was tall, thin, and fair-skinned with hair she kept short and tight. Several years ago, her husband, deciding that 28 and blond were more interesting than 50-something and salt-and-pepper, had left. Not long after that, Nir was looking for a new receptionist/executive assistant/office manager/personal barista.

Mila Wooters came walking through his office

door and ticked every box—everything he'd hoped for with the bonus of being an exceptional baker, a well-schooled city historian, and a self-appointed life coach. That last gift had led to his giving her the nickname Aunt Mila. But even though she could be a little intrusive at times, it was nice to know that someone in Antwerp cared about him.

"Yes, really. Coffee has caffeine, which I could desperately use right now. This has about half a kilo of sugar, and that will put me to sleep in the next thirty minutes."

She slid a mug toward him. "Oh, hush and drink your cocoa. Besides, that whole caffeine thing is a myth."

"It's a . . . What?"

But Mila just waved her hand toward the computer screen.

Giving up, Nir clicked Play, and the frozen image of Israeli prime minister Benjamin Netanyahu began moving. He spoke in Hebrew, and it took the English translation a moment to sync in.

"Good evening. Tonight, we're going to show you something that the world has never seen before. Tonight, we are going to reveal new and conclusive proof of the secret nuclear weapons program that Iran has been hiding for years from

86

the international community in its secret atomic archive."

"Secret atomic archive," repeated Mila. "Sounds very James Bond-y. I wonder if the ayatollahs have a lair."

Nir hushed her and took a sip of the cocoa. For a moment he forgot everything happening on the screen. The liquid in the mug was so thick and creamy, as if it had been made from the milk of a butter-fed cow. And the chocolate? Well, they were in Belgium, after all.

"Oh, where's my coffee?" Mila quietly mocked him.

Realizing he'd missed some of what the prime minister had said, he backed up the video.

". . . to show you Iran's secret nuclear files. You may well know that Iran's leaders repeatedly deny ever pursuing nuclear weapons. You can listen to . . ."

The prime minister continued his detailed presentation, complete with slides and charts. Nir had received a heads-up a few days ago, telling him Netanyahu was ready to go public with everything learned from Operation Deep Sleep. But because he already had a full day of work planned, Nir hadn't been able to watch it live.

Yael Diamonds was Nir's business venture and served as his European cover. He'd started the business in 2012 with a little financial help from the Mossad, and it had quickly taken off. Soon he was able to pay back the Israeli government's loan, and now he owned the business free and clear.

Nir's plan was to finish most of his work, then watch the video on YouTube. When Mila heard what the video was about, she decided to stay late too. Sometimes Nir thought she had to suspect his other life, particularly when he disappeared for days or weeks at a time. But she never asked questions, and more than anything else, that made her a keeper.

"A few weeks ago, in a great intelligence achievement, Israel obtained half a ton of the material inside these vaults. And here's what we got. Fifty-five thousand pages. Another 55,000 files on 183 CDs."

"Breaking into vaults and stealing secret files? It doesn't even sound real," Mila said.

Nir grunted his affirmation as he watched the prime minister revealing shelves full of binders and rows of CDs affixed to a large posterboard. His mind drifted back to the helplessness he'd felt when Nicole was in trouble. Then he thought about how, when he'd finally seen her again, he'd somehow taken a terrible situation and made it worse.

From what he'd been told, once the South African Department of International Affairs and Cooperation had become involved, the wheels had moved quickly. An angry call from the South African ambassador in Tehran reached the right person in Iran's government, and within five hours Nicole was on a plane home to Milan.

It took Nir a little longer to extract himself from his team in Azerbaijan. Three days passed before he caught up with Nicole at her flat.

When she answered the door, he couldn't believe what he saw. The left side of her face was darkly colored with blue, purple, and black. Her left eye was swollen and bloodshot, but at least it was open.

"Nicole," he'd said as he wrapped her in his arms. He wanted to just hold her, but after a few seconds, she pulled away.

"Come on in. Sorry for the way I look. It hurts to put on makeup." She walked past her kitchen and eased herself down onto the soft sectional. Nir closed the door and followed.

"No, please. I'm the one who should be apologizing. I tried to get here sooner, but there was no way."

When he sat next to her, she turned toward him, hugging a pillow as a fluffy wall between them. He was getting a weird vibe from her, but he figured it was from the trauma. Who could blame her after what she'd gone through?

"You got here as soon as you could, I'm sure."

An awkward silence followed, something that rarely occurred between them. He wanted to fill it with something. "I got the run-down, and it sounds like you were amazing. I can't believe how hard you fought."

"Why can't you believe it? What do you think I should have done?" she asked, for some reason defensive.

"I mean I was just surprised that you broke a policeman's nose." He felt like he was tumbling down a deep hole in this conversation, but he couldn't keep from adding, "You could have ended up in prison or who knows what."

"You think I don't know that? Trust me, they made the options very clear to me. But you weren't there, were you? You don't know what you would have done up against that car or chained to that metal chair." Her eyes were beginning to flare as she pulled the pillow tighter against her body.

"No, I wasn't there, and I don't know. I'm just saying it was a huge risk."

"Well, I made it, didn't I? And I brought out the information."

If they were being technical, she didn't bring out any information. She just helped the team acquire it. But given her reaction to nearly everything he uttered, that was a point he should probably leave unaddressed.

"Listen, Nicole. I'm sorry. I'm not sure what I said to send this conversation sideways. I'm just so glad you're safe. And just so you know, there's no way I'm going to let you take that kind of risk again."

It quickly became evident that of all the wrong things he could have said, that was the wrong-est.

Standing quickly, Nicole sidestepped the coffee table and backed away from the couch. *"Let?* You won't *let* me?"

Nir stood just as quickly. "I'm sorry. Wrong choice—"

"Who are you to let me do anything? Are you my husband? Are you my father?"

Nir made another attempt to defend the indefensible, but it was no use. So much fear and pain and grief and anger had built up in her, and all it needed to pour out was a target. His poor choice of words had put the bull's-eye squarely on his chest. He stood there silent while she ranted for a good two to three minutes before turning and stomping into her bedroom, then slamming the door. Stunned at what was coming out of her mouth—not all of it truly directed at him—he remained standing in the same spot, unsure of what to do before finally walking out of her flat.

He'd tried calling her a couple of times in

the past three months. The first time she hadn't picked up. The second time she'd answered, but her hostile one-word answers to his questions had made him wish she'd just let his call go to voice mail.

"Following the new directive of Iran's Minister of Defense, the work would be split into two parts, covert and overt. A key part of the plan was to form new organizations to continue the work. This is how Dr. Mohsen Fakhrizadeh, head of Project Amad, put it. Remember that name, Fakhrizadeh. So here's his directive, right here. And he says: 'The general aim is to announce the closure of Project Amad,' but then he adds, 'Special activities'— you know what that is—'Special activities will be carried out under the title of scientific know-how developments.' And in fact, that is exactly what Iran proceeded to do."

"Okay, he just lost me there," Mila said. "What's this Project Amad?"

"Project Amad was Iran's nuclear program they claimed to have shut down something like fifteen years ago. 'Really, we promise. No more nuclear program for us. Scout's honor.' The UN and the international community immediately bought into it, because, especially for the UN, anything Israel hates they love."

"But the prime minister is saying it wasn't shut down. And this Farky-guy is the one who kept heading it up."

Nir chuckled. "It's Fakhrizadeh. He's known as the Father of the Iranian Bomb."

"That's quite the title."

"He's earned it. Bibi is saying that despite the fact Fakhrizadeh said they shut down the program, they just hid it and kept it going. Which is what Israel has been saying all along. Now we have the proof."

". . . lies and Iranian deception. One hundred thousand files right here prove that they lied. So here's the bottom line. Iran continues to lie. Just last week, Zarif said this: 'We never wanted to produce a bomb.' Again: 'We never wanted to produce a bomb.' Yes you did. Yes you do. And the atomic archive proves it."

Nir took another draw from his mug, both savoring and regretting its contents.

Mila had obviously checked out as Netanyahu wrapped up. She caught him looking at her and said, "I was just trying to imagine what it would be like to have the threat of a nuclear bomb hanging over your head like your family in Israel would if Iran developed a nuclear bomb. I grew up in the Soviet era. We'd have drills where we'd all duck under our desks in school as if that would help anything. But we always figured that if Brezhnev or Andropov detonated a bomb, it would be on the Americans. We're too close here in Belgium. All the fallout would eventually blow into Moscow."

"I do think of that," Nir said, admitting the truth. "But not often. In Israel, when you grow up surrounded by countries filled with people who hate you—even want to kill you—you kind of get used to the feeling. But you're right. With the nukes, it's different. We've been able to fight off the armies that have attacked us. But there's not much you can do if a nuclear bomb detonates in Tel Aviv."

"And you really think it would happen?"

"One hundred percent. Whether by Iran itself or one of their proxy militias. The ayatollahs get the bomb, it's going to make its way to Israel."

Mila stood and collected the mugs. "Well, then, that prime minister of yours better get off his backside and do something about it."

I wish it were that easy, he thought. *I'm proud of what we pulled off at that warehouse. But what did we really accomplish? This only proved what everybody already knew. The U.S. president will probably pull out of the JCPOA, but the rest of the West is committed to that terrible Iran*

nuclear deal. Even the missions the Mossad oper-
ates only temporarily slow down Iran's progress.
We're dealing with symptoms, not the disease.
Somehow, we need to do something that will
make a real difference.

Nir shuffled some papers around on his desk, trying to focus on his work. Mila walked back in, and, after chastising Nir for working late too often, she said good night and left him alone. Rather than working, though, he sat and brooded—first about Nicole, then about a nuclear Iran, then about Nicole again.

He briefly considered trying to call her, but then he decided taking the train to his neighborhood, strolling to his favorite pub, and spending the next few hours doing his best to forget all about the woman was a much more sensible idea.

Still, as he got up and walked to the door, he knew that there were some things in life that even a pint and a game of darts couldn't block out of your mind. Nicole was number one on that list.

CHAPTER 12

Saad Salim dove into the pool, then glided in the cool water. Already it was 30 degrees Celsius with the humidity approaching 90 percent, so any time in the water was better than time spent only lounging beside it. Surfacing after a quarter of the length, he began a long, graceful stroke.

Much of his youth had been spent in a pool, at first just playing but eventually swimming competitively. He'd had hopes of representing his country in the Olympics, but then his family fell out of favor with then-King Fahd. A relocation from Saudi Arabia to Doha, Qatar, had essentially left him without a home country.

After four laps, he lifted himself out of the water. A steward held a robe for him, and he slipped it on before padding barefoot to the elevator, where an operator punched a button lowering them three levels. When the doors opened, he stepped into his master suite. With a sleeping area, a large sitting room, and a mini theater, this one room took up much of the yacht's center deck. Walking past his oversized king bed, he entered the en suite, where he stripped off his swim trunks, stepped into the shower, and let the multiple heads wash the chlorine from his skin.

When he stepped out, he paused to admire his body in the full-length mirror. Despite having reached his mid-fifties, he was still fit with just the faintest outline of the six-pack of his youth still on his abdomen. Rather than submit to the vanity of hair coloring, though, he'd let the beginnings of gray sow themselves through his full head of hair. And although the skin on his clean-shaven face was dark and tight after years spent outside overseeing his oil fields, he still could pass for a man a decade younger.

Going to his closet, he lifted a pair of white linen pants off a hanger, then grabbed a light-blue cotton shirt. After dressing, he slipped on a pair of boat shoes, leaving his socks in the drawer, and made his way to the upper deck for breakfast. He had 24 crew on board this boat, and for now, they were all there to serve just two people—him and one other.

When he exited the elevator, he saw his guest sitting at a table with a flute that held orange juice, no doubt mixed with champagne—their usual. Spread out in front of him sat bowls of fresh fruit and baskets of pastries.

Saad had heard the helicopter land on the forward helipad late last night, but he hadn't come out of his suite to greet the man. Even though the general was his friend, he'd instructed his head steward to direct him to a guest suite and let him know the master of this yacht would meet him at breakfast the next morning. A certain decorum was important for everyone to remember who was who in the overall hierarchy.

The man noticed Saad coming toward him and quickly stood. "Good morning, my friend."

Seeing the general in shorts and a flowered shirt buttoned only halfway up, it was hard for Saad to picture him receiving the salutes of battle-hardened soldiers of the Islamic Revolutionary Guard Corps.

"General Mousavi, I am glad to see you have arrived safely." He shook the man's proffered hand. "Welcome back to the *Ibn Tamiyyah*."

Ibn Tamiyyah was not the name painted on the prow of the boat. In fact, he'd shared that secret name with very few. Anyone gazing at Saad's yacht cruising by would read the words *Cafala Bahr*. *Cafala* was a combination of the first two letters of his three daughters' names—Cantara, Fariha, and Lateefah. The Arabic word for "sea"—*bahr*—was added to make it sound more like a boat's name.

While the craft was under construction, however, Saad had sought a name that did honor to Allah and to his faith as a Salafi Muslim. He could think of no better moniker than that of the greatest of the Salafi jurists, the fourteenth-century *Ibn Tamiyyah*, also known as *Shaykh al-Islam*. So much of reform Islam could be traced back to his wise teachings, including those of the Wahabis and others who knew the importance of true *jihad*.

Undoubtedly, the great Muslim scholar would have been horrified at so ostentatious a display of wealth as a $650 million yacht. Yet many of the meetings held on board spread the reach of Islam and furthered the man's vision of power through conflict. Sheikhs and caliphs, military men and heads of false-front NGOs, politicians and scientists had all been on this yacht. Even Mohsen Fakhrizadeh, whom Netanyahu had gone on about in that speech yesterday, had been on his boat twice with his wife for meetings with scientists from Egypt, North Korea, and some European nations.

The problem was that sailing a yacht around the world with the name of one of the fathers of the jihad movement painted on its side would be a good way to get torpedoed by a U.S. submarine or targeted with an Israeli limpet mine. So it was *Ibn Tamiyyah* to his chosen few and *Cafala Bahr* to everyone else.

Saad continued. "I hope you have found your accommodations to your liking."

"As always, your generosity is unparalleled, and your hospitality knows no bounds."

"Please, return to your meal." Saad indicated the general's chair, then sat opposite him and spooned some fruit into a bowl. "For now, it is just the two of us, Arash. Tonight, we will be joined by others whom you may find much more attractive than I."

"You keep yourself quite fit, my friend, but I'm afraid your body does not curve in the most necessary places," the general said with a wink.

The two carried on the small talk etiquette required throughout breakfast. Then finally, Saad said, "Did you watch that Jewish circus yesterday?"

"The prime minister is a fool and a dog. Yet I must admit this is a victory for the evil side. The Supreme Leader is desperately angry. He is looking for arrests and executions."

Saad pulled back from a croissant he'd been reaching for. "Are you—"

"Oh, no. I am in no danger. The clowns in the security branch who thought it wise to hide all our nuclear secrets in a warehouse with no guards at night are the ones in peril."

Reaching again for the pastry, Saad said, "That truly is a baffling choice, and it has given quite the victory to the enemy."

The general refilled his flute, this time skipping the orange juice part of his mimosa. "*Inshallah*, the victory will be short-lived. Already we are spreading the word that the documents are false. Many in the UN will buy it."

"But they are irrelevant. What matters is that the deranged U.S. president will use it as a pretext to destroy the nuclear deal."

"This is true, which is why we must always think long-term, Saad." Taking a ring of orange, he perched it on his glass, then took a sip. "We must survive only four years of this fool, eight at most. Then the next administration will come in and undo what he has done, much the same way he has undone the actions of his own predecessor. That is why the American system of government is so illogical."

"But it is also unpredictable, Arash. There is no telling what this man will do in the next four years. I believe you and your friends best keep your eyes open."

The general laughed. "I know, but some lines even the Americans will not cross. I was speaking with General Soleimani about this very thing just yesterday. He believes there is nothing to worry about. I tend to agree with him. Our nuclear program will progress. We will achieve our bomb, and then the world will quake."

"You know the situation better than I do. I will have to trust you. Now, down to our real business. Tell me about the UAV training taking place with your militias in Iraq and Syria, and then let me know where my money can make the most impact."

SEPTEMBER 2020 [TWO YEARS LATER]

CHAPTER 13

lear," said a female voice through Nir's com.

"*Root*," he replied, acknowledging that he'd received and understood the message.

Liora Regev's remote disabling of the alarm system from the team control room back at Mossad headquarters in Tel Aviv allowed Nir to insert a tool into the lock. Quietly, he manipulated the slender piece of metal until he felt all the tumblers disengage in the beach condominium's sliding glass door. He nodded to Imri Zaid, who knelt and inserted a thin bar under the base of the door. With another nod from Nir, Imri leveraged the handle of the bar, lifting the door and disengaging the kick lock with a pop.

Nir slid the glass open, and once he and Imri had both slipped inside, he gently closed the door behind them. He clicked his com twice and then twisted on a small penlight. The two operatives began walking through the Airbnb rental.

"Entry acknowledged," Liora said. Nir had no

doubt that the rest of his analyst team surrounded her, following the action and ready to jump in at a moment's notice.

Well, not quite the rest of the team.

Nicole had committed to working Milan Fashion Week, so he'd cut her from the op. When he told her he was going ahead without her, she was understanding. She was understanding about a lot of things these days. Some of it was due to the healing of their relationship during a recent operation in the United Arab Emirates. But much of her changed attitude came from what she called her "new relationship with Jesus."

After her experience in Iran, she was a wreck. She spent some time with her twin brother, Christiaan, a former drug addict who had kicked his habit by going to a church or a religious 12-step program or something. Nir wasn't totally sure what. He just knew Nicole had escaped to Cape Town a basket case and come back a new person. And whether it was Jesus, seeing Christiaan, or spending some time in her home hemisphere where the water circles the drain counterclockwise, he didn't care. He was just happy that she was happy.

Nir and Imri made their way between the living area and kitchen toward the two bedrooms. Outside, but close by, his Kidon ops team waited. Yaron Eisenbach—still Nir's second and an old-school agent who had more operations under his belt in his mid-forties than most have in a full career—was down the beach to the left keeping watch. Right of the condo was a massive Russian Jew named Dima Aronov, who most called Drago after the Soviet boxer in *Rocky IV*. In an SUV four blocks away sat Doron Mizrahi. In his late twenties with a shaved head and a bushy beard, his Millennial perspective on life was both a deep well of cultural insight for the team and a constant source of irritation.

The man softly gliding through this expensively decorated beachside condominium with Nir was on his rookie operation. After one of the team's members was determined no longer fit for active procedures following a gunshot wound during the operation in the UAE, the Kidon team had sought a replacement. Three of the guys sent to Nir never made it past the initial interview. The fourth had accidentally shot Dima in the chest with a SIM round during a training exercise, and the Russian had personally led him off the course by his ear.

Now they had Imri, and so far Nir was impressed. When they'd sat in Nir's office, the young man told the story of his great-great-grandfather, Alexander Zaid, who was a hero in the early years of Zionism.

After the turn of the twentieth century, he and some others founded *Bar Giora*, a Jewish self-defense organization. Many of the early settlements found themselves constantly raided by Arabs, and these men were determined to stop them. Then in 1909, he helped found *HaShomer*, "the Watchmen," the premier defense organization until the founding of the *Haganah* in 1920. Eighteen years after the formation of that benchmark military organization, Alexander Zaid was on patrol in the Jezreel Valley when he was ambushed by a group of Arabs and murdered by a Bedouin, who was himself later tried and executed.

Nir had already known the story and had even seen the statue of the man erected near Beit She'arim National Park. He'd just wanted to hear Imri tell it in order to get a bead on him. There was no doubt of the young man's passion, and Nir respected his desire to follow in his ancestor's footsteps as a watchman of Israel. The jury was still out, though, and Nir was hoping his initial impressions would prove to be right.

Between online blueprints of the condominium and the photos posted with the Airbnb advertisement, the two operatives knew where they were going. When they reached the master bedroom, they both drew their weapons. Nir's IWI Jericho 941 was ready with one in the chamber. The weapon's safety was engaged in between operations but never during. Very gently, Imri turned the handle and pushed the door open.

Nir stepped in. To his left stood a tall fern,

and beyond that, a large wardrobe. Two steps away, directly in front of them, was a half-meter-tall, dark-wood platform upon which lay an undoubtedly comfortable mattress. Two forms were stretched out under an oversized thin comforter. Nir approached the one nearest him. A quick flick of his penlight showed her to be a pretty blond woman in her late thirties. While he knelt next to her, Imri walked behind him for a better angle from which to train his gun on the other person.

Nir holstered his weapon and tucked his light into his pocket. Then from an armband wrapped around his left upper bicep, he removed a syringe. He really wished the woman had been on the other side of the bed so he could make the injection with his right hand. But he'd practiced both ways, and covering her mouth with his right hand, he used his left to quickly insert the needle into her neck. The result was immediate. No struggle; she was just out. Still, he kept his hand over her mouth for a count of 40.

Turning toward Imri, Nir nodded. The new Kidon agent lowered his gun, and Nir walked to the other side of the bed. He removed a photo from a pocket in his cargo pants, held it up to the sleeping man's face, and lit both up with his penlight. No doubt about it, it was him. Nir tucked the picture and the light away and drew his gun once again. Then he waited to let his eyes acclimate to the soft moonlight passing through the gauzy curtains into the room.

The man lying on his back was Dr. Horst Lindner, a German nuclear physicist with a PhD from Johannes Gutenberg University Mainz and post-doctoral work at the U.S. Department of Energy's Institute for Nuclear Theory located on the University of Washington campus. Considered one of the leading minds in centrifuge development, his career had been on a strong, if not meteoric, track. Then quite suddenly, he quit his job and disappeared from all the assemblies and functions and symposiums where those in the world of nuclear physics tend to gather. Six months later, he moved from his tract home in Seattle to a mini mansion in the suburb of Laurelhurst.

That's when the Mossad put eyes on him. They'd been watching him for a year, recording his *two months gone, one month home* schedule and his regular flights to the Middle East, particularly to Tehran. Some snooping within Iran uncovered that Dr. Lindner was now one of the primary physicists involved in the engineering of uranium centrifuges in the nuclear facility in Karaj.

Nir and Imri were here to put a stop to that. It wasn't that the man was doing anything illegal. It's just that in the eyes of the Mossad, the doctor had made a very poor career choice.

CHAPTER 14

02:40 / 2:40 A.M. CEST

N ir pointed his pistol at the man's face.

"Dr. Lindner. Oh, Dr. Lindner."

The deep breathing of the German physicist never changed.

Nir turned to Imri. "Heavy sleeper."

Imri shrugged.

Extending the barrel of his 9mm, Nir tapped the man on the forehead.

Lindner groaned and made a sleepy swipe across his face.

Nir tapped a little harder, and the man's eyes snapped open.

"Augh!" he cried, scooting back into his wife.

Nir hushed him. "Quiet, Dr. Lindner. Your children are in the next room. You don't want to wake them, do you?"

"Who are you? What do you want?"

"My name is irrelevant. What I want is to talk to you."

As if suddenly noticing that his wife hadn't awakened, he turned to look at her. "Ilse," he said, shaking her. When there was no response, he turned back to Nir. "What have you done to her?"

111

"Nothing much. Just gave her something to help her sleep a little better. She'll wake up tomorrow unaware we were here at all—unless you and I can't come to an agreement tonight. Then she'll likely wake up to a mess."

"Please, don't hurt my family. I'll talk. Whatever you want."

"Good. I appreciate that."

Nir turned to see Imri walking back in through the bedroom door. He'd holstered his gun and was carrying two chairs from the breakfast nook. He set them in the middle of the floor facing each other.

"Please, sit," Nir said, holstering his own gun, then sitting on one of the chairs. Without turning to look, he knew Imri's weapon was back in his hand.

Lindner slipped from under the blanket. The only clothing on his "dad bod" was a white pair of briefs. He bent down to retrieve a T-shirt and shorts from the floor, but Nir stopped him.

"Those won't be necessary. We won't be here long."

The man's hand lingered mid-reach, and Nir knew this moment would determine the direction of the encounter. If Lindner defiantly continued his grab for his clothing, then whether the activities of the night would remain verbal or become physical would be up in the air.

With a sigh, Lindner pulled back his hand, then walked to the chair and sat down.

"Now, you asked me who I am. I represent a nation whose millions of citizens are at risk of annihilation due to your work."

The physicist looked confused. He stammered, "I-I don't know what it is you think I do. I am a consultant for TAPROGGE, a cleantech energy consultant. I have been on an extended contract in the Middle East . . . mostly in Iran and the Gulf States. I promise. That's all I do."

"So you don't work with centrifuges?"

"What? No!"

"And your office is not in Karaj?"

The confidence in the doctor's voice seemed to be building. "Certainly not. I have been there, of course, as part of my job with TAPROGGE. But that had nothing to do with centrifuge production."

"So I'm completely mistaken?"

"I'm sorry. It's true."

Nir threw up his hands. "It is I, then, who must apologize to you. Here we have broken into your rental condo. Injected your wife with a narcotic. Threatened you with a handgun. And it was all based on faulty information." Nir shook his head. "I must tell you, I am so embarrassed."

The doctor gave a weak smile. "It is really no problem. I promise to tell no one that you were here."

"That is a relief." Nir prepared to stand. "Well, my friend and I should go. But before we do, may I ask you one more question?"

"Of course. Ask whatever you want."

"Do you think they'll call him Dad?"

Dr. Lindner looked confused. "Will who call who Dad?"

"Your two sons in the next room. Will they call your wife's new husband Dad? I mean, she is fairly young and still quite attractive. I can't imagine her not remarrying after you're gone. Your children, too, are young. After a few years, those boys will forget your voice, then your face. Soon you will be just a distant memory, a smile on an old photograph."

The scientist was shaking now. "I-I told you, I'm just a consultant. I don't—"

"Stop lying to me."

Nir's voice was tinged with violence now. Lindner needed to know what he was up against. "Your work is assisting Iran in achieving a nuclear weapon. When they get one, they will use it on us—on my family. An old saying from the Babylonian Talmud says, 'If someone comes to kill you, rise up and kill him first.' But this is your lucky day. I am rising up only to tell you that if you do not leave your service to the Iranian regime, I will come back. And then I will kill you, and quite possibly I will kill your family as well."

"No!" When Nir shushed the doctor, he repeated in a loud whisper, "No. I will never go back to Iran. I promise. Just don't hurt me or my family. I'll never go back."

"Do you believe me when I say that if you are lying to me, I will find you and I will kill you?"

The man vehemently nodded. "I do! You found me here, so you can find me anywhere, right?"

"Exactly. No wonder you're a doctor. You're very smart." Nir stood and looked down at the man who was doing his best to control his emotions. "Do not disappoint me, Dr. Lindner. I will kill anyone who threatens my family or my country, and I will do it without remorse."

As he was about to exit through the bedroom doorway, Nir turned and said, "Oh, and be sure to take your family to visit the Jardin boutanique d'Èze. I hear their collection of succulents is quite amazing."

The doctor broke down, and Nir could still hear his sobs as he followed Imri out the condo's rear door and onto the stony beach. They put up their hoods and made their way to the van. The only words that passed between them was when Imri chuckled and said, "Their collection of succulents is quite amazing?"

"I felt bad about the wife. Thought she might like it."

Yaron was already at the van, and Dima ambled up 30 seconds later.

After daybreak, most of the team departed on separate flights for their circuitous trips home. By nightfall, all would be back in Israel, except for Nir. When mid-morning arrived, he climbed into his rented convertible BMW M440i and headed northeast along the coast of the Ligurian Sea. Two-and-a-half hours later, he made a brief stop for some bread and cheese in Genoa. Then turning north, he traveled inland for another 90 minutes before the spire of the UniCredit Tower came into view. The tallest building in Italy, the skyscraper dominated the skyline of Milan.

CHAPTER 15

Even on an average day, Milan was a city of beautiful women, young and old. During Fashion Week, though, you couldn't walk a city block without being disdainfully ignored by the thousand-yard stares of a dozen world-class supermodels.

But the long-legged struts weren't what drew Nir's attention as he rested on a bench surrounding the base of a large statue of King Victor Emmanuel II, uniter of all Italy. Across the plaza, rising 108 meters into the sky, stood the Metropolitan Cathedral-Basilica of the Nativity of Saint Mary—or simply, the Milan Cathedral. A classic Gothic design, it was breathtaking in its ornate detail. Spire after marble spire jutted high into the sky.

Using his phone, Nir had looked up the history of the church and was amazed to read that, although work on it had begun in 1386, the structure had not been declared complete until 1965, nearly six hundred years later.

It took Noah only a hundred years to build his massive ark. They should have hired him as foreman for the project.

Something caught his eye, and he smiled at what he saw. *The only thing more beautiful than a massive marble cathedral.*

He stood and opened his arms. "Nicole," he said as they embraced.

When they separated, he could see the look in her eyes didn't match the smile on her face. "Want to sit for a second?"

"No, let's walk. I've got to let off some steam." She slipped her arm under his, which gave him a little relief. He didn't seem to be the one she was upset with.

"Bad day at the office?"

She gave a humorless laugh. "Females are just the worst."

"Don't I know it."

Nicole slapped his arm. "I get to say that. You don't."

They strolled across the plaza toward another large structure. Nir figured she'd let him know what was going on when she was ready. They walked through the doors, and he was surprised to find stores lining the walkway.

"What is this place?"

"The Galleria Vittorio Emanuele II. It's like a nineteenth-century shopping mall."

Nir felt like he'd walked into a steampunk lover's dream. Although the names on the signs were all modern and high-end, the store façades made it look as though they were walking down the streets of old town Milan. Covering them from high overhead was an intricate dome and vault system of iron and glass. "This place is amazing."

"It is. It makes me feel like I should be wearing a long dress with a bustle and carrying a parasol."

"Speaking of your last fashion show, are you ready to tell me what happened?"

She gripped his arm a little tighter. "Not funny. You know, it's not a big deal. The other model was probably having a bad day, and I was in the wrong place at the wrong time." Suddenly, she had a little bounce to her step. "But now I'm in the right place at the right time, right here next to you."

"You sure you don't want me to flush her goldfish or make her disappear?"

"Wow, those are my two options? Fish-i-cide or homicide?"

"I have a very limited skill set."

Nicole laughed, then stopped to look up at the canopy. "I love walking through here. It's hard not to feel transported back a century and a half. More innocent times. Less evil in the world."

Nir shook his head. "I don't know about that. Every era has its own evil. It just comes in different forms."

"Well, aren't you a little ray of sunshine?"

"I know. I'm sorry. It's just that this last op has got me thinking. What are we really accomplishing? We take a guy out of Iran's nuclear program, but with the kind of money they're paying, a hundred more are waiting to jump into his place."

"Kind of like Whac-A-Mole. Every time you hit one head, another pops up."

"Exactly. I don't know, Nicole. I'm getting tired of feeling like I'm just playing a dumb arcade game that gets us nowhere. The stakes are too high. The danger is too real. I feel like if we're going to do something, we need to do something big."

"What about what happened in Natanz?"

Back at the beginning of July, an explosion had ripped through the Iran Centre for Advanced Centrifuges in Natanz, Iran. This facility was there to calibrate the centrifuges used to enrich the uranium needed to create a nuclear weapon.

"No doubt, Natanz was brilliant. First, they fill construction materials with explosives, then they pose as wholesalers of those same construction supplies. They get the Iranians to purchase the stuff, the Iranians install the explosives into their own centrifuge hall, and then a year later— boom! If it hadn't really happened, nobody would believe it."

"Exactly, and that was a huge setback for their nuclear program."

"True, but it's still the same thing. It just slowed them down. We need to do something to actually halt Iran's progress. Slowing them down just delays the inevitable destruction of Israel. Eventually, even the tortoise reaches the finish line."

They started walking again.

"How was the *tenachesh mi*?" Nicole asked.

Nir smiled at her growing Hebrew vocabulary. *Tenachesh mi* meant "Guess who?" and that was what his team had taken to calling their occasional middle-of-the-night visitations.

"The good doctor assured me he's feeling a call to a new career path."

"I'm glad of that. I sometimes feel bad for how terrified they must be in that moment, but I know it's better than the alternative."

"I don't feel bad for them at all. They know exactly what they're doing. I doubt there are many people alive who don't know Iran is pushing for nuclear weapons, and when they get them, they're going to use them on us."

Nicole stopped to look in the window of a sweetshop, where chocolates of many designs sat on intricate racks. "I don't know. Some of them just don't seem to think ahead. They only see the money."

"Would you like something from this shop?" Nir asked.

Nicole laughed and moved on. "No. Just looking. Wishing I didn't have an athletic wear photo shoot at the end of the week."

"Then it's good we're leaving. I was gaining weight just looking at those."

They walked past several more shops, then Nir said, "You know, I don't really care if they've thought it through or not. The result of their work is the same. Whether you kill millions intentionally or unintentionally, millions are still dead."

"That's fair. I just have motives on the mind. There's this preacher I've been watching online."

Nir groaned. Again, he was happy for the big change in Nicole's life. And if it was her Jesus that made the difference, then that was perfectly fine with him. He just wished she didn't feel the need to talk about it all the time.

"Just listen to me. Something might actually break through that cynical, *Bible-schmible* wall you've put up in your brain," she said, laughing and tapping the side of his head. "So this guy was talking about how when Christians are judged before God, their motives are what will be judged. It's not so much about what you do but why you do it."

"Okay. Interesting. Go on."

"You can do the wrong things for the wrong reasons, and that's wrong. You can do the right things for the wrong reasons, and that's wrong too. The only actions that count are when we do the right things for the right reasons. Everything else will be burned up."

Nir thought about that for a moment. "What about doing the wrong things for the right reasons?"

It was Nicole's turn to think as they exited the opposite end of the galleria. "I don't know," she finally said. "I'm not sure if motives can turn something wrong into something right. That slips into an *ends justify the means* philosophy."

"Well, if you get a verdict from on high for that one, I'd like to know. Because that's pretty much where I spend my life."

CHAPTER 16

16:45 / 4:45 P.M. CEST

They walked silently for a while, Nir enjoying the feel of Nicole's hand on his bare arm. A large tiled square spread out in front of the classic Teatro alla Scala opera house, and they stopped in its center to admire a statue of Leonardo da Vinci. Taking a right onto Via Alessandro Manzoni, they continued for block after block, passing shops, cafes, and museums.

The conversation soon picked up again with Nir filling Nicole in on his diamond business and Aunt Mila's latest admonitions against his lifestyle choices. Nicole laid out her upcoming schedule that would take her to Stockholm, London, New York City, and Dallas.

When they reached Via Monte Napoleone, they took a right. Nir stopped. He could not remember the last time he felt so out of place—and actually poor. Lining the narrow street were high-end shops selling clothing that would probably cost him a year's salary just to try on.

"Welcome to *Lifestyles of the Rich and Famous*," Nicole said with a laugh, sliding her hand down to take his. She gave him a tug that put his legs back in gear.

"What is this alien world, and why have you brought me here?"

"Oh, come on. It will be fun. Maybe I'll let you buy me something." He saw the twinkle in her eyes.

"Maybe a souvenir keychain, but even that will probably max out my credit card, and I've got some pretty high-limit credit cards."

As they walked on, Nicole talked about some of the designers with storefronts along the road. Some she'd modeled for, but most were still out of her league. Not all the stores sold clothing. Nir saw art galleries, restaurants, and jewelry stores as well. He recognized some of the names of the jewelers and wondered if any of his diamonds had made their way into their vaults.

Eventually, the conversation moved back to their other activities, the work that didn't involve runways or bling.

"Do you have anything you can tell me about coming up?" Nicole asked.

"Something big is coming in November, but I can't say too much because you'll be out saving the world one photo shoot at a time."

"I know." She sounded a little embarrassed. "I just felt like I need to spend some time rebuilding my presence in the modeling world for the last part of the year. And our higher-ups agreed."

"I get it, I get it. Like we talked about before, it's a good move. I just wish I had you on this op.

It's going to be new and cutting edge, and it will most certainly make the news."

"So intriguing. Can't wait to find out about it."

Nir thought a moment, then said, "I can tell you it will involve AI in a major way."

"Artificial intelligence? Now I'm even more intrigued."

"Exactly. Again, cutting edge. But AI is also the downside to the operation, because who is our team AI expert?"

Nicole laughed. "Oh no. Lahav."

Lahav Tabib was a brilliant analyst. But he was also a little bit crazy and a whole lot irritating. He could speak more words in three minutes than Nir would say in a whole day. Typically, Nir counted on Nicole to keep Lahav under control, but with her gone, he would have no buffer.

"Yeah, and get this. He'll be deployed with my Kidon boys when we go in. I'll probably have to find him a desert camouflage pocket protector for his BDU," Nir said. He really couldn't picture what Lahav would look like in a battle dress uniform.

Nicole stopped laughing. "Nir, is that a good idea? With his mouth and lack of self-awareness, how are you going to keep him quiet?"

"Threats, mostly, I guess. Maybe gaffer tape? I don't know. I just know this op is so technical and complicated that he needs to be on the ground with us."

For a while, they were both silent again.

Nicole suddenly stopped in front of a gallery and pointed to a painting in its window. "I know her!"

"Um, I do too. It's Marilyn Monroe. I hate to break it to you, but she's kind of a big deal."

"No, you goof," she said, punching his arm. "I know the artist. Alicia Marcos. She and I shared a flight once from Frankfurt to New Jersey. She was on her way home to Houston, Texas. We really hit it off, and we've kept in touch and gotten together a couple of times since then. This is her work. See her name in the corner?"

The picture was a modern take on the Hollywood star. Very raw. Very colorful. And she was biting down on a contemporary pair of Oakley sunglasses. But what intrigued him most was the canvas. "What is that painted on?"

"That's the coolest part. Alicia paints on a mixture of cement, and I don't know what else. It's a whole process. And not only does it look awesome, but it lasts, even where it's wet or humid. See, it's got that high-gloss finish, which is really a protectant. Many of her clients are yacht owners—Texas oil barons, movie stars, Bollywood actors. She's one of the few in the world who use this technique, so when they want to decorate their yachts, she gets the call."

A spark of an idea formed in Nir's mind. Likely, it would be impractical—and quite probably, impossible. But he wouldn't know for sure until he got a little more information.

"Where did you say your next shoots are?"

"Stockholm, London, New York, Dallas. Just in and out at each. Why? I can see the gears turning. What's going on in that twisted mind of yours?"

"Since you'll be in Dallas, is there any chance you might be able to pop on over to Houston?"

"It's Texas. I don't think any two cities are within pop-able distance. But sure, I could add a few days to my trip."

A smile spread across Nir's face. "Interesting. You and I need to do some serious talking. Let's grab something to eat. But not here. I don't want to have to mortgage my business for a plate of pasta."

"Okay, Mr. Bond, I'm in." Then she grabbed his arm again as they looked for a cab.

OCTOBER
2020
[ONE WEEK LATER]

CHAPTER 17

ONE WEEK LATER
CAFALA BAHR, MIRABELLO BAY,
SEA OF CRETE, GREECE—
OCTOBER 5, 2020—20:15 / 8:15 P.M. EET

Saad swirled the Hibiki 21 Years Old whisky, then brought it to his nose and inhaled deeply. With his financial reserves, the price of the expensive liquid wasn't even a minor rounding error. But he was a man who appreciated fine things, and he wanted to savor this moment. He sipped and let the whisky's flavor of sandalwood, dried fruits, nuts, and smoke cover his tongue and palate. This was the final bottle from the case hand delivered to him by the chief distiller of the House of Suntory when he was off the coast of Osaka last year, and he wanted to make it last.

Unfortunately, it was difficult to be in the moment with loud music and tittering laughter. Two men—his *invited* guests—were moving their bodies in various ungainly gyrations 20 meters away on the helipad, which doubled as a dance floor. The six women giggling and swaying with much more skill were all being paid for their attendance.

One of the ladies, a tall blond wearing a short and sparkly two-piece halter dress, slapped the bare chest of IRGC general Arash Mousavi. Pulling her close, he whispered something in her ear. She feigned shock, which she then transformed into a well-practiced look of anticipation.

Saad shook his head as he sipped at his drink. It was just beginning to cool off after an unseasonably hot day, and he enjoyed the chilly burn of the liquid. Mousavi was still a fool when it came to women, but he was Saad's in-road to the Islamic Revolutionary Guard Corps. The general was high in the Quds Force of the IRGC, and he'd moved even closer to the top with the assassination of Qasem Soleimani at the beginning of the year.

A great tactician, he was ruthless when it came to his leadership of Iran's proxy militias in Iraq and Syria. When Saad put his money in the hands of Mousavi, he knew it would be funneled into the right places—all except for the portion the general skimmed off the top.

Of course, his friend didn't know Saad was aware of his graft. It was a little bit of information he kept stored away for when it might be needed.

Reaching into a bowl of mixed nuts, Saad took a handful and popped a couple into his mouth. Off in the distance he saw towering lights moving across the water. That would be one of the cruise ships that plagued these waters. It was difficult to find a more beautiful and cultured collection of islands than those that stretched north of him in the Aegean Sea. But often, sailing these waters felt like driving a car down a freeway filled with tractor trailers. Everywhere you looked, 18-deck monstrosities churned up wakes as they passed.

The music changed to some horrid British-sounding pop song, and his other guest began using his champagne flute as a microphone. The expensive contents sloshed and spilled as he sang. Although Saad despised the man, he had to admit he had a good voice. It wasn't just high-level karaoke quality; he had some talent. The paid audience, however, reacted as if he were the second coming of Justin Bieber or Shawn Mendes or whoever was popular these days. Saad's kids could have told him, but he couldn't remember exactly how many years it had been since any of his three daughters were of the age to still live at home. He did know it had been more than two years since any of them had bothered to contact him.

They resent you for being gone while you make the money. Then once you give them the money, they are the ones who disappear.

Noticing that no one had cleaned up the spilled liquid, he snapped his fingers. The bartender who'd been standing nearby hurried to him.

"Yes, sir."

"Go tell one of those new Filipinos to clean up that mess on the dance floor before someone slips and breaks a bone. Let the fools know they have

133

one job to do, and right now they aren't doing it."

"Yes, sir." The man ran off.

Thinking back to his children, Saad realized he couldn't completely blame them for abandoning him. He had no doubt that his ex-wife had plenty to do with their view of him. She'd been a good woman, just naïve. She didn't understand that men who live in his kind of world play with a different set of rules when it comes to family, time, and monogamy. Admittedly, he had not been the best of husbands, but at least he hadn't insisted on having other wives—unlike the buffoon singing on the dance floor. His four submissive wives had born him a total of eight children, although five were girls and two of the three boys appeared to be complete dunces.

Saad had his corporate intelligence team do a full background on Ali Kamal before he allowed him on the boat. He was a prince in the royal family, which was not unusual. The House of Saud bred like rabbits, and each spawn was considered royalty and given an outrageous amount of money.

Saad's father had experienced quite a few run-ins with the "royals" during his years in Saudi Arabia. In fact, one of those royals, the current King Salman, had run to then-King Fahd to report some offense supposedly committed by Saad's father. That was what led to his family's flight to Qatar.

Kamal was an idiot, but he was, as Vladimir Lenin talked about, a useful idiot. This was because he hated the Saudi royal family with a passion that may have even exceeded Saad's own. Although a royal himself, Kamal, too, had experienced a falling out. In November 2017, Saudi Crown Prince Mohammad bin Salman ordered the arrest of four hundred of the nation's elite, among them Prince Ali. Along with the others, he was detained in the opulent Ritz Carlton in Riyadh. But it was no vacation.

The first night they were all blindfolded, and most were beaten. Kamal was left hanging by his arms in his room. His wrists had been tied together with the rope passed over the bathroom door and secured. The next day the interrogations began, and the questions and violence lasted for weeks before he was finally released.

Many of the business leaders lost their fortunes with more than $100 billion collected from them by the government. Because of his bloodline, Kamal was able to keep his wealth but not his status. Banned from the royal palace, many considered him a social pariah.

By all rights, Saad thought he should feel bad for the man. But he was such a loathsome creature that it was difficult to hope for anything but the worst for him.

Again, though he is an idiot, he truly is a useful one. How else can I learn about what is

135

happening in the Saudi royal family? And there is most certainly truth in the old adage that an enemy of my enemy is my friend.

Avoiding the spill still on the ground, Kamal rounded up four of the women, and the five of them danced their way off the helipad and toward the elevator.

He takes four and leaves two. How very Saudi of him, Saad thought, glaring at the man.

General Mousavi waved to a steward, who turned down the music. Then sauntering toward Saad with a woman under each arm, he said, "It seems that our friend is a bit of a glutton when it comes to women."

"He is who we know him to be."

"Since your money is paying for all this, I feel that I should give you your pick," said the Persian. Looking from one side to the other, he added, "Do you prefer blond or brunette?"

"They are both yours tonight, my friend. I had an early morning, and I think I can use some rest."

"Well, if you insist," the general said with a laugh. "Good night, Saad. Sleep well."

"*Fe sahetek.*" Saad saluted him with his glass, then drained the rest of the contents and, in the bartender's absence, poured himself another. The steward was quick to shut down all the upper deck lights at his boss's request, and then Saad tilted his head back and looked up at the stars.

CHAPTER 18

ONE DAY LATER
OCTOBER 6, 2020—10:30 / 10:30 A.M. EET

*Y*ou can tell a lot about a person by how they sit in a room, Saad thought as he lowered himself into a plush high-backed chair. General Mousavi sat to his left on a couch. His legs were crossed, and his arm rested above the pillows. Kamal was to his right. His back was against the arm of the couch, and his feet were up on the white cushions. Each man had a bottle of sparkling water and a bowl of fruit on a table next to them. All were dressed for a day on the upper deck, which likely wouldn't happen because of the cool rain falling outside.

Probably for the best. Some discussions are best held indoors.

Saad poured water over a large cube of ice in a glass. "I trust you gentlemen had a pleasant night?"

The paid entertainment had been loaded onto one of the ship's tenders and taken to shore early this morning.

"I would trade three of my wives for just one of those girls," answered Kamal.

Saad laughed along even though he found the

joke distasteful. Actually, there was little about this man that he didn't find distasteful.

"My night was excellent," said Mousavi. "And I thank you."

Looking at Kamal, Saad said, "I have invited you here, Ali, because I think we may have some interests in common. Surprisingly enough, I think that may be true of our Iranian friend as well."

"Any enemy of the royal family is a friend of mine."

"I can understand that. I must admit, I have been very disappointed to watch Saudi Arabia warming up so much to the Zionist Occupiers."

"Me too! Trust me. The king is a doddering old fool. And the crown prince cares only for power and money. He is everything that is wrong in Riyadh. There are no principles left in the royal palace."

Mousavi said, "First the United Arab Emirates normalized relations with the Occupiers due in large part to the Abraham Accords and the Zionists' part in stopping the drone attack on the Burj Khalifa skyscraper in Dubai. Now the rumor is that Sudan, Bahrain, and Morocco could be the next to cave to the pressure."

"Along with my country," Kamal said. "Our disgusting behind-the-scenes flirtations with the Jews are an open secret in the Middle East."

"It's true," said the general. "Quite honestly, *habibi*, I have been in high-level discussions where we have spoken of placing your country ahead of the Jewish Occupiers on our kill list." He lifted an orange wedge to his mouth.

Kamal sat up, his feet now on the floor. "Don't you include me with those heretics. Allah gave them power and resources, and look what they have done with it. They have squandered their influence in the name of riches and decadence."

Saad stifled a smile by popping a large purple grape into his mouth. *Riches and decadence? This is the multimillionaire prince who took four women to his quarters last night. The lack of self-awareness is astounding.*

The Saudi continued his rant. "If we cut off the head of the royal family, plenty like me would be ready to step in. We are the faithful. We are the true followers of Allah." Turning to Mousavi, he said, "You and I, General, may have major doctrinal differences. And truth be told, in any other venue we might hate each other. But as we sit here this morning, you are my friend. Why? Because we share the same enemies."

"Which are . . ." asked Saad.

"The Saudi royal family, Israel, and the United States." Kamal ticked them off on his fingers one by one.

"And you are comfortable if my ordering of that list differs from yours?"

"As long as we are all committed to wiping out

them all, I don't care what order you personally put them in."

Saad dropped another grape into his mouth, then said, "Tell me, General, what is your country's view of the upcoming U.S. election?"

Mousavi groaned, eliciting a smile from Saad. "I just wish it would happen and be over with. It feels as if we are in limbo until they do."

"How so?"

"If the current president stays in power, life is much more difficult. Of course, we continue our nuclear development and our support and training of the militias. It's just that we must be diligently covert about it. Also, this president is much more likely to sanction any action the Zionists take against us."

"And if the other one is elected?"

The general smiled as he tilted his bottle to fill his glass. "We think we know what we are getting with him. When he was vice president, he was very favorable toward us. Even now he is campaigning on a return to the JCPOA. If he plays along with his party, then it will be very good for us. We'll ratify a new nuclear deal, which will essentially allow us to work *carte blanche* enriching our uranium. It will also be more difficult for the Zionists to gain approval for a military attack on our nuclear infrastructure."

"That brings up a question, General." Kamal was back on the couch again with his feet up.

"When you finally achieve nuclear weapons, will you use them? You can imagine my curiosity, because I recognize that my country may be on the receiving end of one of your missiles. But you need to know that if the royal family is removed, the leadership that takes its place will be much more amenable to your ayatollahs. Yes, we will have our faith difference. However, as we are showing now, that should not hinder our working together against a common foe."

The general sipped his sparkling water, then returned the glass to the table. "Let me address the second part of your statement first. Yes, I agree that we could work together, and I will pass your assurances on to those who need to know."

Kamal gave an appreciative nod.

"As to whether we would use our nuclear weapons, that has not been determined."

Saad suppressed an eye roll. This was an ongoing discussion between the general and him, and the Iranian had always said that weapons are made to be used, not just polished and displayed.

The general continued. "However, if we use them, it would likely not be as you think. Yes, we are developing our missile technology. However, we are also putting much research into developing small, portable weapons. Imagine one of those finding its way into the hands of a Palestinian freedom fighter in Gaza."

Kamal laughed and clapped his hands. "It would be glorious."

"That is why my friend here is pouring some of his billions into training our militias in the handling of portable nuclear devices," Mousavi said, lifting his glass toward Saad.

Kamal lifted his own and drank. Then addressing the general once more, he said, "Speaking of your militias, if we act against the Saudi regime, can you give me the support of the Houthi rebels? I will make a promise to them to stop the air attacks into Yemen. They will be free to do whatever they want in their own country."

"That, my new friend, I believe I can deliver to you." He stood and walked to Kamal, and the two men clinked their glasses together.

Saad stood as well. "I think that concludes our business for now. I don't know about you, but I'm ready for a swim in the indoor pool."

CHAPTER 19

ONE WEEK LATER
EIGHT ROW FLINT, HOUSTON, TEXAS—
OCTOBER 14, 2020—18:30 / 6:30 P.M. CDT

The first flavor coming through was the freshness of the corn tortilla. Then the toastiness of the masa was followed by the char of the onions, the brightness of the crema, and the "pow" of the cilantro. Listed on the menu as a brussels sprout taco, the eponymous vegetable took a back seat to the surrounding players. Nicole indulged in a second bite even before she'd completely swallowed the first.

"This is remarkable," she said, her mouth half full, returning what was left of the small taco to her plate.

"Isn't it, though?" Alicia Marcos covered her full mouth as she responded with a laugh. The remnants of the taco she held revealed shrimp, carrots, some kind of white root vegetable, and little black specks that looked like peppercorns or sesame seeds. "I'm so glad you encouraged me to try someplace different. I get into such a routine when I'm in work mode."

Alicia's ancestors had migrated north from San Luis Potosí three generations back, and she carried their coloring in her bronze skin and jet-black hair, which she kept shoulder-length, probably to keep it out of her paints. On the shorter side yet thin and wiry from all the exertion required by her artistic medium, she would be considered everyday beautiful. Her face might never grace the cover of a magazine, but the joy of her wide smile and the brightness in her rich brown eyes would cause any man to thank the Lord for blessing him with such a gorgeous wife.

"Speaking of work mode, you've got a little . . ." Nicole reached her hand across the small bar table and indicated the left side of her friend's jawline.

Alicia laughed. "What colors? I'm assuming some blue."

"And a little bit of red."

The artist shrugged. "That's my life. I've found paint splatters in places that seem contrary to the laws of physics. I used to go over myself in a full-length mirror after cleaning up, but now I just do a quick glance and figure that whatever I miss is an occupational hazard."

"I love it! I wish I could do the same. So much of my life is having to sit perfectly or walk perfectly or just be perfect. Perfection is as obnoxious as it is unattainable."

Alicia took a sip of her drink. The women had ordered the same one because the name was so intriguing. A house specialty, it was called *There's Always Money in the Banana Stand*, and it was a mixture of two kinds of rum, lime juice, pineapple juice, banana syrup, and egg white. Nicole had no idea what egg white was doing in a cocktail, but she couldn't argue the result. If this was what the banana stand was serving, it's no wonder they were flush with cash.

"I had to get to that point with my art, too—you know, giving up on perfection. There was always one more brush stroke or one more texture. I could add another highlight to the hair or a shadow on the dress. Finally, I had to start giving myself permission to walk away. To just say, *It's done!*"

"I'm a little envious. I want to be at that place, too, but I guess the industry I'm in just doesn't allow it. Although I'm better now than I used to be." Breaking off a piece of a corn chip from a basket, Nicole dipped it in a bowl of green salsa. But before putting it into her mouth, she continued.

"I still pursue perfection to gain other people's approval in a professional context. I have to. God has given me a job, and I want to do it well. But my true affirmation, what makes me content with who I really am, no longer comes from others. It comes only from God." She dropped the chip into her mouth, then broke off another corner.

"Exactly! One hundred percent. Critics will

always be around to tell you you're terrible. You're a terrible artist. A terrible person." Leaning forward, Alicia lowered her voice. "A lady in my church—in my *church*—came up to me one Sunday morning and said she'd seen a photo of my art online and couldn't believe a Christian would paint a picture of Marilyn Monroe. Why? Because she was a hussy. Then she said since I thought Marilyn Monroe was so wonderful, I must be a hussy too."

Nicole almost spit out the remnants of her chip. "She actually used the word *hussy?*"

"She did, right there by the coffee bar in the foyer."

"I thought I'd been called every name in the book for some of the photo shoots I've done, but I've never been called a hussy."

"Well, if you want that square on your bingo card stamped, come to my church. I've got a lady I can introduce you to."

Nicole sipped her drink, trying to loosen some of the sprouts lodged in her back teeth. "There's just such a peace knowing I don't have to prove myself to God. He already knows how messed up I can be, and He still loves me. All my doubts, all my fears, all my bad decisions—despite all that stuff, He stays with me."

"Amen. Now, speaking of *staying* with you, you haven't said a thing about your Belgian jeweler friend. Is he still staying with you?"

Nicole felt heat come to her cheeks as she looked down with a smile.

Alicia laughed. "Apparently the answer is yes. I don't know that I've ever seen you blush before, girl."

"Stop," Nicole said, laughing too. "If by *staying* you mean does he stay with me when he's in Milan, then the answer is no. But if you're asking if we're still a thing, then that answer is yeah. In fact, Nir's one reason I wanted to get together with you today."

Alicia's already big eyes grew even wider. "What? Do I need to start looking for a sky-blue chiffon bridesmaid's dress I'll never wear again?"

"No! It's nothing like that," she said with another smile, but it quickly disappeared from her face. "It can't be anything like that, at least not yet. I've told you before. He doesn't want anything to do with Jesus. He's fine with my being a Christian, but he says it's not for him. I can't marry a guy if the number one thing in his life isn't the same as the number one thing in mine."

"You're right, although I know it can't be easy. Just be patient. There's no telling what God will do. So if it's not the 'Wedding March,' what is it?"

Nicole sipped her drink again, using it as an excuse to prepare herself. These next minutes would determine whether the plot she and Nir were hatching would ever get off the ground. A no from Alicia, and they were dead in the water.

At first, as Nicole listened to Nir lay out his idea for an operation, she was resistant. Alicia was a friend. Nicole didn't want to use her or lie to her or put her in any danger. But as they talked some more, she realized she wouldn't have to actually lie to Alicia, at least not any more than she usually did as someone who lived a secret life as a computer hacker and analyst for the world's premier intelligence agency.

Nicole would be able to tell the truth, just not the whole truth. She'd have to keep some minor details from Alicia—like the fact they'd be secretly hiding explosives in her artwork in order to assassinate terrorists.

Ultimately, it would be a positive for Alicia. Through the connections Nir would make for her, many more paintings with the Alicia Marcos signature would find their way into expensive beach homes and luxury yachts. Currently, she wasn't exactly a starving artist, but Nicole knew she wasn't rolling in money either. The early 2000s-era Nissan she drove up in made that clear.

Quit trying to justify yourself, Nicole. Remember, the Hebrew midwives lied to save those babies, and God blessed them. Sometimes a wrong word uttered for the right reason can be a good thing.

That thought brought to mind the conversation about motives she'd had with Nir a couple of weeks ago, but she couldn't think about that now. She had a mission—and she had to be cool about it.

Leaning forward, then taking on a conspiratorial tone, Nicole said, "My jeweler guy, as you call him, and I were walking down the Via Monte Napoleone in Milan when we saw one of your pieces—the Marilyn, the one with the Oakley sunglasses. It was displayed in a gallery window."

"Oh, that was Gallo Milano. My friend Matteo Franco showed it for me there. It sold five days ago."

"Nir will be disappointed, because he loved the piece. He was blown away, not just by its beauty but by the creativity of materials." Nicole reached across the table and touched her friend's hand. "When Nir saw your painting, the wheels in his brain started turning. That's just the way he is. He's like a business ninja. Long story short, for a ten percent finder's fee from each piece you sell, he thinks he can make you a millionaire by this time next year. And that's just the beginning."

CHAPTER 20

He'll get us all killed," Yaron said. Although his ops second was short and stocky, his standing body dominated the table.

"I'm sitting right here," Lahav said, looking like he'd walked out of computer nerd central casting, complete with thick black plastic glasses and a mostly full pocket protector. "If you have something to say, say it to me."

Yaron turned toward the man and leaned over the table, his face red with anger. "You are going to get us all killed," he said, emphasizing each word with a point of his index finger.

Lahav pretended to turn a crank as he slowly raised a finger of his own. Yaron started to climb across the table toward him, but Dima and Doron grabbed hold of his shoulders and pulled him back down to his chair. The fourth member of Nir's Kidon team, Imri, remained calmly seated at the farthest side of the table away from Nir, watching the events with amusement.

On the analyst side of the table sat Dafna Ronen

and Liora to Lahav's left and Yossi Hirschfield to his right. Dafna and Liora were on their feet threatening to use their extensive computer skills to do something very nasty to the title of Yaron's home if he touched Lahav. Yossi had his feet up on the table with a laptop perched on his long legs. White earbuds had been inserted in his ears.

Nir was at the head of the table, and Efraim Cohen, the assistant deputy director of Caesarea and Nir's good friend, sat to his right. Although Efraim had gone a little soft in the midsection, prior to reaching his fortieth birthday this year, the man had been part of several dozen risky missions and was likely the best shot in the room.

"I like your hands-off leadership style," he said to Nir, nodding toward the mayhem taking place around the table. "Do you usually step in before or after bloodshed?"

Nir glared at him, then yelled, "Okay, knock it off!"

Everyone ignored him.

Efraim took on a professorial air and said, "You know, I once heard a man say that in every leader there's—"

Nir grabbed a large bowl of pistachios Liora had provided for the meeting and hurled it across the room. It pinged off the head of the life-sized Chewbacca mannequin that stood next to Lahav's desk and today wore a hat stenciled with the words *Furry World Tel Aviv 2020*. The metal bowl clattered to the floor followed by what sounded like a very brief yet very intense hailstorm.

All heads turned toward Nir except for Yossi's. His eyes never left whatever he was watching on his computer as he said, "I'm not cleaning that up."

Nir paused for a moment, hoping the silence would lower the emotion in the room.

"Listen, I didn't invite Assistant Deputy Director Cohen here—"

"Isn't that Assistant *to* the Deputy Director?" asked Yossi.

Snickers rippled throughout the room.

"Yeah, what's with the sudden use of titles?" Doron asked in a transparent attempt to bait the room into a meaningless discussion in order to lower the temperature of the discourse.

"I'll tell you what," Dafna said, pointing at Yaron. "I've got a title for that guy."

Unfortunately, she proceeded to announce the title, and the whole table erupted again.

"You're a regular Dale Carnegie," Efraim said as he put his arm around Nir's shoulders. "Never seen so much influencing of people."

"You're not helping."

Gradually, Nir gained control of the mob and said, "Listen, Yaron, normally I agree with you. The operative's place is in the field, the analyst's place is back at headquarters. But this is different."

"Why? What makes this different? Just because it's artificial intelligence? Ooh, suddenly it's too fancy for us mouth-breathers to handle?"

Lahav replied with a placating tone. "No, you're right, you're right. It's true that we don't always give you boots-on-the-ground guys enough credit. Just tell me this, though. What if you're all set up, the target is coming, and you suddenly realize your flux capacitor has gone down and you don't have enough jigawatts to power it back up? What would you do?"

"I can't tell you right now," Yaron said with a condescending tone. "But if you do your job, then by the time of the operation, I will know exactly how to get enough jigawatts to start up the flux capacitor."

"There's no such thing as a flux capacitor, you *mefager*," Lahav said as he leaned back in his chair and spread his arms as if he'd just announced "Checkmate."

This time the hands were on Yaron's shoulders before he could clear his chair.

"I heard you can only get that many jigawatts using lightning," Yossi said amid the ensuing chaos, still focused on his laptop.

Efraim stood and slammed one palm on the table. "Okay, everybody stop. I've got a limited amount of time, and you guys are wasting it.

Lahav is going with the ops team, so shut up and accept it."

As he sat back down, he turned toward Nir and whispered with a wink, "It's all about influence, *achi*. I'll get you a copy of Carnegie's book."

Nir shook his head and sighed. "Okay, can we please act like adults? We've got six weeks before we're on the ground in Iran. We need to be a solid team watching each other's backs. You don't have to agree with all the decisions made. You just need to make them work. Understood?"

Nods of agreement all around, some more emphatic than others.

"Okay, now I have something else to run past you all. And that's why Efraim's in here. Yossi, close your laptop before it follows the flight path of the pistachio bowl."

The full-bearded, man-bunned analyst gave an exasperated sigh and obeyed.

Nir began by giving them the background of walking the streets of Milan with Nicole, ignoring all the catcalls and kissing noises from the Millennials who made up his team of analysts. When he got to the part about seeing the Alicia Marcos painting, he clicked a remote, and a photo of the painting appeared on a large double monitor set that hung over Liora and Dafna's joined workstations. The Kidon members had to turn around in their chairs to see it.

"*Esh*! Marilyn. I love her," said Dafna.

Tattooed, overly pierced, and sporting blue and purple hair on the half of her head that wasn't shaved, she was the visual opposite of the tiny, dark-haired, ultra-cute Liora. Yet despite their external differences, the two of them had a remarkably symbiotic connection as they worked, and they often joked that they finished each other's sandwiches.

Liora piped up. "Nicole's friend is amazing. I've never seen anything like this. It's like Warhol meets pulp-fiction cover art meets NYC Club Kid."

Nir had to admit that was a really good analysis. The best descriptor for the painting he'd been able to come up with was *colorful*.

Imri spoke up. "The gloss is *metoraf*—seriously, it's really incredible. And what's it painted on? That's not a regular canvas."

"Exactly." Nir was glad to see the new guy was weighing in. "It's a cement-based medium, specially designed to hold color in wet and humid environments."

"That's an oddly specific answer. Want to tell the rest?" Yaron said.

All the hostility was in the past now that the page had turned to what might be a new operation.

"Where might one want waterproof and humidity-proof artwork?" Nir asked.

"The shower?" Dima said, immediately looking

as though he regretted his offering. When all eyes turned to him, he said, "Sorry, your words no translate good to Russian."

Imri spoke up again. "I'm thinking either coastal areas or high humidity places like East Asia or the Indian subcontinent."

"Good. And Alicia does have some clients there. But this is very specialized, unique stuff specifically designed not just for humidity but for wetness."

"So I'm guessing boats or cruise ships," Liora said.

"Not cruise ships," Dafna said, the excitement of the process coming through in her voice. "They go as cheap as they can get away with. You're thinking about yachts. Big old Bezos-sized personal luxury cruisers."

"Bingo," said Nir. "How many bad actors—big-money guys running arms or funneling cash to militias—have their own overly indulgent water-bound playpens?"

"Pretty close to all of them," Yossi chimed in. "I've had to track quite a few of them in the past. They're all over the Med, the Persian Gulf, the Indian Ocean."

"I still don't get it, though. What's your play, boss?" Liora shrugged. "Are you going to culture them all with modern art, thereby taking away their desire for violence and mayhem?"

"*Sababa*," Dafna said, high-fiving her friend.

"Definitely out of the box," Doron said with a wink across the table.

"We can call it Operation Art-Masculation."

Cheers greeted Lahav's suggestion, and Nir had to calm them down again.

"Liora, you're partially right. I do want to get this artwork onto the fancy yachts of these bad guys. But I don't plan on just cement and paint and a big wooden frame."

"*Esh!*" Efraim cried, clapping his hands as he jumped up. Everyone turned toward him, startled. Pointing at Nir, he said, "Natanz, you scruffy-faced mastermind! You want to Natanz them."

Everyone got it immediately. Putting explosives into building materials, then selling them to the Iranians so that they themselves installed the bombs into their own nuclear facility was one of the most brilliant operations ever pulled off by the Mossad. And now here was the possibility of pulling off a sequel. The room was hyped.

"So how will we get explosives into the artwork without detection? And then how will we get the paintings on the boats?" asked Yaron, voicing the obvious questions.

"I've got some ideas. But I'm hoping, Yaron, that since you're our explosives expert, you'll help me think through the first part."

"I'll try, but I'm less an expert on making the bombs than I am at making them go off."

Nir gave a dismissive wave. "Well, let's sit and

talk anyway. As for the distribution, I'm already working on it. Well, Nicole is."

He settled back in his chair. "She met with Alicia in Texas last night, telling her that yours truly, a big-time jeweler with connections around the world, is interested in helping her sell her paintings to some very rich people with very big yachts. Of course, no mentions of future explosions will be made to Alicia. No commitments yet, but Nicole has her thinking."

"*Me'uleh*! That's our girl," said Liora.

Nir knew both she and Dafna had a special place in their hearts for the lone Gentile representative on their team full of Jews.

Efraim stood. "Okay, this is all very cool stuff, but remember it's not your priority at present. Put any spare time you might have on it, but right now your eyes are on Iran. We've got six weeks to get ready. Once that's over and done with, you can give me what you've come up with, and I'll take it to the *ramsad*."

CHAPTER 21

TWO WEEKS LATER
YAEL DIAMONDS, ANTWERP, BELGIUM—
OCTOBER 27, 2020—14:40 / 2:40 P.M. CET

Squeezing the tweezers in his hand, Nir lifted a dark-green gemstone and placed it on a small, black-velvet pad.

"That one doesn't look as bright as those other two," said Nicole, leaning close to the table. "Is it a lesser-quality stone?"

Alicia Marcos was also examining the gemstones. "I don't think so. The richness of this emerald is pretty remarkable. The others are glossier, more transparent, but . . . I don't know. It's like with the other two, God said, 'I'm going to show you green.' Then with this one, He leaned in and whispered, 'Okay, now I'm really going to show you green.' "

Nir laughed. "I need to hire you as a salesperson. And you're exactly right about the stones. Each of them is just under 9 carats. Those two will cost you about €45,000 each. That third one will set you back €100,000."

Nicole pulled back as if afraid of some unspoken *You break it, you buy it* rule. "You have

159

got to be kidding me. Why? What makes it so special?"

"A couple of reasons." Nir lifted the emerald with the tweezers again, then positioned it under a large bronze-rimmed magnifying glass mounted above the table. Adjusting the light, he encouraged the women to lean in. "First, it's an untreated emerald, which means no oil or resin has been used on it. That keeps it pure with no foreign substances absorbing into it. Most every emerald is thoroughly worked over, so an untreated emerald is rare."

"If cleaning it up makes it less valuable, why do it?" Alicia asked.

"Because most emeralds need it. They need the sparkle and the shine—the glossy, as you say—because inside they're filled with inclusions." Using his left hand, he tweezed up one of the other two stones. "Can you see inside there? All the little flaws? Those are the inclusions. Often we call them *the garden* because they look like little plants or moss."

Both women indicated they could see them.

"Now look inside the untreated emerald."

"Hardly any inclusions," Alicia said. "It's like it's been cleaned inside."

"Exactly, but the clean is natural. Every now and then a stone comes along with so few flaws that the gemologist will pull it out for special treatment—or special lack of treatment, as the case may be. I've seen less than a dozen untreated emeralds in my career, and this is the first Yael has owned."

"Fascinating," Nicole said. "So what will be done with the stone?"

"I was thinking of making it into a ring for this girl I know," Nir said with a grin.

"Yeah, right. You do that, you can expect to see it on eBay the next day."

"Nicole." But Alicia's scolding had come with a laugh.

"I actually have a buyer for it already. It's arranged for transport to an Indian city that will remain nameless."

"You and your secrets," Nicole said as Nir stowed away the gemstones. The three exited the vault, which Nir proceeded to seal tight. When they entered his office, a heavenly scent reached their noses. Three mugs of Aunt Mila's cocoa sat on Nir's desk.

Nicole turned toward the open door that led to the foyer and Mila's station. "Mila, I told you I can't indulge in this kind of stuff."

"I heard you," his assistant called from the other room. "I just disagreed. All three of you could stand to have a little more meat on your bones."

"It's useless arguing with her," Nir said. "She's going to win, so just accept it."

Alicia gave no such complaint. She looked like

she'd been gifted with one of those metabolisms that allowed people to eat or drink whatever they wanted without gaining an ounce. Lifting one of the mugs, she returned to the leather chair where she'd been sitting before their vault excursion and settled in.

After taking a sip, she called, "Mila, this is amazing. What is that in there? A little touch of nutmeg?"

Mila walked to the doorway. "Well, yes it is, and thanks for noticing." She nodded toward Nir. "That one on the other side of the desk guessed my secret ingredient was *Christmas spirit*." Then muttering loud enough for all to hear, she said, "Gracious, he's helpless as a whelp."

"Thank you, Mila," Nir said. "Now, please close the door behind you."

"Thank you, Mila," the ladies chimed as the door closed.

"Sorry. You can't get good help these days."

"Oh, please." Nicole rolled her eyes. "You'd be lost without her. She's the best thing you have going for you in Antwerp."

Nir chuckled. "Yeah, she kind of is. So, ready for business?"

Alicia spoke up. "First, let me say thank you for flying me here all the way from Texas. This was my first time crossing the ocean on a private jet."

"It was nothing at all," Nir said, thinking she

really should be thanking the Israeli government for her transatlantic flight. "I appreciate your taking the time to come here and listen to my proposal. Am I right that you have business in Milan after this?"

"I do. I'm going to visit the owner of the gallery where you saw my Marilyn Monroe painting."

"Excellent. Well, you and Nicole can share the Gulfstream down to Italy. Then when you're ready, I'll arrange a first-class seat on a commercial airway for your trip home. Just give Mila your details before you leave. Is that amenable?"

"It is. In fact, if I can speak freely . . ."

Nir nodded.

Alicia seemed as if she was gathering her thoughts, then spoke. "Okay, not only is it amenable, but it's a little too amenable. Honestly, if Nicole wasn't part of this, I would have bugged out a while ago. My daddy always told me if something looks too good to be true, it probably is. And this whole thing looks just way too good to be true."

Nicole looked ready to speak, but Nir gave her a quick glance. He knew how to handle this. He was the businessman. "I get it. Sometimes I come on a little too strong. Maybe it's from growing up on a *kibbutz* in Israel where hard work was always expected of us. Or maybe it's just me following the advice my dad ingrained in me."

"Which was . . ."

"If something is worth having, then go out and get it and don't stop until it's yours."

Now Alicia appeared to be thinking about Nir's words. Meanwhile, Nicole stared at him with wide eyes like he'd just put his foot into his mouth and then deep into his throat. Before he could figure out what terrible thing he'd said, though, Alicia leaned forward, and when she spoke it sounded like the depth of her Texas accent had been turned up to ten.

"Well, I'm not sure if I should be flattered or horrified. But one thing I can tell you is that no one will ever *have* this Texas girl. I'm not some little gem you can tuck away in your vault, Mr. Tavor. I've never considered having a business partner. I don't need a business partner. And if you think you can fly me here in your private jet and show me your pretty rocks and I'll just swoon and sign whatever papers you have, you can kiss that little fantasy goodbye."

Finished, the intense look in her dark eyes making it clear she'd meant every word, Alicia leaned back and took a sip of her cocoa. But when she pulled the mug away, a little dot of Mila's homemade whipped cream sat on her nose.

Nir knew he should be reeling from her tirade and apologizing profusely for choosing his words so poorly. But instead, he was in a desperate struggle not to laugh. Yet if he so much as giggled after she'd just poured out her emotions like that, the whole operation could be tanked. Still, that little white dot sat there on the end of her pert little nose, taunting him.

He glanced at Nicole, who was so focused on shooting daggers at him that she obviously hadn't noticed the offending cream. He looked back at Alicia. The visual was so absurd, so incongruous with the situation, that he was powerless to hold back.

Nir put his elbows on his desk and his head in his hands. Then his whole body convulsed, and it all poured out.

CHAPTER 22

15:05 / 3:05 P.M. CET

When Nir looked up, both women's eyes had grown enormous.

"Nir," Nicole said, truly scolding him as shock covered her face.

"I'm sorry," he said, trying to get out the words as he pointed at Alicia. "I'm so, so sorry. I just—"

He lost control again.

Nicole looked at Alicia and saw the problem. "Oh, for heaven's sake, Nir. You're like a child." Leaning toward her friend, she pulled her sleeve up into her hand and cleaned Alicia's face. But Nir saw her grinning while she was doing it.

"Did I have . . ." Now Alicia was using her own hand to wipe the tip of her nose.

Meanwhile, Nir was caught up in an ongoing mixture of laughter and apologies. Soon, the two women were laughing too. They grew so loud that Mila came knocking on the door.

"Is everything okay in there?"

Only Nicole could gain enough control to weakly blurt a yes.

Finally, Nir breathed hard three times and spoke. "I am so very sorry, Alicia, both for laughing and for messing up with my words.

That's the other thing I get from my Israeli upbringing—I'm sometimes a little too blunt with what I say. I was just trying to tell you I love your art and would like to come alongside you, doing what I can to help you get it on many more walls."

Alicia, too, was gaining control. "And I'm sorry I overreacted. Being raised a Texan means I tend to live with a chip on my shoulder. Let's just erase the misunderstanding and begin with, 'Okay, Mr. Tavor, will you please share with me your business proposal?' "

"Gladly, but let me first make clear that this isn't just *my* proposal. You'll get two for the price of one," he said, nodding toward Nicole. "I'll offer my financial investment and connections. Nicole will offer her . . . Um, I think I'm about to say the wrong thing again, but here goes. Nicole will offer her face."

Nicole gave a nod of affirmation.

"You don't need any help with your art. It's spot-on. Unique. It fits a niche in the market. Where you need help is with marketing and capital. Marketing, because I don't think you're effectively communicating to your niche. Capital, because once the marketing kicks in, you'll need to crank up your inventory."

"What is the niche you believe I'm not reaching? People already know my art is good for wet and humid climates."

"True, but that's way too broad. That's not a niche; it's a full-on weather system. The niche you fill is yacht art. I know enough people who own the fanciest of boats, and they're constantly having to replace fittings, furnishings, decorations—really, anything that can deteriorate. The water and salt get in, and within a couple of years everything is destroyed."

"I get it. But so many of the yacht owners like to redecorate all the time anyway, and it's not like many of them notice the cost."

"True. That's what makes your product unique—if you're okay with my calling your art a product. Just in the business sense, of course. Your Marilyn on an owner's wall will be the statement piece he shows off to his guests. 'I've had this hanging here for a decade now,' he'll say. 'What?' his friends will respond. 'Impossible!' Then he'll go on to tell them just how smart he is to have invested in it. It's an ego thing, and if there's one word that describes a mega yacht owner, it's *ego*."

"That's true. I've met enough yacht owners. But mega yachts are a limited market. Only so many exist or will ever exist. Getting to yacht owners isn't too difficult, but breaking through to mega yacht owners is impossible."

Nir leaned forward, causing the jewelers loupe hanging around his neck to clink against the glass desktop. "That's why you need to emphasize the

168

unique nature of your niche. You can work harder and sell ten €5,000 pieces to ten yacht owners, or you can sell two €50,000 pieces to one mega yacht owner."

Alicia laughed. "Why would anyone pay €50,000 for one of my pieces?"

"Because you would ask them to. Again, it's about ego. Would the yacht owners you've met rather show their friends the €5,000 painting on their wall or the €50,000 artistic masterpiece? To these guys, your art is worth whatever your price."

Nir could tell Alicia was getting it, and from his peripheral vision, he saw Nicole wink at him.

"So if we were to do this, how would we start?"

"Well, you know the old adage that it takes money to make money. I need something from you."

He watched her expression change as her guard went up.

"Don't worry, I'm not asking you to give me $20,000 so I can release the $4 million I have tied up in the Nigerian courts. You said it's impossible to break into the mega yacht world, but I can get you there. What I need from you is three paintings. I want to give them away to three friends of mine to seed the field."

Nir already had the three who would receive the paintings in mind, and none of them were actually friends. But they were men with connections, and that's what was important.

One would go to Anatoly Kvashnin, a Russian oligarch who made his money in fertilizer after the fall of the Soviet Union. He'd been funding a Chechen militia that had made its way into Azerbaijan and was stirring up trouble at the behest of the Russian government. In return for intelligence and special forces access into the country, Israel had promised the Azerbaijani government they'd cut off the funding for the militia. Nir and Yaron had staged a *tenachesh mi* on Kvashnin's yacht while it was moored off Cyprus.

It turned out that, when he had a gun pointed at his face, the Russian wasn't interested in ideology—only money and self-preservation. So Nir had promised to spare his life if he halted his funding of the Chechens and fulfilled one favor with no questions asked at the time of Nir's choosing. Nir was now going to call in the favor by sending him a painting with instructions signed *Your night visitor*.

The second man would be a Jordanian billionaire, Marouf Ensour, who made his money in road construction and was an established Mossad asset. The last painting would go to Takeshi Kitamura, the owner of a Japanese tech company, whom Nir met when the man was shopping for diamonds for each of his four daughters.

170

Nir continued. "In exchange, each man receiving a free painting will be asked to display it prominently and spread the word of their acquisition. Like you said, it's a fairly small community, and word will get around quickly."

When he paused, Nicole jumped in. "That's where you and I come in, Alicia. We need to create a packet to distribute to the owners of the world's top one hundred personal mega yachts. If we time it right with the buzz, we'll get some interest. Then it will be up to you and me to go make some visits."

Alicia seemed overwhelmed, as if she were still trying to process it all. "Why would you do this?" she finally asked, looking only to Nicole. Apparently, she'd decided she had Nir figured out. He was about the money.

Nicole reached over and grabbed Alicia's hand. "First, you're a friend. A good friend. And I don't have a lot of those in this world. Second, quite frankly, the money could turn out to be really good. And, third, it's an adventure. Girl, we'll be visiting mega yachts all over the world. It'll be crazy fun. A lot of work, but crazy, crazy fun."

Nir was amazed at Nicole's performance. But maybe she was so good at it because it wasn't really a performance for her. She genuinely liked Alicia, as did he. He really hoped none of their bigger plan would blow back on her. If all went well, this would turn out to be a great deal for Alicia, for Nir and Nicole, for the State of Israel, and even for the three men given the free paintings.

It was a win all around—except for the men who would eventually be blown up on their yachts by explosives-laden artwork. This was decidedly not a good deal for them.

NOVEMBER
2020
(ONE MONTH LATER)

CHAPTER 23

ONE MONTH LATER
AL ASMAKH TOWER, DOHA, QATAR—
NOVEMBER 24, 2020—
10:30 / 10:30 A.M. AST

Saad had instructed Mousavi and Kamal to use the draft box for their shared email account when they needed to communicate with him. This morning the box was empty, but that was fine. Although he wanted inside information from both men, he had a busy schedule. Sometimes it was hard to keep his overall mission from interfering with his everyday work. A message from either man too often distracted him for the rest of the day.

Rolling back from his desk, he walked across the tiled marble floor to the full-length windows that made up the walls of his office. He was on the 28th floor of the Al Asmakh Tower, which was not the penthouse of the building, nor was it in the city's tallest skyscraper, although he could have easily afforded either. Saad had chosen this location for the headquarters of his company, ASEnergy, because among a bizarrely futuristic skyline, the Al Asmakh was a retro-looking throwback.

Inspired by the American Empire State Building, its art deco design came right out of the early twentieth century. Well before the high-rise opened its doors, Saad had purchased rights to the 26th, 27th, and 28th floors, and now, three years into his occupancy, he couldn't be more pleased. When it came to boats, he wanted cutting edge. When it came to office space, a little artsy aesthetic was a nice change.

He looked out toward West Bay. His view of the water was only slightly obstructed by the Burj Doha Tower. Although similar in height, the two structures couldn't have been more different. While Saad's building looked to the past, the cylindrical Doha Tower appeared to have been transported from a futuristic science fiction novel. In his opinion, it was fortunate that the Al Asmakh didn't fit the overall aesthetic of the Doha skyline, a city he thought was trying too hard to be modern.

At the far reaches of the bay, almost out to the open waters of the Persian Gulf, he could see the *Cafala Bahr* where it was moored. Only five days of meeting with the board and entertaining potential clients left before he could step aboard one of his tenders, which would shuttle him out to *Ibn Tamiyyah*, his boat's true name. Then it would be off to the Malay Peninsula for the next month.

As he watched his yacht rocking in the water, his

mind returned to the meeting he'd had last month with Mousavi and Kamal. His business, both the energy work in public and the freedom-fighting work in private, was all about relationships. He was a people person, and he drew other people to himself. Over the years he'd become a good judge of character. He knew whom he could trust and whom he couldn't. From the first meeting he could tell who had the skills to get the job done and who would flounder.

Kamal was not a quality person, which was glaringly evident. He could, however, be Saad's link into the inner circle of the Saudi rebel movement. Not only could this make him a significant amount of money in weapons purchases should an actual rebellion take place but also leave him in a strong position if the ruling family was overthrown. And as long as he stayed in the background, he needn't be afraid of repercussions should Kamal and his unhappy friends never get their movement off the ground.

A knock on his door pulled his thoughts back to the present.

"Come in," he called.

His secretary walked in carrying an oversized white envelope. She was followed by a young man he didn't recognize. In his hands was a large wooden box.

"I'm sorry to interrupt you, Mr. Salim." She then whispered something to the young man, who put the box on the long conference table that ran along the far side of the window wall. After he completed his task, he looked to the woman, who with her hand indicated he could leave. He hustled out the door.

"What have you brought to me, Noora?" Saad asked, stepping toward the box.

"It just came in, and I knew you would want to see it right away."

He recognized the Japanese character meaning "harmony" painted on the side even before he read the words *Hibiki Suntory Whisky* stenciled next to it.

"Ha! Takeshi, how did you know I was out?" When Saad had found it necessary to upgrade the technology in his pumps, he'd turned to SEKEI Inc., a Japanese company owned by Takeshi Kitamura. The two quickly bonded over their love for their yachts and had since been each other's guest on the seas. Kitamura had been the one to arrange for the Hibiki distiller to hand deliver Saad's previous store of Japanese whisky.

"Mr. Kitamura also asked that this be given to you with his compliments." Noora held the envelope out toward Saad.

"Just put it on my desk. Then find me a crowbar or something to leverage this open," he said, putting his hand on the lid of the box. It shifted under his weight, causing him to momentarily lose his balance.

"I took the liberty of having the nails removed from the top of the crate."

Saad smiled. "Noora, have I told you lately that I love you?"

"I'm sure my husband will be happy to hear that," she said, raising her eyebrows. She walked out, closing the door behind her.

Excitedly, Saad removed the lid from the crate and placed it on the table. Next came handfuls of crinkle packaging, which he scooped out and dumped next to the lid. When the first glass-capped cork came into view, he took hold of it and carefully lifted the bottle out. After transporting it to his desk, he crossed the room to his bar, then removed a ball of ice from the freezer and dropped it into a glass, enjoying the anticipated *clink*.

He returned to his chair and slowly began to work the cap until he felt it give and heard a slight pop. Before he laid the cork down, he closed his eyes and deeply inhaled its scent. For a moment he was transported back to the upper deck of his boat. Tilting the bottle, he watched the amber liquid cascade off the ice and pool in the bottom half of his glass. He swirled it around a few times to chill it before taking a sip.

A smile came to his face, and he let out an audible "Ahh."

As he was taking a second taste, his eyes caught sight of the envelope Noora left on his desk. Putting the glass down, he pulled the square over. The eggshell-colored material was familiar to him, but he didn't know why. It came to him when he opened the envelope and saw threads fraying from the edges. It was artistic canvas. His daughter Fariha had gone through a stage when she wanted to be a world-renowned artist. A small fortune in materials and art lessons later, she decided she wanted to be a world-renowned singer instead.

Intrigued, he removed the envelope's contents. The first item he noticed was a square of cement with a glossy coating approximately 10 x 12.5 centimeters. On it was painted a miniature caricature of Marilyn Monroe. She was biting a pair of Oakley sunglasses. It was irreverent, sexy, and overwhelmingly appealing. It was also familiar, and he tried to remember where he'd seen it.

Then that came to him too. The gist of a story published in the online newsletter of a high-end, members-only yachting organization was about some new canvas technique that allowed art to survive on the waters. Saad had been skeptical until he'd seen a photograph of his friend Takeshi standing next to that same Marilyn painting, titled *Oakley Marilyn*. He'd installed it on his yacht and was singing its praises.

The concept was certainly intriguing. The canvas was some kind of cement compound, likely the stuff he was holding in his hand. The paint was applied to the cement, then a thick gloss coating was added to protect the artwork. Mold, mildew, salt deterioration were all a constant battle on his yacht. It wasn't a big financial drain, but it was a drain.

This might be something worth looking into, he thought as he laid the cement piece down and picked up a brochure. On the cover, two women stood next to a full-sized *Oakley Marilyn.* He recognized the woman on the right from the article. She was the artist, and under a headshot of her was the name Alicia Marcos. When he saw the second woman's photo, his breath caught. She was exquisite. Her blue eyes were the color of ice, and they were staring right through the camera lens into his own. He read her name—Nicole le Roux.

Dropping the brochure onto his desk, he turned toward his computer and did a Google search on her. He quickly learned she was a model from South Africa who currently lived in Milan. Clicking from *All* to *Images* offered him row after row of photos of her. Some professional, some candid. Some sexy, some girl-next-door. Soon he found himself lost in the repetition of sliding to the bottom of a page, refreshing, then sliding to the bottom of another.

When he reached the end of the available photos, he turned back to the brochure. He skimmed through it page by page, looking for her. Then on the back cover, he found one final photograph of Nicole and the artist. They were standing in front of a new painting, this one a glamorous woman staring through her fingers. Across the bottom were the words *Let us come tell you why you should own a Marcos*. A phone number was listed.

Saad pressed a button on his phone.

"Yes, Mr. Salim?"

"Noora, come in here, please. I need you to set up a meeting for me. I'm in need of an artistic makeover for the *Cafala Bahr*."

CHAPTER 24

Is there a coffee maker around here?" Lahav asked. He was dressed in desert camouflage and had a helmet on his head that looked like a giant mushroom cap perched on a narrow stem. Nir had made the decision to go with the desert camo instead of civilian clothes. He figured his team had a much better chance of blending with the surrounding countryside than they did with the Iranian residents.

"Watch me," Dima said. "I'll barista you some field coffee." He walked to a table that held several dozen bottles of water. Cracking one open, he scooped some brown crystals out of a can, funneled his hand over the opening, and dumped them in. After replacing the cap, he shook the bottle until the crystals dissolved.

"Here you go," said the Russian, tossing the bottle to the analyst.

Lahav grimaced. "I'll pass."

"Suit yourself."

Doron joined the conversation. "Come on. You used to be in prison. Don't you guys make hooch in your toilets or something?"

"Don't remind me. Found out that little fact the hard way." Lahav shook his head.

At the time the analyst was recruited for Nir's team, he was serving time for shutting down the power grid in Eilat. He'd warned his superiors it was vulnerable, and when they disagreed, he proved his point. Eilat got an upgrade to its power grid, and Lahav got five years at Maasiyahu Prison. Two years into his stay, the Mossad gave him an offer he couldn't refuse.

Nir had been nervous having him along on the operation. He was weird, and Nir was concerned about how he would blend in with his ops guys. Could this strange young intellectual savant control his idiosyncrasies and act like a normal person for just a while? So far, the answer had been yes, and the guys actually seemed to accept him.

"Okay, we're out in three," Nir called.

"*Root*," answered the ops guys as they gathered their things. Lahav, however, mumbled "Crap!" and scrambled to inspect the contents of his backpack one more time.

They were going in fully prepared for a gun battle. Nir didn't expect one. He prayed they wouldn't have one. But he also knew if they were discovered, they would survive only if they shot the bad guys before the bad guys shot them.

Each Kidon man wore full tactical gear and helmet. Strapped to their legs were IWI Jericho

941 9mm pistols with extended mags. And across their chests, each man had an IWI Galil MAR with 35 rounds of 5.56x45mm NATO cartridges in the box magazine and six more mags in their chest rigs. Dima also carried a Mossberg 500 Compact Cruiser AOW 12-gauge in his gear. Finally, each man had five M26 fragmentation grenades easily accessible.

Lahav also wore the camouflage, and Nir was thankful that he was in good enough shape to be able to function in the body armor. Back in Tel Aviv, he'd tested the analyst on the weapons and was only comfortable letting him carry the Jericho handgun. But that was okay. The team was there to protect him, not the other way around.

Checking his watch, he saw it was time.

"Let's go," he said, moving to the stairs that would lead them up to ground level. At the top was an Israeli Mossad agent who had her eyes up to a viewer. Just above her was a flat panel.

This subterranean Mossad outpost here in Erbil sat right in the middle of an upscale neighborhood not far from the U.S. consulate. While the mansions were going up all around, local Mossad agents were digging down, claiming they were creating an elaborate septic system worthy of the eliminations of those who could afford to live in the nearby manors. In fact, a Kurdish oil tycoon whose home was situated just 40 meters from the false cable box paid for much of the underground Israeli base thinking he now had something much greater to flush into than the oversized leach field he ended up with.

"Hold on," the agent said as they crowded around her.

She continued pressing her face against the viewer, then suddenly sprang into action, pulling back a bolt and letting the panel drop inward. She scrambled down the steps and said, "Hurry! Let's go."

Nir went up first. Once at the top, he saw hands reaching down, and a voice said, "Arms up."

He raised his arms over his head and felt the hands clamp on and haul him up with amazing ease. When he was back on his feet, he could see why. Two bearded men, both a head taller than Nir and tightly muscled, were lifting Doron. A sour smell told him he was in some sort of dairy truck. This cargo area had a single light in its ceiling, and apart from the growing number of bodies, it was empty.

Dima was the last one in, and the two men actually grunted when they pulled him up. With heavy Arab accents, they pointed to the open hatch in the floor and said to the Russian, "You close. Latch. Latch."

"Got it," Dima said.

With a practiced precision, each of the burly

men stepped to the hole and dropped through. Dima closed the hatch and slid the two bolt locks in place.

It was a short drive to the Erbil International Airport and the CIA's operational hangar. The U.S. president wanted their target dead almost as much as the Israelis did, so a deal had been worked out between the *ramsad* and the director of the American intelligence agency for transportation into Iran. The president, though, had made it clear to Israel's prime minister that once they were in-country, they were on their own. It was imperative that he be allowed to disavow any knowledge of the operation.

Nir felt the truck brake, and the rear door slid open.

"This way," said a man in a U.S. military uniform. Nir jumped out and followed the marine to a helicopter, its rotor just beginning to turn.

"I thought you marines retired your Hueys," he said, nodding to the chopper that had to be at least 50 years old.

"I think your pilots would beg to differ, sir. Please go on board and strap in."

"Thanks." Nir slapped him on the back before climbing up into the copter, and then instead of sitting, he stuck his head into the cockpit. "Hey, boys, I appreciate the lift. I'm Nir Tavor, team leader."

Without turning, the pilot said, "I'm Captain

J.J. Marks. That *boy* over there is my junior First Lieutenant Caitlin Bader."

You idiot. Nicole is right. When it comes to females, I have absolutely no game.

"Sorry, no offense intended. Just wanted to thank you for giving us a lift. I have to admit, though, I don't think I've seen one of these Hueys since I last watched *Apocalypse Now*."

Marks laughed. "You know what they say about the three-letter agencies. If there's metal out there that works, they'll use it. This girl has got some years on her, but she's aged like a fine wine. She'll get us where we're going—fast and low."

"Just don't start blasting any Wagner out of the speakers."

"Roger that."

Nir moved back into the cabin, counted heads, and then took a seat. They'd be in the air for only about an hour, but that was long enough to transport them to a different world. While a team of Jews would not be well loved here in Iraq, once they landed in Iran they would be in the belly of the beast. And if they were caught, they would undoubtedly be tortured, tried, and executed.

Just have to make sure we don't get caught.

The rotors reached full speed, and he felt that familiar drop in his stomach as the chopper lifted off. No matter how many times he flew, the sensation was always the same.

While the propeller pounded the air outside the cabin, no one made any noise inside. Nir had instructed his team to stay absolutely silent to ensure that no details of their mission slipped into the ears of the two up front. Although the Americans were well aware of the identity of their target, there was no reason they needed to be let in on the technology of the hit. If later the *ramsad* determined he wanted to fill his U.S. friends in on how the operation was accomplished, that was his decision.

The ground raced by just 90 meters below, hilly and barren. About 20 minutes into the flight, Lieutenant Marks keyed the coms and said, "Welcome to Islamatopia, folks. Beware the ayatollahs—they bite."

Another 45 minutes later, and the chopper was touching down.

As the rest of the team piled out, Nir put his head back into the cockpit. "Thanks again for the ride."

"Send one right up Khamenei's keister," Marks said.

"Will do."

When he jumped out, he saw the rest of his team already making their way to a large white panel truck. The terrain they were in was hilly and dirty. Two kilometers to the east would be the city of Sanandaj, the capital of Kurdistan Province in northwestern Iran. Then seven hours' travel beyond that would be their destination.

Two men stood at the rear of the truck, helping Nir's guys climb in. Although Iranian citizens, they were ethnic Kurds and both had been Mossad assets for over a decade. Anytime you work with locals, you put your life at risk. But on paper, these two appeared to be trustworthy.

We'll find out, Nir thought as he walked toward them.

Putting out his hand, he said, *"As-salamu 'alaykum."*

The older of the two took his hand and replied, *"Wa-'alaykum salam."*

He shook the hand of the younger man too. Their resemblance confirmed what Nir already knew—they were father and son.

Speaking in Arabic, Nir said, "Thank you for your help. We have a long journey ahead of us."

"Yes, we do," the father said. "I have put food in the back as well as water. And I know of places where we can stop out of sight every two hours for anyone who might need to relieve themselves."

"That is much appreciated, but I would just as soon not risk being seen. We'll be fine."

The man nodded. "As you wish."

Nir climbed into the truck, and when the son pulled the door down, Nir heard him fasten the latch. It was dark in the box, the only light coming from a small vent window near the cab.

"Did I just hear you tell that guy we don't need bathroom breaks for the next seven hours?" asked Yaron.

"Since when have you started understanding Arabic?"

"Listen, I've learned how to say the word *pee* in many languages."

"Not surprising with how big your prostate must be by now, old man," Doron said.

Lahav seemed agitated. "Wait. Did you say seven hours without a bathroom? I can't go seven hours. I have a delicate system."

"Just pretend you're in solitary and they forgot to leave your bucket," said Imri, joining in the fray.

Laughter filled the back of the truck—but not from Lahav. "Seriously, guys, I kind of feel like I have to go already."

And so it begins, thought Nir.

CHAPTER 25

The lug wrench popped the nut loose, and Nir spun it off. Once it was free, he threw it off into the field, then blew on his fingers to warm them before starting on the last nut. The temperature had reached 11 degrees Celsius, but it was humid, and the moisture was giving him chills.

Through his com, he could hear Lahav and Imri arguing.

"To the left. Your other left, Einstein!" Lahav shouted.

"That *is* my left!"

Nir could hear the slight phase separation between Imri's digitized voice in his earbud and the real thing coming from the back seat of the beater sedan.

Lahav paused. "Oh. Yeah, my bad. But if you guys had parked the car straight, we wouldn't have to be repositioning the camera."

"Quit whining and do your job," Nir said.

So far, Lahav had been remarkably professional during the operation. But now it seemed the stress was getting to him.

The final nut removed, Nir sent it flying after

192

the others. Leaning down again, he pulled the rear driver's side wheel from the car. "Be careful up there, Term 5. I don't know how stable this jack is." *Term* was short for *Terminator*, chosen because of the futuristic nature of this operation's technology.

"*Root.*"

"Okay, the camera is good," Lahav said. "Listen, guys, I want to apologize if I'm coming across as a little abrasive. It's just that I've never—"

"Term 6, shut it. No one is interested in your feelings," Nir said.

"Uh, *root.*"

"Term 2, ready for you."

"*Root,*" Yaron replied.

Nir helped Imri ease out of the back seat. Both were dressed like they belonged in rural Iran, wearing light jackets, dark cotton pants, and off-brand sneakers. Nir was wearing a black wig because he normally kept his hair cut tight to his scalp. Yaron and Doron had joined him in that particular disguise. Imri had glued a beard to his normally smooth face.

A blue Nissan Zamyad pickup pulled onto the shoulder. Covering its bed was a large, dark-blue tarpaulin. Yaron nodded from the front seat. Nir lifted the tire he'd removed from the car and set it in the passenger seat of the truck. Then he followed Imri into the bed, where Doron was already waiting. Once inside, Doron slapped the rear window, and Yaron pulled out. Immediately, he made a U-turn around the center median. Ten seconds later, he turned right.

"Is it staying stable?" Nir asked Doron, nodding to the truck's cargo.

"Holding tight. Been a little bouncy but not bad."

"Bouncy?" came Lahav's voice. "How bouncy? We can't have bouncy."

"Relax, Term 6," Nir said, trying to keep Lahav from getting wound up again.

After the truck had traveled three-quarters of a mile, it slowed and stopped. Then they all jolted back and forth as the pickup eased up and over a high curb. It went forward a few more meters and repositioned itself on a small rise parallel to the curb and a low barbed wire fence. The front door opened and closed, and Nir heard Yaron slap the side of the truck.

That was their okay signal, and the three of them got to work while Yaron walked away.

Bolted to the bed of the pickup was a metal tripod. Fastened to that stand was a FN MAG machine gun. Belgian-made, it fired 600 7.62x51mm NATO rounds a minute and was known for its accuracy and reliability. The person who got in its path didn't stand a chance, as this Mossad Kidon team was hoping to prove this afternoon.

The problem was that this target field was in Iran, an hour east of Tehran. Anyone whose finger was on the trigger of the gun had no chance of escape—unless the trigger of the gun was hours away.

Designed 2,000 kilometers from this location in Herzliya, in the heart of Israel's Silicon Wadi, this killing machine was fully automated. Not only could it be directed and engaged remotely, but the artificial intelligence incorporated into its computerized brain meant it could shoot a fly off the backside of a cow without even eliciting a moo.

After the robotic gun was designed and manufactured, it was broken down into individual pieces. Over the last four months, those parts had been smuggled one by one into Iran. Once it had all arrived, a team of Sunni Baloch engineers had reassembled the weapon and installed it into the bed of one of the tens of thousands of blue Nissan Zamyad pickups that filled the streets of Iran.

While Imri fired up the electronics and began system-checking the cameras, Nir and Doron readied the gun. Lifting the cover, Doron laid in the ammunition belt. Then once he closed it back up, he pulled the cocking lever to charge the weapon. Stepping back, Nir moved in to check everything Doron had just done. He didn't expect to find any mistakes, but in this kind of operation, you check everything twice. Meanwhile, Doron had moved on to ensure that the explosive charge was armed and ready to blow.

"This is Term 6. Everything is a go on my end," Lahav said after a few minutes.

"Everything is a go here. Move to pickup." Nir looked at Doron, who nodded.

"*Root*," sounded off each member of the team—except for Yaron, who was already walking up the road.

After making sure no traffic was coming, Imri and Doron dropped out from the back of the truck. They would follow Yaron's path. Nir hit the timer on this watch, set for four minutes, then began to position the tarp so the barrel of the gun had a clear shot.

So far, all had gone smoothly for Operation Unholy Father. Nir laughed when he first heard the name, mainly because it was so perfect for their target—Dr. Mohsen Fakhrizadeh, known as the Father of the Iranian Bomb. His official title was head of Iran's Organization of Defensive Innovation and Research, or S.P.N.D. As all in the Mossad knew, though, this was just a fancy way of saying he was the one most responsible for the weaponization of Iran's nuclear program.

Fakhrizadeh had been on a Mossad target list for more than 14 years, but he was almost impossible to get to. More than one assassination attempt had been prepared, then aborted. When

Nir heard Netanyahu call the doctor out by name during his vault press conference, he had a feeling Fakhrizadeh had graduated to the top of the Mossad's kill list. He just didn't know his team would be the ones doing the killing.

Even as Israel became more diligent in their efforts to target the doctor, he was allowing his security to become more lax. For a decade and a half, he'd been told he could be killed at any time. But the intel Nir's organization had received was that he was getting tired of hearing it. So many people had cried "Mossad" that he was starting to ignore the cries. This slipshod security reached into his carpool, and he'd begun to drive his own vehicle, relegating his protection team to cars in front and in back of his own. Nir and his agents would be counting on that sloppiness today.

Nir's watch beeped. He climbed out of the back of the truck and started walking up the road. Soon, he heard a vehicle slowing behind him. The side door of the van was already open. He stepped in, and Lahav closed the door behind him.

"This is so cool," said the analyst, obviously excited. "It's like real secret agent stuff."

"Go sit down before you blow a blood vessel."

Nir opened the door for Imri and Doron, then again for Yaron before moving to the front passenger seat opposite Dima, who was driving.

"Hi, sweetie," Nir said to the Russian whose

disguise consisted of a woman's headscarf and a long black dress. Dima glared at him. "Wow, hon, you don't seem happy."

Nir heard laughter in his coms as he reached to pull out his earpiece. "Great work, guys," he called back. "Relax for the drive. Our babushka here has promised us a smooth trip."

Let's hope it's smooth, Nir thought. *Three hours from now we'll be past Tehran and set up in Kaveh Industrial City. And three and a half hours from now, the unholy father will be meeting his unrighteous end.*

CHAPTER 26

KAVEH INDUSTRIAL CITY, MARKAZI PROVINCE, IRAN— 15:20 / 3:20 P.M. IRST

Term Lead, be advised that Father's ETA is seven minutes. That's seven minutes."

"*Root*," Nir answered Liora's update. He tried to picture their crowded team control room. He figured a minimum of 30 people were packed in, watching and listening to everything done and said. Because this was such an important operation that would probably be reviewed and analyzed for years to come, Nir had insisted that everyone do and say everything strictly by the book.

If there had been room in the van, he would have been pacing. And despite the cold outside, he was sweating profusely. One reason was that he and the team had changed back to their full gear, and its weight was a continual workout. Yet he knew most of his discomfort was from nerves. It was essential that nothing keep Doron from pressing that trigger.

Dima remained in the front seat. Lahav had his eyes on the many small monitors arrayed in front of him. Imri and Yaron both watched their own monitors, connected to tiny cameras mounted on the outside of the van, allowing them to see anyone coming toward them. Only Nir had nothing to do except wait and worry.

I guess that's what leadership is. Your only part is to sit and hope no one else screws up.

"Term Lead, be advised that Father's ETA is five minutes. That's five minutes."

"Got a dirty approaching from the south," Yaron said. Nir quickly moved behind him.

Yaron continued, "Military-aged male. Empty hands. No signature." Nir leaned in close, but he, too, didn't see the outline of a weapon. Still, he removed his 9mm and stepped toward the van's rear doors.

They were positioned in an alley between a cellulose factory and a transportation company. Kaveh Industrial City was a bustling manufacturing area, so it wasn't surprising that a pedestrian would be moving past. But Nir wasn't taking any chances.

Yaron spoke again. "Be advised he has partially unzipped his jacket and is reaching inside."

Even though he knew what position it would be in, Nir still fingered his gun's safety to make sure it was off.

"Dirty is coming alongside in 3 . . . 2 . . . 1."

Silence filled the van as the man walked past. By the time he reached the camera by the rear door, his hand had come back out of his jacket holding a pack of cigarettes and a lighter.

Lahav laughed with relief. "Phew, that was close."

"Shut up," Doron hissed with venom in his voice. Three minutes passed before the team began to loosen up and Nir reholstered his weapon.

Lahav was back at his monitors, but Nir could see he was shaken by Doron's rebuke. He walked to him and put his hand on the young man's shoulder. "You always have to let a situation breathe. The cigarettes could have been a signal. Remember, it's never safe until it's safe. Lesson learned. How's it looking?"

"Everything looks good here." His voice was a little shaky.

Once again, Liora sounded in the coms. "Term Lead, be advised that Father's ETA is one minute. That's one minute."

"Okay, boys, let's go hunting," Nir said, then settled behind Lahav.

Dr. Fakhrizadeh had spent several days with his wife at a home they owned along the Caspian Sea. This was a regular excursion they took once or twice a month—always the same route there and always the same route back.

So sloppy, Nir thought. *Nothing kills you faster than routine.*

The seconds counted down slowly as they waited for the convoy of cars to register on the small camera mounted on the stranded car with the three wheels.

"Term Lead, Father should be approaching the scout."

Distant shadows appeared on the monitor. They grew and took shape until Nir could make out two cars in a line. From Liora's reports and because of the eight months of collected intel, Nir knew two more cars were in the convoy. They were just blocked by the camera's perspective.

As the lead car slowed, Nir got a close look at the front-seat occupants. The one in the passenger seat was the head of Fakhrizadeh's security team. That was a good sign that the doctor was actually in the procession.

The first car began its U-turn around the median, giving a clear view into the second car. It was a black Nissan Teana sedan, as they'd expected. Nir could make out the passenger first—Sadigheh Ghasemi. The camera then resolved on the driver, Sadigheh's husband, Dr. Mohsen Fakhrizadeh.

"Father ID'd," came Dafna's voice. "We have a positive on Father."

"Are you one hundred percent positive?" came a gruff male voice. Nir recognized it as that of the *ramsad*.

"Look at the ring," Lahav called. "The red agate!"

On the fourth finger of the man's left hand

draped over the steering wheel was a large ring set with a bright-red stone. It was identical to the ring worn by the Supreme Leader Ayatollah Ali Khamenei. It was also a twin to the one that had remained on the severed hand used to confirm the assassination of General Qasem Soleimani.

"Mission is a go," said the *ramsad*.

"Mission is a go," Liora repeated.

"Mission is a go," Nir announced to his team.

The next two cars also slowed and made their U-turns.

"Lead car is turning right from Firuzkuh Road onto Imam Khomeini Road. The others are following," Liora narrated.

Three quarters of a mile up Imam Khomeini Road, their blue Nissan Zamyad sat parked on a rise by the side of the road. Nir waited with anticipation. Only one more hurdle had to be jumped.

"Term Lead, first car is accelerating and leaving the pack."

That was it. It was at this point each trip that Fakhrizadeh's head of security went ahead to ensure all was safe at the doctor's house. "*Esh!*" sounded quietly throughout the van.

"Lahav, you're on," Nir said.

The analyst didn't acknowledge his words, so intent was he on the collection of monitors. Red lines and squares were bouncing around each screen.

"Get ready, Doron," Lahav said. Nir refrained from chiding him for not saying *Term 3*.

The lead car raced by the truck, and the three remaining black sedans were clearly visible. The lines and squares were slowing down. In turns, they became stationary, then broke free again.

"Steady . . . steady . . ." Lahav said.

One by one the squares on the ten monitors locked into place. When the last one stabilized, all turned green.

"Fire!" he called.

The picture on the monitors shook violently but briefly. In that short burst, 15 rounds struck Fakhrizadeh. The car veered to the left and rolled to a stop. The doctor's wife burst out of the passenger door screaming, untouched physically by the gunfire. Nir felt a pang of sympathy for her, but then he remembered she likely knew exactly what her husband was doing in the nuclear program.

Lahav zoomed in with the operational record camera. The view confirmed that Fakhrizadeh was indeed very, very dead.

"Kill confirmed," Nir said. "Blow it."

Lahav pressed a computer key, and the monitors went blank.

Liora's voice sounded a moment later. "Destruction incomplete. I repeat, destruction incomplete."

CHAPTER 27

15:30 / 3:30 P.M. IRST

All the elation of a mission fulfilled was sucked from the van. The explosives in the truck bed were supposed to completely destroy the vehicle and the weapon. As Liora narrated the view from the satellite, it sounded like neither was accomplished.

"Term Lead, what happened?" It was the *ramsad*.

"We're determining that now." Nir turned to Doron with his eyebrows raised.

"I can only tell you it should have worked." The agent's face was red with anger and, Nir was certain, embarrassment as well. "I've been blowing bombs for over a decade. There's no reason that amount of explosives should not have done the job."

Yaron nodded in agreement. "I checked it out too. It was more than enough. Either something was faulty with the materials or it was tampered with."

"When would it have been tampered with?" Nir asked. "We've had eyes on it since we arrived in Tehran."

"It would have to be before we got here," Doron said.

That idea seemed far-fetched to Nir. He looked down for a moment to collect his thoughts. "Sir, we have no explanation. The explosives were checked by more than one operative and confirmed to have been sufficient. We suspect possible outside interference."

There was silence on the coms for a full minute. Finally, Liora came on. "The *ramsad* said he will discuss it with you when you return and to get your team back in one piece in the meantime."

That sounds like it will be a fun discussion. Maybe I can stay here in Iran. Homestead a little plot of land outside of Isfahan.

Dima started the van's engine.

"At least we killed the guy," Lahav said quietly, a bit of wonder in his voice. "I mean, we really, really killed that guy."

Nir looked around and saw the discouragement on his men's faces. Maybe this was the moment he needed to be a leader. "You know, Lahav, for once I agree with you. We really, really killed that guy. The Unholy Father met his just demise. Good work, guys. You did an extremely professional job."

The mood lightened, briefly. But soon a pall fell over the group again. For the next 50 minutes they drove west along the Hamedan Freeway in silence. After passing Gharqabad, they pulled off the pavement and drove into the hills. Ten minutes of bouncing over a barely cut road brought them to the box truck. The father and son were waiting for them.

Before leaving the van, Doron set a detonator for an explosive charge that would remove any evidence left in the vehicle. Nir resisted the urge to tell him not to screw this one up. That would do no one any good.

The men were exhausted, and they stretched themselves out the best they could in the old truck. It was five hours back to Sanandaj, where hopefully a helicopter would be ready to fly them back to safety. Nir laid down, put his head on his pack, and closed his eyes.

He woke to a hand shaking his shoulder. "Nir, wake up." It was Doron.

"*Ma nishma*?" Nir asked, wondering what was up.

"We've got a problem."

Instantly, he was fully awake. Jumping to his feet, in the light of a battery lantern he saw Imri and Yaron speaking quietly near the sliding door. That's when Nir noticed they were no longer moving.

A quick glance at his watch told him only two and a half hours had passed. "How long have we been stopped?"

"About five minutes. We felt them take an exit off the freeway. Then we bounced on some rough road for a couple of minutes before stopping."

Nir was a little embarrassed that he'd slept

through all that. "Any word from the cab?"

"That's the thing. They always signal us when they stop—two hits on the side of the truck. This time there was nothing."

Lahav was awake by now. "Guys, are we trapped in here? I hope not, because I'm going to get really claustrophobic really fast."

"He's right, we need to get out of here," Dima said.

"How?" asked Imri. "The door is latched from the outside, and I'm not seeing any way to open it from in here."

Lahav's breathing was speeding up. "Seriously, we've got to get that door open. Besides, I really have to pee. I mean, it's serious!"

"Lahav, man up!" Nir shouted. "Figure out a solution rather than whining." Then he saw it. "Okay, Lahav, you want to get out of here? There you go." He pointed at the tiny plastic window in the ceiling of the truck.

"*Achi*, I don't think even Liora could fit through that," Lahav said, eyes wide.

"We don't need Liora to fit through it. We need you." Turning to Imri, he said, "Get up on Dima's shoulders and get that plastic shell off there."

Imri pulled a multi-tool out of a cargo pants pocket and passed it to Dima. "Hand that to me when I'm up." Dima took it, then squatted. Imri climbed on his shoulders and began working the screws.

"Okay, strip down," Nir said to Lahav.

"What? Why?"

Nir was probably enjoying this more than he should. "You'll need to shed every millimeter you can. Besides, those are new camos. I don't want you tearing them up. *Yalla*! Let's go."

"Just pretend it's intake day at Maasiyahu Prison and they're giving you another strip search," Yaron said, obviously relishing their hazing the analyst.

A thump sounded through the box, and Nir turned to see Imri back on his feet. Looking up, he saw that the clear starry sky of a late fall night showed through the hole, and the cool air wafted the stale air from the container.

Lahav had hold of the waistband of his boxers when Nir quickly said, "You can keep those on."

"In fact, please keep those on," said Dima. Then he squatted, offering his shoulders.

As Lahav rode the Kidon agent's shoulders toward the hole, Nir said, "Stick only your head through first, then tell me what you see."

Dima wedged his hands under Lahav's backside and lifted the man until he could see through the open ceiling.

"I don't know. It's dark. Give my eyes a second to adjust. I see hills and dirt and rocks."

"So we're still in Iran," Doron said, joking.

"What about people? Do you see the man and his son?" asked Nir.

"I don't think so."

"Okay, Dima, push him through."

It turned out Lahav was slight enough to slip through easily.

"Probably could have kept his clothes on," Imri said with a grin.

Yaron grinned as well. "Yeah, but what fun would that have been?"

Lahav stuck his head back through the hole. "They're definitely gone. No sign of them anywhere."

"*Yalla*! Just open up the back of the truck," Nir said, a sinking feeling in his stomach.

"Oh, yeah. Just give me a minute first."

"What do you need a minute for?" Nir yelled, knowing exactly what Lahav was going to do. But the man had already pulled his head back out. "Open the door!"

"This is not a good situation," Yaron said. "I have a feeling we won't be alone for very long."

Nir had been thinking the exact thing. They hadn't just been abandoned; they'd been left for someone else. There was no telling when that *someone else* would get there.

"*Yalla*! Let's go," he yelled, pounding the wall of the truck.

A minute later the metal from the latch clanked, the door slid up, and Lahav stood there with a relieved look on his face.

CHAPTER 28

SOUTH OF DASH BOLAGH, KURDISTAN PROVINCE, IRAN— 19:10 / 7:10 P.M. IRST

N ir jumped from the back of the truck, and the rest of the team followed.

"Make sure we have everything out of there, then lock it back down," he said. "I'm going to raise headquarters. I want everyone geared up, locked and loaded, and connected to the coms."

"*Root*," sounded throughout the group.

"Imri, go see if they happened to leave us some keys," he said, knowing the chances were slim.

"*Root*."

Stepping away from the truck, he said, "Term base, you there? Term Lead to Term base."

Yossi's voice came on. "Term Lead, this is Term base. Go ahead."

"We have a problem. Our chauffeurs have abandoned us."

"They what? Hang on."

As Nir waited, he heard Yossi say, "Dafna, you and Liora need to get back here now!"

Imri trotted up to his side. "Not only are there no keys, but they cut the gas line. This truck isn't going anywhere."

211

Nir was about to curse when Yossi said, "Give me your coordinates."

After checking his GPS, Nir rattled off a latitude and a longitude. "We've got a clear sky and a half moon, so we've got some light. It's rolling hills and open spaces. I can just make out a decline, which makes me think there may be a stream or a dried wadi to the north."

Yossi was always very hard on his keyboards, and Nir could hear him pounding away. "Okay, I've got you three kilometers directly south of the village of Dash Bolagh, just southeast of the border to Kurdistan Province. Unfortunately, I don't see any way to get live eyes on you. No satellites around or available."

"Do you see anywhere we can get some cover?"

"I don't. They did a great job dropping you in the middle of nowhere. You've got a road to the west and the freeway to the north."

"Okay. Hang on, Term base." Turning to his team, he said, "I'm thinking we go northwest. See if we can get some cover there. Once we get near a road, maybe we can find someone who can be persuaded to let us borrow their car."

"*Root*," they all replied—except for Lahav.

"Wait a second," he said. He dug around in one of his cargo pants pockets and pulled out a small black disc, then ran to a boulder to which he attached the object. When he came back, he said,

"Okay, now we have eyes on the truck. We'll know if anyone shows up."

"*Achla*," Nir said.

Yaron clapped the analyst on the back, which made him beam with pride.

Nir started moving and said, "Okay, let's go."

As they jogged along, he asked, "Term base, can you get our ride to pick us up here?" He already knew the answer he'd likely get from Yossi.

"Our foreign friends have strict orders that it must be SKP or not at all."

Before they left Erbil, it was again made very clear that the CIA was doing the Mossad a huge favor crossing the border into Iran. They would risk going as far east as Sanandaj, Kurdistan Province, but absolutely no farther. This whole event had "international scandal" written all over it.

"And how far are we from Sanandaj?"

"You're 130 kilometers from there."

This time Nir did curse. There was no chance they could make that trip on foot, especially if people were on their trail.

"At least ask. And let the *ramsad* know what's going on. Maybe he can pull some strings."

This time Liora's voice answered. "Will do, Term Lead."

They hiked for about 30 minutes before Nir held up his hand. He moved his finger to his lips as he listened. From the south came the soft sound of engines. His view of them was blocked by the hills, but the low rumble made it clear diesels were among them. Nir waved his hand, and they began moving again.

"Stop, guys." It was Lahav. His face was lit by the glow of a large cell phone as he moved next to Nir. "They're at the truck."

Nir counted three jeeps and three large transport trucks on the screen. But by the angles of other light beams, it appeared more were out of camera range. Troops were piling out of the trucks and lining up.

"Term base, this is Term Lead. We're monitoring IRGC activity back at the truck. Multiple jeeps and trucks. At least 40 dirties, likely more."

Once the IRGC soldiers were in position, a command must have been given because all the rifles were raised to firing position. Then the soldiers opened fire. For a full eight seconds, automatic weapons riddled the truck. The side panels and rear door splintered, then shredded, then disintegrated. The vehicle dropped suddenly as the tires burst.

As the Mossad agents watched what was almost their death, a faint sound—like the sound of a distant sparkler fizzling—reached their ears. The men were silent.

Once the firing stopped and the smoke cleared, they watched as the IRGC soldiers began to realize that the truck was empty. Where they'd expected to see mangled bodies, they saw only the detritus of their barrage. Hands started pointing as orders were given. The troops loaded back in the trucks while a handful of men began examining the area. It wasn't long before their tracks were discovered and more pointing took place.

The picture flashed brightly once, then twice. The bearded face of a soldier who appeared to be in his mid-thirties filled the screen. His hand reached out, and he plucked up the camera. They briefly saw a flashlight before the screen whited out again. When the flashlight was moved, another face filled the screen, this one older with a thick, graying mustache. As he examined the camera, his expression turned from curiosity to anger. The camera dropped to the ground, then the picture went black.

"He owes the State of Israel 2,400 shekels," Lahav said.

"Term base, how's our transport looking?" Nir asked.

"Still a no go. The *ramsad* is trying to arrange an alternative. Right now, you're on your own."

"Keep me posted." Turning to his team, Nir said, "We've got maybe 15 minutes before we have visitors. I don't think it will be the full force at first, because they've got to find us. But they know the direction we're going. Once we engage,

I would expect that within ten minutes we'll have 50 or more angry dirties on us."

"We've got to get ourselves some cover," Yaron said. "Or at least some high ground or something."

"Unfortunately, we're stuck on this moonscape."

Suddenly, Imri shushed them. "Listen."

Nir strained to register what Imri had picked up. Then he heard it. "What is that?"

"Think back to your *kibbutz* days."

Imri was right. Nir had heard that sound every day growing up.

"Sheep," Nir said with a grin.

Lahav rolled his eyes. "I hate to break it to you, but a bunch of sheep aren't going to do much to stop bullets."

"No, they aren't. But if you weren't such a city boy, you'd know that by this time of night, the sheep aren't still out grazing. They're back in their . . ." He left the sentence hanging for Lahav to finish.

"Pen."

"Exactly. Due east, Imri?"

"Due east."

"Lead the way."

With Imri on point and Dima bringing up the rear, the Kidon agents and the analyst took off at a low jog, searching for the source of the bleating.

CHAPTER 29

Get out of here if you want to save your lives," Nir said in Arabic. He had to give some respect to the three young shepherds. Despite the fact they had only one rifle and two long staffs, they were standing their ground against six heavily armed men dressed in military fatigues.

"What about our sheep?" asked the one with the rifle. "We want to take our sheep."

"There's no time. You leave without your sheep or you die with them."

"We want our sheep."

"Boss, we don't have time for this," Yaron said. The other team members were already scouting the best cover among the three small stone buildings that made up the sheep pen and shepherds' hut.

Nir reached into his pocket and pulled out a wad of rial notes worth just under two thousand dollars—the entire stash headquarters had given him in case they were somehow stranded in Iran. "Take this and get out of here."

The man with the rifle nodded to one of the other men, who raced up and grabbed the cash. All three then ran off, leaving their sheep behind.

"Everybody's got their price," Nir said.

"Shouldn't have let them go." Yaron was kneeling behind a low stone wall, checking his Galil machine gun. "Now they'll let everyone know we're here."

"Who are they going to call? The IRGC?" Nir moved to a spot ten meters away.

"Good point."

"Term base, this is Term Lead. Be advised that we've taken shelter at a sheep pen at . . ." Nir reached in his pocket for his GPS but couldn't find it. "Doron, give her our coordinates."

Doron did so, then Nir continued. "We expect company very soon. At least 50. Any sign of our helo friends?"

"Negative," said Liora. "We can't even raise them on the phone anymore. I think they've stopped taking our calls."

Nir couldn't help feeling betrayed. The two marines had seemed like they understood the wider brotherhood of ops. Granted, they could only do what their superiors allowed them to do, but still . . .

"Keep trying. Term Lead out."

Headlights crested a hill 80 meters away. A jeep took the rise, followed by a truck. They paused as if they were planning their approach.

Nir looked to his left. He could just make out Lahav behind a windowless wall that made up one of the three sides of the open shepherds' hut.

He was sitting with his legs tucked up and his head on his knees.

To his right he locked eyes with Yaron, who raised his eyebrows and gave a small smile. They both knew none of them would likely survive this. And for any who did, their fate might even be worse—captured, interrogated, tortured, executed.

Looking forward, Nir saw that both vehicles had begun to approach their location.

"Don't waste rounds, guys. Take only good shots. Wait for my order."

As he lined up his rifle, Nir's mind drifted to Nicole. He wondered if she was praying for him right now. While he didn't buy into all that Jesus stuff, she certainly did. Right now, he'd take all the help he could get. The two of them once had a conversation about dying, when she'd said she wasn't afraid to die because she knew where she would go. He wished he had that same kind of confidence. If this was his last night on earth, he had no idea what would happen to him after.

Nicole's God—or Jesus, I guess—if You're really there, I could use some help here. If You get me out of this, I promise to really listen to Nicole next time she talks about You. Protect me, but most of all protect my men.

The squeak of brakes cut through the quiet night. He heard a lot of activity from the truck but couldn't see past the glare of the headlights.

However, in front of the truck, he saw four officers exit the jeep. Nir could hear them talking, but he couldn't understand their Persian words.

Four soldiers appeared in the light and began moving forward while the officers and the rest of the troops took positions of cover behind the vehicles.

Wait for it, Nir thought. *Let them get closer.*

When they were three meters away, Nir fired, and one of the soldiers dropped to the ground with most of his neck torn away. Instantly, four more shots echoed, and the rest of the lead squad went down. Without pausing, Nir directed his rifle at the vehicles and began firing. The IRGC men shot back, and Nir's face was peppered with chips of stone.

He ducked and wiped the dust from his eyes. When he looked back over the wall, he spotted a low target alongside the jeep. One shot took the soldier in the hip and put him on the ground. A second shot finished him off.

Two grenades flew from the opposite side of the sheep pen. One landed near the officers, putting three of them down. The second was perfectly thrown toward the transport truck's external fuel tank. A fraction of a second after the grenade blew, the truck did too. All gunfire from the IRGC soldiers stopped.

"Doron, Dima, clear the area."

"*Root,*" they said. Nir saw them up and moving

toward the burning truck, rifles ready. Moments later, he heard two shots, followed seconds later by another double tap.

"Cleared," said Dima. "All hostiles are down."

"Collect whatever weapons and ammo you can salvage, then get back," Nir said. "This was the easy round. Anybody bleeding?"

"Just a little." Nir looked over and in the light of the fire saw blood smeared across Yaron's forehead.

"My arm got tagged, but it's just a graze. Lost a little flesh is all," Doron said.

"How you doing, Lahav?" Looking to where the analyst had been shaking, Nir was surprised to see him with his Jericho 941 in his hand, looking around the wall toward the truck fire.

"It's really different from *Assassin's Creed*."

All the guys laughed. Nir said, "Yeah, just a bit different from a video game." Noticing Lahav's slide was locked back, he added, "You may want to change your mag."

"Oh, yeah. Thanks."

"Get ready, everybody. The rest should be here any moment."

CHAPTER 30

B ut they didn't come. And with each minute that passed, the unease in Nir grew.

Five minutes.

Ten minutes.

Then it hit him. "Guys, they're flanking us. Get to the vehicles now. It's our only possibility of surprise."

The whole team sprinted to where the transport truck had burned itself out. Yaron propped his arms on it, then quickly pulled them back. "*Tembel*," he said.

Nir looked over to see why Yaron had just called himself an idiot, then saw him blowing on his forearms.

"Burned myself," Yaron said.

"I guess someone had to do it."

"Hey, boss, I'll bet you falafel to fez that this jeep still runs," Doron said.

Nir looked it over. It was a little scorched from the explosion, but it appeared to be in one piece, and the tires had air. The bright headlights let him know that the battery was still good. Looking in the front seat, he found keys dangling from the ignition.

"Excellent, but you drive like an old Talmudic rabbi. Dima, when we're ready, I want you behind the wheel. The rest of you in the back seat."

"*Root.*"

Gunfire erupted from the other side of the sheep pen as round after round hit right where they'd been taking cover. The screams of wounded and dying sheep cut through the din. The guns of the Kidon team, however, were pointed in the opposite direction, ready for anyone coming over the original rise. Twelve shadows suddenly appeared against the starry sky. The Israelis cut them down before they had a chance to fire their weapons.

"Okay, into the jeep," Nir said.

The men piled in, and Dima turned the key. Remarkably, the jeep's engine started. He hit the accelerator, and Nir could hear curses from the back seat as gravity heaped the men together.

"What direction, boss?" Dima asked.

"Away. Can you see without the headlights?"

"I can see enough." The Russian reached down and the road ahead suddenly went dark.

The terrain was rough, and the men were jostled hard as they hung on to anything bolted down. Then suddenly, the ground disappeared from below them, and they dropped into a dry wadi. Dima managed to keep control and drive along the flat surface.

"We've got company behind us," Imri said.

Nir turned around and in the distance saw the shadows of three jeeps angle into the wadi, followed by one truck, then a second. When the third truck took the embankment, it teetered to the right, then tipped over.

One down, Nir thought. They had a half-kilometer lead, but it was shrinking. It appeared that the IRGC drivers had more experience night driving in this type of terrain.

The wadi suddenly angled to the left. Dima tried to make the turn, but he was going too fast. The jeep ran up the embankment, became airborne, and landed hard. After a loud metallic snap, it abruptly stopped. All the men were thrown forward, and Nir barely missed hitting the windshield face first.

"Everybody out!" he yelled.

They all piled out of the jeep and took a position behind it. The jeeps and trucks came closer and closer. Ten meters out, they hit their brakes in a cloud of dust. To the roar of the diesel engines were added the shouted orders and the sound of soldier after soldier jumping from the trucks and taking position.

Nir and his men were in a hopeless position. This was it—no way out.

"Blaze of glory, *chaveret!*" he shouted into his com.

"Blaze of glory!" everyone repeated.

Music began playing through his communication system. Nir was so surprised that he didn't recognize what it was at first. Then it hit him—"Ride of the Valkyries" by Richard Wagner. That's when he realized that the commotion he heard wasn't just coming from the trucks in front of him. Turning around, Nir saw a Huey cresting a ridge. The mini-guns mounted on either side of the chopper opened up, firing at a rate of four thousand rounds per minute. First the bodies began falling, then the vehicles began exploding. Only 45 seconds later, not a single IRGC soldier was left alive.

The Huey angled around and put its skids on the ground. Nir waved his team to the helicopter, and they climbed in. Once he'd counted all five, he jumped in himself. Immediately, the chopper took to the air.

Nir moved to the cockpit and put his hand on Captain Marks's shoulder.

"If I had external speakers like in the movie," the captain said, "I would have really made an entrance."

"No, it was perfect. Duvall had nothing on you." After a moment, he added, "I heard you guys stopped taking our calls."

"Had to maintain radio silence. President didn't want to take a chance of anyone discovering our little Persian soiree."

Nir was surprised that the decision for their

rescue had reached all the way to the Oval Office. "Could have at least let our side know you were coming."

"What? And spoil the surprise?"

Nir laughed. "Well, thanks. First round is on me back in Erbil."

"We'll take you up on that."

"Oorah," said First Lieutenant Bader.

Moving back to the cabin, Nir sat down. Imri was checking Doron's arm. Yaron was cleaning blood off his face. Dima was watching Nir with a stupid grin, and Lahav was sitting and shaking.

"Lahav, secure and holster your weapon," Nir said.

Lahav looked at his hands as if just now realizing he was still holding his pistol. He obeyed.

Dima leaned forward and put his hand on Nir's leg. "That's years of good living right there, my friend."

"It was years of something."

But deep down he wondered if any part of their survival had to do with that little talk with God. *Who knows? Can't think about it right now. Nicole will have an answer. I'll ask her later.*

Nir tilted his head back, and despite the fact that the Vietnam-era helicopter was racing at a very unsafe speed at a ridiculously low altitude, he savored the flight.

CHAPTER 31

FIVE DAYS LATER
MOSSAD HEADQUARTERS,
TEL AVIV, ISRAEL—
NOVEMBER 30, 2020—09:10 / 9:10 A.M. IDT

Meeting in five," Nir said as he walked into his team's workroom.

"*Yesh*! He's back," Liora shouted, jumping from her chair and running toward him. Dafna followed her, as did Yossi, while a smiling Nicole remained at her workstation. After a couple of hugs and a fist bump, Nir took the long way to his office, starting to the left rather than to the right.

The workroom for his analysts was large and open. He passed three empty desks no one used right now, then came to Nicole's extremely clean and organized area with its numerous keyboards and monitors. These were the tools she used to break into the supposedly impenetrable systems of various governments, satellites, commercial enterprises, and private citizens. He touched her shoulder, and she touched his hand.

"Hey," he said.

"Hey."

Next he came to where Liora and Dafna had

pushed their workstations together, creating an oversized electronics mass that constantly flashed and beeped and whirred as they analyzed thousands of images from satellites and cameras every day. He had no clue what at least half the machines did or how they worked. He just knew these two Millennials were the best he'd ever seen at digging through tons of visual coal to find a hidden diamond.

Next was Yossi, whose board shorts, tank top, and flip-flops went well with his oversized beard and man-bun. His intel analysis was unparalleled in Mossad headquarters, especially now that Nicole had given him access to the computer systems of most of the world's leading intelligence services.

Nir pointed to one of the monitors. "What's that?"

"Haleiwa Surf Challenger. North Shore Oahu. They've got some gnarly barrels and closeout bombs. Bucket list, man."

"Find me someone nasty to bump off there, and I'll bring you along."

"*P'tsatsa*," Yossi said with a grin.

Finally, Nir came to Lahav's dark workstation decorated in Star Wars chic, complete with hanging TIE fighters and that full-sized Chewbacca who had seen better days. By the time they'd arrived home, it was obvious the young analyst was truly shaken. Nir had given him a week off and ordered him to two sessions with one of the in-house counselors.

Reaching into his bag, Nir pulled out a ball cap. The team traded off putting hats on the Wookie. The one Nir placed on his head now read *Erbil Beach Club*.

Nir looked into his office and saw a stack of papers that needed his attention. Instead of walking in, though, he closed the door and took his seat at the head of the conference table.

"Okay, bring it in," he called out.

"We still have two minutes," Liora said. She was rapidly typing on one of several keyboards on her desk.

"Did I say five minutes? I meant three, which means"—Nir looked at his watch—"it's time."

Liora gave an exasperated sigh and pushed the keyboard away. Before rising, though, she pulled open a file drawer, then brought out a large metal bowl and plunked it on her desk. Then she lifted out a very large bag of Skittles, which she tore open before noisily emptying it into the bowl.

All the while, she was mumbling, "They give you work to do. Then you can't get it done because they fill your day with stupid meetings all the time." Walking to the table, she slid the bowl to the middle.

"You okay?" Nir asked.

"I'm good."

"You sure? Because you seem a little unhappy."

"I'm sure."

"You know, we don't need a snack every time we meet."

"Okay, Boomer."

"Boomer? How old do you think I am?"

"Age is not a number; it's an attitude," she said, snatching a handful of candies. She held one up to throw to him.

He glared at her, but she wouldn't put the candy down. The rest of the team arrived at the table and saw the standoff.

"Nir! Nir! Nir! Nir!" they chanted.

Even Nicole had joined in. With a sigh, he opened his mouth.

Liora threw the candy, and it bounced off a front tooth and skittered across the table to the floor. Sounds of disappointment filled the room.

"That one is on you and your big old buck teeth," Liora said.

"What? I don't—" Wait. Was she grinning at him?

"You are so easy."

There were nods of agreement around the table, and he could hear Nicole say, "It's true."

Shaking his head, he said, "First, I want to thank you guys. And that's not just from me but from all the ops team. We wouldn't have made it out of there without you."

"Well, we would have missed Lahav," Dafna said with a smile.

"Liar." Yet Nir had to admit that, as irritating as the man could be, Lahav had garnered his respect in Iran.

"Let's get right to it. Despite the fact that I didn't blow up the robotic gun and almost got my team killed, the *ramsad* has okayed our continuing to develop the plan for our killer art."

Cheers sounded around the table.

"We need an update from you, Nicole, and then we have to do some serious brainstorming. First, though, I want to give you all our mission name."

All four analysts drum rolled the table with their hands.

"Operation Bezalel."

Three of the analysts hit their imaginary cymbals with great flourish, while Nicole said, "Huh?"

"I got this," Yossi said. "Listen, my New-Testament-reading Gentile sister. In Exodus, when God told Moses to build the tabernacle and the ark of the covenant, He gave him an artist with the skills to make it beautiful. That man was named Bezalel."

"I read the Old Testament too," Nicole said.

Nir raised his hand. "Okay, I'm going to veto that tangent, Nicole. Instead, why don't you fill us in on where we are with the marketing for the paintings we'll need for our newly christened Operation Bezalel?"

"Just because I haven't memorized the name of

231

every old guy out of Exodus doesn't mean I don't read the Old Testament," Nicole muttered as she spread out some notes on the table. Looking up, she said, "Yossi, remote."

He obliged. Nicole pressed a button, and a photo appeared on the screen.

"This is Alicia Marcos. As you know, she's our artist, and she lives in Houston, Texas."

"Yee-haw," Liora said with a laugh.

"That's a stereotype, but whatever."

The mood in the room changed in an instant. Nir hadn't seen snippy Nicole in quite a while. Not since before her big spiritual change. Judging by the way the rest of the team was looking down at the table, they hadn't seen it either. He was about to say something, but he saw her staring down at her hands. He knew exactly what she was doing, because he'd been around her other times when she was silently praying.

After a moment, she looked up and said, "I'm sorry, Liora. And the same goes to the rest of you. I've been running so hard and not getting enough sleep. But those are just excuses. There's no reason to have snapped at you."

But Nir knew there was a reason. She'd been embarrassed at being the only one who didn't know the name Bezalel. It was tough being the only Gentile on a team full of Jews, all of whom had the Torah taught to them since before they were old enough to listen. But it was more. She was new in her faith and didn't know all she wanted to know. If she couldn't remember a Bible verse or come up with an answer to a question, she seemed to feel she was letting God down.

Dafna reached over and took hold of her arm. "We all have days like that, girl. No harm, no foul."

Liora and Yossi quickly agreed, and Nir smiled some encouragement toward her.

Nicole did a quick mascara-saving eye dab with her index fingers, and said, "Skittle me?"

"You bet!" Liora pulled a red candy out of her pile and tossed a bull's-eye right into Nicole's mouth. Turning to Nir, the Millennial said, "That's how it's done, Bucky."

Nir shook his head.

Nicole picked up her report. "So with the help of some of Nir's friends in Antwerp, Alicia and I were able to put together an amazing marketing packet." The picture changed to show the canvas envelope, sample mini-art piece, and the cover of the brochure.

"*Achla*, Nicole. You should be a model or something," Yossi said. The rest of the team added their affirmation.

"Yeah, yeah, yeah. Anyway, we seeded the market with three free paintings given to rich guys who promised to get the word around. And they did. We sent fifty packets to owners of mega yachts, and we've heard back from twenty-two."

"How many of those fifty were on our bad guy list, and how many of them responded?" Nir asked.

"Thirty bad guys. Eight have responded."

"Not bad, not bad. In fact, pretty good." His excitement for this operation was building. "What's next?"

"Next is selling. I've had my agent hold any modeling bookings for now, and Alicia and I are making sales calls. We've met with six yacht owners so far, two of them bad guys, and one has purchased two paintings. The guys back in Alicia's workshop are starting work on his order."

"Who's the purchaser?" asked Dafna.

"Khalid Al Kooheji, a Bahraini oil guy who's been funneling money into Palestinian weapons for about a decade. Let me tell you, that guy was a pig. Beautiful boat, really bad manners."

Nir felt a twinge of protectiveness and maybe a bit of jealousy. He put it out of his mind, though. Nicole had proven she could take care of herself. He had already learned the hard way what being over-protective could get him.

"Great work. What's next?"

"Alicia is leaving Houston tomorrow for Dubai. I'll meet her there, and then we have a few sales meetings lined up."

"Wining and dining on yachts worth tens of millions of dollars. Sure you don't need a short brunette to tag along?" Liora asked.

"Wish I did. I'd love to have the both of you," Nicole said, including Dafna.

"Okay, last agenda item," Nir said. "And it's kind of a biggie. We've got the paintings. We've got bad guys buying the paintings. Now, how do we get explosives into the paintings before they're shipped to their new owners?"

Like air leaving a balloon, the enthusiasm in the room died.

Yossi spoke. "Okay, so you were basing this whole idea off Natanz and the explosives planted in the building materials. What about doing the same kind of thing and putting it in the frames?"

"Unfortunately, the success at Natanz has ensured we can never pull off another Natanz. The frames will most certainly be checked by the yacht owners' security teams well before they're ever allowed on the boat."

"What about the paint?" Dafna asked. "I know we've done work with liquid explosives."

Nicole answered this time. "Another good thought. But like a lot of artists, Alicia mixes her own paints. And she's not in on this."

The minutes went by as one idea after another was presented and shot down.

Then a smile spread across Liora's face. "How much does one of Alicia's paintings weigh?"

"I have no idea," Nicole said, then turning to Nir, "Do you?"

"No. But she uses cement along with other substances, so I'm sure they're heavy."

"So you've both seen the paintings up close. Still, you have no idea what they weigh. What about how thick they are?"

"Oh, I don't know," Nicole said, using her hands to demonstrate a range of width.

Liora was almost bouncing in her seat. "But you have no idea exactly, do you? Okay, here it is. On the back of each painting we lay a sheet of explosives. We can do sheets of explosives, right?"

She looked at Nir, who nodded his affirmation.

"*Achla*! So, then, over the explosives we lay a false back made out of the same material as the rest of the painting."

"*Sababa*," Dafna said. "No one will notice the extra weight, because no one knows how much one of her paintings is supposed to weigh."

"What about the detonator?" Yossi had a handful of Skittles, and he tossed one at each of the three women, who all caught them in their mouths.

Liora chewed, then said, "We make the false back thick enough to allow a small cutout for the detonator, but still thin enough to only add minimal variable in the weight. Because of the type of materials, I would guess that there is no standard weight for the paintings. You can get all sneaky and make sure of that, Nicole."

"Definitely, but it makes sense," Nicole answered. "Alicia has said to me that it's not a science. 'I'm an artist, not a physicist' is the way she puts it."

"What about a seam?" Nir asked. "Like on the edge that will show the layers."

Again, it was Nicole who answered. "There won't be a seam. Alicia told me she's had problems with deterioration on the edges. Also, a couple of times corners have been chipped in moving the paintings. So now she has her team put a thick epoxy around the rim."

Nir thought for a moment, then said, "Liora, I think you've come up with a brilliant idea. But we still have one big question. How in the world will we get all that—sheets of explosives, a false cement back, and a detonator—on Alicia's paintings? Do you have that problem solved too?"

Liora smiled as she emptied a fistful of candies into her mouth. As she chewed, she managed to say, "I have no idea, Mr. Kidon Agent. That's your job, right?"

CHAPTER 32

AROMA ESPRESSO BAR, TEL AVIV, ISRAEL— 15:20 / 3:20 P.M. IST

Nir carried two full ceramic mugs to the corner table where Nicole sat waiting for him. Their usual spot, it gave them both a clear view of the front doors and all the windows. And, tucked away as it was, it was unlikely they'd be overheard.

"Is it feasible?" Nir asked, taking a sip of his latte.

"I've seen Alicia's workshop. It's really big. It has to be because curing the materials and creating the artwork is done in several stages. Once it's painted, she has a whole separate process for protecting the paint with this glossy sealant and finalizing the canvas. Then there's the packaging for shipping. I was shocked when I saw her space. She has, like, three or four people working for her."

"Again, is it feasible?"

"There has to be a way, but that's much more your mind than mine."

"It takes a criminal to think like a criminal?"

Nicole laughed. "Something like that."

"Okay, I'll get my gang of hooligans together,

and we'll talk it through. But any way you look at it, I think a trip to Houston is in my future."

Nicole held her own latte in her hands as though she was enjoying the warmth of the mug. She took a sip, then put it down. "So did the *ramsad* really go after you?"

"It wasn't pretty, I'll say that. But he did recognize that something weird had to have happened, because the whole thing doesn't make sense. Who benefited by the gun not being fully destroyed? And who would have gained by our playing catch-the-bullet in that box truck? The obvious answer to both questions is the IRGC. But that makes no sense in context, because if the IRGC were involved, they would have thwarted the whole attack, and Fakhrizadeh would still be alive today."

Nicole leaned forward. "Well . . . maybe just before I left headquarters to meet you here, your team of merry analysts and I found something you can share with the *ramsad* to make him a little less grumpy."

Nir raised his eyebrows as he finished off his latte. "As you like to say, color me intrigued."

"You know how in most places it's *Follow the money?* In Iran, it's—"

"Follow the bodies."

"The bodies have started piling up." She lifted her phone from her purse, swiped around a little bit, then showed the screen to Nir.

"He's ugly. Who is he?"

"This was one of the Baloch engineers who helped assemble the gun."

"Was?"

"He was found dead in a hotel room, tortured and then eviscerated alongside his mistress, who happened to be a Kurd. Our Baloch friends tell us he was the one who tampered with the explosives so the charge was directed away from the gun. *Why?* you might ask." Nicole paused, obviously enjoying the reveal.

Nir waited, then realized action was required on his part. "Why?"

"Here. You may need this so you can follow me." She swapped her mostly full mug with his empty one. "Okay, the Baloch engineer liked to pillow talk his mistress about his secret projects. You know, show how important he was. Little did he know she was connected into the Kurdish resistance. She told the Kurds about the robotic gun, and they decided they really wanted the technology."

"Who wouldn't?"

"The problem was that the head of the engineers was very protective of the plans, allowing each person to see only their part of them. Since the bad-egg engineer couldn't just abscond with the plans, the Kurds went to Plan B. They had some compromising information on a Persian guy in the weapons analysis department for the Iranian

240

military. If this guy could just see the weapon, he could lay out plans to replicate it. Still with me?"

"Barely."

"Try to keep up, old man. The Kurdish mistress lovey-doveyed her Baloch engineer into tampering with the explosives so the gun wouldn't be destroyed. Then she promised him a ton of money from the Kurds if he could use the information from their weapons analysis guy to recreate the robotic gun."

"That was a lot of words. I think I get it, though. So was it the Baloch or the Kurds who then wanted the IRGC to kill us in the truck?"

"Neither."

Nir threw up his hands. "Okay, I need another latte."

Nicole laughed. "That second incident was about both bodies and money and was totally separate from the first."

"*Oy vavoy*, I might actually need a little something from my uncle's secret cabinet to pour into my coffee."

Nicole rolled her eyes. "The leader of the Arab community next to where your Kurdish driver and son lived had been trying to ingratiate himself to the IRGC, because when you have the big bullies on your side, you can be a bully too."

"It's called being a toady. The kids I learned English from on the *kibbutz* taught me that word."

"Well, it fits. The Arab guy had spread the word that he would pay good money for information the IRGC might find interesting. The father and son told the Arab they just might know where six Mossad operatives could be found. The Arab told the IRGC, and there you go."

"Amazing. Two betrayals, two different actors. Everybody and everything is for sale in the Middle East. Any idea what happened to the Kurds?"

"This part is just rumor from the Kurd community right now, but word is the IRGC wasn't too thrilled about one of their squads being wiped out by a mysterious helicopter incursion. They needed scapegoats, and the driver and son fit the bill, as did the Arab guy. Sounds like they may not still be among the living."

Nicole stood and lifted both mugs. "Hang on," she said, then walked to the counter. A few minutes later, she came back with just one mug and placed it in front of Nir.

"Thanks."

Sitting, she reached across the table, took his hand, and looked right into his eyes. "Now, in all honesty, how close was it?"

"Honestly? If that CIA chopper hadn't come in all *Apocalypse Now*, I wouldn't be here."

She held his eyes, then leaned back in her chair and looked down at her lap.

"I know what you're thinking, Nicole. What

would have happened to me if I hadn't made it out of there alive? Well, you might be interested to know I actually had a talk with your God when I was in the midst of it."

Nicole looked up and raised her eyebrows.

"I did. I don't know if it had anything to do with how the battle turned out. But if so, then I owe Him one—a big one."

Nicole smiled and shook her head. "You still don't get it, Nir. It doesn't work that way."

"What do you mean?" He'd thought Nicole would be excited that he'd prayed, but as usual, she liked to zag when he thought she'd zig.

"Think about it. What do you have that God needs?"

Nir started to answer her question several times, but each time he stopped before the words came out. Everything that came to mind seemed silly or petty.

She continued. "People think God works on some kind of barter system. *You scratch my back, I'll scratch yours.* But it doesn't work like that. It can't work like that. It's like a three-year-old offering you something for your BMW. What could he possibly have for a fair trade?"

Nir laughed. "Remember, I'm a Jew. There's always a deal to be made."

Nicole smiled and shook her head. "Not with this, Nir. One time Jesus sent His disciples out to tell people about Him. He gave them this whole list of instructions, and then He ended by saying, 'Freely you've received; now freely give.' That's the order of things. It's not a transaction. It's not *I've got to give something so I can receive something*. You're not buying anything. Salvation is a gift."

"You see, that's what doesn't make sense to me. It's a losing proposition for God. If I go down the street and give someone a thousand shekels, then tell him, 'Now, go give that one thousand shekels to someone else,' what do you think will happen? He'll be sporting a new watch, and I'll be out a thousand shekels. That's human nature."

Nicole laughed. "You're exactly right. But it's not God's nature. I can give you money, but I can't change you inside. Yet that's the change God makes. He gives you salvation, but then He also changes who you are. Think about it. I'm here trying to convince you to take the thousand shekels God gave me."

Nir leaned back in his chair, then took the now-lukewarm latte and downed it in one long draw. He chuckled and shook his head as he set the mug back down. "Girl, you have been studying."

Nicole smiled proudly.

"I promised you I would listen. I'm listening."

"That's all I can ask."

Nir stood. "But I'm done listening for now

because I just heard two very interesting stories I would like to repeat to the *ramsad*. Maybe I'll be able to convince him to hate me just a little bit less."

DECEMBER 2020 (FOUR DAYS LATER)

CHAPTER 33

FOUR DAYS LATER
CAFALA BAHR, SINGAPORE STRAIT,
OFF SENTOSA ISLAND, SINGAPORE—
DECEMBER 4, 2020—16:15 / 4:15 P.M. SGT

As the copter descended toward the helipad, Saad leaned toward General Mousavi and shouted so he could be heard. "I want you to be on your best behavior. These are professional businesswomen."

"Aren't all the women you bring professionals?" Mousavi responded with a lecherous smile.

"Different kind of profession. Different kind of women. I just need you to determine if they are who they say they are."

"With pleasure."

"I appreciate it. This whole deal has moved fairly quickly, and I just want to make sure it's all on the up-and-up."

The black Sikorsky S-76C emblazoned with the name and logo of ASEnergy softly touched down on the yacht, and the doors remained closed as the rotor slowed to a stop. Saad's anticipation was getting the best of him, and he chided himself for acting like a schoolboy with a crush. This was business, and he needed to treat it as such.

Thus far, the day had been good. Arash arrived that morning, and together they'd celebrated the victory in the previous month's U.S. presidential elections. It wasn't just the outcome they applauded, however. The whole process had left America a divided nation. A divided America is a weak America, and Iran was taking full advantage of that truth.

Mousavi admitted that the Zionist assassination of Dr. Fakhrizadeh had been a terrible blow to the nuclear program. The global distraction provided by the U.S. elections, however, had compensated quite a bit, because it would open the door for ramping up their enrichment process. And while the loss of the doctor was significant because of the progress already made, it wasn't as devastating as if it had happened ten years ago or even five. Iran was racing toward a nuclear weapon, and they were confident they would achieve that goal in the next six months.

Now he hoped a good day was about to get even better.

The helicopter doors opened, and a female crewmember stepped out, followed by the male pilot. Standing at the bottom of the steps, he held up his hand and helped the first passenger down. It was the artist. When she was on solid ground, his hand went back up, and then Nicole le Roux stepped out.

Saad's insides fluttered. The woman was even

more magnificent in person. Tall and shapely. And when the light wind rolled across the Singapore Strait and caught her hair, the scene could have been right out of a commercial. She removed her dark, oversized sunglasses, and her ice-blue eyes caught his. Her face spread into a wide smile, and she waved. In his peripheral vision, he saw Mousavi waving back, and he realized he was just standing there like a love-struck teen.

Get control of yourself.

He smiled, turned on the charm, and began walking toward the women.

"Welcome to the *Cafala Bahr*," he said as he reached them. He shook the artist's hand first, then took hold of Nicole's. Looking into her eyes, he said, "I am Saad Salim, and you are most welcome on my humble vessel."

The artist laughed. "This boat is anything but humble."

Saad shrugged. "What can I say? I have been blessed. This is my good friend Arash. I have invited him because he has a good eye for art and for people."

With a strong Texas twang, the short brunette said, "Perfect. We're people, and we've got art. I'm Alicia Marcos, the artist, and this is my good friend Nicole le Roux. She has a good eye for con men and bull crap. Unfortunately, on our little visits of late, we've met with plenty of both."

Saad laughed. "Let me assure you that I do not invite con men onto my boat. And I have an excellent staff that cleans up after our bulls very well."

"Excellent. Sounds like I didn't need to pack my boots after all," Nicole said.

Saad was surprised by her voice, a smoky alto that was sultry and intriguing. He could feel his obsession level rising. It had been a few years since he'd lost control to that mania, and when he did, it never ended well.

"Please, come. Let me show you my boat, including the walls where I just might need an artist's touch." He held out his arm to Alicia, who took it, and they walked toward the elevator. Nicole and Arash followed similarly linked.

"*Cafala,*" Alicia said. "Is that an Arab word?"

"No, but *bahr* is. It means 'sea.' *Cafala* is just the first two letters of each of my daughters' names combined."

"Oh, that's sweet."

Just before they entered the elevator, a steward stepped forward with four flutes of orange-pink champagne on a silver tray. He watched Alicia give a quick look to Nicole, who gave a small shake of her head.

Very interesting. She is not just the business partner. She also seems to be the bodyguard. Could she be more intriguing?

He leaned forward and said conspiratorially, "I

know it can be a dangerous world, and one can never be too careful. Please, feel free to choose whichever of the glasses you would like. Then Arash and I will try ours first."

Nicole smiled. "You are the first to make us that offer. One client near Sicily demanded that we leave his boat immediately because we wouldn't drink whatever it was he offered us. Thank you."

Nicole and Alicia each chose a flute, then waited as the men took the others and sipped their champagne.

"Let me extend that agreement to anything else I offer you, whether it be food or drink. I want you to feel this is a safe place."

"Much obliged," Alicia said, then added after sipping, "Oh, this is good. What is it?"

"Louis Roederer Cristal Vinotheque Rose 2000."

Saad watched how the two women handled their champagne glasses. It was obvious to him that the Texan wouldn't know a rosé from a noir. Nicole, however, held hers to the light, which gave her a clear view of the rare color and extra-fine bubbles.

"Please," Saad said, motioning the group into the elevator, where the operator took them down a level.

For the next 40 minutes, he escorted them deck by deck, letting the women admire the seven bedrooms—each with its own balcony—the outdoor pool and the indoor pool, the spa room, the cinema, the vast kitchen and dining room, the crew quarters, and the bridge, where they met the captain and chief steward. He even took them down to the lowest deck so he could show off his garage with its two tenders for going to shore, its variety of playtime watercraft, and his mini-submarine.

When they finished the tour in the salon, Alicia dropped onto an overstuffed couch. "That was incredible! Most definitely the biggest and fanciest boat we've seen, and we've seen . . . How many others, Nicole?"

"Twelve." Nicole settled into a chair.

"Twelve. But yours, Mr. Salim, takes the cake."

"Please, call me Saad. And I know you've settled in, but if you would indulge me, I would like to show you two more things."

"Of course," Nicole answered as she stood again.

Alicia rose as well, and Saad led them across the large room and pointed to a bare white wall. "There it is."

"My goodness, that's a sad-looking wall," Alicia said with a smile. "I bet a little color, maybe some classical beauty, would liven up this whole room."

"That, of course, is why I have invited you here." Saad walked them to another bare wall.

"I'm afraid this wall suffers from the same melancholy malady."

"Alicia's portfolio is with our bags," Nicole said. "If you will direct us to our rooms, we can return and show you your options."

Saad waved his hand. "That is business. At one time my business had to come before pleasure, but one of the benefits of success is that I can now reverse that order. Let us just enjoy ourselves tonight. Tomorrow, we will sign whatever needs to be signed." He turned toward the man waiting near an open door. "My steward will show you to your rooms so you can change and freshen up. When you are ready, you will be shown to the dining room."

For several hours, Saad carried out his charm offensive. At times he even amazed himself with the subtlety of his wit and the perfection of his timing. As the evening carried on, he transferred his attention from Alicia to Nicole. Arash, as they had planned, took the cue and engaged the artist.

After dinner, they returned to the upper deck to enjoy the night sea air. Standing by the outdoor pool with drinks in hand, the four admired the distant Singapore skyline.

"What a beautiful night," Saad said. This was his signal to Arash, who picked up on it right away. Yes, this was business, and these women were professionals, but he'd also confessed his infatuation with Nicole to his friend—and his hope that he could make some sort of connection with her tonight.

Turning toward Alicia, the Persian general pointed toward the skyline and said, "Can you see the Guoco Tower?"

"Which one is it?"

"Why, it's only the tallest building in Singapore. Come. I'll show you." He led her around the pool and toward the railing surrounding the deck.

"She is a delightful young woman," Saad said, turning toward Nicole.

"So talented."

"Some women create beauty. Some women have beauty bestowed upon them."

Nicole smiled. "You're going to make me blush."

"I'm sure it would only enhance your magnificence."

Nicole laughed and stepped toward Arash and Alicia.

If she gets to them, my one chance will be lost.

He reached out and took hold of her hand, stopping her progress. When she turned, he noticed the fire in her eyes. This was something new—a fresh level of intrigue.

He pressed on. "Listen, Nicole. I am a man with more money than I can spend in many lifetimes. I have boats and cars and mansions and businesses. But it all means nothing because I don't have anyone to share it with."

Although she was tugging her hand, he held on. He was too caught up in the moment.

"I can give you the world. A woman like you deserves nothing less. Look around you. All this can be yours."

"Let go of my hand."

But instead, he pulled her toward him, then kissed her full lips. It was exquisite. But then he was stumbling backward, trying to regain his balance. His legs caught on a pool chair, and he tumbled over, hitting the deck with his back, then his head. Pain radiated throughout his entire body.

Rolling to his side, he saw Nicole striding toward the elevator with Alicia racing to catch up with her. A steward stepped in front of them, barring their way, until Saad raised his head and called out, "Let them go. Take them to their rooms."

He laid his head back down and closed his eyes. A steward sprinted over to help him up, but he chased him away with a curse. A few moments later, he heard a creak in a nearby pool chair, followed by Arash's voice. "So how'd it go?"

Opening his eyes, he saw his friend with legs stretched out, smiling at him. Arash offered him the drink in his hand, which Saad took and downed in one toss.

"You know, you could just take her. You've got

more than enough resources at your disposal to clean up any resultant mess."

Saad threw the empty glass into the pool and pulled himself into a chair. "You Persians. How did you ever build an empire? You have no tact."

Arash laughed and signaled for the steward to bring two more drinks. "Who needs tact when you have power and money? That is the lesson you, my friend, must learn."

But that's not who I am. This was simply the first battle. I may have lost this skirmish, but I will win this war. Nicole le Roux will be on my arm one day, not because she will be forced to be but because it will be her greatest desire.

CHAPTER 34

Alicia closed the door to her room and locked it.

"What happened?"

"I'm such an idiot!" Nicole cried. "I totally saw it coming. His little cue to his buddy. The 'Oh, have you seen the big building?' as he led you away. I knew it, and I still let it happen." She dropped backward onto the bed. "I tried to get away, but he was holding on. And then he kissed me! The pig kissed me right on the lips. Ugh. He tasted like whisky and breath mints."

"That sounds like a country song."

Nicole popped her head up and saw her friend giving her a sympathetic smile. She laughed. "Yeah, I guess it does. Oh, Alicia, I'm so sorry. I've totally screwed this up."

Alicia laid back on the bed next to her. "How did you screw anything up?"

"I pushed the jerk into a bunch of chairs, and he went down hard. Probably gave him a concussion."

"I caught the last part of the show as he was on his way down. It looked pretty funny to me."

Nicole laughed again. "I guess it was in an *I*

259

can't believe what I just did sort of way. One minute he's *Oh, I can give you the world,* and the next his boat shoes are flying into the pool. But there's no way he's buying any of your paintings now. Two sales down the drain. That's real money."

Nicole's disappointment was much deeper, though. Saad Salim was on the bad guys list. He provided funding to terrorist organizations and was involved in the acquisition and distribution of weapons. His was one boat Nir had really wanted to load up with explosives in case there came a time they were needed.

"You're right. You should have just slept with him. That would have guaranteed the sale."

Nicole sat up. "What?"

Alicia followed suit. "That's what you just said. Because you rejected his advances, I lost a sale. The implication is that I would rather have had you sleep with him so I could off-load some paintings."

"I don't see the connection," Nicole said, although it was becoming clearer to her as she thought about it.

"You know, I think this technically makes me your pimp. Good to know I have career options in case this whole artist thing doesn't work out."

Nicole laughed and swatted Alicia on the arm. "Stop it. You've made your point."

"I'm just happy you're okay. And I'm sorry our

260

plan to sell my art has put you in a situation like this."

"I knew what I was getting into. Besides, you had to deal with Arash. Notice we never got a last name? There's something creepy about that guy. I just haven't figured out what it is yet." She flopped back onto the bed. "Mind if I sleep in here tonight?"

"Be my guest." Alicia lowered her voice. "By the way, after traveling all the way to Singapore, there's no way I'm leaving here empty-handed. I'm stealing all the full-size soaps and shampoos from the *en suite*."

"Do it! And I'm totally packing that robe. Did you feel how soft it is?"

"I didn't even see it."

The two women talked for a while, and then Alicia collected Nicole's bag from her room.

THE NEXT MORNING

The bed had been big enough for them both to have plenty of space, so Nicole woke the next morning surprised at how fitfully she'd slept.

She and Alicia debated going to breakfast. There was no telling what kind of mood Salim would be in. Would he be angry? Repentant? Out for vengeance? Finally, they decided if he wanted to harm them, he would have done it during the night.

Still, before they left Alicia's room, Nicole went into the bathroom and removed a Gerber Terracraft tactical knife with a four-inch fixed blade from the false bottom in her makeup kit. She'd balked at packing it, but Nir had insisted she have it along for these sales calls on strangers' boats. He'd been right. She strapped it to her upper calf under her orchid-pink linen Cabo pants.

Once their bags were packed, a steward stationed not far from Alicia's room told them breakfast was on the top deck. As soon as the elevator opened, Nicole heard Saad's voice.

"Ladies, welcome to another beautiful day in the South China Sea." The two men stood next to a table filled with fruit and pastries and what appeared to be a mimosa at each place setting. "Please, come sit down."

Arash and Saad had each taken position behind a pulled-out chair. Nicole sat in the one in front of Arash. Then once both women were in place, Saad said, "Before I sit, may I first say how sorry and embarrassed I am at my behavior last night. I wish I could blame it on the alcohol, but I was wholly in my right mind. I've just been dealing with some family and business pressures, and I let them cloud my judgment. I am without excuse, and I beg your forgiveness."

Nicole said nothing, but Alicia answered. "You

were a real jerk last night, and where I come from, people have been shot for less than what you did."

Saad smiled. "Yes, the Wild West of America."

"I'm not talking America. I'm talking Texas. In my state, we tend to give people second chances, but my mom used to tell me *Sorry is as sorry does*. So I look forward to seeing if your apology is genuine."

"I hope I may be able to prove the veracity of my words to you."

Arash had already taken a seat on the other side of the table, and Saad joined him.

"Please, tell me more about your Texas," Arash said. "And then your art."

Nicole knew those two topics would set Alicia off chattering, so she just listened to her talk while she ate. Out of the corner of her eye she could see Saad taking quick glances in her direction. Thirty minutes into the meal, Nicole was relieved to hear the copter returning to the helipad. As it drew near, two of the stewards ran over with a large, clear acrylic sheet the size of a wall.

"I love to see it land," Saad said while peeling a pre-cut banana segment. "This allows me to watch it without the rotor wash scattering fruit and croissants across the upper deck."

Nicole kept her eyes on the two young men, wondering what life journey had led them to a mega yacht holding an oversized windbreak for a billionaire.

Once the helicopter had set down, she said, "Well, I guess our ride is here."

But Saad held out his hands. "Wait. We still haven't talked business."

Alicia spoke up. "We just thought—"

"I was a fool for what I did last night. But I would be an idiot if I let you leave here today without purchasing your artwork."

Alicia glanced at Nicole, who nodded.

"Okay. What do you have in mind?"

"I want the Marilyn biting the Oakleys. And I would like the Latin fruit bowl."

Alicia looked excited. "We have those prints in inventory. *Oakley Marilyn* is $500,000, and *Fruit Bowl* is $350,000."

As the sales had mounted, Nir had urged Alicia and Nicole to gradually increase the prices to see what the market would bear. This was the highest Alicia had ever gone.

Saad smiled. "I'm afraid you don't understand. I don't want prints. I want your originals. How would it look if I showed off your work to someone in my salon, then had to admit they were just reprints. Saad Salim does not do reprints."

Alicia looked stunned. "The originals are not for sale."

"Oh, come on. Everything is for sale. Tell me how much you want."

Nicole jumped in. "You heard her. They're not for sale. Just because you're rich doesn't mean you can buy anything you want."

Saad looked at Nicole and said, "Two million dollars for the pair."

"They're not for sale," Nicole growled.

"Five million."

"You can stuff your five million in your little mini-submarine," Alicia said.

"Seven million."

Nicole couldn't imagine what point this man was trying to make with this whole staring-at-her-while-bidding-with-Alicia thing. Was he trying to buy the paintings—or her?

"They're not for sale," she said.

"Ten million dollars."

"Sold!"

Nicole whipped her head toward Alicia, only to see her standing and reaching across the table to seal the deal with a handshake.

"What?" cried Nicole.

As Alicia and Saad shook hands, the artist said, "But you pay for the shipping."

Saad, who was now looking at Alicia, said, "It's only fair. Send the necessary papers to my assistant, and we'll work out the details."

"You bet. It was a pleasure doing business with you. Now, if you don't mind, I think me and my girl are gonna get ourselves off your little speedboat here." Spotting one of the stewards, she said, "Hey, Jeeves, wanna get our bags?" She then proceeded to spread out one of the cloth napkins and load it up with pastries. She folded it over and slipped it into the beach bag she'd set next to her chair.

"Thanks for the snacks," she told Saad.

Nicole was still dumbfounded. She stood and followed her friend toward the helicopter. Behind her, the two men said their fare-wells, but she didn't bother to acknowledge them.

Once their bags arrived and they were strapped into the helicopter, she turned to her friend. "What just happened there?"

Alicia beamed. "I just sold three thousand dollars' worth of paint and cement for ten million—to that idiot!"

Nicole wasn't sure if she should be excited or angry. "What about artist integrity? What about his being a sleazeball?"

Alicia took hold of Nicole's face with both her hands and turned her head so they were looking directly into each other's eyes. "Nicole, it's ten million dollars! Heck, I'll just paint another one. I'll have Marilyn biting a pair of Dolce & Gabbanas this time. And the fruit bowl? Who knows? All I know is my life just changed forever."

Nicole was laughing by now. She wrapped her arms around her friend, and they hugged.

"Congratulations, honey. I'm so happy for you."

"And I'm so happy for *you*. Remember the finder's fees? Ten percent for you and ten percent for that hunk-a-stud you have." Once sales had taken off, Nir had renegotiated with Alicia so that Nicole would receive her own ten percent rather than sharing the fee with him. Nicole's worry that her friend would now resent having to part with two million dollars was relieved when Alicia sighed and said, "Somehow, I guess I'll just have to find a way to manage with eight million. What's a girl to do?"

"And don't forget the money from all your other sales. Pretty soon you'll be able to buy your own mega yacht."

When they landed at Singapore Changi Airport, a limousine picked them up at the hangar to take them to their terminal. Once there—after a quick stop in the women's restroom, where Nicole unstrapped the Gerber knife, wiped it clean of fingerprints, and left it in a trash can—they were ushered through the VIP security doors. They said their goodbyes, and Alicia boarded her 21-hour ANA flight to Houston via Tokyo— but not before upgrading from business class to first. An hour later, Nicole boarded a flight to Frankfurt.

After landing in Germany 13 hours later, she changed the destination for her final leg from

Milan to Tel Aviv. And by early afternoon the day after she left Singapore, Nir was hugging her by baggage claim at Ben Gurion International Airport.

CHAPTER 35

TEL AVIV, ISRAEL—DECEMBER 6, 2020— 15:15 / 3:15 P.M. IDT

After laying Nicole's bags in the trunk of his black Škoda Superb, Nir opened the passenger door so she could get in. Her exhaustion was evident in her few words and slow movements. He wished he could take her back to her guesthouse to rest, but she had too much time-sensitive information. A couple hours with him and a few more with the team, then she could sleep all she wanted.

As he pulled out of the parking structure, he asked, "You want some coffee to wake up?"

She thought for a moment. "No, I've been sitting down for so long. I'd rather stretch my legs."

"A walk it is. Just close your eyes for a bit right now, and if you fall asleep, I'll wake you when we get there."

Nir expected her usual push back, saying she wasn't tired. But she closed her eyes, and he soon heard steady breathing. A half hour later he pulled into a parking space by the Homat HaYam Promenade. He was debating whether to wake her or let her sleep when she saved him the choice by stirring.

"Feel better?"

"Just enough to take the edge off." Looking outside the car, she said, "Jaffa. Perfect choice."

They stepped out of the car and walked to the patterned brick walkway.

"Left or right?" asked Nir.

To their left was Old Town Jaffa with its centuries of history. To the right was the skyline of Tel Aviv with its ever-present construction cranes. Old and new—the ongoing contradiction of Israel. Directly in front of them was the Mediterranean carrying on its breeze the sound of surf and the smell of open water.

"Let's go right."

As they set off, Nir said, "So you and Alicia made three stops, right?"

"We did. Two near Hong Kong and one by Singapore. One good guy and two bad guys."

"And . . ."

"Well, the good guy was really a bad guy, just not in the ways we care about. The Hong Kong bad guy was actually a good guy. I mean, he was very nice and a great host. It's just that whole funneling of Chinese weapons into the Middle East thing. Anyway, first guy didn't buy, but the second guy did."

"Excellent. He was the one we wanted. What about Singapore?"

"Well, there we had the good, the bad, and the just plain ugly."

Nicole told him about her time with Saad Salim and the mysterious Arash. When she came to the confrontation by the pool, he was furious. But he caught himself before he vented. He'd played knight in shining armor before with Nicole, and it hadn't worked out so well. So instead, he forced a laugh and a high five when she relayed how Salim had tumbled over the chairs.

"One out of three sales isn't bad," he said.

Nicole took his hand. "Well, here's where it gets really interesting." She described breakfast the next morning, the negotiation, and the shocking result.

"Ten million dollars? I mean, I love Alicia's work. But ten million dollars?"

Nicole just laughed. "It's crazy. It's like he'd worked himself into a frenzy and was going to win no matter what. I don't know if it was to prove something to himself or to me."

"It was to you. Without a doubt. He'd been rebuffed, but he doesn't lose. I'm guessing he still thinks he has a chance with you."

Letting go of his hand, Nicole ran a finger under his chin. "Maybe he does. You should have seen the size of his yacht."

"Yeah? Did you see the size of my Škoda? That monster has four doors and power steering."

Nicole laughed. "You know our cuts are one million each."

"And I'm sure the *ramsad* will thank us very much for our donation to the cause."

They walked in silence for a while, enjoying the cool air and bustle around them. At one point they sat on a bench and watched the surfers doing their best to catch rides off the low waves.

"So what's going on in that mad-scientist brain of yours?" Nicole asked.

"Same stuff that goes through it every day— just trying to take over the world." Nir kept his eyes toward the Mediterranean.

Nicole smiled. "Seriously. What are you thinking about?"

He leaned forward so that his elbows rested on his knees. "Okay, I'll tell you. But it will just add to my reputation as the worst buzzkill in the history of buzzkills." He turned toward Jaffa, then toward Tel Aviv. "I'm just thinking that if the Iranians get their nuke, all this could be gone."

Nicole laughed. "I'm sorry. What you just said is terrible, and I feel horrible for laughing. But you're exactly right. You truly are the worst buzzkill in history."

"I warned you. But you know how I go on and on about how we're just slowing down their nuclear program instead of stopping it. This right here is what's on my mind when I'm saying it." Pointing toward Tel Aviv, he added, "That city right there will be the first to go. Well, maybe after Riyadh."

"So you think it will be Tel Aviv and not Jerusalem. Seems like they'd want to strike at the heart of the nation, not just at its wallet."

"Oh no, they won't touch Jerusalem. The Holy City is not their target; it's their goal. For them, Jerusalem belongs to Islam."

"But how can they say that? Jerusalem belonged to the Jews way before Islam existed."

A small, fluffy dog on a long retractable leash trotted up to Nir and sniffed his shoes. He reached down to scratch the animal's head, but as soon as he touched it, the owner whistled. The dog hurried back as the owner glared at Nir.

"Have a nice day," Nir called as he sat up on the bench. Then turning back to Nicole, he said, "They have two main reasons for saying Jerusalem is theirs. First, it's holy to them because it contains the Al-Aqsa Mosque and the Dome of the Rock, the location from which they say Muhammad ascended into heaven. Second, when Jerusalem was conquered, it was declared *waqf*, which is a sacred and permanent dedication of something to Allah."

"I've heard that word before, but I've never known what it meant. So in their minds you Jews have taken for yourselves something that belongs to God."

"There you go. But again, that's just for Jerusalem. They point to countless other reasons and excuses and historical events for why they think all Jews in Israel need to be wiped off the face of the earth."

Nir nodded to a family walking along the beach. Even though the afternoon was cool, the two toddlers were barefoot and kept running to the edge of the surf and back with each wave. "I can't watch that without thinking *What if?* Tehran is getting close with their ballistic missile technology. Once they develop their warhead, they'll have the ability to drop a missile right in Tel Aviv. Even if the place where those little kids are playing somehow remains outside the blast radius, it will still be rendered unusable for, like, a hundred years or something."

"That's hard to imagine."

"But that's just traditional nuclear weapons. How long until the mullahs put a suitcase nuke or a dirty bomb in the hands of their terrorist militias? Hamas, Hezbollah . . . both would love to walk one of those into Haifa or Netanya. The Houthis will turn Riyadh into rubble. All Iran's goals can be achieved, and they wouldn't have to fire a single missile."

They watched in silence as the family made its way down the beach.

After looking at his watch, Nir stood and said, "We better head back to the car."

Nicole joined him, and they started back in the direction of Jaffa.

"Even the job the guys and I just did with Fakhrizadeh, what did it really accomplish? Rather than racing at 100 kilometers an hour, their nuclear program slows to 60 an hour. Even with Operation Bezalel, it feels like we're in a vast wheat field pulling up weeds one at a time. But the bottom line is if we don't find a way to shut down Iran's nuclear program, by one means or another, by one group or another, at one time or another, we'll lose tens of thousands if not millions of people. Guaranteed."

Nicole slid her hand under his arm. "Different subject, same subject. When is the last time you took a vacation?"

Nir laughed quietly. "Maybe back when I was 13."

"Maybe you need to think about one. In fact, I'd even say you need to consider taking a hiatus."

"Come on, Nicole. How do I take a hiatus when there's so much to do?"

"First, you're not Superman. And, second, you just got through saying what you're doing isn't making that much of a difference anyway."

Nir halted and looked at her. "As you're so fond of saying, I get to say that. You don't."

Nicole stood on her toes and kissed him on the cheek. "I'm the girl. I get to say whatever I want." Then she walked on, leaving him standing there.

After a moment, Nir hustled to catch up. When he had, he raised his eyebrows and grinned. "Okay, reverse psychology duly noted. Well played, Jedi Master. Listen, I know I'm making a difference. It's just discouraging to see less progress than I believe we need to make."

She took his hand again. "I get it."

"I wish our government would decide to shut down the Iranian nuclear program once and for all, while we still can."

She swung his hand and sung, "If wishes and dreams were candies and creams, we'd all have a merry Christmas."

Once again, Nir stopped to look at her. But this time the expression on her face made it clear she was teasing him.

"You're lucky you're pretty," he said, looping his arm around her shoulders as they started strolling again.

"You're lucky I'm pretty too," she said, then bumped him with her hip.

CHAPTER 36

MOSSAD HEADQUARTERS, TEL AVIV, ISRAEL— 17:10 / 5:10 P.M. IST

Nir took a seat at the head of his team's conference table. This afternoon a snack bowl held miniature chocolate candy bars, and he grabbed a handful. He was five minutes late for his own meeting, but he'd been on the phone with Efraim Cohen passing on Nicole's news that the Mossad would soon be two million dollars richer. It was one of his rare happy calls with superiors.

His mood changed when he saw the table of analysts glaring at him for keeping them waiting. "I was on the phone. Any of you who can beat me arm wrestling, feel free to complain. Otherwise, stow it, and let's get going."

"Arm wrestling, no. Sudoku, yes," said Liora.

"Beautiful. That will come in handy when we have an enemy we can defeat only with brute puzzle power."

Liora rolled her eyes. "Leave it to you to miss my subtle way of saying that while you may be stronger than me, I am much, much smarter."

Dafna nodded. "He missed it because, despite

his being stronger than you, you truly are much, much smarter."

"You're smart, huh? How about I show you my Trivia Crack record?"

"Oh good," Dafna said. "It's 2015 again."

"And apparently he's 13," Liora added.

"You're never going to win with these two," Nicole said to him. "Just admit defeat and move on."

Nir pointed to the two younger women. "This is not a defeat; it's an armistice for the sake of time. Now, I gave you guys a task. For almost a year we've been calling this room team headquarters, which is boring even for a mental Neanderthal like me. I asked you to come up with a new name that's catchy and fits what we're doing here. So what is its new name?"

Once again, a drum roll sounded on the table. Then Dafna pressed the remote, and Nir read the name.

"Carl?"

Four of the analysts yelled "Carl!" while Nicole just smiled and shook her head.

"What does it even mean, and why are you yelling it that weird way?" Nir asked, but the analysts just kept calling out the name.

"I think it has something to do with *The Walking Dead*," Nicole said. "It's a TV show. You'd like it. A lot of people die . . . and un-die."

"But that's *shtuyot bamitz*."

"Okay, you lost me on that one. Something about juice?"

Dafna explained. "It means 'nonsense in juice.' It means something is total nonsense. Which Carl is not."

"But why is it in juice?"

"Who knows? That's just the expression," Nir said. "It makes as much sense as this stupid name."

"You told us to come up with a name, and we did," Liora said.

"Is it an acronym?"

"Nope. It's just Carl," she answered, causing Dafna, Lahav, and Yossi to break into calls of "Carl!" again.

Looking across to Nicole, Nir said, "What were you saying about burnout?"

Nicole winked at him, then said, "Okay, everybody, rein it in. The boss has a point. It is a bit obscure. So let's spell it in all caps so everyone will think it actually means something and they'll be frustrated when we don't tell them what it is."

Cheers of "*Esh*" and "*Sababa*" sounded all around.

Nir just shook his head. "CARL it is. Now, let's see if we can get as much work done in CARL as we did in our team headquarters."

"I'll start," Nicole said.

She proceeded to fill them in on the same

information she'd passed on to Nir. When she gave them the Saad Salim story, violent threats were voiced against his person, his boat, and his financial empire. The anger turned to cheers when she let them know about Alicia's sticking it to him to the tune of ten million dollars.

Nicole concluded her report by saying, "Now, here's the one negative. Our timeline just blew up. Before, we were looking at two months to get the explosives mounted to the artwork. Now, we're looking at two weeks since this guy wants the originals. He's not the patient type."

Cries of panic came from around the table.

Nir said, "I know, I know. That's what my little chat with Efraim was all about. But after some threats on both sides, we came to a mutual understanding."

"Meaning you got him to agree with you," said Yossi.

"Well, yes, but I agreed with him agreeing with me." Nir unwrapped one of the little chocolate bars and popped it into his mouth. "It's not as impossible as it seems. While I was on the phone, Efraim checked with the bomb folks. They already have the generators we need standing by in a warehouse. Our little lab of horrors will finish up the explosive sheets in a couple of days. But we'll have only eight, so we need to choose which bad guys will get them."

Groans of disappointment this time. They'd all been counting on more.

"Listen, I'm bummed too. But at least that's more than half of what we wanted. In every operation, you have to adapt. Let's just be smart about who gets them." He unwrapped a second candy bar and tossed it into his mouth, then immediately regretted it. Looking at the wrapper, he read Elite Bittersweet Chocolate. He spit the offending "treat" back into the torn wrapper and threw it toward the trash can. It missed and splatted on the ground.

"Stay classy," said Dafna, as Nir wiped his fingers on his pants.

"Who eats . . . Never mind. The sheets of explosives will be sandwiched in a false back in the generators. The detonator will be hidden as part of the machine's electronics. The cement backs will be stored in a false bottom in each crate. And they'll fudge the weight of the generators to hide the extra kilos."

"Obviously, we don't have time for them to be transported by ship," Lahav said. "Are we going to fly them to the States?"

"We are. But not directly to Houston. When a major, early-winter storm hit the Ohio Valley last week, one to two feet of snow took out power lines and caused outages. That gives us an excuse and ability to fly them into the States through Cleveland. We have a factory-owning friend of

281

the nation in Columbus who's agreed to order the generators as our cover. Then we'll truck them down to Houston."

"I'm impressed," said Yossi. "Those folks on the second floor know what they're doing."

Dafna chimed in. "Now comes the hard part. How do you get the sheets from the generators to the back of the paintings?"

"Good question. Step one is getting Alicia away from her workshop—like out of town away. Not only do we need enough time to affix the sheets, we need . . . how long for the epoxy to dry around the edges, Nicole?"

"Twenty-four hours."

"And that clock starts after we put the sheets on. So we'll need Alicia gone for a couple of days, and we'll have to do it on a weekend so the crew isn't around."

"Getting Alicia gone will be a problem," Nicole said. "Flying in the helicopter from the yacht to the Singapore airport, Alicia said she was done with travel for the time being. She's exhausted and just wants to be home for a while."

Dafna turned to Liora, and with her pinky sticking out, said, "We chatted in my private helicopter as we left the mega yacht, and Miss Marcos said she was simply exhausted."

"How lovely it is to be able to fly high above all the peasantry," Liora added, striking the same pose.

Nicole threw the balled-up wrappers from two candy bars at them. "Anyway, I don't know how we'll get her away for that time."

Nir turned to Yossi. "I've got an idea. Use your little boat locator site and tell me where the *Mayan Princess*, the *Manatee Baby*, and the *Rock-a-Little* are right now."

As Yossi typed, Nicole said, "Nir, I told you. She's not interested in any more travel."

"That's unfortunate for her, because I'm going to one hundred percent guilt her into making one more trip. If it wasn't for my brilliant idea, she'd still be one of those peasants you guys are now helicoptering over," he said with a grin.

"Boom!" Lahav said.

"Got them," Yossi announced. "*Mayan Princess* is off Trinidad. *Manatee Baby* is near Cyprus. And *Rock-a-Little* is alongside St. Martin."

"*Mushlam.*" Nir slapped the table. "Gabriel Calvo, who owns the *Mayan Princess*, and Don Bernier, who owns the *Rock-a-Little*, both owe me favors for services rendered, which shall remain nameless. Nicole, I can get you ladies on both, and they're right there in the Caribbean. Alicia will barely have to fly at all. That should give us two nights in Houston to get this done."

Nicole gave him a haggard look. "Nir, she's not the only one who's exhausted."

"Suck it up, Buttercup," he said with another

grin, letting his enthusiasm cloud his common sense.

"Ooh, someone's going to get it!" Yossi cried. The rest of the team added their comments.

Nicole glared at him, held up her index finger, and said, "That is your one." But when everyone else turned to see Nir's reaction, she gave him a wink.

"Okay, let's wrap this up so I can go to my office and commit ritual seppuku. We've got the materials. We'll have the time. Now we just need to find a way into Alicia's workshop for six hours or so on a weekend."

Nicole shifted in her seat, then tentatively said, "I was holding off saying anything, because it sounds so bad, and it's probably nothing, but . . ."

"Speak up, Nicole," Lahav said. "You know we try to maintain a judgment-free zone."

Nir almost laughed. Lahav was on the receiving end of most of the judgment that took place in CARL. Thankfully, most times he was blissfully unaware he was wearing the target.

"When I visited Alicia's warehouse workshop, she introduced me to her team. They were a great group of guys, very nice, seemed like hard workers—"

"Just say what you're going to say," said Nir, recognizing her stall.

"Okay, so I also met one of the complex

security guards, and he stood out from the rest of the guys because he was the only one who didn't seem, you know, Hispanic. His name was Tommy Cohen. I remember it because of Efraim's last name. And just looking at him . . . He looked, I don't know, kind of Jewish."

Yossi's eyes were like saucers. "Looked kind of Jewish? Nicole, that is the most anti-Semitic thing I've ever heard anyone say in my life."

"And we thought you were becoming one of us," Liora said, then broke down with a fake sob and hugged Dafna.

Nicole dropped back in her chair. "Why do I even try with you guys?"

Everyone started laughing, and Nicole soon joined in.

"Tommy Cohen, huh?" Nir said.

The flush from Nicole's face was starting to fade. "Yeah, I thought it was an unusual combination, especially when I saw the name on his uniform said Tomaso. That's a name I'm more used to seeing back home in Milan."

"Interesting. Yossi, do a deep dive on Mr. Cohen's life. See if he's got any friends and family here in Israel. Is there any information we can exploit in our Italian Jew's life?" Then Nir broke into a very poor Marlon Brando imper-sonation. "Maybe I'll visit our friend when I'm there and make him a falafel he can't refuse."

"I hate that." Liora shook her head as she

rose from the table. "Never say that again."

"That was the worst. Doesn't even qualify as a dad joke," Dafna said, following her friend's lead.

Yossi and Lahav both gave him disappointed looks before walking away.

Only Nicole remained at the table. "I thought it was kind of funny," she said with a smile.

"Really?"

"No. Now suck it up, Buttercup, and get to work."

She stood and left him.

CHAPTER 37

TWO WEEKS LATER
LA PORTE, SOUTHEAST OF
HOUSTON, TEXAS—
DECEMBER 17, 2020—15:45 / 3:45 P.M. CST

When the Suburban pulled up to the nondescript warehouse, Nir turned from the front passenger seat and said, "Okay, guys, full gear in. I don't want anything left in the vehicle when I head out."

"*Root*," said Imri while the rest of the Kidon team began collecting. They'd spent the night at a nearby hotel, but tonight they would stay at a different one.

Confident that one of the guys would carry his gear, Nir gathered the four large orange and white bags emblazoned with the word *Whataburger*. When he'd contacted the leader of the Mossad team inside, the man told him the fastest way to win over the passionate loyalty of the men and women there was by means of cheeseburgers and fries—Whataburger cheeseburgers and fries, to be precise.

How very American of them, Nir had thought.

When they were still pulling up, he'd sent a message to let the man know he and his team were arriving. So as they approached the door, he wasn't surprised when it opened from the inside. A short, paunchy man who appeared to be in his mid-seventies stood in the doorway. A sparse ring of white covered the lower quarter of his scalp, and a wide smile had spread across his face.

"Come in, come in," he said.

Once inside, Nir put out his hand. "I'm Nir Tavor."

The man grabbed his hand and shook it vigorously. "Of course you are. Your reputation precedes you."

"My reputation? In training, it seemed like we couldn't go two days without a story about the great Avigdor Neeman."

The old man laughed. "Lies and exaggerations, I'm sure." After being introduced to the rest of the Kidon team, he said, "Ah, you brought the food. My team has been working nonstop since five this morning. They will appreciate this very much."

He led them into the large open warehouse. Eight green industrial generators sat positioned around the room, and each one had a pair of techs working on it.

Neeman leaned toward Nir. "I keep them in pairs. Not as efficient, but it greatly reduces the chance that something will accidentally go boom."

Clapping his hands loudly, he got everyone's

attention. Nir wondered if startling them all like that increased or reduced the chances that something would go boom. When the techs looked up, he said, "Our friends are here."

Their expressions were a mix of awe and fear. They knew what Kidon was, and they knew what Nir and his team did.

Then Neeman added with a big smile, "And they brought lunch."

That seemed to break the ice, and all 16 techs came forward. It was like they were thinking, *How bad could these Kidon guys really be if they came bearing cheeseburgers?*

"Good call on the food," said Nir.

"I've learned a few things over the decades. Now, let's you and I go talk."

The old man's mood change didn't escape Nir. *This guy is as Mossad as it gets. You never know what's real and what's deception.*

He followed Neeman into a side office, where he'd placed two chairs next to a table that held two glasses and one tall blue bottle of El Massaya Arak. The old man motioned for Nir to sit down. "I thought you might want a little taste of home."

"For a taste of home you serve me Lebanese liquor?"

"To me, anything to the east of the Mediterranean coast tastes like home," Neeman said as he squatted at a mini-fridge and removed a bottle of water.

"When was the last time you were back?"

"In 2008 for the 60th anniversary of Statehood. I keep telling my wife we'll go back for the 75th, but I don't think she'll be able to. She's not as mobile as she once was." He poured two fingers of the arak into each glass, then held up the water bottle. Nir nodded.

"I'm sorry to hear she's struggling." Nir watched the water turn the liquor a cloudy white.

Neeman lifted his glass. "To our comrades we carried home."

Nir clinked the glass with his own, then swallowed the liquid. It tasted like licorice, anise, and fire.

"I heard you were retired," Nir said.

"I heard you were dead."

"Sounds like we were both wrong. But seriously, I was surprised when I was told I'd be working with you."

"Don't start again with that gushing about me being a legend. The *ramsad* called me and asked if I would do him a favor. How do you say no to that? Besides, I live in a condo in a planned community in Florida filled with old people. The most exciting thing I do these days is chase the ducks with my golf cart. Not quite the same as a high-speed pursuit through Berlin."

"I'm sure there's a story behind that reference."

"Not as exciting as the story of a high-speed chase through rural Iran," Neeman said with a longing look, as if he'd go back to the front lines of the espionage war if only his aging body would let him.

"For a man chasing ducks in Florida, you seem to be incredibly well-informed about current operations."

The old agent just shrugged his shoulders and smiled. It was hard for Nir to picture the cold-blooded killer in this mild-mannered grandfather, but he knew he'd been part of a Kidon unit that, all in a five-year span, had assassinated Gerald Bull, the Canadian who was working on a supergun for Saddam Hussein; Atef Bseiso, PLO head of intelligence and participant in the 1972 Munich Olympics massacre; and Fathi Shaqaqi, the founder of Islamic Jihad, a Palestinian terrorist organization.

Neeman tilted the arak bottle toward Nir's glass, but he covered it with his hand. "I'm going back out tonight."

"Well, then with your permission . . ." He poured the arak into his own glass as Nir nodded his assent. "Now tell me, what is your great plan for getting my team into this artist's workshop without getting caught?" He lifted the glass to his lips.

"Well, that's still in flux."

His glass stilled, the old man's expression didn't change. But Nir noticed his face begin to redden. The glass returned to the table.

"I have eight people in there who are risking their lives, their careers, everything they have. I've got a high school volleyball coach. I've got a housewife. I've got a manager of an Applebee's. They're moms and dads who are missing the final night of Hannukah with their families to be here. If they're caught, they'll likely lose it all along with their freedom. I want more than *in flux*."

Now Nir could see the warrior. But despite this man's past and experience, Nir was still the man at the top of the org chart for this operation. "Apparently, it's been a while since you were on the tip of the spear, my friend. *In flux* is the way Kidon operates."

Neeman slammed the table with both fists. "You are Kidon! I am Kidon! Those people out there are not Kidon! They're regular people using their training to help protect Israel and her citizens. And they are trusting you to protect them as they do it."

Nir leaned across the table. "Avigdor, it is in flux." He emphasized each word as he said it.

Neeman locked eyes with him, and they stared at each other until the old man sat back. Lifting his glass again, he said, "They told me I'd like you." He tossed the contents into his mouth and swallowed. A harsh "Ahh" followed. Then he pointed at Nir. "You have three more nights. After that, those people are going back to their real lives."

CHAPTER 38

17:10 / 5:10 P.M. CST

Imri and Nir kept their eyes on the guard shack. It was stationed inside a rolling gate, the only access through a razor-wire-topped, chain-link fence that circled the 12-warehouse complex. Inside the shack two men were talking, one of them Tommy Cohen. He'd been alone until ten minutes ago, when the man they presumed to be his shift replacement arrived.

Nir sipped his coffee. It was cold outside, but the heavy jacket he wore and the contents of the thermoses Avigdor Neeman had given them made it bearable.

"Looks like he's leaving," Imri said a few minutes later. They watched as Cohen crossed the parking lot, then disappeared behind one of the warehouses. After a short time, an old white Ford F-150 pickup pulled up to the gate. Using his binoculars, Nir confirmed the license plate and that the driver was Cohen, changed out of his uniform. The gate slid open, and Cohen waved to his coworker before driving off. Imri gave him a lead, then pulled out behind him.

They were fairly confident they knew where he was going. A local Mossad agent had been tailing him for the last week. Nir had heard the term *dive bar* before, but he'd never been in one. As they pulled into the parking lot of Hawk's Place in nearby Pasadena, he felt like that was about to change. An American flag was attached to the door, and another one was emblazoned on the sign next to the bar's name. Classic rock of a vintage Nir wasn't too familiar with carried through the doors and into the parking lot.

Cohen exited his parked truck and entered the bar.

Imri found a spot next to six motorcycles and parked the Suburban, then Nir said, "You go in first and find a corner. I'll follow in five."

He looked Imri over top to bottom. The young agent was wearing a dark-blue untucked T-shirt, jeans, and Western boots, likely similar to what most of the men in the bar wore. Somehow, though, he still looked like a Lebanese terrorist. "And try not to look so foreign."

"You're one to talk. Just hope no one in there has ever watched *Fauda*, or they'll nail you as Mossad as soon as you step through the door."

Nir was dressed much like his partner, and he knew the man was probably correct. "Let's just try saying things like *Ya'll* and *Get 'er done*."

Imri laughed. "That's the advice you give me? Aren't you supposed to be some kind of super-agent or something?" He slipped out of the SUV and closed the door behind him.

Nir watched him go in. *He's turned out to be a great addition to the team. Quick thinker. Doesn't take himself too seriously. Deadly instincts.*

A couple left the bar and climbed into a nearby pickup. Nir was relieved to see the man was sporting the jeans and T-shirt look. He'd debated between this and the snap-button patterned shirt and cowboy hat, but he sensed that Houston had a different sort of vibe. It appeared he'd made a good decision.

His phone vibrated. *Empty seat at bar next to him.*

Nir responded with *K*. He got out of the truck, walked to the door, and stepped inside.

The music had quieted. Now the racket took the form of voices. The place was bigger than it looked, and it was packed. Just inside sat two poker tables, each surrounded by a full complement of eight people. Further to the right were a couple of pool tables and an empty DJ set-up complete with oversized speakers and a disco ball currently unlit. The outside wall was lined with video games and poker machines. The video games weren't being used, but the poker machines were. The walls were covered with memorabilia from sports jerseys to neon beer signs to flags of all sorts, including a Texas state flag, various U.S. flags, and an enormous Confederate flag with a Harley Davidson on it.

It was such a mishmash of décor, Nir thought a

little taste of every bar in every state in America might be there. The only constant throughout was the smell of stale beer, no doubt spilled on the wood floor.

Nir noticed a few folks watching him as he ambled to the bar, but no one seemed interested beyond mere curiosity. To his left, he spotted Imri, who was pretending to examine the label on his beer bottle.

Nir sat on a red vinyl swivel stool next to Cohen, and when he signaled for the bartender, the woman came toward him. Everything about her—from her faded apron to her sleeve tattoos—gave him the impression she'd been working this bar for the past 30 years and knew what you wanted better than you did.

Sure enough, before he could say anything, she pulled a bottle of Budweiser from a vat of ice, popped the cap with a wall opener, and set the drink in front of him.

"Thanks." He took hold of the bottle, acknowledging the accuracy of her pick—though he would have preferred an amber Goldstar.

"I'll run you a tab," she said, then walked away.

On the widescreen above the bar, ESPN was previewing that night's game between the Los Angeles Chargers and Las Vegas Raiders. Nir had spent much of his flight to the States studying American football just to prepare for this conversation, and he was feeling pretty confident. According to his prep team in Tel Aviv, the NFL was the one universal language between all bar guys.

Tilting his bottle toward the screen, he said to Cohen, "Still can't get used to saying Las Vegas Raiders. Why can't teams just stay where they belong?"

"Guess if that were true, I'd still be rooting for the Oilers and not the Texans."

And just like that, Nir was completely out of his depth. *Who the heck are the Oilers? They weren't on the list of league teams.*

Without taking his eyes off the screen, Cohen continued. "Actually, wouldn't mind having the Oilers again, especially in their heyday. I'd take a Glanville or a Bum Phillips over O'Brien any day."

Nir was back on solid ground. He had no idea who the first two guys were, but he knew the last. "Too bad they couldn't have fired O'Brien before he gave away DeAndre Hopkins."

"Amen to that." Cohen tilted his own Budweiser toward Nir, who tapped it with his.

They talked more football, and when Cohen finished his beer, Nir signaled for two more.

"By the way, my name is Nate Andres." Nir stuck out his hand.

Cohen took it. "Tommy Cohen. Tomaso Cohen, in fact. But I'm guessing you already know that."

Nir laughed—but only to mask the sinking

feeling inside his chest. How had the man seen through him? "Why? Are you famous or something? Like a YouTube star? *Tommy Talks Texans*. That's actually not bad. You can have it." He chuckled and took a draw from his bottle to hide his concern.

Cohen was smiling—but not from Nir's joke. "You know, I've been coming to this bar for two years. This is the first time any dude has bought me a beer."

Nir was about to say something, but Cohen interrupted. "No, no, no. Wait. You know what else? And here's the good part. When some guy does buy me a beer, he sounds exactly like my uncle Levy, who lives in Haifa."

Nir was busted. There was no sense keeping up the ruse. But maybe he could still salvage this side mission. He had to.

Smiling, he leaned back on his stool. "Would it have helped if I'd said *Get 'er done* a few times?"

Cohen smiled again as he set his bottle on the bartop. "This is just so bizarre. I have another uncle—Omer. He lives out west in Tarzana, and we used to stay at his house for family vacations, like when we'd go to Disney or to a beach out there." He extended his hand with only his thumb and first two fingers sticking up. "He was missing two fingers from his right hand. I never had the guts to ask him about it when I was a kid, and my parents refused to talk about it. Then when I was a teenager, I finally got up the courage. I'm like, 'Hey, Uncle Omer, what's up with your hand?' You know what he said?"

Nir just shook his head, wondering where all this was going.

"He told me he was special forces. You know, *Sayeret*. And that he'd lost the fingers during the First Lebanon War in '82. I was in awe. Suddenly, my uncle was like legend to me. Once that ice was broken, he started telling me all sorts of stories about special forces operations and intelligence stuff. Some he was involved in but most he wasn't. Anyway—and here's where it gets to the weird part—he once told me if some guy with an Israeli accent ever sits next to me in a bar and buys me a beer . . . You know what he said?"

"I can't imagine."

"He said, 'That guy is Mossad.' Now, here you are, and here's my free beer." Cohen lifted his bottle again and took a long pull. "So what do you think of that, Mr. Double *O* Seven? Or should I say *efes*, *efes*, *shiv'a*?"

For being knee-deep into just his second bottle of beer, the security guard seemed on the verge of drunk. Nir wondered if he would find empties if he looked in the cab of the man's truck.

Nir's phone vibrated. *Everything ok*

299

He texted back. *He made me but think I can still work it*

"You calling in reinforcements?" asked Cohen.

Nir slid his phone back into his pocket. "No. Just telling my sniper he can lower his weapon."

CHAPTER 39

18:15 / 6:15 P.M. CST

The Italian Jew ducked and looked around the bar.

"Calm down. It's a joke. So did Uncle Omer tell you anything else?"

"He said if it happened, it would be the best day of my life or the worst. Or both."

Nir tilted his gaze back toward the TV. "Sounds like Uncle Omer was pretty smart."

"He was smart, all right. Not lucky," he said, putting up three fingers. "But smart. So is this my best or my worst?"

"That depends one hundred percent on you, *achi*." Turning toward the man, he said, "Here's what I have to offer you. First, you are currently a little over $63,000 in arrears in child support."

Cohen's mood instantly changed. Now he was angry rather than scared. "How do you know that?"

"How do I know that? Really? Come on, Tommy boy. Channel your inner Uncle Omer. So that $63,000 debt goes away, as does the case family court is building against you right now." Cohen's mouth dropped open. "Yeah, you didn't know that part, did you?"

301

The man looked down at the bar and shook his head. "When you say *goes away,* does that mean the debt disappears or that my ex gets the money? Maria is a good woman and could really use it. It's not her fault she got caught up with a deadbeat."

"Good question. Shows you've still got a heart. You're right, it's not her fault. Maria will get every last penny. Plus a little extra for having to deal with a *mefager* like you."

"No need to get nasty." Cohen signaled for another beer.

When the bartender reached for a bottle, Nir called, "He's switching to Coke." She popped the cap from the bottle anyway, but when she saw the look on Nir's face, she set the beer in front of him. Then scooping some ice into a glass, she shot some Coke into it and set it in front of Cohen.

"Second, *achi,* your credit rating of 582 gets bumped up to 810."

"You can do that? Wait, dumb question. Don't answer that."

Nir smiled. "You're learning. Third, 50K gets dropped into your bank account. Now, does that sound like the best day of your life or the worst?"

"I don't know yet. I haven't heard what you want from me in return."

"Two things. First, I need access to one of the warehouses you guard two nights from now for six hours. If you ask me, one man alone in a shack at the entrance gate with no one patrolling the rest of the complex is beyond poor security, but that makes this whole thing easier for us both."

Cohen looked crestfallen. "But I'm not working Saturday. I can't get you in."

"Are you telling me you can't figure out a way? Come on. What would Uncle Omer do?" Nir held up three fingers.

The security guard swirled the ice around in his Coke as he thought. "I guess I could trade with another guard. But what happens when whatever you're stealing is discovered missing? Switching shifts will look totally suspicious." He pulled back. "Are you going to blow something up?"

"We're not stealing or blowing up anything, and we're not going to hurt anyone. If all goes well and you do your part, no one will ever know we were even there."

Cohen thought a moment more, staring down at the bartop. "I suppose I could get you in and out. I know how to shut down the lot cameras too. Those things malfunction all the time. I could tell my boss they just fritzed out." He looked up. "You said two things. What else do you want me to do?"

"I want you to go into an alcohol treatment center. Forty-five-day residential. We'll pay for it."

Nir had no authorization to offer that, but he'd find a way to make it happen even if he had to pay for it himself. During his mandatory service in the Israel Defense Forces, it was stressed to him and all the other soldiers that Israel leaves no one behind. Using Cohen, then abandoning him in his alcoholic state, felt like he would be deserting a Jewish brother.

Cohen was immediately defensive. "Listen, I don't need any treatment. I just like to drink. I do it because I want to, not because I have to."

"Sorry, but that's the deal, Tommy. You can't see it. I can. And if I hear you checked yourself out before the 45 days were up, the credit rating drops to where it was, and the cash goes away. Understood?"

Cohen kept swirling his Coke, but then he took a deep breath and turned full on toward Nir. "Listen, you may think money is all I care about. Sure, it's a problem, and I'm ready to take the offer. But I'm adding one more stipulation, and it isn't up for debate. You say yes or the deal is off. Got it?"

Nir didn't answer.

"I love one thing more than money, my ex-wife, the Houston Texans—heck, anything else. That's my daughter, Lily. That girl is my life."

"If she's your life, then why are you drunk in a dive bar on the last night of Hannukah instead of with her?"

Cohen's temper flared. "Don't you judge me." Then just as quickly, his anger was gone, replaced by an obvious regret. "You're right. I should be with her. I'm not because of my own bad choices. Because maybe I do drink too much. Anyway, I love Lily more than anything, but she's caught up with this guy. Arturo something, but he goes by Banger. He's bad news. She's only seventeen, and he's, like, twenty-five or thereabouts. He's done time for auto theft and drugs. He's going to mess her up, but she won't listen."

Tears were in his eyes now. "And that's my fault. If I'd been around, she wouldn't have gone looking for love other places."

Nir wasn't totally following. "So what do you want us to do? Are you asking me to kill somebody? Who exactly do you think I am, some hired assassin?"

Cohen looked all around, as if trying to spot eavesdroppers. In a whisper, he said, "No! I don't want anyone . . . made not alive. I just want it made clear to Arturo that he needs to stay away from Lily."

Nir shook his head. "I'm afraid you have me confused with somebody else."

Cohen reached past Nir and took the bottle of beer. "I'm afraid you have me confused with someone else too."

Nir grabbed the man's arm and squeezed until

Cohen let go of the bottle. Nir released him, and he pulled his arm back.

"I'll trade with one of the other guys," Cohen said, "and then I'll be on a 12-hour shift Saturday, 5:00 p.m. to 5:00 a.m. What warehouse do you need to get into?"

"Alicia Marcos's workshop."

Cohen looked surprised. "Not at all what I expected. That crew's always been so nice . . ." He closed his eyes and sighed, then looked Nir directly in his. "Okay, when you come, I'll shut down the cameras and let you through the gate and into the workshop. But if you haven't visited Arturo before you come, don't bother. Instead of opening the gate, I'll be dialing nine-one-one."

He grabbed a pen from on top of a signed check next to him, then reached over the bar and lifted a napkin off a stack. He scribbled something on it, then slid it to Nir. "Here's Arturo's number. I got it from Lily's phone. I figure you can find him with that."

"You know we only have one night for this."

Cohen slid off the barstool. "Then you better get busy."

The man walked out the door, and a minute later, Imri sat in the vacated seat, bottle in hand. Nir filled him in.

"We going to do it?"

"We have to." Nir started laughing. "This

reminds me of something my grandfather used to say."

"What's that?"

"We Jews will find a deal in anything."

"Fair enough," Imri said, then finished his beer.

They stood, and the bartender walked over to settle the tab. But before she had a chance to ring them up, Nir pointed to her and said, "You, my dear, have beautiful eyes."

Immediately, all the harshness left her face, replaced with a wide smile. Nir pulled a hundred-dollar bill from a stack and set it on the bar. The two men walked out.

CHAPTER 40

ONE DAY LATER
FRESNO, SOUTHWEST OF
HOUSTON, TEXAS—
DECEMBER 18, 2020—
23:40 / 11:40 P.M. CST

"CARL, Lead. Any more activity?"

"Negative," Liora said. "We've had a bird on it for four hours. Only one car in. Unknown number of occupants."

"Got it." Nir resisted the urge to say *Root*. If anyone happened to break through their encrypted communication, this operation could not have the stamp of Israel on it anywhere. Not only could discovery cause an international incident, but he could potentially lose his job. He hadn't even told Avigdor Neeman, instead deceiving him by saying the guys were bedding down early in preparation for Operation Bezalel tomorrow night.

"Any sign of the suits around there?" he asked.

A new voice came on. "I'm going for more of the T-shirt, blazer combination, so I know you must not be asking about me."

Efraim Cohen. Nir's heart sank.

"So, Lead, may I ask what in the name of

Theodor Herzl's ghost are you doing there?"

"You're twenty years too old for T-shirt, blazer. And you know exactly what I'm doing here and why, because apparently I have an analyst team filled with big mouths."

"Sorry," Liora whispered.

Nir glanced at Yaron in the driver's seat. The op just shook his head.

"Listen, it has to be done. You know that," Nir said.

"What I know is that you are about to carry out an unsanctioned operation on foreign soil. That's an issue, and if you're discovered, it can become an international incident." Nir could hear frustration in his voice—but also resignation.

"Come on. I'm a walking, breathing international incident. That's why you love me."

"This isn't funny, Lead."

Yaron sure thinks it's funny, he thought but didn't say as he watched his driver laugh.

"Okay, officially I am telling you not to do this."

"And unofficially . . ."

Efraim paused. "She's seventeen, *achi.* Just don't get caught. And don't kill anybody."

"And that's why I love you too. Lead is rolling."

Nir nodded to Yaron, who pulled the Suburban back onto Palmetto Street from the factory parking lot where they'd been waiting. "Gear

309

up," he said to the rest of the Kidon team in the back seats.

Because they all flew in commercially, they didn't have their usual gear. But a local Mossad asset had given them access to her small arsenal. Each man was carrying a Glock 22 handgun with a suppressor, which carried 15 .40-caliber rounds in the mag. Every man also had a KA-BAR Straight Edge with a 7-inch fixed blade and a can of pepper spray. Dima alone carried a nickel-plated Remington 870 12-gauge shotgun. All were dressed in black, and each pulled their balaclavas over their faces.

"Next left onto Cleveland Street, then two blocks up on the left," Liora told them.

Yaron turned the SUV, and they rolled up the semi-residential street. Nir had emphasized they were there only to scare Arturo—Banger. No one should get hurt apart from a few necessary bumps and bruises.

"There it is," he said, pointing to what looked like a stolen real estate sign painted over with the words *Auto Repair*. They pulled over 50 meters up. As they slid out of the vehicle, Nir said, "Doron, light."

Doron's pistol popped, and the streetlight above them went out.

"Sound off," Nir said, making sure everyone was ready with their designation.

"One," Yaron said.

"Two," Doron added.

Dima followed with "Three."

Imri, as the new guy, was designated last. "Four."

"On me," Nir said, and they set off up the road. There was open space around them, although just a block to their right was the busy FM 521 Road. Reaching the property line, they skirted the long drive. Up ahead was a metal building with a large roll-up door and a small standard door next to it. One large spotlight was mounted to the apex of the roof, shining down on the driveway.

Nir pointed to his eyes, reminding his team to be on the lookout. If these guys were involved in drugs and this was an auto theft chop-shop, there was no telling what sorts of weapons might be inside. With handguns pointed toward the ground, they fanned out alongside the entrance.

Nir tried the door. Locked. He pointed to Doron, who came forward and knelt in front of it. Inserting a device into the lock, he began flicking it. Twenty seconds later, he gently turned the handle, gave the door a slight push, and then stepped back.

Nir eased open the door and slid in, then stepped forward to make room for the rest of the men. At least eight cars in various states of disassembly sat inside, plus a number of roll-away toolboxes and several engine hoists. Around a corner to the left, Nir could hear voices.

He pointed for Doron and Yaron to clear the rest of the building, and Imri and Dima followed him. He inched forward and peeked around the corner. A massive television hung on a wall, and a First Person Shooter game played on the screen. Sitting on a torn and greasy-looking couch in front of the TV were three men in coveralls, each holding a controller. They were laughing and swearing at one another, and on a table in front of them sat at least three dozen beer cans—no doubt empty—various bongs and pipes, and a large bag of what looked to Nir to be weed. He also saw three handguns and an AR-15 painted jungle camouflage.

Lifting his hand, he pointed for Dima to take the far guy and Imri to take the one in the middle. Then raising his gun, Nir fired a suppressed round into the center of the television.

"On the ground! On the ground!" The three black-clad operatives moved forward as the terrified men on the couch dropped to the floor. While Dima and Nir held their guns on the men, Imri zip-tied their hands behind their backs. Dima then reached down and, one by one, lifted the bound men by their hair and dropped them back onto the couch. Meanwhile, Imri secured the handguns and rifle.

"Man, you can't do that to me!" said the young man nearest Nir, his dark hair greased back and his mustache razor thin. "I don't care if you're

SWAT or whatever, cop. You can't lift a dude up by his hair."

The name on his coveralls read *Arturo*. His sleeves were rolled up, revealing arms with no smudges, matching the clean condition of his hands.

This is the boss of the operation, all right. Nir leaned over and slapped him hard across the face. "Speak only when I ask you a question."

Arturo looked shocked. It was like he knew the cop game and was realizing this wasn't it. "Dude, you can't do that! It's police brutality."

Nir slapped him again, and the sound echoed throughout the shop. Blood trickled out of Arturo's mouth.

Nir leaned closer. "I didn't ask you a question, did I?"

Arturo was fuming. His face was red, and he was breathing hard.

Nir slapped him again. Arturo lunged up, but Dima's massive right foot suddenly appeared on the man's chest, forcing him back down onto the couch.

Nir stepped back. "That time I did ask you a question. You're not very smart, are you?" He emphasized the last words by tapping the man hard on the temple.

When Arturo didn't answer, Nir raised his hand.

"I just didn't understand what you were saying,

bro," Arturo spat out, cowering. "You come in here and shoot my TV. Then you cuff us. What are you doing? Is this a raid? All I have is weed, I swear."

Nir held up his gun. "You ever seen cops with suppressors, genius?"

The other man's eyes got really big now. "Are you cartel? Oh man! I swear, I only deal small. I boost cars—that's my thing."

Nir spit on the floor. "I eat cartel for breakfast, little boy. I don't care about your drugs. I don't care about your cars. I care about one thing. Lily Cohen."

"Who?" Arturo's eyes looked down when he said it. No doubt at all that he was lying.

"Lily. Cohen. The teenage girl you've stolen from her home because you aren't man enough to get a woman your own age."

"Man, I don't know who told you that." Arturo was getting a little of his swag back. "But I don't know the chica. Do I look like I need to mess with teenagers?"

The guy next to him said, "Dude, just tell him where she is. These guys are bad news."

"Shut up, bro!"

As these two were talking, Yaron said through the coms, "Lead, we found her in one of the back rooms. She's beat up pretty bad. Two is with her. I'm clearing the rest."

Furious, Nir reached for Arturo. But as he did,

he heard a bang to his left. A compact man with scruffy beard had kicked in a side door and was aiming a shotgun directly at Nir. Nir lifted his Glock, knowing he'd never get a shot off in time.

A pop sounded from the other side of the building, and the side of the man's head blew out.

He dropped.

CHAPTER 41

Yaron still held his gun in firing position as he moved toward the prone man.

"One, continue clearing," Nir said. Then pointing to Imri, "Go." The operative broke off to secure the dead man's shotgun and clear outside the door.

So much for nobody dying, Nir thought, angry.

"What did you do? What did you do?" Arturo was crying. The other two men were shaking, pushed as far back into the couch cushions as they could go.

Grabbing Arturo around the neck, Nir lifted him, then flung him against the wall. With his hands zip-tied behind his back, the man had nothing to slow his momentum. He hit hard, and then crumpled to the floor. The broken television separated from its mount and crashed on top of him.

Taking hold of the man again, this time by the collar, Nir pulled him up. "You want to know who killed your buddy? That was you." He began dragging him over to where his friend lay dead. "That was you with your drugs. That was you with your stolen cars. And most of all, that was you with beating on little girls."

"Come on, man. I'm sorry. I'll leave her alone, I promise. I swear on my mother's grave." Arturo was sobbing now.

"Right side clear," Yaron announced in the coms.

Nir reached the body, then took hold of the back of Arturo's sweaty head. "Look at him. Look at him! You did this. This was all you!"

Tucking his boot under the dead man's body, he rolled him over so he was faceup.

"Half his face is missing because you're a pathetic punk. And unless you want to end up like your idiot friend"—Nir looked at the blood-soaked coveralls—"Wesley . . . unless you want to end up like Wesley here, you will never go near that girl again. Do you understand me?"

"Yes."

"Do you believe me?"

"Yes."

"Outside clear," said Imri.

"Do you believe I will kill you without blinking an eye?"

"Yes."

Nir let go, and the man collapsed to the ground. "Team, let's go."

Dima said to the two still on the couch, "I want you to count slowly to five hundred. If I see movement in here before I think you've reached that number, I will come back in, and I will kill you. Do you understand my words?"

They both nodded.

"After that, take your dead buddy there and go throw him in a lake or something. Got it?"

Both men nodded again.

Doron was already outside when they left the building. Lily looked tiny in his arms, like a child. Even with the discolorations and swellings on her face, Nir could see she was a very pretty girl. Imri was the last one out, and they all moved toward the SUV.

Once inside, Nir broke the communications link. As they drove off, he removed an encrypted cell phone from the glove compartment and called Efraim.

"What happened?" asked the deputy director when he answered.

Nir gave him a full run-down. Efraim was furious about the shooting, but after some back and forth, he seemed to realize there'd been no choice.

"And you're sure you're untraceable?"

"We're ghosts."

"I'll have to tell the *ramsad*."

"Figured you would."

"How's the girl?"

"She's pretty beaten up, but she'll be okay. We're taking her to her father now."

Efraim was silent, then said, "You did a good thing tonight, *achi*."

"Yeah, I just don't know if the *ramsad* will see it that way."

Yaron had taken it upon himself to tend to Lily. Once they were at the SUV, he'd put his hand on Doron's shoulder, who'd stepped back. Yaron had a daughter her age who was battling her own demons. For the next 45 minutes as they drove across Houston, the older man's voice could be heard in a soft whisper. Every now and then Lily would say something, but it was mostly him.

When they arrived at Tommy Cohen's apartment, Nir stepped out of the SUV. They'd all removed their balaclavas early on in the trip in order to lower the fear factor for the girl. Nir waited as Yaron said a few more things to her, and she nodded after each sentence he spoke. Then he kissed her forehead, and she stepped out of the car. Nir put his arm around her shoulders and walked her to the door.

It flung open after the first knock. Tears streamed down Cohen's face as he wrapped his daughter in his arms. He was apologizing to her, and she was apologizing to him. In the midst of it, Cohen looked at Nir and said, "Thank you."

"Are you going to do what you said?"

"I'll take care of it tomorrow night."

Nir gave him a hard stare. "That's not what I'm talking about."

"I swear, man. I'm getting treatment. My boss is happy about it. Even says he'll save my job for me. So as soon as Lily is really settled back with her mom, I'm going in."

"You better."

Nir turned and walked back to the SUV. *No one left behind.*

CHAPTER 42

ONE DAY LATER
LA PORTE, SOUTHEAST OF
HOUSTON, TEXAS—
DECEMBER 19, 2020—21:00 / 9:00 P.M. CST

The next night, the team drove up to the warehouse complex in a box truck. Yaron, Avigdor, and Nir sat in the cab. In the back with the cargo were the rest of the Kidon operatives, as well as Avigdor's tech team. As the fence bounced open, Yaron rolled down the window. Cohen stepped out of the guard shack.

Looking at Nir, he said, "I can never thank you enough—"

"What's done is done," Nir said. Avigdor didn't know about the events of the night before, and Nir wanted to keep it that way.

"Anyway, Lily asked me to give this to the older man." He reached in with a small photo of the girl—a head shot, like the ones taken for yearbooks.

Yaron took the photo from his hand and slipped it into a cargo pocket on his pants. "I'll make sure he gets it."

"Thank you. So the front door to the Marcos workshop is unlocked. Best you can, try to leave the place like you found it."

Following the directions Cohen then gave them, they identified the correct building. The door was unlocked as promised, and Nir stepped in and turned on the lights. The teams immediately began unloading the truck. Nir had his Kidon team carry in the heavy rectangles of cement, leaving the moving of the explosives to the experienced hands of the tech team.

Inside, everything was exactly as Nicole described. Different stations had been established for each stage of the creation process. The area they were looking for was down to the right next to a series of three roll-up doors. This was where the finished products were prepared for shipping. The techs began identifying the paintings that matched the correct shipping addresses. Meanwhile, Nir sent Yaron and Doron to watch the unlocked door. He kept Dima and Imri close for any heavy lifting.

Avigdor walked toward him. "We have a problem. All the copies are accounted for and ready to ship, just as le Roux had discovered from the artist. However, the two originals aren't here."

Of course they aren't, you idiot, Nir thought, chastising himself. *Why would Alicia keep ten million dollars' worth of paintings in a warehouse with so little security? I really need to talk with her about upgrading her workshop.*

"Get your team working on the others. Let me make a call."

Taking out his encrypted phone, he punched in a number. He could hear steel drums and laughter in the background even before he heard her voice.

"Nicole le Roux."

"Nicole, Nir."

"Just a second." Then she called out, "It's just my agent. Give me a quick sec. What? No thanks, Heather. If I ate another shrimp, I'd grow a shell."

A moment passed, then she spoke, her tone much more serious now. "Is there a problem?"

"Hopefully only minor. The originals aren't here. I can't believe I didn't think of that."

"I didn't either. Um, hold on. I'll call you back in five." She ended the call before Nir could respond.

True to Nicole's word, Nir's phone rang five minutes later. "Go," he said.

"That's new. You been watching *Criminal Minds* or *CSI* or something?"

Nir smiled. The fact that she was joking with him meant good news. "So?"

"They're in her office. I think I'm getting a little too good at this whole art of deception."

"Art of deception," he said as he walked across the workshop. "I see what you did there. And we still have a problem," he added as he arrived at the office. A keypad was inserted above the door's lock, and the door looked like it was made of steel.

"Oh, you mean the combination? Problem for you, but not for me." She rattled off a ten-digit number. "When I was there, I videoed her punching it in when I was pretending to be texting."

"Who are you? Pretty soon we'll have you making dead drops in Gorky Park." Nir punched in the numbers, and the door opened with a *shoosh*. "I'm in." He looked around and realized Alicia wasn't quite as lax on security as he had thought. This room was essentially a big steel vault. He began walking back toward Avigdor. "Sounds like you're having a good time."

"It's always a good time on the *Rock-a-Little*."

"Well, get back to your mai tais and your limbo or whatever you're doing."

"Watch your back, Nir."

"I always do." He ended the call.

The work wasn't fast, but it was smooth. As Nir watched, the techs laid a 15-millimeter-thick sheet of rubberized, organic compound RDX, an explosive usually used for mining, on the cement back of each painting. A detonator containing a passive signal receiver was connected to the explosives using a thin cord of the chemical PETN, and then they affixed a cement false back with cutouts sized just perfectly so it could lay flush against the painting. Finally, a protective sealant was added around the edge, essentially just extending the already existing sealant applied by Alicia's team.

When the detonator received a signal, Avigdor had explained, it would trigger the PETN cord. The smaller explosion of the PETN would set off the RDX with enough force to send any mega yacht sky-high, then down to the bottom of the sea.

As Nir watched the process, part of him felt pride. This vision he'd had from just a simple walk through Milan was now coming to fruition. Soon these bombs would be in the yachts of eight really bad guys. Would they ever be used? Who knew? But at least they'd be there if needed.

Another part of him, though, felt ashamed—maybe even a little disgusted—at this whole scheme. An idea had popped into his head, and now human beings could die because of it. It was hard to really feel proud about that. Sure, the people targeted were bad guys, but who was to say he wasn't a bad guy too? *Aren't good and evil just based on which side you're on or which religious texts you read?*

Nicole would vehemently disagree with that. She would say there's right and wrong. If you're on God's side, then you're right. If you aren't, then you're wrong. He wondered which side he was really on.

I'd sleep better if I knew I was on the right

side. However, is that IRGC soldier in Iran sleeping well because he knows that, based on his scriptures, he's in the right? Nicole and the IRGC guy can't both be right, can they? Otherwise, there is no right and wrong. Truth is just arbitrary.

Avigdor walked up. "Want to tell me what's rattling through that brain of yours?"

"Absolutely not."

"Good." The old man placed his hand on Nir's shoulder. "Then instead, maybe you can tell me about your little escapade last night. Did it have anything to do with the passing of that photograph in the truck?"

"You have got to be kidding me. Who told you? I can't believe one of my team spilled it."

"Oh no, *achi*. I heard it from the *ramsad* himself."

Nir threw up his hands. "The *ramsad*? Beautiful."

"Don't worry. He's not as mad as you think. He said you killed only one person, which is apparently some kind of record for you."

"Great. Now I'm getting smack talked by the *ramsad*."

Avigdor laughed. "Come. We're nearing completion. Tell me while there is still time. I live for a good story."

JUNE
2021
[SIX MONTHS LATER]

CHAPTER 43

The reports coming through on the operation were good. Sitting behind his desk, the door to his office not quite closed, Nir scanned satellite photos of the damage and was impressed at what one explosive-laden quadcopter drone could do. The targeted building was part of the Iran Centrifuge Technology company, or TESA. Located outside the city of Karaj, just an hour's drive northwest of Tehran, TESA was responsible for the production of the fine-tuned pieces of machinery necessary to enrich uranium to a weapons-grade level.

As usual, Iran claimed it had thwarted the attack, but a thwarted attack doesn't bring down the roof of a building like he saw in the photo. What had to be especially enraging to the IRGC was the fact that quadcopters have such a limited range. They had to suspect that this damage was caused by their own citizens.

And they'd be right about that. The ayatollahs would be amazed at how many people hate them enough that they would come alongside outside forces to sabotage their own government. But this is nothing compared to what we pulled off in our latest attack on Natanz in April.

The Natanz operation was classic Mossad. Nir would have loved to have been part of it, but it wasn't his type of operation. It was an intricate plot carried out over the long-term, so there was no need for a Kidon-style strike. Mossad agents posing as dissidents approached ten scientists who worked at the Natanz nuclear facility, which was still recovering from the construction materials blast in July of last year. Over time, they won them over to their side and convinced them to sabotage their own nuclear plant. Using both quadcopters and food deliveries, pieces of an explosive device were smuggled in. The scientists assembled the parts, then detonated the bomb.

It wasn't the size of the blast that caused so much damage but where it was located. The bomb went off alongside the main power supply for the plant. The ensuing blackout shut down the centrifuges in the uranium enrichment center, causing the machines to overheat. Ninety percent of the facility's centrifuges were destroyed, setting Iran's nuclear program back by months.

He tucked the photos and report back into a folder, then reached for an envelope. After unwinding a red string, he opened it and scanned the contents—something about rumblings with Putin in Russia. His mind, though, drifted back to the Iran operations.

Once again, the damage cost them only months. Those months will pass, and then we'll be right back where we were with a soon-to-be-nuclear-equipped Tehran and a giant target right here on Tel Aviv.

Tossing the papers onto his desk, he leaned his head back and closed his eyes. No matter how many times he flew, he still fought jet lag whether he was going east or west. During the April Natanz attack, he'd stayed in Antwerp working at Yael Diamonds. But when he heard about the TESA operation, he wanted to be here to watch. Using the excuse of having to buy diamonds at the exchange in Ramat Gan, he'd flown in three days ago.

The team, minus Nicole, had watched the action via satellite. This time Liora provided a huge bowl of caramel corn, and it was addictive. He still felt a bit of a sugar hangover after the massive quantities he'd eaten.

His mind drifted to Nicole. Right now she existed in his life only through phone calls and the occasional Zoom—well, on a secure Zoom-like video chat system she'd created just for them. Because she'd taken so much time off for Operation Bezalel, she felt she had to dive deep into modeling in order to reestablish herself in that world. Every time they talked, it seemed she was in another part of the globe. He didn't know how she did it.

He wondered if he should be clearer with her about his feelings. Was it time for them to go to the next level and make a commitment of some sort? One side of him said absolutely, one hundred percent, without a doubt. But he knew that was because he missed the part of their relationship that ceased when she became a Christian and got her new set of morals. Yeah, it would be nice, but that motive wasn't strong enough for a life commitment.

And she'd already made it clear she could never make a lasting pledge to any man who didn't believe the same way she believed.

I could just pray some prayer with her and all would be good. But I don't make empty commitments. If I say I'm going to give myself to something or someone, I'm going to do it. And the truth remains that I'm still not convinced about her Jesus. Besides, she has one of the greatest ingrained lie detectors I've ever seen.

His mind went back to one of the secure video calls he'd had with her in March. She was wrestling with the deceit sometimes needed with her work in the Mossad. In particular, she was feeling guilty about hiding so much from Alicia Marcos.

"Sometimes it feels as though I become another

person. It's like what I've heard people who go on reality shows say. 'I'm really an honest person, but here I lie and cheat and steal. Yet it's okay, because it's all just part of the game.' And I get that. But this isn't a game. It's real life."

"But it kind of is a game, Nicole. Just with higher stakes. I remember a story about David from when I grew up. This was before he was king and Saul was coming after him. I think Saul had tried to attack him with a spear or something. But David went to where the priests were, and he was really hungry, so he had them give him and his men the sacred bread that was only for the priests. Technically, both David and the priests were in the wrong, but my teacher said it was okay because it was for a greater good."

Nicole had laughed. "Jesus used the same story talking about the Sabbath."

"Jesus and I must have gone to the same *yeshiva*."

"I understand the greater good. I know sometimes you need to play a part. I just wish there wasn't so much of it in the Mossad."

"Unfortunately, it's who we are. It was even in our motto."

Nicole looked surprised. "What motto? The Proverbs motto on the Mossad seal?"

"That's the one."

Nicole shook her head. "I don't think so. I memorized it in training. It's Proverbs 11:14—'Where there is no guidance, a people falls, but in an abundance of counselors there is safety.' "

"That's what it is now, after they changed it. That's why I said *was*. The first one came from Proverbs 24:6. I think your English translation says something like *With wise counselors*—or maybe it's *With wise guidance—you can wage war*. An alternative translation of the Hebrew, though, says, 'By way of deception you can wage war.' In Israel, we've always known we can never be the strongest. So instead, we need to be the smartest."

" 'Wise as serpents and innocent as doves' is what Jesus said."

"Yeah, I'm with Him, at least on the first part. We've got to be smarter than the rest. Another time Solomon, I think, talks about a city being under siege. The king and the warriors realize they can't fight their way out. Then along comes this wise old man. He tells them what to do, and the city is saved. Not surprisingly, the old man is forgotten, but that's okay because everyone survived."

Understanding showed on Nicole's face. "You're saying we're the old man. We use wisdom and trickery to defeat strength and weapons."

"Exactly. And I have to say that for an old man, you're looking pretty good."

Now, as Nir sat at his desk, he could almost

picture an old man in a raggedy robe walking up to the *ramsad* and saying, "You know, if you can convince ten scientists to smuggle in some explosives, you can blow up the nuclear plant's power system and destroy all the centrifuges." He smiled at the mental picture as he picked up the Russia memo again.

"Boss, you have to get in here now," Yossi called from the workroom.

CHAPTER 44

Yossi sat at his workstation. Liora and Dafna stood next to him looking at his computer screen. Lahav remained at his workstation wearing oversized headphones, manipulating the schematics of some sort of machine on his own computer.

As Nir looked at Lahav, Liora said, "Leave him. He thinks he's discovered an exploitable weakness in the steerable warhead mechanism of Iran's Khorramshahr 2 ballistic missile."

"I understood about every third word of that sentence," he said, walking toward Lahav.

No doubt rolling her eyes, Liora called after him. "Lahav maybe make big bad missile go crash-y boom into ground."

"That much I got." He tapped Lahav on the head, startling him.

As the analyst slipped off his headphones, electronica music thumped at a volume far above any manufacturer's recommended levels.

"*Yalla.* Let's go. Yossi has something."

"Sure, *Ha'mefaked.*" Lahav bounced to his feet.

"Quit calling me *sir,*" Nir said as he moved to Yossi's workstation. "*Ma nishma?*"

The analyst turned toward them. "Okay, I'll try

336

to explain this in a way all of us can understand." Nir noticed he was looking right at him as he said it. "Over the last year and a half, I've developed algorithms to learn and analyze repetitive words and phrases that exist in the enormous amount of chatter we pick up."

"Yossi make computer smart-smart, listen to talkies out in sky," said Dafna, putting her hand up to her ear.

"Okay, enough." Nir resented the fist bump she got from Liora.

"I then divided those words and phrases into topics that seemed to be of particular interest to the bad guys. I've picked up subjects like convoy size, shipping methods, transport modes, plumbing repairs. But one topic they really like to talk about is bombs. Blast radius, to be more precise. It's like a competition. *My blast is bigger than yours.*"

"Absolutely no comments from any of you," Nir said.

"Typically, the numbers are within a certain range. I've seen anywhere from 50 to 300 meters."

"Sounds about right." Nir pictured that distance expanding all around from the epicenter. "Maybe even a little more with a large truck bomb."

"Exactly. Then suddenly, I see this." He pointed to the screen, where he had a number highlighted in red.

337

"Eight hundred meters?" Nir said. "Holy crap! Are you sure that's right—not just a typo?"

"Wish it was, *achi*. It's appeared three times in the chatter, and once it was bumped all the way up to 950."

"Eight hundred meters. That's . . . what? A full mile diameter? Can you think of any conventional explosive that can do that?"

"That's what I've been looking for. But a semi full of fertilizer couldn't even do that. I hate to say it, but it's got to be nuclear."

Nir shook his head. "And this is militia traffic you're talking about. You're saying Iran's proxy militias have deliverable nukes, like a suitcase nuke."

Yossi shook his own head vigorously. "No! *Mamash lo*! I only said it's coming up in the chatter. Again, I'm trying to piece things together, like doing a jigsaw puzzle without the box photo for reference. Best I can come up with is that training is taking place for how to handle these kinds of bombs. Like they don't have them, but they're expecting them, and they want to be full-on ready when they do get them."

"Give me a location, Yossi. Where are these guys?"

"I don't know for sure, but best I can tell is there are three different sites—and they're all involved."

Nir started moving toward the door. "I'm

heading to the *ramsad*'s office. By the time I get there, I want at least one location texted to my phone. And, ladies, I want enough satellite photos of the place that it kills my phone's storage." Halting before he stepped into the hallway, he added, "And, Lahav, when I get back here, you're going to tell me everything I ever need to know about suitcase nukes."

He walked out without waiting for a response. Slipping his phone out of his pocket, he said, "Call Efraim mobile."

"Calling Efraim mobile," his phone responded.

After one ring, he heard, "Nir, *ma nishma?*"

"What's up is that I'm on my way to the *ramsad*'s office, and I think you ought to join me."

He could hear a desk chair rolling back and hitting something. "Slow down. Let me meet you first so you can fill me in."

"No time."

"*Achi*, what is going on? Can you at least tell me on the way to his office?"

"Not over the phone. Meet me there."

He ended the call because there really was no time to talk. He had to strategize how to overcome one major obstacle if he was to get in to see Ira Katz immediately, and her name was Malka Bieler. Over the last 20 years, the Mossad had seen three *ramsads*, but only one *ramsad*'s executive assistant. To get past her and into the chief's office, you either needed an appointment, an act of the Knesset, or some firepower greater than your standard military-grade rifle.

Nir had none of these at the present time.

He stopped at the entrance to Malka's office. Through her open door, he could see the pathway to the *ramsad*.

"Want me to distract her so you can make a run for it?"

Nir jumped. Efraim stood behind him.

"It will never work. There's one of her and only two of us. We're hopelessly outnumbered."

Just then the door to the *ramsad*'s office opened, and the man himself stepped out. He was holding a file folder.

"*Ramsad*!" Nir called out, rushing through the open doorway. "I must speak with you."

With remarkable speed for her age, Malka was on her feet blocking Nir from reaching the head of the Mossad. "Excuse me, young man. I don't know what you think this place is, but I can assure you it's not a rock concert or a play-ground."

Nir was so taken aback by the two incongruous and out-of-context comparisons that he lost his train of thought.

Efraim jumped in. "I'm so sorry, *ramsad*. I'm not sure what this is about, but I do know barging in unannounced is not typical Nir behavior. It must be important."

Malka took a step closer to them. "It's so important that you can't go through protocols and establish a meeting? Three members of the Knesset are scheduled to be here in seven minutes. So if you'll excuse—"

"Thank you, Malka. Let them through, please."

To her credit, the woman didn't argue. Instead, she stepped aside and contented herself with staring daggers at Nir. "Seven minutes," she hissed.

The men followed the *ramsad* into his office, and Efraim closed the door. Once their leader sat behind his desk, he motioned for them to sit in the two chairs positioned in front of him.

"Now, Tavor, what is so important that I'm going to have to deal with an angry Malka for the rest of the day?"

"I'm sorry, *Ha'mefaked*, but this couldn't wait. I have strong evidence that Iran is training members of their proxy militias in the handling and deployment of suitcase nukes."

The *ramsad* sat up straight. Never before had Nir seen this man, who was always so calm and cool, look shocked.

"You what?" asked Efraim.

"Show me your evidence," the *ramsad* said—a demand, not a request.

Nir walked the two men through Yossi's algorithms and the numbers his intel had registered. Neither man responded.

"So?" Nir finally prompted.

The *ramsad* settled back into his chair. "I'm afraid your definition of *strong evidence* and mine are quite different. Is there anything else? Do you know what militias are involved? Do you know where they are?"

Nir felt a text vibration from his phone. Looking down, he read, "They're at 33.092 latitude and 36.361 longitude."

"Not surprisingly, that helps me not at all."

The phone buzzed again, and Nir read, "It's about three kilometers southeast of El Sharayah, Syria, in the Daraa Governorate."

"Within spitting distance of our border. That's not ominous at all," Efraim said.

"Do we know who they are?" asked the *ramsad*.

Nir's phone buzzed again, and he hoped for another fortuitous answer. Instead, he got a satellite photo, then another, then another. Soon his phone felt like an electric razor with one photo text after another popping up.

Efraim held up his phone and spoke. "Just got a text from Yossi. He said the ladies are blowing up your phone with satellite pics, so he tried me. He believes the militia is *Liwa' Al-Arin*. He sent me some facts. About six hundred members. Leader is an up-and-comer named Waseem al-Masalma. Used to be called Brigade 313."

"Heard of them," said the *ramsad* to himself.

"Tightly allied with Hezbollah. Heavily

involved in their drug trafficking. Fights for the regime when called upon."

"Okay, enough," the *ramsad* said. "This is interesting and certainly concerning. If it's true, it changes the nuclear game and ups our timetable for finding a long-term solution to Iran's nuclear program. I can't, however, take one analyst's algorithm to the prime minister." He leaned toward Nir. "I need definitive proof that they're prepping militias for receiving and deploying suitcase nuclear weapons. Can you find it for me?"

"I can, *Ha'mefaked*. And I know right where to look. About three kilometers southeast of El Sharayah."

Efraim shook his head. "*Achi*, I knew you were going to say that."

"Okay, Tavor, approved. Liaise with the military through Efraim for any equipment or transport you need. Good work. Now get out of here and apologize to Malka on your way out, not that it will do me any good."

"Thank you, *Ha'mefaked*," Nir said as he stood.

Once through the door, he found Malka sitting behind her desk. She glared at him. Putting on his best smile, he said, "I'm very sorry, Malka. I promise to make an appointment next time. By the way, has anyone ever told you that you have beautiful eyes?"

But what had worked so well with the Houston

bartender had probably just made the situation with Malka exponentially worse. She didn't move a muscle, not even to speak.

Nir hurried away, Efraim close behind.

CHAPTER 45

FOUR DAYS LATER
CAFALA BAHR, INDIAN OCEAN,
OFF MAHÉ ISLAND, SEYCHELLES—
JUNE 28, 2021—14:15 / 2:15 P.M. SCT

The pain radiating from Saad's right shoulder blade down his arm was exquisite. Then, as the fists slid across his scapula, he felt the sensation all the way down to his toes. The hands lifted, then began their journey down his shoulder one more time. He wondered if his guest was enjoying this as much as he was.

A low groan came from the next table. Apparently, the answer to that question was yes.

At times, he felt that keeping two highly qualified masseuses on the boat was excessive. But he consoled himself with the truth that being a billionaire meant indulging in extravagant luxuries. It's not like it made any difference at all to his fiscal bottom line. And moments like this made it worth every *riyal* he spent.

"It's good?" he asked. His diction was a little distorted from his face being lodged into the massage table's cradle.

"It is heaven, *habibi*," answered Ali Kamal. "I may have to buy one of these for myself."

"The massage table?"

"The masseuse."

Saad laughed. He disliked so much about this man, but at times he was almost tolerable. This morning had actually been quite enjoyable as they rode WaveRunners around Saint Anne Marine National Park. While personal watercraft were forbidden in the wildlife preserve, money has its privileges. Whenever they would pause and drift, the crystal clear water gave them perfect views of coral reefs, tropical fish, and the occasional reef shark.

By the time they returned to the yacht, they were exhausted. After a light lunch of fruit and fresh-caught fish, the two had showered, then met at the spa. The helicopter was already on the upper deck waiting to take Kamal to the airport in Victoria later this afternoon. From there, his private jet would take him away to places Saad was neither aware of nor cared about.

Once the massages were complete, the two men wrapped their towels around their waists and moved to the steam room. Opening the door, Saad was met with a hot wet blast that smelled of cedar and eucalyptus. After walking in, he ladled some water onto a pile of hot rocks. The heat and humidity in the state-of-the-art room was fully regulated by a thermostat, but he still liked the feel of making his own sizzle and steam.

They each took a seat in the back corners.

"Tell me, Ali, how your plans are progressing," Saad said. All the necessary preliminaries were over, and he could now finally address the reason he'd invited Kamal to his boat.

"The numbers are growing. I have five other members of the royal family, and seventeen key business leaders. Most important of all, I have three generals who, although they have not committed, are at least listening."

"That seems like a lot of people in the know for a cabal. Aren't you risking someone turning on you?"

"*Habibi*, you don't know the depth of the hatred that exists in Saudi Arabia for the royal family—and particularly for the crown prince."

Saad shook his head as he leaned back to let the heat envelope his whole body. "I know that hatred. You forget my family history."

"I am aware of your history, and that is why I say you cannot fully understand. You are one generation removed from the fear and humiliation that can be wrought by the kings and their sons. Your father may know the hatred. You cannot."

As much as Saad resented the man's statement, it was true. His pain was of someone who had watched a loved one beaten down by the regime. He was, as Kamal had said, one level removed.

Kamal broke the silence. "The crown prince holding his own family members prisoner in that hotel was beyond the pale for any twenty-first-century ruler. It's like he thinks he's some modern-day Saladin. All-powerful, with complete autonomy to do whatever pleases him."

Saad looked at the other man, who was leaning back with the fingers of his hands interlaced behind his head. "Was it as bad as everyone says at the Ritz Carlton?"

Kamal turned to him. "It was worse than you could imagine. There was no warning. I was invited to a gathering, then suddenly I was hanging by my hands and being used as a punching bag. Tortures of all sorts were employed. I was pepper sprayed several times and beaten often. But I know it was much worse for those who do not have royal blood."

"That sounds plenty bad to me."

Kamal stood and stepped down to the rocks. "The thing is, the physical abuse wasn't the worst part. It was the humiliation. The disrespect." He ladled water and inhaled deeply of the steam. "Being treated as less than human, as if your life mattered not at all."

Much like the way you treat my staff and those women I bring on board—and most likely your wives as well, Saad thought but didn't say.

"Enough of that." Kamal waved the subject away with his hand. "Yesterday I was thinking this whole coup would be so much easier if I could get the West on my side. But they have a strange love/hate fascination with this man.

348

Think of when he had Jamal Khashoggi killed. Some condemned what he did to the journalist, but so what? Those are just words."

"Oil speaks louder than murder."

"Exactly." Kamal stepped back up the cedar benches to his former perch. "Soon, both the American and British press forgot all about him, and once again they're posting glamor shots of Mohammed bin Salman on their front pages. It's like he has them bewitched. Which is why he will never be held responsible by anyone on the outside. Retribution can only come from inside Saudi Arabia."

"Do you have any idea when you will be ready to exact this retribution?"

"I don't know," he said, sitting. "Soon. I need the generals to commit first."

"Is there anything I may do to help?"

"Honestly, it is not from you I need help. I had hoped General Mousavi would be here. I need the Houthis."

Saad shook his head and chuckled. "The Houthis unfortunately seem otherwise pre-occupied these days. They have their drones from the IRGC, and they are making full use of them on your country's refineries."

"That is why the general must connect me with them. All that effort and firepower could be used so much more strategically. Why swat at flies when you can remove the whole pile of manure?"

"I will pass the message along. But do let me know if I may help you in any way. It is true that I am a generation removed, but I assure you that the rivers of my hatred run very deep." He stood. "Now come. Let's get cleaned up, and I'll meet you in the salon. I want to show you two amazing paintings by a modern-day master—originals. They are worth ten million dollars, and I have them right here on my boat."

CHAPTER 46

Nir steadied himself. It had been a long time since he'd jumped out of a perfectly good airplane, and he hadn't missed the experience at all. Yet here he was in the back of a Beechcraft Super King Air that had been converted to an Israeli Air Force reconnaissance plane. It patrolled the skies above Israel, occasionally straying into the airspace of other nations, as had not so accidentally happened tonight.

He'd really hoped his assault team would be able to fly in the new Oron spy plane, a modified Gulfstream 550. It had been part of the Israeli Air Force's fleet of planes for only three months and was supposed to be amazing. But the IAF said it wasn't suited for this mission, and they were right. The Gulfstream was an airborne early warning and control aircraft and would be flying at a much higher altitude than the 3,700 meters they were currently flying. Anything lower than 9,000 meters would catch the eye of any radar operator and make him wonder what that plane was up to.

Besides, neither Nir nor anyone on his Kidon team was qualified for that kind of high-altitude jump. It was likely, though, that the five special forces commandos on loan from *Sayeret Matkal* had racked up double-digit jumps from that height. Those guys were as elite as they come.

"Two minutes," said the pilot.

It had taken a week to iron out all the logistics for the operation. Nicole had flown in, and he was happy to have her on the com. The hope was that they would be in and out, and that Nir and his team would return with the evidence necessary for the *ramsad* to brief the prime minister on the suitcase nukes.

"One minute."

Nir turned to look at his men. Because the two teams had never worked together, they'd kept the call signs easy. Every Israeli kid knows how to count to ten in Arabic, and since they were going to Syria, Nir used that knowledge. He was *wahed*—number one. Yaron was *ethnein*—number two. And on down the line they went.

"Stay close. Keep control," Nir told them. "We've got a three-kilometer hike once we're down. We don't want to add to it by drifting off course."

"*Root*," came the men's acknowledgment.

Nir's team was geared up as they normally were with helmet, body armor, tactical vest, and Galil rifle. The *Sayeret* team had brought their own tactical gear, including their IWI Tavor TAR-21 bullpup machine guns. Everyone on the team carried a Jericho 941 9mm in their holsters.

"Open the door," the pilot said.

A jumpmaster pulled open a side door, and the sound of the twin turboprops became deafening. Nir watched the red light above the door. Everything was instinct now. *Watch, react, do. Thinking will only mess you up.*

The red light extinguished, and the green light popped on. The jumpmaster pointed at Nir, and he fell out of the aircraft, the noise of the plane evaporating quickly. Because the night was dark, the sensation of the fall was muted. His sense of hearing recognized the sound of air rushing past, and his sense of touch could feel the lightness in his body, but without the sense of sight, his brain had no reference point with which to process the information.

Nir watched the glowing timer on his wrist. When the number reached 45 seconds, he opened his chute and began his float. Four minutes later, he was on the ground. He collected his parachute, then waited for his team to gather.

"CARL, *wahed*. We alone?"

Nicole answered. "*Wahed*, no other heat signatures near. A vehicle is approaching from six kilometers west, but it's pinging as our asset coming to get your chutes."

"Copy." Turning to the team now with him, he

flipped down his night vision goggles and said, "Let's move."

They kept a brisk walking pace and covered the distance to the *Liwa' Al-Arin* training base. Nir had hoped they would find the leader, Waseem al-Masalma, here. But this afternoon Dafna had spotted him on a bank surveillance camera in the city of Daraa.

Maybe next time, Waseem.

"Wahed, CARL. You're 30 meters out."

Nir held up his hand, and the team halted. He could just begin to make out the shapes of the buildings through his night vision. *Tis-a* and *ashara*, nine and ten, were his *Sayeret* snipers. He pointed to them, then indicated this was where they should set up. The rest of the team got low and followed him as he slowly moved forward.

When they reached 15 meters out, they went to ground. Nir clicked his com twice.

Nicole responded. "I have three signatures patrolling. Two in front of you on the east side and one to the south. All should be in targeting range."

Nir knew the snipers would have already acquired their targets by now. He gave a single click, paused, then gave three more. Two muffled pops echoed, followed by a third.

"Targets down," said Nicole.

The men remained in the dirt. Although the pops would have sounded like gunshots to a trained ear, they were still unexpected noises in the night. Nir waited to see if anyone came out to investigate.

"No movement," Nicole said. "Still have three more guards patrolling the north and west sides."

Nir had expected that based on previous surveillance. He tapped *sitta*—six—the leader of the *Sayeret* team, who was on the ground next to him. Immediately, the commando popped up and began circling the perimeter of the five-building complex. The remaining members of his team, *sab-a* and *thamanya*, followed him. They would use their knives to noiselessly remove the threat of the other terrorists.

Crouching, Nir moved forward, and his Kidon team followed him. As they passed the perimeter of the camp, he saw a nearly headless man lying to his right. Nir stepped around the body and headed for the first building.

CHAPTER 47

SOUTHEAST OF EL SHARAYAH, DARAA GOVERNORATE, SYRIA— 03:15 / 3:15 A.M. EEST

Of the five structures at the site, Liora and Dafna had identified two as barracks and one as an oversized storage building. That left two options for finding the necessary evidence. The camp was dark, which was standard practice in the area. No use advertising your location to weaponized drones or F-35s.

At the first building, Nir could see light leaking through the edges of some ill-fitting blackout shutters. Flipping up his night vision goggles, he peeked through. Two men were talking and chopping vegetables at a long prep table. Beyond them, he could see more tables surrounded by chairs.

Nir turned back and shook his head. Then lowering his goggles again, he led the team to the second building. This one had a locked door, which was a good sign. The lock and the latch were poor quality, though, and Dima popped it open with his tactical knife. The men filed in and quickly cleared the building.

Using a red flashlight, Nir and Yaron began

looking through documents, while Imri, Dima, and Doron collected items. Three clicks came through Nir's com, followed by one more. The *Sayeret* boys had taken care of the remaining guards. They would remain near in case the operation turned upside down.

So far, Nir wasn't spotting anything interesting. The majority of the contents on the desk were receipts, uninteresting memos, old newspapers, and adult magazines. *"Thalatha,* you find anything?"

Doron, who was three, said, "Nothing apparent. Maybe on hard drives."

Nicole spoke. *"Wahed,* be aware two have left building one and are moving toward barracks one."

Nir clicked his response. *This is not good. This is probably our only shot. If we come out of here empty-handed, the next time intel turns up suitcase nukes, it could very well be too late.*

Then a thought struck him. If these men were training with actual suitcases, they wouldn't do it in an office or a workroom. They weren't scientists; they were terrorists. Just the delivery system. *Offices are for planning. Storage buildings are for training.*

"Keep looking. *Khamsa,* with me."

Imri followed him to the door. Nir peeked out, then moved. With his weapon up, he passed one barrack and then another, slowly and smoothly approaching the storage building. Upon reaching the door, he saw that it opened out. He tried it and found it unlocked. He motioned for Imri to move to the other side and take hold of the knob. His fingers counted down, three . . . two . . . one. Imri pulled the door open, and Nir stepped inside.

The building was dark except for a single light above a long workbench across the cement floor. A man with his back to them sat on a stool working on something. The light was enough to cause a flare in Nir's night vision, so he tilted his goggles up.

As his eyes adjusted, he took stock of the room. Two pickups and one box truck had been parked by a large rolling door, and a small armory was contained behind a chain-link fence to the left. Nir counted at least four rows of AK-47s, ten to a row. The man and the workbench were on the far wall, and to the right sat a series of shelves containing tools, auto repair supplies, and five bags that ranged in size from briefcase to steamer trunk.

Nir clicked his com four times.

Nicole quickly responded. "*Wahed*, are you sure? That gives you only three minutes."

Nir clicked four times once again.

"Copy, *wahed*," she responded, but Nir heard the concern in her voice.

Turning toward Imri, Nir pointed to his eyes and then to the man on the stool. Then he pointed to himself before walking two fingers in the direction of the man. Imri nodded, and Nir slipped his fixed blade knife from its sheath. Slowly moving between the two pickups, he drew closer and closer. Four meters, three meters, two meters.

A door opened to his right. A militia soldier walked in, and Nir's eyes locked with his. The terrorist drew his sidearm, and Nir threw his knife, the blade catching him in the chest just as he pulled the trigger. Nir felt a searing pain on the side of his head as the gunshot echoed throughout the building. The man at the bench swiveled on his stool, only to drop to the floor as a round from Imri's gun caught him under his eye.

"Get the cases," Nir yelled to Imri. "Everyone bug out!"

"Where are you?" Dima called.

"We're coming! Just go!" Nir was running toward the cases too. "Leave the trunk."

"*Wahed*, you have two minutes," Nicole said.

Reaching the cases, Nir quickly opened the briefcase, finding various components and wires. He slammed the case shut.

Imri snatched the two larger suitcases, leaving Nir the briefcase and a carry-on. They ran out the door the now-dead man had walked through, and just as they made it out, a door inside slammed.

"They're going for the armory," Imri said as he

ran. The door had opened to the far side of the storage building, opposite the barracks. In front of them was the mess hall, and beyond that, open space.

The two men who'd been chopping vegetables burst out of the building, each with a rifle at the ready. Nir let go of the bags and dove to the ground. As he rolled, he reached for his pistol. Then letting his momentum carry him up to his knees, he fired two rounds into each man. They dropped.

Nir holstered his pistol and snatched up the two bags. The shouts were increasing as the militia camp woke up. Gunfire started popping off.

"*Wahed*, you have one minute!"

The two men cleared the perimeter of the camp and ran with all their might into the barren wilderness. Nir had no idea where the others in his team were, but he knew they would be clear. They were trained to follow orders, and he was confident that's what they had done.

Nir heard the missiles, but he never heard the jets. Two streaks passed directly over their heads. The blast from the impact lifted both him and Imri up into the air. They flew, landing hard.

As he lay on the ground, trying to recover his breath, Doron ran up to him. "Are you okay?"

"*Khamsa.* Where's *Khamsa*?"

"I'm good," Imri said. "Ankle hurts like a mother, though."

"*Sitta*, your guys?"

"Present and accounted for," reported the head of the *Sayeret* team.

"*Wahed*, your head is bleeding like a sieve. You sure you're okay?" Doron asked again, reaching into his tactical vest and pulling out a roll of gauze. He began to quickly circle it around Nir's head.

Nir tried waving him off. "I'm good. We need to get moving. You can look at my head after we get some distance behind us."

"But boss—"

"Listen, our friends in the sky just took care of any evidence of our being here. We don't want someone finding us here now. Besides, we've got seven kilometers to hoof to get to the LZ for pickup."

Doron tied off the improvised bandage, then helped Nir to his feet.

He took a step and stumbled a bit.

"You don't look so good," Dima said.

"I'm fine. Make sure that one can walk," he said, pointing to Imri, who was limping unsteadily. "Carry him if you have to."

"You try carrying me, I'll shoot you," Imri said, stepping away from the Russian.

The *Sayeret* guys picked up the bags, and the team began their long trek to where a helicopter would pick them up and fly them out of Syria.

CHAPTER 48

AROMA ESPRESSO BAR, TEL AVIV, ISRAEL— 16:45 / 4:45 P.M. IDT

How do you drink that abomination?" Nir asked, nodding to the iced coffee Nicole was carrying.

She placed a ceramic mug in front of him. "It's 34 Celsius out. How do you drink hot coffee on a day like this?"

"I like how you informed me you're using Celsius," he said with a laugh.

Nicole rolled her eyes. "I'm in so many countries that announcing Celsius and Fahrenheit has become second nature. It's like living in two worlds. I've become a master at converting feet to meters, gallons to liters, pounds to kilos—and back again."

"Impressive skills. But what I meant by asking how you drink that abomination is actually more of an existential question. You see, I believe if God had wanted us to drink cold coffee, He wouldn't have invented boiling water."

"That's *shtuyot bamitz.*"

"*Nonsense in juice!* Look at you with your Hebrew. Still, the fact remains that you think my logic is nonsense only because your brain has been addled by cold coffee. It makes perfect sense to me." He leaned back in his chair and sipped from his mug.

"I think it's much more likely that your brain was addled by that bullet," she said, pointing to the bandage on his left temple. "That was a little too close a shave."

"Speaking of shave, you like the new look?"

When the nurse said she needed to shave where the bullet had grazed him in order to stitch up the wound, he'd sweet-talked her into removing the hair all around his head, leaving only some tightly buzzed hair on top.

"I think you've watched *Heartbreak Ridge* a few too many times."

"Oorah." Nir took another sip.

"Seriously, that was a little too close. Between Iran and Syria . . . I don't know. How many close calls do you get?"

He lowered his mug to the table. "No, I can't talk about that. If thoughts like that get into my mind, I'll freeze up someday."

Nicole had a habit of slowly twisting her straw in cold drinks, which she was doing now. "On the field of operation, yes, I agree. You've got to just go on instinct. But in these downtimes, you need to ask yourself the *what-ifs,* Nir. What if that bullet had been millimeters to the right? Where would your soul be right now?"

Nir waved his hands. "Please, Nicole. I'm tired.

I don't think I'm up for one of these big eternal soul discussions. Seriously, I just got shot this morning."

Nicole stared at him, but then a sad smile spread across her face. "You're right. Just because it's on my mind doesn't mean I have to burden you with it. There's a time and a place. This is neither."

Nir reached over the table and took her hand. "Thank you. Now, what did you hear about the contents of those cases we pulled on the op? I got wind that it's good news."

"I guess that depends on how you take it. While you were in the infirmary, I got a call from the second-floor lab. Inside each case were wires and parts pieced together so they look like a bomb. The lab woman said they were put together like a lower-secondary class was given a science project to build a suitcase bomb."

Nir pictured what he'd seen in the briefcase. That sounded about right. "How do we know they're supposed to be suitcase nukes? Couldn't they just be practicing to set off conventional bombs?"

Nicole lifted her phone and made a few swipes, then passed it across. Nir saw a photo of a yellow and black radiation warning triangle.

"Now I remember," he said. He recognized that sticker. It was in that same briefcase. In the craziness of the event, he'd forgotten it was there.

"Each one of the cases had one or more of those stickers."

A concerning thought struck Nir. "Does that mean we may have been exposed to something?"

Nicole shook her head. "No, they were only for show. Like, 'Hey guys, don't forget these are supposed to be nukes.' So what happens now?"

"Hang on," he said, standing. They had a usual routine where he ended up drinking Nicole's drink after he'd finished his. But her buying iced coffee had thrown off the ritual. At the counter, he ordered a second cappuccino and asked the woman to deliver it to the table. When he got back, he said, "Now the *ramsad* goes to the prime minister, hopefully to tell him it's finally time to permanently shut down Iran's nuclear program."

"Can we do that?"

"With enough firepower. It will cause a major international incident, and we'll be paying for it publicly for a long time, but behind the scenes a lot of people will be happy we finally did something definitive."

Holding her straw stationary, Nicole swirled her mug to spread the cold around. "Will Iran declare war?"

"They might. They've got plenty of missiles stockpiled. But they would hesitate to go all out with their conventional weapons."

"Why's that?"

"First, there would be little international backing. Again, while publicly nations may be sympathetic, most will be glad they don't have to worry about a nuclear Iran anymore. But more importantly, you must remember that while they may not be a nuclear power, we are. Likely, what will happen is we'll have rockets showered on us for a while from the north and the south, so it will probably be a good idea for you to stay away. But unless Russia gets involved . . . and they might. They keep inching their way farther and farther south in Syria. But unless they engage, we'll survive it."

"So if the prime minister approves this, how long until you think the strike will happen?"

"That really depends on the Saudis."

Nicole froze with her straw still in her mouth. "The Saudis? What do they have to do with any of this?"

"Pull up a map of the Middle East on your phone."

"You have a phone," she said, picking hers up, then starting to thumb in a search.

"Yours is right there. Mine's all the way down in my pocket."

Nicole stopped and glared at him. He gave her an innocent smile.

Turning her attention back to her phone, she pressed a couple more buttons, then set it down between them.

"Okay, look between Israel and Iran. What do you see?"

"Other countries, of course."

"Exactly. We can't get to Iran without flying over other countries. But if we take the northern route, that means—"

"I get it. Flying over Syria and Iraq."

"Exactly. Syria essentially belongs to Putin, and as we just said, he's a wild card. We can't know if he'll make the IAF pay on the way back from Iran, make Israel pay later, or just say, 'Sucks to be you, Khamenei.' But any way you look at it, he'll exact some sort of price out of Israel."

"What about the central route over Jordan, then Iraq?"

The barista delivered his coffee, which Nir received with a "Thanks." Then turning back to Nicole, he said, "Good question, because it seems the most logical route. But we're touch-and-go with Jordan's King Abdullah. He's in a tough place. He's Western enough to be hated by the Arabs and Arab enough to be distrusted by the West. He makes semi-nice with Israel for his own preservation, but he has too many militant Arabs and Palestinians in his country to allow our air force to fly over for a major attack on fellow Muslims. Giving permission for that is a good way to get himself assassinated."

"So that leaves the southern route and Saudi Arabia."

"And thanks to the Abraham Accords, we actually have a relationship with them. It's not necessarily formalized yet, but the back channels we've had with them for years no longer have to remain so hidden."

"Can we trust them?"

Nir laughed. "Absolutely not. The royal family is corrupt, and the crown prince is as shady a dude as you'll ever find."

Nicole threw up her hands. "Okay, now I don't get it again. Why would we depend on a government we can't trust run by shady characters?"

"Because they need Iran's nuclear program gone as much as we do. They know if Iran doesn't bomb them themselves, they'll give the Houthis a nuke so they'll do the dirty work in their stead."

Nir took a sip of his drink. "So the *ramsad* will go to the crown prince on the prime minister's behalf, present him the evidence, and ask him to let us fly our air force over his country on our way to knock the snot out of Iran's nuclear program."

"Such an elegant way of putting it," she said with a wink. "Do you think the crown prince will say yes?"

"I don't know. It's a big ask. He'll know the pros, but he'll also recognize that he'll pay a price internationally and with the Houthis.

Those Yemeni rebels are already making his life miserable, like being perpetually bitten by a swarm of sandflies. If he does say yes, he'll want something big for it."

"Of course, because, as you love to say, everything in the Middle East is a deal."

Nir laughed. "Spoken like a true Jew! Nothing is ever given or received for free. He'll ask for some intelligence or technology or weaponry or something."

"Will the prime minister agree to the price?"

"I guess it depends on what it is. But probably yes. We're not really in a strong bargaining position."

"The Middle East is so weird."

"As opposed to your African home, where everything is so stable all the time."

Nicole laughed. *"Touché."* She took another pull from her straw, then sat back looking at him with a smirk on her face.

"Tired of shoptalk?" Nir asked.

"Dreadfully."

"Good, because I have something I want to talk about."

Nicole leaned forward. "Sounds ominous," she said with a glint in her eyes.

"I just . . . it's . . . Okay, so when we were jogging back to the LZ to get picked up by the *Yanshuf* and flown out, there was nothing to do but bleed and think for an hour and a half. Want to know what I thought about most of the time?"

"Aunt Mila's cocoa?"

Nir laughed. "No, I thought about you . . . about us. I thought about this, these coffees, and the rare times we get to see each other. I thought that if that round had been a few millimeters to the right, I would have died not telling you exactly how I feel about you."

"Stop." Nicole was dead serious. "We can't have this conversation."

Exasperated, Nir leaned back. "Why?"

"You know exactly why, Nir. We've been over this so many times already."

"Okay, I do know why. I just don't get it. I know Jews who are married to Muslims. I know Muslims who are with Christians. And I know Christians who are with Jews. Why does it seem like everyone can make it work except us?"

Nicole paused, and he could tell she was collecting her thoughts. "I can't speak for those other people. All I know is that Jesus is the most important person in my life."

"*Sababa.* You've said that. I get it. I'm cool with that."

"You say that now. But how many more conversations like the one I tried to have with you earlier—"

Nir had opened his mouth to interrupt, but Nicole put up her hand. "How many more of those kinds of spiritual conversations can we have before you just get tired of it and end things between us?"

"I don't know. A better question is why we have to keep having these conversations. Why are you not content for you to believe what you believe and for me to believe what I believe?"

"Because it doesn't work that way, Nir. Okay, think of it this way. What if that coffee mug was made out of lead?"

"That would make for some pretty nasty coffee." He laughed.

Nicole didn't smile. "Let's say I told you using that lead mug would kill you, but you still came in here and used it day after day. You loved that lead mug, and you were determined to keep drinking from it. Then one day you got so frustrated with my telling you to get rid of it that you told me you never wanted to hear me talk about it again. What should I do?"

Nir didn't answer. This was not the way he'd hoped this conversation would go.

"Would the loving thing be to just shut up about the mug so we could get along? Sure, I'd have to watch you killing yourself one day at a time, but as long as we had some laughs together and I didn't offend you anymore, it would all be good. Or would the loving thing be to risk our friendship, risk our future, risk everything we had so I could save your life?"

The impossibility of their relationship was

sinking in. Nir saw no prospect that Nicole would ever budge on this point. Any hope he had for a future with her was fading into nothing.

"But you're not saving my life, Nicole," he said quietly. "I'm not dying."

"Maybe not physically. Spiritually, though, you're already dead. I'm just trying to show you how God can bring you back to life."

Nir shook his head and sighed. "I don't get it. We used to have so much fun together. Now it's like you've become this one-note violin."

Nicole stared at him, and for a long moment neither of them uttered a word. Then a tear trailed from one of her ice-blue eyes. "It's the only note that really matters, Nir."

She stood and walked out of the café.

JULY
2021
[THREE WEEKS LATER]

CHAPTER 49

THREE WEEKS LATER
MOSSAD HEADQUARTERS,
TEL AVIV, ISRAEL—
JULY 23, 2021—08:30 / 8:30 A.M. IDT

Nir took a seat on one side of the conference table and nodded to the two men already there. They were leaders of Kidon teams like his, and that told him who would likely be filling the two empty chairs to his left.

"Got any idea what this is about?" he asked the man to his right.

"Not a clue." Lavie Bensoussan, a late-forties operative, was missing his right ear, lost to a knife thrown by a Palestinian in a tunnel under the border wall with Gaza. Nir had served under Lavie when he was first brought into Kidon. "But I'm guessing one of those five chairs across this table is for the *ramsad*."

Nir had flown home to Antwerp a couple of days after that disappointing discussion with Nicole. She'd already left Tel Aviv, off to a show in Lisbon. They hadn't spoken again, and Nir wasn't exactly sure where their relationship stood now. Were they still friends? Had they fallen back to how it was after the Iran vault operation?

He would find out soon enough. She'd flown in this morning, and he would see her in CARL once this meeting was over.

The other two Kidon leaders entered and took their places. Nir fist bumped the man who took the chair on the other side of him, the only one besides himself still in his mid-thirties.

Moments later, a door opened opposite them, and Nir and his fellow Kidon leaders stood. The first person out was Efraim Cohen. He was followed by Assistant Deputy Director of Mossad Karin Friedman, Deputy Director Asher Porush, and Ira Katz, the *ramsad*.

Then came a surprise guest, Prime Minister Oren Geller, who had been in office for only a month and a half. So far, Nir was unimpressed with him.

The leaders sat.

"Sit," said the *ramsad*. "Prime Minister Geller, I'd like to introduce you to the leaders of my five Kidon teams, Ravid Efrat, Irin Ehrlich, Lavie Bensoussan, Nir Tavor, and Zakai Abelman."

"Gentlemen," Geller said.

"*Ha'mefaked*," they answered.

Geller continued. "Only three weeks after I took office, Ira came to tell me that one of you—"

"Agent Tavor," said Katz.

Geller waved him off. "Had come to him with evidence that Iran was training militias for suitcase nukes. As much as I had hoped that one of our allies would be able to reason with the regime in Tehran, this information proved to me otherwise. It appears there will not be a political intervention to stop the Iranian nuclear program. And there is one truth that all of our intel over the years has made quite clear—when Iran goes nuclear, they will use it."

He leaned forward just slightly, as if to be certain they'd hear him well. "We may have been able to interfere with their missile capabilities, but the idea that they plan to disseminate these weapons to their militias to deploy is unconscionable. This tactic will also be nearly impossible to stop once they are in their hands. So it's time that we end the Iranian nuclear program once and for all."

Finally, Nir thought. *I've been waiting to hear those words for years. Sure, we'll pay a price, but no cost is too high to keep a nuke from going off in Tel Aviv or Haifa or Ashdod.*

Geller continued, now leaning back in his chair. "I dispatched Ira to Riyadh to speak with King Salman about using his airspace. Not surprisingly, it was the crown prince who showed up to the meeting. I think that old king makes even the new U.S. president look spry. The crown prince said he was open to discussions, but he would hold them only with me. So I called Ira home."

Nir saw the *ramsad* bristle every time Geller

used his first name. It was no secret that these two did not like each other, and many believed that if this prime minister lasted more than a year, Ira Katz would be out.

"At the Saudis' invitation, I had already planned on visiting Neom, their future technology city by the Red Sea. We moved up the date, and the crown prince met me to show me around. Then when we spoke privately, he told me the price for letting us make use of their airspace—a single life."

That caught Nir's attention. He thought since they'd been in Neom, which was supposed to become the greatest planned "smart" city in the world, the price would be Israel's water extraction and purification system or their chip technology or some other Israeli scientific discovery.

He caught Efraim's eyes. The man's look was hard with warning. Whatever he was about to hear would be extremely difficult and dangerous.

Geller nodded to the *ramsad*, who took over. "The target is a member of the royal family, and the information you are about to receive is everything we have on who he is."

Friedman stood and slid a thin folder to each man. Nir opened his and read the name, but he didn't recognize it.

The *ramsad* continued as Nir closed the folder. "His stipulations are, first, that he does not want the man harmed on Saudi soil. In fact, he

378

doesn't want him even touched on Saudi soil. He will have to be lured away for the hit. Second, he wants to make sure the world knows we eliminated him."

"What?" asked Bensoussan. "He wants us caught?"

"No. He just wants our fingerprints on it. The crown prince has had enough bad press to last a very long time."

Ravid Efrat, who had to be pushing 60 and was so rough he gave sandpaper a rash, asked, "So this Saudi prince chooses the victim, then demands that we serve as both hitman and patsy? All so we can fly our planes over his giant sandbox on our way to Iran?"

"That's the deal."

"And do we know why he wants this man killed?"

"No. He refused to say."

Efrat nodded. "Yeah, I can live with that."

Nir felt chills on his spine at the gruff man's words. The truth was he was intimidated by all these guys—except for Abelman, who was more of a peer. They were legends. They were older and wiser, and they'd seen and done things Nir had only heard about after hours over bottles of Goldstar.

Again, the *ramsad* spoke. "The wheels are already set in motion for our attack on Iran, and word has been dispatched to our assets in-country. This must happen. We cannot take this back without losing an unacceptable number of our Iranian agents."

He quickly looked into five sets of eyes. "I am giving each of you and your teams twenty-four hours to come up with a plan that will lure the target outside of Saudi Arabia, where he will be dispatched in a manner that says Mossad. We will meet here at this time tomorrow. Make sure your plans are foolproof, because, again, we cannot fail. Do you have any questions?"

"When is the strike happening? What's our time window?" asked Nir.

"The timing of the strike is *eyes only*. Your deadline is August 24, a month from now. If this guy is still breathing after that, we'll have to call off the strike, and some of our people in Iran will die."

Geller looked down his side of the table. "Are we done here? I have another meeting to get to."

They all stood, Nir's side followed suit, and everyone filed out of their respective doors. Once in the hallway, Efrat said, "Nothing like a good competition to get an old man's blood flowing. How about the winner buys a round for the rest?"

Bensoussan said, "I'm in on that. But only after the dirty is in the ground."

The five men agreed to the wager, then separated to see what their teams would come up with.

CHAPTER 50

eeting in 3 Nir thumbed on his phone, then hit Send and shot the text off to Liora.

It felt like he was a kid and the sun was going down to start the first day of Hanukkah. He had to force himself to keep from jogging to CARL. *Why do I want this so much? Of course, there's the competition, which is awesome. Gives me a chance to prove I belong among this elite group. But it's more than that. This big play of finally taking out Iran's nuclear program? I've been harping on it for years. I can't just sit idly by and watch it get done. I need to be part of this.*

As he approached CARL, he spotted multicolored streamers fluttering over the open door, creating a crepe paper curtain. He groaned.

Another birthday. Why today of all days?

Inside, the analysts were all sitting around the conference table, each wearing a pointy paper party hat. Except for Dafna, who reigned resplendent with a plastic silver birthday crown. A large, decorated sheet cake sat in the center of the table, and at his place, a party hat waited for him.

"Yeah, that's not going to happen." He slid the offensive headgear aside as he plopped into his chair.

"Told you," Liora whispered to everyone, then began to quietly sing. "Every party needs a pooper, that's why we invited you . . ."

Nir had no time for this stupidity. And he was about to shut the party down when he remembered who this band of misfits were and how they operated. This team comprised cut-ups and cast-offs. They didn't fit the Mossad mold, but they were too good at what they did for the higher-ups to let them go. So they were assigned to him, and somehow he'd pieced them together so they were the best team of analysts in the building. But he had to let them be them.

He began singing a different song. *"Ha'yom yom huledet, Ha'yom yom huledet, Ha'yom yom huledet le Dafna . . ."*

After the first two words, the whole team joined in the birthday song. Across the table, Nicole was looking right at him with a big smile. Apparently, he'd made the right choice. He hoped that smile also meant everything was okay between the two of them. They sang the verse, then the bridge, then the verse again, ending with a loud "Hey!"

"But I'm still not doing the hat," Nir said.

"Sababa," said an ecstatic Dafna as she stood to cut the cake. "It would look weird on that bizarre hair tuft you have growing on top of your head."

He'd begun to grow accustomed to his marine cut. "I like my hair tuft."

"Okay, Boomer," Liora said.

"Don't start with the Boomer stuff again. It makes no sense."

"It's *shtuyot bamitz*—nonsense in juice," Nicole announced with great flourish, and everyone cheered her Hebrew.

They laughed and joked for the next 15 minutes while they ate cake and drank sodas.

When Nir could wait no longer, he said, "Let's rein it in. Believe it or not, we still have jobs to do."

Yossi quickly sliced off seconds of the cake for himself and Lahav, then sat down. All attention was on Nir.

"First, congratulations to all of you. Because of this team's hard work in Syria, getting that evidence of the suitcase nukes, the prime minister has okayed an operation to destroy the Iranian nuclear program."

The team cheered. Due to their intel work day by day, more than most people in the country they knew why it was so important to stop Iran now before they achieved weaponized nukes.

"The Saudi crown prince is even going to let us use his airspace. But he wants something in return."

"A hot tub?"

"A cricket team?"

"A penguin?"

"No, he wants a man killed."

By their expressions, it was evident that they hadn't been expecting to hear that. But why would they? He hadn't.

"What? Are we the royal Saudi hit squad all of a sudden?" Liora asked.

"I thought he'd just want some technology thing," Dafna said. "Like turbo camels or the latest in beard oil science or something."

"Ooh, I'd take some of that beard oil stuff," Yossi said while stroking his long hipster facial hair.

"Who is the *he* the crown prince wants killed?" asked Nicole.

"I don't know much about him, and the crown prince wouldn't say why he wants him killed." Nir held up the folder he'd been given. "This is all we have, and it's just the basics. Name, age . . . assorted facts. You know, like drinking piña coladas and getting caught in the rain."

"I don't even want to know what he likes to do in the dews of the cape," Lahav said, wagging his eyebrows.

"It's *dunes on the cape,*" Yossi said.

"What do you mean? It's *dews*. It's midnight, and the dew has settled on the sand, and—"

"Hey!" Nir sailed his party hat at them. Unfortunately, it caught air and fell to the floor well short of its target. Still, it was enough to get their attention. "Don't make me regret letting you eat sugar. Focus."

The whole team mumbled their apologies.

"Anyway, what I'm saying is that this folder contains what we would expect from a basic Mossad examination of this dude's life. It's more than anyone else could get, but way less than we can get. So I want the CARL deep dive."

The analysts all broke into a cry. "CARL!"

"Exactly. I'm giving you two hours. When I get back, I want everything about him those other guys aren't smart enough to uncover."

He could see they were excited and ready to go. Time to drop the final bomb.

"And just so you know, the other four Kidon analyst teams are doing the same thing. Whoever comes up with the best plan will be tapped to carry it out. Now, those guys think they're smarter than us."

Lahav said, "Yeah, I know a couple of the guys on Zakai Abelman's team. They're—"

Before he could finish, empty paper plates and used napkins were flying toward him from around the table.

"Forget Abelman's team," Dafna said. "We're going to win this, you chin strap."

"And I tend to agree with Miss Dafna," Nir said. "So you've got two hours. What are you doing sitting at the table? *Yalla*! Let's go."

The team stood and hustled to their workstations. Nir picked up his party hat and placed it on Chewbacca's head. When he turned, he saw Nicole gathering the trash spread all over the floor. He hurried over to help her.

"Is *chin strap* even an insult?" he asked.

Nicole laughed. "Who knows? By the way, allowing them that party was so smart. They'll work straight through the next twenty-four hours on the buzz alone."

"*Achla*, I just had to remember who they are." They walked to a trash can side by side, then dropped the plates and napkins in. "So, are we okay?"

Nicole smiled. "We're okay. I shouldn't have walked off like that. Sometimes when I'm feeling all the emotions, I'd rather just escape than let them show."

Nir leaned against the wall as he spoke. "I understand that. I apologize for calling you one-note. That was wrong, and it came out of a combination of exhaustion and near-death adrenaline. Like I told you before, I listen and take to heart everything you say. It just probably wasn't the best time."

Nicole raised her eyebrows as she nodded. "And I take responsibility for that. Now, I'm assuming you're about to go fill in the ops guys, but first . . . Something about this bothers me. If the crown prince just wants us to go kill some innocent person for him, I'm not down for that. The only way I can justify what I do is that proverb you always recite to me, the one about rising to kill first. But that's predicated on the fact that the target is coming to kill you. That's when you rise up and kill first."

"I hear you, Nicole. But you need to remember one of the Mossad's other commitments. As far as is possible, we will kill no innocents. Think of Fakhrizadeh. Wouldn't it have been easier just to drop a hellfire on his car from a drone? Instead, we went through this elaborate scheme with a robotic rifle because we didn't want to harm his wife. Did she know all that he was involved with? Probably. Does that make her morally complicit in his actions? Maybe. But *maybe* isn't enough for the Mossad. We err on the side of innocence. So we took out the guilty and spared the possibly innocent."

"And that's top-down? You're saying the *ramsad* never would have agreed if the target wasn't a bad guy—and everyone around him too?"

"That's what I'm saying. And if I personally ever feel this new operation is at all iffy in that regard, I'll pull out. The *ramsad* has four other options for someone to run with it."

Nicole smiled. "Thank you. That's what I needed to hear."

He watched her go to her workstation, then left CARL. His next stop was the boys who'd be pulling the triggers.

CHAPTER 51

The rest of the cake didn't stand a chance once the ops guys arrived. They divided the remaining two-thirds into four massive slabs as soon as they sat down at the conference table. The analysts were still working, and Nir had been looking at something on Lahav's computer when he turned around just in time to see Yaron drop the last of the cake onto a plate and slide it down to Imri. When Lahav saw the arrivals, he walked over, and they all fist bumped him.

That's good to see.

Nir waited a few extra minutes to call the meeting so the ops guys could get rid of the evidence of their cake theft. But when Yossi turned and asked, "You ready for us, boss?" he felt compelled to call them in.

The analysts came over, and Liora and Dafna just stood behind their chairs. The ops guys were grinning with full mouths, chewing away at Dafna's cake.

"This is *metoraf*," Dima said, pointing at the cake with his fork. "Seriously—so good!"

"Really? The whole thing?" Liora asked.

"There wasn't that much left," Yaron said, his mouth still full.

"Like way more than half," Dafna said in her most accusing tone. "Come on, that was *my* cake."

"Happy birthday," Dima said. His heavy Russian accent and mouth stuffed with cake made his words barely understandable.

The women dropped into their chairs.

"I don't even get it," Liora said. "How do you even eat that much cake? You got a llama back there you're feeding?"

"We're growing boys. We need nourishment," Dima replied.

Nir stepped in. "Enough about the cake. Dafna, the guys have already told me they're bringing in the treat of your choice for a day-after-birthday celebration tomorrow. Right, Yaron?"

Yaron leaned toward Nir and whispered, "It's only a stupid cake."

"Right, Yaron?" Nir repeated loudly.

Yaron turned to Dafna. "*Sababa.* Just let me know what you want."

Yossi said with a laugh, "Oh, she is going to make you pay."

Nir took over the meeting. "I filled the ops team in. It's been two hours. Let me hear what you have."

Liora began. "Name, Ali Kamal. Age, 48. He's the eighth son and ninth child of the late Prince Mutaib bin Abdulaziz Al Saud, and who knows what number grandchild of King Abdulaziz, also known as Ibn Saud."

"Ibn Saud was the father of a bunch of other kings, right?" asked Doron.

Dafna answered using her notes. "He fathered King Saud, who reigned in the '50s and '60s, and King Faisal in the '60s and '70s, and King Khalid in the '70s and '80s, and King Fahd, who brought it all the way up to 2005. Then King Abdullah took over and was on the throne up until 2015."

"Another son of Abdulaziz?" asked Yaron.

"Of course. When he died, King Salman took over—another Abdulaziz son. But when he goes, which everyone thinks won't be too much longer, Salman's son Mohammed bin Salman will take over."

"The infamous MBS," Liora said. "He of the sexy beard."

"I thought that was me," Yossi said.

Ignoring him, Dafna added, "It will be the first time since 1932 that neither Abdulaziz nor one of his sons is on the throne."

"So I got a little lost in there," Nir said. "And, Liora, cool it with the knowing look to Dafna—it got genuinely confusing. What exactly is Ali Kamal's relation to the Saudi throne?"

Nicole spoke up. "When they told me all this, I had to work it out in my head too. Ali Kamal's real name is Ali bin Mutaib Al Saud. He's a grandson of King Abdulaziz. That makes him a nephew of the current king, King Salman, and a cousin of MBS."

"But MBS wants him offed?" asked Imri.

"I guess when you have that many cousins, you don't care if you lose a few."

Yossi jumped in. "It's all tied to a falling out that started with Mutaib bin Abdulaziz, Ali Kamal's father. Mutaib was always a bit of a dissident. A pesky fly buzzing around his brothers calling for reforms and a constitution. In order to keep him out of his way, King Khalid named him Minister of Municipal and Rural Affairs in 1980, a post he held until 2009."

"Okay, boring. Jump ahead," Nir said.

"When he left the post to his son, Mansour, Mutaib immediately became a pest again. Abdullah, who was now the king, wasn't having it. He exiled him, which seemed just fine with Mutaib. He bought an entire floor in Trump Tower in New York City and lived there until he died in 2019. The man it wasn't fine with was Ali. He was angry with the king for exiling his father, and he was angry with his father for shaming the family. In fact, he stopped using his father's name and instead calls himself Ali Kamal."

Liora stepped in. "The shame his dad brought to the family began to fall on Ali. He stopped being invited to gatherings. Many of his uncles and cousins no longer took his calls. Then came the night at the Ritz Carlton in 2017."

"He was one of the guys held at the Ritz?" Imri asked. "No wonder he's not a fan of MBS."

Nicole said, "And MBS is obviously not a fan of his. We think Kamal might have something going against the Saudi royals, like a revolution or a coup. It's got to be something big. Ostracizing a family member is one thing, even if it is one of your hundreds of cousins and even if you are Saudi, but having them killed just because you don't like them is another."

"Any other new basics we need to know about him?" Nir asked.

"Four wives, ten children, two of them just babies. Has a mansion outside of Riyadh. Owns a fleet of cars, none of which cost him less than six hundred thousand riyals. Owns vacation homes in Marbella, Spain; Vallauris, France; and Jeddah, along the Red Sea."

"Oh, to be rich and Saudi," said Yaron.

"No doubt." Nir shook his head. "Those are good to know as possible sites we could lead him to. So that's all the stuff the other teams probably already know. Tell me what they don't know."

Liora spoke up. "Well, our South African sister used her hackabilities and got us into the Saudi phone company. We were able to track Kamal's phone pings so we could follow his movements."

Dafna jumped in. "The guy really gets around. Probably that whole *four wives* thing. Home is not his happy place. We focused only on his movements outside of the country. We wanted to see if there was a pattern we could exploit. He was out of the country twenty-three times in the last year. Four times to New York City. Twice to each vacation home. Once to Hong Kong. Once to Manila. Five times to Bangkok, which is a bit creepy. Once to Paris and once to Berlin. Then he was in the ocean four times."

"What?" It was evident that Nicole hadn't heard these findings yet. "What do you mean *in* the ocean?"

"His phone pinged from out on the water four times. Which meant . . ."

Nir took it up. "Which meant he was either a really good swimmer with a waterproof phone or he was on a boat."

"*Achla*! You're smarter than you look," Liora said. "So we got Yossi to use his ship-finding software, and it turns out the same boat was at each location—the *Cafala Bahr*."

"Why do I know that name?" Nir asked.

Nicole had a wide smile across her face. "I'll tell you why. Saad Salim."

"There you go," Yossi said.

"The originals guy!" cried Nir. "That's the sleazeball who—"

"Yes, I remember," said Nicole coolly.

Nir took the hint. She didn't want to go over that again. "What's the connection? How do they know each other?"

"We don't know yet," Liora said. "But there's more."

"*Achla*! Bring it on."

"We wanted to know if anyone else of interest was on that boat while he was there," Dafna said. "So we checked out all the other signals. Most of them stayed with the yacht, obviously from the crew. Then there was Salim. But one other signal has shown up there over 20 times in the last two years. Three of those were when Kamal was there. We followed it, and each time it went back to Iran."

"Wait a second," Nicole said. "I think I met this guy. What's his name?"

"General Arash Mousavi, head of the Intelligence Division of the Quds Force of the IRGC." Nir said the last part of that sentence along with Dafna. Turning to Nicole, he said, "You never told me you met Arash Mousavi."

"I never knew I met Arash *Mousavi*. I just knew the guy's first name. I hadn't heard of him until now, and honestly, I'm getting a little creeped out that I was on a yacht with someone you know by name." Her face had turned pale, and Nir could see fear in her eyes. He knew that, mentally, she was probably right back in that interrogation room in Iran. Dafna went over and squatted next to her, putting her arm around her.

Nicole kind of laughed and said, "I'm fine. Really. Go on."

But Nir was glad to see Dafna remain with her.

"So we've got a terrorism financier, an IRGC general, and a Saudi prince," he said.

"Sounds like the beginning of a bad bar joke," Dima added.

"True. But what's the connection? I guess if Kamal really is planning a coup, then it would make sense. From what I remember, Salim has a grudge against the royals for how they treated his dad too. So either he's in on it or he's just the go-between. You've got Kamal wanting to take down the Saudis. But unless he has a bunch of generals on his side, he can't pull it off."

"The Iranians hate the Saudis, but they're not going to fight in a coup," Doron said.

Lahav spoke up. "The Houthis will. They're already trying to take down the Saudi government."

"Exactly," Nir said, pointing to Lahav. "So picture this. We get the Saudi and the Iranian on the yacht together with Salim and let our lovely paintings take care of the rest. Kill three bad birds with one stone. The world will say, 'Oh, there goes Israel again, blowing people up.' MBS will say, 'How dare you do that to a royal?' while behind closed doors he's saying, 'Nice job. Feel free to use our airspace as your playpen.' Which we will gladly do, destroying Iran's entire nuclear program in one fell swoop. *Esh*! It's absolutely perfect."

"You make it sound so easy, *achi*," Yaron said.

"But one big question remains. How are we going to get all three of these guys on Salim's boat, all at once, in our short window of time?"

They all sat in abnormal silence as the wheels in Nir's head finished turning. Then he said, "I have some thoughts about that, but I doubt any of you will like them."

AUGUST
2021
[ONE MONTH LATER]

CHAPTER 52

Nir was going to sweat. There was no getting around it. Looking out the window as the plane landed, by the heat shimmers on the runways it was evident that the temperature had reached the full 42 degrees Celsius predicted. London had been half that temperature when he'd left Heathrow that morning.

The Qatar Airways Airbus touched down with a jolt, then began its taxi to the terminal. Nir wished the pilot would take his time. He was not looking forward to what awaited him. It was a good plan. It was a necessary plan. But it still stunk rocks that he was here as the primary player in the plan.

The CARL team hated the idea when he presented it to them. They argued it. They fought it. But eventually, he wore them down. In the end they accepted it not because he as their leader demanded they accept it but because it was the one plan they'd come up with that could work.

The reaction was similar when he took the idea

to the *ramsad*. He'd been the last Kidon leader to present, and the other teams had given some solid options. But they weren't great ideas. His was a great idea. The *ramsad* pointed out all the possible flaws. Efraim Cohen went apoplectic, saying that's just not the way the Mossad operates. Old Ravid Efrat had even called him a "punk cowboy." But in the end, they'd given in, and the *ramsad* greenlighted his plan.

Three of the other team leaders offered to go in Nir's place. Efrat, however, had just shaken his head and labeled him a fool. But that night, it was the old agent who had dished out the money for the round of Goldstars Nir owed for winning the competition. When Nir pointed out they weren't supposed to celebrate until after he came back, Efrat said they better do it now just in case.

After collecting his carry-on, Nir exited the plane. Immediately, he was wowed. Less than ten years ago, Hamad International Airport had replaced the old Doha International, and everything he set his eyes on still looked new and cutting edge. On the flight over, in the in-flight magazine *Oryx*, Nir had read that just that month Skytrax had named HIA the number one airport in the world.

Let's see if that extends to their immigration process. In all my travels, I have never seen one efficiently run.

Once again, his expectations were exceeded. In

400

a country that sees far more international travel than domestic, the Qataris have immigration down to a science. Despite 500 passengers on his flight, he stood in line only ten minutes. The agent took his United Kingdom passport under the name Thomas Martin, ran it through the computer, stamped it, and passed it back all in the span of 45 seconds. Customs was just as easy with his carry-on.

When he exited the airport, the brutal heat hit him like a communal bread oven on a *kibbutz*. It forced the air out of his lungs. Thankfully, though, the sun was starting to go down. Maybe the city would become tolerable in the next couple of hours.

Spotting a line of cabs, he walked to the first one in line. In Arabic, he asked, "How much to take me to the Mandarin Oriental?"

"That's very far. Eighty riyal."

"I'll give you twenty."

The man looked shocked. "Do you even know what a riyal is? Please. I'll do it for sixty, but no less."

Nir shook his head. "I know exactly what a Qatari riyal is and what it's worth. I'll do it for 30."

"Fifty. I can't do it for less. I'll lose money on my gas."

"Sorry. Have a nice night." Nir turned toward the second taxi in line.

The man stopped him. "Please. I have a family. Thirty-five, and we have a deal. I have a very nice car. Very cold air conditioning."

Nir looked at the man, then said, "Okay, thirty-five, even though you and I both know you're pulling five more than you should."

The cab driver smiled and shrugged as he opened the rear door. Nir slid in bag first.

Dafna had told him to expect a 20-minute trip. That gave him some time to process through all that had happened and what was about to take place.

Soon after the plan's approval, the *ramsad* had set more than 150 Saudi assets on the task of digging up information on why the crown prince would be after Ali Kamal. Yossi, though, had made the breakthrough.

An unusual pattern of phone calls from the father of Kamal's driver to numbers in Yemen had begun over the past several months. With some access help from Nicole—into the computers of the General Intelligence Presidency, the primary Saudi Arabian intelligence agency—Yossi discovered those numbers had been flagged for being related to the Houthi rebels. He then cross-referenced the timing of those calls with the location of Kamal's phone. He realized that for every one of the Houthi contacts, Kamal's phone was at the same location as the phone registered to his driver's father.

So Ali Kamal was reaching out to the Houthis. The question was why, with only two logical answers. Either he was supporting them in their cause or he was trying to recruit them to his. Nothing in Kamal's history pegged him as a traitor to his country, so they assumed the latter. He simply wanted the royals out.

Based on that information, the *ramsad* set up a meeting between his envoy and the crown prince's chief of staff. The purpose was to communicate information too sensitive for any method but person-to-person. If the information was satisfactory, then the envoy would be taken to the crown prince. The location was set for Doha, and Nir was designated as the envoy.

Now here he was in Qatar preparing for a meeting tomorrow, during which he would ostensibly communicate two pieces of vital information to the Saudi crown prince's number two man. First, he would reveal the name of the one conspiring against the royal family. Second, he would reveal the date and time for Israel's planned air strike on Iran's nuclear program.

Of course, it was all a ruse, designed to draw out his true target. The crown prince already knew the name of the person conspiring against him, and Nir would likely never have the opportunity to communicate any attack information to the Saudis.

And this is your brilliant plan, he thought, shaking his head.

It was dusk when the driver pulled up to the hotel. No sooner had the car come to a halt than Nir's door opened. A porter wearing a long white jacket and a small mocha-colored hat welcomed him in English. Nir punched a tip into the cab's electronic pay system and stepped out. The long driveway was well lit, as was the beautiful marble façade of the hotel.

"Do you have any bags?" asked the young man.

"Only what's on my shoulder," Nir responded in his practiced Estuary English accent. "Just point me in the right direction."

"Just inside the doors, you will find check-in. Enjoy your stay at the Mandarin Oriental."

The porter closed the door to the cab and slapped its roof. The car pulled off, and Nir walked into the lobby, slowing to take in all the beauty and accoutrements one would expect in a five-star hotel. Its large atrium rose many floors up into the air, and all around dark woods contrasted with the white marble. The walls themselves were covered with long windows tinted orange, brown, and yellow, which probably gave a much more stunning effect during the sunlight hours than they did this time of the evening.

"Sir, would you like a moist towel?" A young

woman stood next to him holding a tray with three rolled-up cloths.

"Thank you," he said, unrolling one, then using it to wipe his face, neck, and hands.

The woman held out a basket, and Nir dropped in his towel.

"Sir, would you like juice?" He spun the other direction, and there was another young woman holding a small silver tray on which stood four flutes of golden liquid.

"Thank you," he said, taking a glass.

I could get used to this treatment, he thought as he made his way to the front desk.

"May I help you?" a young man behind the counter asked.

"Checking in. Thomas Martin." Nir set the glass on the counter and reached for his passport.

"Welcome, Mr. Martin. We have your room all ready for you."

Four minutes and a glass of juice later, Nir stepped into an elevator. Room 486 said his card folder. He punched the button with the 4 on it.

If I can just get a good night's sleep after all this flying, maybe I'll be ready to face tomorrow. He'd started yesterday morning at Ben Gurion Airport in Tel Aviv. After leaving Israel, he'd been to Frankfurt, Essen, Berlin, Frankfurt again, Helsinki, and London. Now he just wanted a beer and a bed.

The elevator dinged, and he stepped out, noting

his room was to the left. At the end of the hall, he held the keycard to the reader, heard a click, and turned the handle.

The door flew open, and a fist drove into his solar plexus. Nir doubled over, gasping for breath. Two sets of hands grabbed his arms and pulled him into the room, while another pair drove his head toward the floor. He plowed forehead first into the carpet. Before he could even fight back, he felt a sharp jab in his neck. Still sucking hard to get air, he lifted his eyes. He had only a second before a black hood was pulled over his head, but he saw at least three other men in the room besides the ones who'd assaulted him.

Directly in the center of his line of sight was one more item he wished he hadn't seen. A large steamer trunk in the middle of the floor, its lid open.

That is going to hurt, he thought before all went black.

CHAPTER 53

THE NEXT MORNING
DOHA, QATAR—AUGUST 23, 2021—
06:15 / 6:15 A.M. AST

Voices. They sounded echoey and distant. And they weren't speaking right. The words were garbled. Confused.

Nir sucked in a deep breath, then another. The voices were growing louder, clearer. He realized the words weren't jumbled. They were just in another language. Arabic. He chanced opening his eyes, cautious about the possible brightness. But there was no great glare. As he looked around, it appeared the only light source was from a line of windows two thirds of the way up on three of four walls.

He spotted two men dressed in black wearing balaclavas over their faces. Noticing that Nir was conscious, one of them walked out a door, closing it behind him. The second raised a rifle in Nir's direction.

"I will shoot," he said in broken Hebrew.

"Your Hebrew sucks," Nir responded in Arabic, surprised at how croaky his voice sounded.

Well, it's obvious they know who I am. And so it begins . . .

He'd been stripped to his boxers and was sitting on a folding metal chair. His hands were bound behind him, and when he tugged on them, he heard chain links rattling. He assumed his numerous aches and scuffs were from being transported in the trunk he'd seen back in the hotel room. He had no idea how long ago that had been.

Absolutely nothing can happen in these next hours to make them anything less than terrible. Prepare yourself. Endure. Survive. Get under their skin. Then pay them back.

The door opened. Four well-armed, black-clad, masked men walked in and took up positions, two on each side of the door. They were followed by two more men, one older than the other. Each was wearing a white Saudi *thawb*. On their heads they wore the traditional red-and-white-checkered *ghutra*, held in place by the black cord of the *igal*. Neither man was masked, and both wore full beards.

"He speaks Arabic," the man with the poor Hebrew skills said.

"Good to know," said the older of the men.

They stood in front of Nir and looked down at him. The younger one wore a look of disgust while the older looked amused.

"You want me to pose? Maybe talk sexy to you?" Nir asked.

"I don't think you are in a position to be

making jokes, Mr. Tavor," said the older man with disdain.

"They say if you don't have your humor, you don't have anything." Nir looked down at himself. "I'd say that's pretty true for me right now."

Now the man smiled. "Yes, that is certainly true for you. Unfortunately, I also don't think you'll maintain your humor for much longer."

"Try me."

"Oh, I will." The man snapped his fingers, and one of the men in black brought a chair and unfolded it. Sliding it in front of Nir, the man sat down.

"What did you do to your head?" he asked, pointing to the row of staples where Nir had been shot.

Nir hadn't realized they'd pulled off the adhesive covering. "Cut myself shaving. Thanks for caring."

The man glared at Nir. "Why are you in Qatar, Mr. Tavor?"

"I'm an air-conditioning salesman. Making a killing."

"Ilyas," the man called out. One of the other men in black began walking toward them. With a flick of his wrist, he telescoped out a black, metal baton, then struck Nir across his shoulder blades. The pain felt like the man had just snapped him in half.

"Oh, that sucked," he said through gritted teeth. "Good thing you hit like a girl, Ilyas, or that would have really hurt."

Again, the baton struck his shoulders, followed by a shot to his right side.

This time Nir couldn't speak. The pain had taken all his wind.

The old man spoke. "Now, if you're through with your little games, I have some questions I want to ask you."

"I'm all ears," Nir said through clenched teeth.

"Once again, why are you in Qatar?"

"I'm an air-conditioning—"

The boot of the black-clad man connected with Nir's chest, toppling him over backward. His head hit the cement of the floor, and he saw flares in his vision. The baton connected with the bottom of his bare feet once, twice, three times, and then a fourth. Nir's vision momentarily grayed from the pain.

One of the other men ran over to help set Nir and his chair upright again.

Oh, Nicole, I hope you're praying to your Jesus right now, he thought, picturing her with her head bowed like she did before they ate together.

His head was hanging to his chest, and he was trying to keep his feet from touching the floor. "Ilyas," he growled, "one of these days you and I are going to have words."

His abuser stepped forward, but the older Saudi held up his hand.

"Okay, Mr. Tavor. You've proven you're a tough man. If anyone asks us, we'll say yes, he was very impressive. But you and I both know you will eventually tell me what I want to know. Everyone has their breaking point."

Nir took several deep breaths, then looked up at the man. "Listen, I appreciate your offering to give me a reference next time I'm applying for a job, but you've got to understand that I have no clue what you're talking about."

The man sighed. "And yet you provoke us. Why are you Jews always so exasperating?"

"Tell me about it. Why do you think I never got married?"

"Consider yourself blessed. I married four times."

Nir shook his head. "You Saudis. Everything in excess."

"Maybe so. Now let's try this another way. It is obvious that I know who you are. What may surprise you is that I also know why you are here. You have come to meet with a member of the Saudi crown prince's staff."

"Boom. You caught me. Now that that's settled, how about we call it a day?"

"And the reason you planned to meet was to pass some information to him. First, you were going to tell him a man named Ali Kamal is plotting a coup against the royal family."

"Plotting against the royal family? What kind of an idiot is this Ali Kamal?"

"I am Ali Kamal." The man was angry now.

"You don't say. I pictured you thinner."

Kamal reached over and cuffed Nir on the side of the head. His ear started ringing, and his jaw stiffened.

"Not bad for a fat old man," he said.

Kamal paused as if he was trying to gain control of his anger. Then he said, "I imagine you are surprised that I intercepted your mission. You must understand that I am very well connected, and I have powerful friends. Now, as you can imagine, I can't have you taking my name to the crown prince's staff."

"You do know there's a whole country of people just like me right on the other side of Jordan from you? Been there since 1948. You don't think they'll just send somebody else?"

Kamal laughed. "That's the beauty. Of course you Jews will send somebody else, but by then it will be too late. Because you are my bargaining chip. You are what is going to get me the army I need to take the royals down."

It was Nir's turn to laugh. "Really? Me? I mean, I'm handsome and all, and you can probably tell I've been working on my pecs, but I'm really not much of a bargaining chip. Israel won't fight a war for you just to get me back, and I can't think of any other country where I'm that hot of a commodity."

Kamal's bravado was back now. "Oh, I can. You're all smart and smug, but I know more than you think. I know the other piece of information you're bringing. You're here to inform the crown prince of the date and time Israel will attempt to destroy Iran's nuclear program."

Nir let the surprise show on his face. "I hate to break it to you, *habibi*, but we aren't in the habit of passing on our military plans to any country, particularly to you Saudis."

"You will if you need our airspace."

Nir said nothing.

"Ha! You thought I was a fool. But you will tell me what I want to know, and I will pass it to my Iranian friends in exchange for their giving me the Houthis as my army."

"I don't know what you're talking about," Nir said quietly.

"Suddenly, you're not so smug. Tell me, Mr. Nir Tavor, agent of the Mossad, who is the fool now?"

Kamal swung, connecting with Nir's cheek and making his head snap sideways. A second punch opened a cut under his eye. After a third punch, Kamal cried out and grabbed his hand.

Spitting blood onto the man's white robe, Nir said, "Aw, did my face hurt your little hand, you soft tub of pig fat?"

Ilyas stepped behind Nir. A rope whipped around his neck and cinched tight, and Nir gasped for air. Tighter and tighter it was pulled until he felt like his windpipe would snap.

This isn't the way it's supposed to go, Nir thought through panic. *If I die here, it's all lost. Please, God, make it stop. Not for my sake, but for all those who need this plan to work.*

The rope went slack, and when Nir felt a glancing blow of the baton across his skull, sharp pain radiated down his spine.

Ilyas whispered in his ear, "Please keep resisting."

The rope went taut again. Nir arched his body upward, trying desperately to find air. His lungs burned. His mind began to give way to the helplessness even as his body thrashed.

"Stop!" The rope loosened, and Nir gulped in air. He didn't recognize the voice that had just saved his life. But then through his watery eyes he saw the younger man in the *thawb* and *ghutra* walk toward him. He began examining the crease under Nir's right pectoral muscle.

Oh no, here it goes, Nir thought, preparing himself. This was the whole reason for his antagonizing his captors. He needed them angry, so that they would really work him over. All for these next few moments.

The man pinched the skin, then pinched deeper. "Bring a knife," he said.

Ilyas stepped toward him and unfolded a blade.

"Cut there," the man said. "That little bump alongside the scar."

Ilyas did, and Nir cried out. The Saudi reached around the incision, then cut deeper. Nir could feel him rooting around with the tip of the knife under his skin.

"Got it," Ilyas said. "It's a tracker. I told you we needed the ability to check him for devices."

"We need to go immediately," said the younger Saudi in white, concern on his face. "His people know where he is."

Ilyas slammed his fist into Nir's right temple, and he sprawled to the floor. A hand grabbed Nir by the hair and lifted his head. It was Kamal. "You think you've survived this? You've only made it much worse, you Jew pig. Now I'm going to call my Iranian friend, and he's going to bring the professionals. You're going to wish you had told me what I wanted to know so I could have just put a bullet in your brain." He threw Nir's head back down to the cement.

As his vision turned from gray to black, Nir heard Kamal say, "Get the syringe and the trunk. We're taking a trip."

CHAPTER 54

CARL, MOSSAD HEADQUARTERS, TEL AVIV, ISRAEL— 06:37 / 6:37 A.M. IDT

W e lost the tracker," Liora shouted as she began frantically typing on her keyboard.

Nicole had seen it disappear on her monitor as well. The thought of what Nir must have had to endure for the tiny capsule to be discovered and removed sickened her.

She called out, "Wait ten minutes, then initiate the ping for the secondary."

She caught Lahav looking at her from across the room. He mouthed the word *Sorry,* and she nodded.

One of the biggest questions with Nir's plan had been how to get Kamal out of Doha. Why wouldn't he just torture Nir until he got his information, then kill him there? As they'd met around the table, Lahav looked at Nir and said, "I have an idea, but you're not going to like it."

"When have we ever liked any of your ideas?" Yossi had said with a wink.

Lahav ignored him. "We're planning on inserting a tracker under your skin, right?" he said, still looking at Nir. "In fact, I put the order

416

in for it this morning. What do you think the chances are they find it?"

"Eighty percent? Ninety?" answered Nir.

"Try one hundred, unless they're totally *dafuk*. Everybody watches Netflix. Everyone knows intelligence services chip their operatives. It's like the one part of action movies that's actually true."

"So you're saying don't chip me?"

"No, I'm saying recognize that they're going to find it and turn it to our advantage."

"How?"

"By chipping you twice. The first one, we'll expect them to find and remove. Then the second . . ." Lahav stopped and took a deep breath. "I'm sorry, *achi*. I just ran past that removal part. That's going to totally suck for you."

"It is what it is."

Nicole listened to Nir's stoic response, and she struggled to maintain the same sort of composure. Inside, though, she was anything but calm. She wanted to get in Nir's face and yell, "Don't do this! You'll get yourself killed. And I couldn't live with myself if I let that happen." But she knew he needed to do it. The country needed him to do it. And he needed her help so he could do it.

"Keep going, Lahav," Nicole said as matter-of-factly as she could.

"So we put the first one where it will be found and the second where it won't."

Liora pointed at Lahav. "And for the second, we won't plant the same kind. We'll do a passive beacon, one that won't transmit. You know, the ones that can only be pinged by us."

Nir agreed to the plan, and Nicole had come up with putting the first one on his chest. Picturing herself in that interrogation room, she knew the torso was the logical beginning point for their harsh activities. The fact that the tracker was now gone proved her assumption correct.

Now the thought of someone taking some rusty knife and digging around in Nir's chest brought bile into her throat. She swallowed hard and took a long drink from her water bottle, giving a quiet gargle to clear the taste.

Protect him, Lord. Give him strength to endure. Don't let them take his life. Show Yourself to him.

It was Nir who came up with the insertion site for the passive chip. He had one of the Mossad's medical staff come in, then instructed him to open the scar on the side of his head from where he'd been shot in Syria. "Below the skin and against the skull" was the order he'd given for inserting the thin piece of coded foil. The doctor then stapled the wound back together so that if anyone took a wand to Nir looking for metal, they would think the staples had triggered the device.

Brilliant, but horrific as well. This was not

normal. None but a small handful of people in this world would say, "Oh sure, it's a great idea to cut open your head and insert some coded metal so we can still follow you after you're kidnapped and tortured and your first tracker is torn from your body."

But that was the operation, and so far the operation was going as planned. For the past 45 minutes, she'd been trying to hack into a Chinese satellite. But it was giving her fits. Maybe because her mind was in Doha instead of in Tel Aviv.

Nicole turned up the volume on the monitor connected to Nir's passive tracker. Earlier, she'd opened access to a U.S. GPS satellite, and Lahav had programmed it to ping the sliver of metal for one quarter of a second every half hour. She wanted to make sure she heard it when it did.

"Any movement with Mousavi?" she called out.

"Nothing," Dafna said. "His phone hasn't moved, and the asset outside his house says he's still there."

"Good. And Salim is still moored off Mumbai?"

Liora answered. "His yacht is there, and his phone is there. As soon as you get us that Chinese satellite, we'll confirm he's there too."

"Working on it."

Oh, Nir, what is happening to you right now? I don't even know if you're alive.

Monitoring the team's activities from the conference table were Efraim Cohen and Deputy Director Asher Porush. The two were holding a quiet, animated conversation.

"Nicole, come join us," Porush suddenly called. "We need you."

Her fingers flew rapidly over the keyboard, finishing a line of code. That satellite was still eluding her, but she walked over and took a place across the table from the two.

"Give me your assessment so far," Porush said.

"Everything has gone according to plan. We seeded the information of Nir's mission and arrival five days ago, and it appears Kamal took the bait."

"Appears?"

"His phone is pinging at the same location Nir's tracker is—was. That's strong evidence. However, we don't have a visual, and the *ramsad* will not let us act without visual identification. Otherwise, we would have already taken him down right in Doha."

Cohen added, "And if we did raid Nir's location and Kamal was not there, the whole plan would be busted."

"Got it. So let's assume he is there. You're counting on him moving Nir to Saad Salim's yacht now that his location is compromised."

Nicole answered. "Again, I wouldn't put it that way. *Counting on* is too strong a phrase. *Hoping* would be better. But the *Cafala Bahr* does seem to be the gathering place for promoting their shared interests." She noticed the older man's face and bald head were reddening.

"If you were a gambler, where would you put the odds?" he said.

"I'd say 60–40 it's the yacht. We're watching General Arash Mousavi of the IRGC right now. If we see him traveling to the boat, we'll know we've got them. He's the man Kamal is pursuing right now because of his access to the Houthis."

Porush gave her a hard look. "Those are not good odds when so many lives are at stake."

"They are the best I can give." She gave him a hard look back. "And trust me, I understand the lives at stake."

"If Kamal doesn't head to the yacht, we'll follow where he does go," Cohen said calmly, as if he was trying to keep the temperature down between her and Porush. "As long as it isn't back home to Saudi Arabia, then we're good. When we make a positive ID, we'll take him out."

"What would that mean for Tavor?" Porush asked.

Nicole and Cohen looked at each other, then Nicole said, "We'll do our best to get him out, *Ha'mefaked.*" She quickly stood and walked back to her workstation before Porush could see the emotion in her eyes.

CHAPTER 55

SEVEN HOURS LATER
CAFALA BAHR, ARABIAN SEA,
OFF MUMBAI, INDIA—
16:20 / 4:20 P.M. IST

The helicopter crossed the water from the direction of the mainland.

"What does this fool want now?" Salim asked, dripping sweat from the hot, humid air. If he was this miserable, he couldn't imagine what the general was feeling in his uniform. Since the military man had IRGC troops on board, he didn't feel it proper to change into his usual comfortable yacht-wear. So he stood there with sweat stains soaking through his jacket.

"I don't know what he wants, but I do know I didn't think it was possible for me to loathe him more than I already did. Yet he has proven me wrong." He finished his ice water and held out his hand. A steward quickly replaced the glass with a fresh one. The general pulled the wedge of lemon from the rim, squeezed it, and pushed it down into the ice.

"All he told me was that this meeting was of utmost urgency," Saad said. "Obviously, he told you something more since you have a dozen armed soldiers with you."

"And my interrogator." Mousavi nodded toward the bar.

"That's who that is? If Kamal is bringing some sort of prisoner here, I will personally throw him off my boat. That's not what this vessel is for!"

Saad's company helicopter was just now within earshot.

"Well, then you better get ready to throw him overboard, *habibi*. He told me he had a deal I could not refuse. Then he added that I should bring a bodyguard and an interrogator. Oh, and he said you knew all about it and had given your approval."

Saad was fuming. *This is not Al-Ha'ir Prison. This is not some interrogation cell for the General Intelligence Presidency! What is this fool doing?*

The ASEnergy chopper eased in and touched down. After the rotors slowed, the doors opened, and a steward stepped out, extending the steps.

Ali Kamal bounded out. "Saad! Arash!" he called from the distance, his arms stretched wide. "My friends, it is so good to see you on such a glorious day." He crossed the helipad toward the waiting men.

"Oh, wrong again," Mousavi said to Saad. "He did find a way to make me hate him even more."

Saad counted eight men in desert camouflage stepping out of his helicopter behind Kamal. They had rifles strapped to their bodies. What he didn't see was a prisoner of any sort. Four of the soldiers walked behind the copter to the cargo hold, where they unloaded a large trunk. They picked it up and followed their leader.

"*As-salamu 'alaykum*," said Kamal when he reached them.

"*Wa-'alaykum salam*," the two men dutifully replied.

The men with the trunk arrived and dropped it with a thud.

Saad spoke before Kamal had a chance. "I have been speaking with the general, and he told me you asked him to bring an interrogator. What is going on, Ali? I demand to know what is happening on my boat."

"What is happening is that I have come to make a deal with the general. Quite possibly the deal of the century! I have come to ask for the Houthis, and I want them immediately. In three days, I want all their skinny little bodies and their weapons at my disposal."

Mousavi laughed. "I don't know who you think I am, but I can tell you I don't have that kind of power."

Kamal smiled and tapped the general on his moist chest. "You may not, but you know who in Tehran does. I will trade you the Houthis for what is in the trunk." He gave the box a light kick.

The general's look hardened. "Even if it were full of gold, it would not be enough—"

"Oh, I am offering you something of much more value than gold. It is far more powerful than any weapon. It can be more beautiful than the lithest of women. I am offering you information."

Saad was already tired of Kamal's game. "Enough. Open the trunk and show us this valuable piece of information you have inside."

Kamal snapped his fingers, and one of his men undid a latch and opened the lid.

The rank smell caused Saad to step back before he had a chance to look inside.

"What is wrong with you?" Mousavi said to Kamal, his eyes locked on the contents.

Removing a handkerchief from his pants pocket, Saad covered his nose and mouth. He stepped toward the box and looked in. A man was crammed inside, folded into a tight fetal position but with his arms thrown akimbo because they wouldn't fit in the curl.

"Gentlemen, please let me introduce you to Nir Tavor, agent for the Israeli Mossad."

Saad's stomach dropped. "What? You fool! You absolute moron. You brought a Mossad agent onto my boat?" He began scanning the waters to see if any warships were already approaching.

Meanwhile, Mousavi had taken hold of Kamal's *thawb* and was swearing a blue streak at the man.

Rifles racked in the ranks of Kamal's men, followed by the IRGC soldiers doing the same.

"Stop!" cried Saad, stepping forward with his

arms out. "No more!" He pushed Mousavi and Kamal away from each other. "Tell your men to stand down. Both of you. Now!"

They obeyed, and the soldiers slowly lowered their guns.

Saad kicked the lid to the trunk closed. "Is he alive?"

"Of course he's alive," Kamal answered, angrily readjusting his *ghutra* and *igal*. "He wouldn't be much of a source of information otherwise, would he?"

"Please tell me you scanned him for tracking devices."

"We're not fools, Saad. We found one, cut it out, and disposed of it before we left Qatar, where we captured him." The man sounded so proud of this accomplishment.

"Okay, good," Saad said, mulling his next steps. "Tell your men to take him down to the empty storage hold next to the garage. And get him out of that box. Make sure he's bound securely and use the seawater hose to rinse him down. I don't want him stinking up the entire lower deck. Then throw the trunk into the ocean and make sure it sinks."

Kamal turned toward his men. "You heard him. Be quick." The four who had brought the trunk came forward and lifted it. Saad's chief steward stepped from his respectful ten-meter distance to show the men the way to the storage room.

Still angry, Saad said to Kamal, "Now, let's hear what you have. If you say it is important enough for the general to bring you the Houthis, then it must be incredible. But I swear to you, if it is not, this will be the last time you ever step foot on this boat."

A smile crossed Kamal's face again. "Oh, it is special, all right. But first, General, I must insist that you promise me the Houthis."

"How many times must I tell you? I cannot."

"Yes you can. And you will—gladly—when I reveal my little secret to you."

Mousavi stared at the man as if trying to read his face. "Okay. If this information is as spectacular as you say, you will have your army."

"Splendid," Kamal said, clapping his hands. "Now for secrets revealed. The Mossad agent, Nir Tavor, came to Doha for an express purpose. He was to communicate to the Saudi crown prince's chief of staff some very important information— the date and time the Israeli Air Force is planning to fly over Saudi airspace on its way to Iran to decimate your nuclear program in a massive, unparalleled air strike."

"What?" The general looked stunned.

"See, I told you," Kamal said with a grin.

Mousavi looked unsteady for a moment as he processed this news. But Saad had already run it through. At the most, Iran was only months from joining the nuclear club. But the rest of the world wasn't doing anything about it, so Israel believed it was up to them to shut down the program for their own personal survival.

Kamal was right. This would change the Middle East. If Iran was prepared for the attack, they could do great damage to the Israeli Air Force while drawing on the sympathy of the world. Meanwhile, Kamal could launch his attack on the royal family. If he succeeded, Saad would be friends with a king. If he failed, the man would finally be out of his hair forever.

"Well, General?" Kamal asked.

"This is certainly momentous," Mousavi said. "Yet if the Mossad discovers we have the information, won't they just change the date?"

"It is a good thing you have a sharp mind like mine on your side, Arash. Yes, you prepare for that date and hope it will not be changed. However, my gift to you is not just the Mossad agent's information. It is the agent himself. Imagine the international furor your country will create when you show this man to the world as proof of Israel's evil intentions. This one Jew's confession can have the same power as all those binders and discs stolen from your vaults."

Kamal smiled. "In fact, once you have extracted every last bit of information you want from him about the workings of the Mossad in your country, you can try him for espionage and execute him—publicly, if you wish. No one could deny the justice of that. So what do you think now?"

"*Habibi*," Mousavi replied with his hand outstretched, "you have yourself an army."

CHAPTER 56

CARL, MOSSAD HEADQUARTERS, TEL AVIV, ISRAEL— 13:50 / 1:50 P.M. IDT

The helicopter is five minutes out," Nicole heard Dafna say. Her teammate was following its progress on a large monitor at her workstation.

"Kamal's phone is on board," Liora added. She turned toward a separate monitor and typed on a keyboard. "Nir's next ping is scheduled in seven minutes. His last one placed him in Mumbai. We can't confirm yet if he's on board the copter."

"Very well," the *ramsad* said gruffly.

To Ira Katz, Nicole had reported that Mousavi had been visually confirmed to be aboard Saad Salim's yacht off the coast of Mumbai. She also informed him that Ali Kamal's phone had landed in a private jet at the Maharashtra capital's Chhatrapati Shivaji Maharaj International Airport. Soon after, it had lifted off in a helicopter owned by ASEnergy in the direction of the yacht. However, they were yet to receive a visual confirmation of the man's presence. The last ping from Nir had placed him eight minutes ago in the private hangar to which Kamal's Gulfstream V had taxied.

"Come over here," Lahav called to the *ramsad* as he walked toward Dafna's workstation. That made Nicole cringe a little. When Ira Katz just glared at him, Lahav added, "*Ha'mefaked.*" The old man rose and followed him.

From among the row of pens in his shirt pocket, Lahav pulled a long green one with a metallic end. "Lightsaber," he said to the *ramsad* with a grin. Then he waved it around making lightsaber-y sounds as if he were expecting some sort of reaction. When he received none, he pushed on the end, and an internal laser projected an X-wing starfighter onto Dafna's monitor.

Circling the image around one man standing on the top deck of the yacht, he said, "This is Saad Salim. He is the owner of the boat. Exiled Saudi. Owns ASEnergy, an oil company—no surprise there. Also major financial and weapons supplier to militias, including Hezbollah and Hamas. Probably supplied a whole bunch of the four thousand Katyusha rockets that landed on us from Gaza back in May."

He shifted his starfighter to the man next to him. "This is General Arash Mousavi, head of the Intelligence Division of the Quds Force of the IRGC. He is very close with General Esmail Qaani, who took over Quds force after Mousavi's previous BFF, Soleimani, played catch with a hellfire missile. Torture, murder, rape—he's a real turd. The rest of these guys around here are the IRGC soldiers Mousavi brought. Best we can tell, that's unusual for his little yacht excursions."

"Got it. And I've already read up on Ali Kamal, so there's no need to brief me on him," said the *ramsad*. He looked the young man over. "You're Lahav Tabib. The analyst from the Fakhrizadeh operation."

"Yes, *Ha'mefaked*."

"I thought so. That was some good work."

Yossi started making kissing noises from his workstation but quickly broke into a coughing fit when the *ramsad* turned toward him sharply.

To Lahav, he said, "And this view is from Chinese satellites?"

Lahav pointed to Nicole. "She's the one you want to talk to about that."

She was sitting at the conference table with a laptop open in front of her, watching everything happening, including the exchange between Lahav and the *ramsad*. After spending so many hours at her workstation, she'd needed a different view. She'd wiped everything else off this portable computer and reprogrammed it to be a home base from which she could control all her work, then moved to where she now sat.

"Yes, it's Chinese, *Ha'mefaked*," she said. "Our satellites are good. The Americans' are better. The Chinese satellites are best."

"How much longer will they let you have access to their cameras?"

"Until they realize I have it. I'm guessing we have 15 to 20 minutes before I have to find us another Chinese bird."

The *ramsad* chuckled. "Oh, what we could have done with you during the Cold War."

"One minute out," called Liora.

"Excuse me, *Ha'mefaked*." Nicole waved her hand sideways.

The *ramsad* turned. "No, excuse me," he said, stepping over to where Efraim Cohen was watching after realizing he'd been standing directly in her line of sight to the large monitor showing the satellite feed.

Nicole's heart was racing. *Lord, please let me get a glimpse of Nir. Let me see him being led out of the helicopter or even carried out. Just let me know he's alive. Please protect him. Please reach him. Please encourage him to reach out to You.*

As the helicopter touched down, Yossi said, "Look at Salim and the general's body language. They don't seem all that happy to see their friend. I doubt there's a lot of love lost between them and him."

"It's true," Nicole said. "When I was on the yacht, Salim and Mousavi were quite jovial and casual. Now they're standing straight up and down. No movement toward the chopper at all."

"Could be because of the IRGC soldiers present," Cohen said. "They figure they need to keep it professional."

The door to the helicopter opened, and Ali Kamal followed a steward out.

"He certainly looks happy to be there," Liora said. "Waving his arms in the air like he just doesn't care."

"His friends still seem a lot less ecstatic," Dafna added.

Nicole kept watching for Nir. Uniformed men followed Kamal off, eight in all. But that was it. Nobody else stepped off except the pilots. Four of the men removed what looked like their equipment trunk from the rear of the aircraft and carried it over to where Kamal had met the men.

"Where is he?" she asked.

"Ping in ten seconds," Liora said. She counted down, and a loud electronic chirp sounded throughout the room. A red dot covered most of the monitor.

"What is that?" demanded the *ramsad* as the dot slowly faded.

"That's just the location indicator of Nir's tracker. We're too far away to know exactly where he is on the boat. We just know he's most definitely on it."

If he's there, why haven't we seen him? Why haven't they taken him off the chopper?

On the screen, Nicole saw one of the men who'd carried the trunk from the helicopter raise its lid. Saad stepped back quickly, but Mousavi

434

peered inside. Nicole couldn't make out what was there.

"*Oy vey*," said the *ramsad* softly. That's when she recognized the contents. A body. She couldn't make out the details, but she knew who it was. The dark line of the mended wound on the side of Nir's head was all the proof she needed.

She started to cry. She couldn't stop herself. This man she loved, this hero of the country, had been beaten and stuffed into a trunk. It was more than she could take. She put her head down on the table and wept.

An arm wrapped around her. She looked up and saw it was the *ramsad*. Putting her face into his shoulder, she felt his arms embrace her. All the tension and fear and exhaustion and sorrow poured out through her tears.

"We'll get him back. I promise you," he said in his low, gruff voice.

"We don't even know that he's still alive."

"He's alive. He has to be. They still need his information."

Nicole pulled back, and the *ramsad* offered her a handkerchief. She thanked him, then dabbed her eyes and wiped her cheeks. "But what if they've already broken him? What if . . . what if he already told them all about the timing of the attack?"

The *ramsad* smiled gently. "He can't, my dear. He doesn't know."

Confused, Nicole blinked. "He doesn't know?"

"Of course not. I would never tell him that. Besides, he was the one who first insisted on maintaining his ignorance. He knows the only person who can never be broken is the person who has no information to give."

Relief flooded into Nicole, as did hope. She turned back to the monitor to watch as the trunk was closed and then carried away. "So they still need him."

"Yes, they still need him. These next hours will be very rough going for him. But when night falls, our boys will be there, and they will rescue that man from that boat." A hard look came across the *ramsad*'s face. "And then they will make those men pay for what they have done."

CHAPTER 57

The chill of water jolted Nir awake. He sputtered, tasting salt in his mouth and feeling a raw blast up his nostrils. His eyes burned when he opened them, and through the blur he saw a soldier in an IRGC uniform stepping away and carrying a water hose.

"Mr. Tavor, it's good to have you back with us."

Nir followed the voice and saw Kamal standing with two other men—Saad Salim and General Arash Mousavi. Scattered around were several IRGC soldiers and a few of Kamal's men.

You can't let Salim and Mousavi realize you know who they are. Stay strong. Stretch it out. Give your boys a chance to come get you.

"Kamal," he choked out. Nir cleared his throat and spit. "Good to see you're still around. Still doing that keto diet?"

"See what I mean about the Jewish arrogance?" Kamal said to the other two men.

"Want to introduce me to Dewey and Louie?" Nir said as he pushed himself into a sitting

437

position on the floor, ropes tied to his wrists and ankles pooling at his sides. He ached all over, and raw spots burned where his body had no doubt rubbed against the walls of the trunk Kamal had asked for.

"These men are of no concern to you. They're here to—"

"You're not even going to introduce me to the general in the Quds Force uni? Shame what happened to Soleimani. You know him?" The general's face began reddening. Already Nir was getting to him. "You did know him. I can see it on your face. You have one of those red rings too? Like the one on his runaway hand?" Nir held his own hand in the position Soleimani's disembodied hand had been discovered.

He went on. "Speaking of red rings, what about Fakhrizadeh? I got to watch that one on a monitor. His head just blew apart like an over-ripe watermelon. *Whoosh*." Nir pulled his hands away from his head like an explosion.

Mousavi stepped forward, but Saad put a hand on his shoulder.

"Yeah, listen to your master." Looking at Saad, Nir said, "Does that mean you're the Dr. Evil of this secret lair? Between the saltwater in my face and your trendy boat shoes, I'm guessing we're on the ocean and you're one of those superrich mama's boys who never got enough hugs when you were a child."

Kamal nodded toward Nir's left. Suddenly, his arms and legs were being pulled by the ropes. He was flung back against the wall and stretched until he was hanging spread eagle. All his joints screamed, and it felt like his arms were being pulled from their sockets. He struggled to suck in a breath.

Through gritted teeth, he managed to say, "How da Vinci of you."

Kamal said, "You know, you are the only one who finds your comments amusing."

Nir sucked in another deep breath and nodded toward one of the IRGC troops. "Dude there was smirking."

"Enough playing. I told my friend, the general, that you are carrying information of interest to him. More precisely, that you know when your nation of criminals is planning on attacking his peaceful nation with an air strike. So I would like you to tell him."

Whoever had secured the ropes pulled them tighter. Nir cried out, then said, "Sorry. Had it on my phone. Seem to have lost it."

"Is that the way you're going to play it? You're determined to take the difficult approach?"

Between gulps of air, Nir said, "Don't know what you're talking about. I'm not air force. My work is one-on-one, like with the general's friends."

This time Mousavi didn't stop when Saad put

his hand on him. He strode forward and drove his fist into Nir's abdomen. The pain radiated throughout his body, and he groaned more deeply than ever.

Then Mousavi's hand wrapped around Nir's throat and he squeezed. "You think you can laugh at me, you Jewish dog? You think I will just stand here and take it like my Saudi friend here? He is not a warrior. I am. I have killed trash like you before, and I will kill you too."

The general released his neck and stepped back while Nir coughed and gasped. Then he took his face in his hand and squeezed again. "You came to tell those Sunni traitors when you plan to fly over their airspace to come to my country and attempt to destroy our nuclear program. You will now tell me when this operation is planned to take place. Or I will bring you pain like you've never imagined."

Dropping his hand, he turned and walked back to Saad.

Kamal took a step forward. "So, you see, Jew—"

"You, shut up," Mousavi said, pointing at him. Then he snapped his fingers and called out "Ghasemi!" A small, thin man wearing a doctor's smock walked over. An IRGC soldier followed carrying a table, which he placed in Nir's sightline.

Here it comes. How am I going to survive this?

440

I'm all out of bravado. Ignorance is my only defense, and that's only going to make it worse. Nicole's Jesus, please help me through this. If You protect my life, I'll know it was You.

The man unwrapped what looked like a knife roll, then began removing instruments one by one and placing them on the table. Blades and picks and hooks. Sandpaper, a corkscrew, a small butane torch.

Nir knew the drill. This was all part of the psychology game. But even though it was a game, it still worked. That was why they did it. He was as terrified as he'd ever been. He was helpless, and he was vulnerable to whatever this man decided to do to him.

"Hey, Doc. While you're at it, how about—" Nir's voice faltered as the IRGC soldier returned carrying a cricket bat and some spiny-looking sea creature.

As the doctor continued his prep, he said to the soldier, "Knees and ankles first, please. Carefully."

The soldier left the sea creature, took the cricket bat, and walked over to Nir. The two locked eyes, and the man's gaze remained impassive, dead. He stepped sideways, wound up, and swung. The bat connected with Nir's left knee, and he cried out. The pain was immense.

The man wound up again, and this time the bat connected with Nir's right knee. From his thighs down to his calves, he legs contorted in hideous cramps. The soldier changed his angle, and the bat slammed against Nir's left ankle. His teeth clenched, and his respiratory rate skyrocketed. Thankfully, he had only heard *thwack* but no crack. As long as he had no broken bones, he still had a chance of walking off this boat.

The soldier tried to line up for the right ankle, but he wasn't able to get the proper trajectory. Another of the soldiers stepped up and took the bat. He held it like a lefty and swung. Nir moaned.

"And now it's time to begin," said the man in the smock. He picked up what looked like a dental pick with a sharp hook on the end and walked toward Nir. "Don't tell the general what he wants to know quite yet, though. I'm finally all set up, and I so very much enjoy what I do."

CHAPTER 58

Saad turned and walked out. This was not the kind of man he was, and this was not what his boat was for. The screams followed him down the hall until the elevator doors closed.

He rode up two levels to the salon. Immediately upon entering, he said, "Play Schubert." The flute introduction of Franz Schubert's *Symphony No. 5 in B-Flat Major* surrounded him. Soon the strings joined in and began to drive away the echoes of the wailing man. He poured himself two fingers of Blanton's bourbon and drank it down neat.

Refilling his glass, he ambled toward one of his two new Marcos paintings. While the Marilyn certainly had pop and sexiness to it, he found himself more and more intrigued by the fruit bowl. It was a Latin American take on the old classic. The bowl was painted with some sort of colorful Mestizo design, and it was filled with dragon fruit, tamarillos, loquats, and other produce whose names he had not yet taken time to look up.

How did I let this happen on my boat? he asked himself as he stared at the piece of art. *I blink my eyes, and suddenly it is an armed vessel with a man being tortured in the hold. This is not who I am. I pay for the guns; I don't pull the triggers.*

Downing the second drink, he placed the glass on an end table, then moved to his favorite chair and sat. *They need to go. Tomorrow at the latest. Do not back down. All ties with Kamal must be cut.*

He wasn't sure what to do about Mousavi. The general was a vital connection into the Tehran regime. *Once this is all over and his emotions are calm, we'll have to have a serious conversation about what can and cannot happen on this boat.*

The symphony had just transitioned to the fourth movement when he heard a ding at the elevator. The doors opened, and Kamal and the general stepped out. They were arguing.

"Pause music," Saad said with a sigh.

"I don't think he knows," said Mousavi. "I don't even know that there *will* be an attack."

Kamal shook his head. "There will be an attack, and he does know."

"How do you know he knows?"

"Because that was the whole other purpose for him meeting with the chief of staff." Kamal walked to the bar.

Saad stood. "Wait. What do you mean, *the whole other purpose?* What was the main purpose?"

Kamal paused as he poured. Saad resented the cost of the cognac the man chose.

"Tavor brought two pieces of information to

444

pass on to the crown prince. First and foremost was the timing of the attack. They had to warn the Saudis about when they were going to fly over. Second, the Jews had heard rumors that someone might be plotting a coup against the royal family. Tavor was supposedly bringing the name of the conspirator."

Saad couldn't believe his ears. "Are you telling me your little plot has been uncovered? I said you were telling too many people."

"I don't even know that it was me. Do you know how many coups are plotted against the royal family every year?"

"No," said the general, who looked like he might pounce on Kamal at any moment. "Enlighten us."

Kamal looked trapped. "I don't know either. But no doubt a lot. The chances that they've discovered mine are incredibly slim."

"Yet, there is a chance. And you wanted me to go back to my government and ask them to enlist the Houthis into a plot that is probably already burned? Were you even going to tell us?"

"I didn't think it was worth it. Like I said, it could have been about somebody else."

Mousavi was in a rage. Saad knew he needed to calm this. It wasn't just that these two men could come to personal blows. Twenty heavily-armed soldiers and bodyguards were also on board. If a gunfight started, not only would people be killed but millions of dollars in damage could occur. And even beyond that, the attention of Indian authorities and Interpol could very well have his whole operation shut down.

"I want this man off the boat immediately," Mousavi yelled. "And you can forget any Houthi army. You're lucky I don't just shoot you myself."

"Really? Try it. I've got eight men out there who say you will never get off this boat if you touch me."

"Stop!" Saad had his hands up. "I've already made a decision, and I am still in charge on this boat. Use tonight to try to extract your information. But when the sun comes up, I want both of you, your entourages, and that Jew off my boat. Understood?"

While Kamal glared at him, Saad could see the rage leaving Mousavi. "I'm sorry, *habibi*. This should not have happened on *Cafala Bahr*. You opened your vessel to us, and we have taken advantage of it. We'll leave in the morning."

Kamal remained obstinate. "I'm not leaving until—"

"We will both leave in the morning." Mousavi stared hard at the Saudi until the man nodded his acquiescence. "Good. In the meantime, I'll tell Ghasemi our time is short and to flay the Jew alive if that's what it takes to make him finally talk."

446

CHAPTER 59

THREE HOURS LATER
20:40 / 8:40 P.M. IST

I don't know, I don't know, I don't know," Nir moaned. He was still hanging against the wall, but he couldn't feel the pain in his joints anymore. That had all drifted to the background. Right now, all his focus, his entire existence, was centered on the serrated blade tracing across his abdomen. He knew it was serrated because his torturer was insistent that he admire its shape and craftsmanship before he employed it.

"Just tell me, you stubborn fool," said the doctor as he stepped away. Nir heard the blade clank onto the table. "Let me make it stop," he added. But then he came back.

Nir smelled the alcohol before he felt it. He cried out, then slipped back into his mumbled mantra, "I don't know, I don't know, I don't know."

Mumbled conversation reached his ears. Then the ropes were loosed, and he tumbled to the floor. He immediately balled up for self-preservation. He was clueless as to what bodily fluids he was lying in, but he didn't care. At least he wasn't hanging anymore. Then his arms and legs began cramping, and a whole new wave of agony assaulted his body.

The doctor squatted in front of him. "We'll be back very soon to try again. Use this time to reach into your memory banks for the information we are seeking. And just to give you something to look forward to, when I return, I think it will be time for the torch."

As the man walked away, Nir could hear him giving orders to the two IRGC men in the room. "Clean my instruments and his scraps from the table. And wash down the floor. It smells like a sewer."

Please come, please come, please come. Nir pleaded for his rescuers to arrive.

"What's he saying?" one of the IRGC men asked.

"Who knows? Something in his gutter language."

Nir hadn't realized he'd been speaking out loud. He bit his lower lip to make sure he didn't accidentally start up again.

The second man continued. "You know, I'm thinking this guy really doesn't know anything. After what he's gone through? I would have talked hours ago."

The other man laughed. "Yeah, you would have. Honestly, I don't care if he knows anything or not. He deserves what he's getting. I hope the doc skins him alive."

"If he does, I don't want to be here. Once you see that, you won't be able to get it out of your head."

As they went about their work, Nir tried to shut down. Every nerve in his body was screaming with pain, and all he wanted was a little relief. Another wave of cramping twisted his muscles. Even if that relief meant death, he was ready for it. Nothing awaiting him in the afterlife could be worse than what he was experiencing in his present life.

God, if this is Your idea of rescue, then I think everything Nicole has said about You is wrong. I'm trying to do good, and this is my payment. I offer myself up, and You crush me. Why must I be tortured and die a horrible death just so others can live? I don't get You. What kind of insane plan is this?

But then he pictured those little kids he and Nicole had seen along the beach at Jaffa. He pictured his nieces and nephews, who lived up near Galilee. He pictured a laughing Nicole sipping one of her horrid, iced coffees.

Okay, I get it. If taking my life means life for them, then take it. Please just do it soon. And can You give me some kind of sign that this really is You? That You exist and are really here?

Saltwater splashed on him. Then one of the IRGC men nudged him hard with his foot, and Nir gingerly slid his body sideways. More saltwater splashed, sluicing through every open wound.

"Clean enough," said the guard.

Not the sign I was looking for, God.

He heard them walk across the room. Then the lights went out, and the door closed. He was lying in complete darkness. The first time the doctor and his assistants left, Nir had tested the ropes, finding them secured to the wall with just a little slack. He tugged again weakly now and found them to be the same.

He laid his head down.

A sound woke him. He had no idea how long he'd been out. He opened his eyes, and a small bright light was shining on him from across the room. Confused and still half asleep, he pleaded. "Please, no more. No more."

The light came closer, and Nir saw the shape of a person dressed all in white. Maybe God had answered his prayer by sending an angel.

Then a voice in heavily accented English said, "Friend. Friend."

What is this? Part of the torture? Get my hopes up, then crush them?

The man held out a water bottle and tilted it against Nir's lips. Without thinking, he opened his dry, raw mouth. The cold liquid felt so good. But then he realized anything could be in there, and he spit it back out.

"Friend. Friend," the man repeated, then turned

the light toward himself. He was a young Asian man with a wide smile yet concern in his eyes. He was holding a cell phone. He put the bottle to his own mouth and drank, then smacked his lips and said, "Good." Nir remembered Nicole saying she thought many of the stewards here were Filipino, because they were Asian yet their name tags had Spanish last names.

"Who are you?" Nir croaked.

The man just shushed him and put the bottle back to Nir's lips. This time he drank greedily. As he did, the man pointed at him and said, "Jesus, friend. Jesus protect."

A sound outside made the man jump. He doused the light and hushed Nir. Once more, it was completely black in the room. After a couple of minutes, Nir felt a hand press gently on his arm. The young man spoke, saying words in a language Nir didn't recognize. His tone and cadence made it sound as if it were a blessing or even a prayer.

"*Pagpalain ka nawa ni Yahweh at ingatan ka*; *palinawagan nawa ni Yahweh ang kaniyang mukha sa iyo, at mahabag sa iyo*; *ilingap nawa ni Yahweh ang kaniyang mukha sa iyo, at bigyan ka ng kapayapaan*."

The hand was removed, and a few moments later, Nir briefly saw light across the room as the door opened and closed.

CHAPTER 60

90 MINUTES LATER
CARL, MOSSAD HEADQUARTERS,
TEL AVIV, ISRAEL—
19:45 / 7:45 P.M. IDT

The eight screens mounted high on the walls were all a murky green. Below each one was an identifier: K1, K2, K3, K4, S5, S6, S7, S8. The *K* stood for Kidon, and the team members included, in order, Yaron, Doron, Dima, and Imri. The *S* represented *Shayetet 13*, the batwings, the Israeli equivalent of the U.S. Navy SEALs. When it came to the water, they were the toughest of the tough, and Nicole was very glad they were part of the rescue team.

Below the eight smaller screens was a large, wide monitor. It showed a color view of Saad Salim's yacht from a drone hovering high above. All looked calm and peaceful, a large circle of light in the blackness of the Arabian Sea. Nicole counted six guards patrolling the well-lit upper deck. The helicopter was still on the pad.

"Twenty meters," said Liora.

"Shut down the alarm system," Cohen said.

"*Root.*" Nicole had wormed her way into the yacht's computer system earlier in the evening.

For as vast as the ship was, its internals were fairly simple to navigate. Her fingers flew across the keyboard, and a red light on her screen turned green.

"Garage alarm is off," she reported.

"Open the garage door."

"*Root*," Nicole said, acknowledging Cohen's second order.

A little more tapping, and she watched an animation of a door sliding up. She halted its progress after 2 meters. No use making more noise than she already had.

"Five meters out," Liora said.

Suddenly, the screens on the wall filled with greenish-black images from the night vision body cams on each operative as they stepped up into the boat's garage. On K1 and K2, Nicole watched as Yaron and Doron moved to the tenders and the other watercraft and began disabling them. K4, S5, and S7 shifted around a lot as they removed their scuba gear. Then they swung out the door. The cameras now showed close-ups of the side of the yacht as they suctioned their way up its hull.

Team member S8 remained in the ocean with the underwater scooters. The monitors of K3, Dima, and S6 had Nicole's greatest attention, though. They were the ones with the tracker that would lead them to Nir. But they couldn't go anywhere yet. They needed to give K4, S5, and S7 time to arrive on the upper deck. Imri, K4, was headed for the helipad. The last thing they wanted was for Ali Kamal to escape aboard the helicopter before he had a chance to enjoy the fireworks. The two *Shayetet* commandos would scuttle the lifeboats. Once the three operatives cleared the railing to begin this work, Dima would go.

"Nicole, you're ready for shutdown?" Cohen asked.

"Ready." If there was any problem—gunfire erupted, someone was caught, another boat arrived—she was prepared to shut down the power throughout the entire boat. Lahav had also created a device that would scramble all cell service for a 1,000-meter radius. The tiny apparatus had been released by the rescue team on their trip in, and now it was deployed 30 meters from the yacht awaiting activation. Its only drawback was that it would sever communication with the team. In addition, he'd created a false automatic identification system signal, so to those monitoring the AIS, it would look like the boat was still there and doing just fine.

On the drone monitor, Imri and the *Shayetet* commandos came into view as they drew closer and closer to the top. A triple click sounded on the coms, and a light showed it was from Dima.

"He's got a strong signal," said Yossi.

Cohen answered, "Yes he does."

"K4, you have a dirty approaching your position," Liora told him.

Imri and the commandos paused. The guard looked out over the water, then moved to port.

Liora looked at Cohen, who nodded. "K4, S5, S7, proceed."

Less than a minute later, they were on the upper deck.

"Go, K3!" Cohen yelled.

The picture on Dima's monitor started moving rapidly. It looked very much like a First Person Shooter game with a Galil as the primary weapon. It passed through the garage and out into the hallway. Nicole could remember seeing all this when she'd visited Salim's boat with Alicia. It was surreal viewing it this way now, as the lair of the enemy.

Doors passed on either side. Then Dima came to a "T." To the left, Nicole remembered, was the elevator. Dima turned right. At the end of the hall was a door. A double click sounded, and she saw Dima's hand motioning toward it.

Her leg bounced nervously, and her hands were sweaty. What would they find inside? Was Nir really there? How bad was he? Was he even still alive?

Dima's hand reached for the knob, and he eased the door open. It was dark inside. K3 and S6 stepped in and scanned the surroundings. Two more clicks sounded, and Dima began moving rapidly forward. Suddenly, his monitor was filled with Nir's green, glowing body.

"Shut it down!" cried Cohen. "Shut it down!"

Nicole pulled her eyes away from the K3 monitor and saw a gunfight taking place on the upper deck. *I don't even know if he's alive or dead! Dima, quick, please tell me how he is.*

But she couldn't wait for his report. Her fingers were flying across the keyboard. On her monitor, every system turned from yellow to black. The yacht was dead in the water.

Then the monitors went black.

Lahav called, "Scrambler is deployed. We have three hours until the battery dies and everyone's phone is back online."

Nicole stared at the blank monitors.

Please, Lord, bring him back to me. Protect them all, and bring Nir back.

CAFALA BAHR, ARABIAN SEA, OFF MUMBAI, INDIA— 22:25 / 10:25 P.M. IST

"I will never allow that moron on my boat again. I'm sorry for introducing you to him to begin with," Saad said to Mousavi as they lounged in the salon.

"I have no doubt that Israel has all sorts of plans to try to stop our nuclear aspirations, but I'm also becoming sure of one more thing." The general pointed to the floor. "That agent down there knows nothing about any of them. No one can endure what he has suffered without telling everything he knows."

"I agree with you." *I was such a fool letting Ali bring him aboard. This can only end badly.* "Will you take the Jew with you?"

"Why would I? What could I possibly do with him? 'Supreme Leader, here is a Mossad agent who was in Doha to meet with the Saudis. Should we try him as a spy?' He would throw me out of his office. And General Qaani! I can't imagine what he would do. He would probably demote me to Iraq to train all the illiterate, donkey-riding militias. No, I don't want him. I say we give the doctor one more shot at him, then we dump him in the ocean."

"Then that's what we'll do." Saad put his tumbler against his forehead, and the ice tinkled inside. "Ali is giving me such a headache. I just want him gone for good."

The general leaned toward him and pointed with the hand that held his own glass. "I will tell you this. If he gives us any more trouble, I will personally put an end to him. Maybe I'll make a friend of the Saudi crown prince in the process."

The men laughed.

"Please, just promise me that if you feel you need to end him, do not do it on my boat. I don't want to have to—"

The room went dark.

"What is going on?" asked the general.

"Give it just a moment for the backup generators to come on," Saad said as his eyes adapted to the glow of the night sky coming in through the windows.

But nothing happened. And it was eerily silent. Normally, by now some motor would be humming or air would be blowing. But there was absolutely nothing.

"How long does this usually take?" the general asked.

"Not this long." Pulling his phone out of his pocket, Saad turned on its flashlight. As he did, he noticed at the top of the screen it said *No Service*.

He rose and walked to the bar. "Check your phone to see if you have service."

"I don't. That's strange. I haven't had any trouble before."

In a cabinet to the right of the bar, Saad pulled out two battery-powered lanterns. He pulled them open, and light flooded the room. As he passed one to Mousavi, a realization hit him. Power, backup generator, and cell service all out at once. One is unfortunate, two is bad luck, but three is . . .

"The Israelis."

CHAPTER 61

Nir awoke with the opening of the door. Panic filled him, and his breathing accelerated. He pulled himself back protectively against the wall. But maybe his Filipino friend had returned.

A shadow crossed the floor, then knelt next to him. The glow from outside the door went out, plunging the room in total darkness.

"Nir, it's time to go."

It was Dima's voice. Tears of relief flooded Nir's eyes.

"Coms are down. Secondary protocols."

Nir was momentarily confused until he heard another voice say, "*Root.*"

"Come on, *achi*, we've got to get you on your feet."

The second man began cutting the ropes from Nir's extremities. The pain was intense, and the raw circles around his ankles and wrists caused him to involuntarily pull back.

"*Ani mitnatzelet,*" the man said, apologizing as he continued his work. Nir didn't recognize his voice.

When Nir was free, Dima helped him stand. It had been so long since he had been on his feet that his legs were weak, and his knees and ankles were swollen from the cricket bat. He tried to take a step but stumbled.

"Need me to carry you?" Dima asked.

"I've got it." His arm went around Dima's neck, and the man half led, half dragged Nir out of the room.

"You smell like borscht," Nir said, his head lolling against the Russian's shoulder.

"You don't want to know what you smell like. I can't wait to throw you into the ocean."

Footsteps sounded up ahead. Two suppressed double taps echoed in the hallway, followed by the sound of bodies hitting the ground. In the brief muzzle flashes, Nir saw a soldier in front of them wearing night vision goggles. He wore the coveted batwings of *Shayetet 13* on his shoulders.

"Careful," Dima said, and Nir felt the bodies of the dead men under his bare feet as they passed them.

After another turn, light appeared ahead. As they approached, Nir saw it was from the moon reflecting off the ocean's surface. Two men were waiting, and one more was in the water.

"*Achi*, you look like death." It was Yaron. "And you smell worse."

"I could still knock you out, old man," Nir wheezed.

"Right this way, *Ha'mefaked*," said the man in the water.

Nir looked to Dima, who said, "It's all right. I'm going to strap you to me, and we've got air."

Nir nodded. He felt steady enough to let go of Dima.

Two more shots fired from the doorway of the garage.

"We've got to get going," called the *Shayetet 13* commando as he changed mags in his gun.

From somewhere outside the garage door, Nir could hear unsuppressed shots fired. "Wait. Where's Imri?" he asked, looking around.

Yaron answered. "Taking care of the chopper up top. He and a couple of other batwings will join us as soon as they can."

Doron stepped forward and took charge of him. "Come on. We've got to get you tanked and strapped in."

Three minutes later, Nir and Dima dropped into the water. Nir hadn't realized how many places his skin had opened until that moment. The pain was so intense that he probably would have frozen up and sunk to the bottom if he hadn't been strapped to the back of the big Russian Jew.

Soon, they were moving. Nir had no opportunity to reflect or even think at all as he held on to Dima's back. He didn't like the closed-in feeling of being trapped underwater, and the scuba gear was making him feel claustrophobic. On top of that, the continual movement of the underwater scooter kept the saltwater passing over and through his cuts and gouges. Letting his brain shut down, he lost track of time.

He felt the deceleration before he saw the boats. When they surfaced, he spotted two Morena rigid-hulled inflatables with two men on each one. As they drew alongside, the *Shayetet 13* commandos tied off the underwater scooters and hauled the men in. Nir was pulled in first, followed by Dima. With surprising gentleness, Dima toweled Nir off, then wrapped him in a blanket. One of the batwings handed Nir a communication bud, which he placed into his ear.

"This is Team Lead," he said.

The cheering on the other end was deafening. Once again, tears came to Nir's eyes. *I am not going to cry in front of* Shayetet 13. *I'll dive back into the water first!*

"How are you, Team Lead?" Nicole's voice. For a time, he hadn't known if he'd ever hear it again.

Pushing down his emotions, he said, "Been better. I'll survive. Where's Imri?"

"We have no contact with him. We scrambled the cell service around the boat, which left us without coms. This is the first we've heard from your team since the op started."

Nir's relief at his rescue now turned to agitation. His body screamed for rest and medical attention, but as long as Imri was still out there, he wouldn't leave. The rest of the team was finishing loading in.

"Boss, you okay?" asked Doron.

"I will be when Imri gets here. When and with what are we rendezvousing?"

"We're being picked up by a sub five kilometers from here. They're waiting for us now."

There was a stir in the water, and an underwater craft surfaced, followed by a second and a third. The first pilot removed his mask, and Nir breathed a sigh of relief.

"You think the whole world waits on you, Zaid?" Nir called out.

"Okay, Boomer."

On his com, he heard Liora say to someone, "*Esh*! I told you he'd say it."

Once Imri was aboard, Nir asked, "You get the chopper grounded?"

"It's not going anywhere. How're you doing?"

Nir just nodded. His words were gone. His energy was gone. His will to even sit up was rapidly leaving.

"Preparing to blow the boat," Liora said.

Somehow, Nir had forgotten about this part. The whole purpose behind his capture and torture. The final act that would open the Saudi skies to the Israeli Air Force so they could crush the Iranian nuclear program once and for all. Operation Bezalel was actually happening.

Everyone on the two inflatables turned back in

the direction of the yacht so they could see the distant fireball.

Suddenly, Nir thought of the Filipino steward. And it wasn't just him. A whole crew was on board.

"Five . . ." counted Liora.

No innocents. That's a Mossad creed. Israel doesn't do collateral damage, if at all possible.

"Four . . ."

Nir jumped up and tried to say something, but he broke into a coughing fit.

"Three . . ."

The coughing grew until he fell back to his seat. Doron grabbed hold to steady him.

"Two—"

"Stop," Nir gasped.

"We've got you, *achi*," said Doron.

"One—"

"Stop! You don't understand. It's—"

CHAPTER 62

CARL, MOSSAD HEADQUARTERS, TEL AVIV, ISRAEL— 20:22 / 8:22 P.M. IDT

top!" The power of the *ramsad*'s voice startled Nicole.

"Hold, hold, hold!" Liora called out.

There was silence on the coms and silence in the room. All eyes were on Ira Katz.

"Tavor, talk," the *ramsad* commanded.

"*Ha'mefaked*, we can't launch yet." Nicole could barely hear Nir's strained words.

"I need a very good explanation as to why, because we are one button push away from accomplishing the entire mission—exactly as you laid out, I might add."

"You're right. But I have new information. This will not wash out the mission. It will only delay it."

"Talk."

"There are—" Nir's voice cracked, and there was a pause. "Thanks," he said to someone nearby. When he spoke again, his voice was much clearer. "In the Mossad, we take the lives of the guilty while striving to protect the innocents as much as is possible, right? *Proportionality* is what I was taught in training. If innocents must be caught up in the operation, it must be for a very good reason and there must be no other option. That was true when we planned out this mission."

"I would think that protecting Israel and the rest of the world from a nuclear Iran is a proportional cause," the *ramsad* said.

Nicole wasn't sure where Nir was going with this, but one thing was becoming evident. Her night of worrying about his safety was not over.

"It is. The *proportional* criteria is met. However, now that I've been onsite, I see another option. *Ha'mefaked*, according to our intel, there are typically twenty-four crew on board this yacht at any given time. We didn't think we could save them. Now I believe we can."

Cohen cut in. "Nir, we talked about this. It is tragic, but there is a price for working for a gunrunning, terrorist-supporting billionaire."

"But do they know that's who he is? I thought so before, but now I don't."

"Why?" asked the *ramsad*. "What made you change your mind? You know you're asking men to risk their lives for these people?"

"I know I am. But I'm asking only because it must be done. Our nation cannot protect its existence at the expense of its soul."

Cohen had moved next to the *ramsad*, and the two were now in a hushed discussion.

Nicole had never been so proud of Nir—nor so angry with him. He was right, but a voice inside kept telling her he would pay dearly for this. *Lord, I know I'm feeling doubt, and doubt is a lack of trust in You. Bless Nir and these men for their commitment to what is right. Protect them. Bring them home.*

Nir spoke again. "*Ramsad*, how many times did we have Fakhrizadeh in our sights but held back to protect the innocent? How many times did we have Soleimani dead to rights but left it to the Americans because all our options would harm his children?"

"Quiet, Tavor," Katz said.

"You have the trigger. We will blow the boat. We just have to try this first."

"Nir, shut up," Cohen yelled before going back to his discussion with the *ramsad*.

Then the *ramsad* looked at Nicole. "You've been on the boat. You've seen these people. What do you say?"

Nicole knew her next words could cost Nir his life. But like him, she didn't have a choice. "You've got to let them try."

The *ramsad*'s bloodshot eyes told her the weight of every life on those two teams bore heavily on his shoulders. "Yes, it appears I do, don't I? Tavor, I'm approving this mission. But I have two demands. First, it will be run by the *Shayetet 13* lead. Your team will be part of it, but

I want the best military operators in charge, and that's not Kidon."

"Yes, *Ha'mefaked*."

"Second, under no circumstances are you to be part of it. I want you back on the sub as soon as possible. You're in no condition to be on an assault team. Am I understood?"

No response.

"Am I understood?"

"Yes, *Ha'mefaked*."

"Good, you have one hour. Make it count."

"Thank you. Team Lead, out."

The *ramsad* leaned back into his chair and took his cell phone out of his shirt pocket. "He's going on the raid, isn't he?"

"One hundred percent," Nicole and Cohen said in unison.

ARABIAN SEA, OFF MUMBAI, INDIA— 23:01 / 11:01 P.M. IST

"I need your uniform," Nir said, pointing to one of the batwings who'd been manning the boats.

"*Tiraga*, slow down here," said S5, the *Shayetet 13* squad lead. "I say which of my team strips naked and for whom. So you're going?"

"You stopping me?"

The man put up his hands defensively. "Lighten up. It's only a question. I've just never heard of anyone defying old Ira Katz before."

Nir let his hackles settle back down. "He's a teddy bear when you get to know him."

"Yeah, a teddy bear with a limpet mine inside. Listen, Tavor. I don't recommend you go. You look like a mess, and you're bleeding all over my boat. But I also recognize that you don't give a rip about my recommendation. So as the new leader of this operation, I'm faced with a dilemma."

"Think fast," Nir said, sitting down. "Anyone have an energy bar or something?" One of the batwings pulled one out of a pocket and tossed it to him. Nir missed, but Doron caught it on the deflection.

S5 shook his head. "Listen, with what you just went through, and now you're sitting here looking like someone ran you through a fishhook factory, you're saying you want to go back to the guys who did this to you? That's stupid beyond measure. But I also have mad respect for it, and I'd like to think I'd do the same if I were in your position. So it's not my place to tell you no. Instead, I'm just going to tell you it's a really stupid idea."

"Duly noted." Relief flooded through Nir. He really didn't want a battle with this man. He needed to conserve his energy for the real struggle ahead.

Holding out his hand, he said, "Thanks . . ."

"Azoulai. Omer Azoulai. And you're not taking

the clothes off one of my men. You earn that uniform. I'll put a navy uni on our shopping list from the sub. So you're saying we need to evac twenty-four souls?"

"It's an estimate. How many more inflatables like this are on the sub?"

"They've got a total of five."

"Okay, let's bring two extra. It will be crowded, but they'll manage them ashore. I'm sure the captain and his crew can figure out how to pilot them."

"We're just leaving the boats with them? We don't have time to make them anonymous."

Nir shook his head. "No, keeping them identified will only help. Part of our mission was to make the operation distinctly Israeli. Those boats can serve as our calling cards. Now, you just tell me how we're going to get back on that yacht."

"Yeah, I've got an idea."

CHAPTER 63

30 MINUTES LATER
CAFALA BAHR, ARABIAN SEA,
OFF MUMBAI, INDIA—
23:35 / 11:35 P.M. IDT

Saad sat at the bar on the upper deck and sipped his iced bourbon. Even though the power was out, the freezer had not yet defrosted. The air was thick with humidity, and the temperature had to still be in the upper 20s. *Why does anyone choose to live here? Better question, why did I decide to come here? My curiosity over Mumbai is now officially sated.*

He swirled the liquid in the glass, then finished it off. The bottle was right there, so he poured another. *I'm quite content to get drunk tonight. If anyone deserves it, it's me.*

Turning on his stool, he admired his beautiful 12-million-dollar Sikorsky helicopter that couldn't fly. Spinning, he looked up at the rear of the bridge of his $650 million mega yacht that couldn't sail. Down below, his garage was filled with watercraft whose engines were in pieces. He held up his glass. "Congratulations, Jew-dogs! You won this one." He threw the liquor back and poured himself another one.

"Pour me one too."

Saad turned to see General Mousavi walking toward him. He got up a little unsteadily and stepped behind the bar, then pulled a large ice ball from the freezer and dropped it into a glass. He looked at the row of bottles under the bar and pulled out the Johnnie Walker Blue Label. He set it and the glass on the bartop.

"Here. A night like this, you can have your own bottle. It's supposed to be served neat, but it's just too hot in this godforsaken place for that."

The general smiled as he sat down. "It looks like I have some catching up to do."

"Where's the Saudi?"

"Hiding in his bedroom. He has four armed guards outside his door—all that's left of the eight he brought."

"How many did you lose?"

The general drank his first glass in one shot. "Two. They were good men."

"Do you think the Israelis will be back?"

"I don't think so. They got what they came for. If they did return, though, it would be to slap a mine on the boat or something like that."

Saad jumped up, then stumbled back into the bar. "Do you think they'd do that?"

The general was on his feet, helping Saad back to his stool. "I don't. The Jews have enough of a public relations problem without blowing up the

472

boat of a private citizen off the coast of one of their allies. But . . ."

"But what?"

"But I think your days of yacht ownership are over. The Jews never forget. They'll never forgive you for allowing Tavor to be tortured on your boat. If you weren't on their radar before, you certainly are now. This yacht is too easy a target. You'll never know which will be the night they either show up in your stateroom or just sink the whole thing to the bottom of the ocean. But don't feel too bad. Once Tavor tells them I was here, I probably have a hellfire missile in my near future."

The general downed his second drink and poured himself a third.

The realization of what he'd lost came over Saad. This yacht was his kingdom, his refuge. All the hours he put in at his office in Doha were just so he could disappear for weeks at a time to some new destination. He could fly to Europe or Asia or Australia or the Americas and there would be his home waiting for him just off the coast.

And that Saudi fool had just taken that from him. Saad stood and started toward the stairs.

The general caught up with him and took his arm. "Whoa, where are you going?"

"It's Kamal's fault. He stole this from me. He needs to pay."

Mousavi laughed. "*Habibi*, you won't get by

his bodyguard. You'll end up getting yourself killed on your own boat." He led him back to the bar. "Besides, you needn't worry. Kamal will pay. I will make sure he's a dead man before this year is out. I can even make sure your name is the last word he hears in this life."

Saad sat on a stool with a vicious smile on his face. "Thank you, Arash. I would like that."

"So while you are still somewhat clearheaded, I need to know what we are to do now."

"You mean how do we get off this giant worthless bucket of bolts?" Saad asked with a bitter laugh.

"That's what I mean."

"We can't! That's the funny part. We're stuck, at least for now."

Mousavi's face was beginning to darken, and Saad realized the general had been calm only because he was pacifying a drunk. His serenity had lasted only so long. Pushing his glass away, he tried to force himself sober.

"Can we shoot off any flares?" asked the general.

"No. The last thing we want is attention. I'm not sure why no one has been sent to us yet because of our AIS losing power, but I'm perfectly happy they haven't. I don't want the Indian Coast Guard coming aboard and finding armed men and freshly made bullet holes."

"So what do we do?"

"Nothing. Just enjoy the last night on board the yacht the best we can. In the morning, my office will try to contact me as they do every morning. When they are unable to, they will dispatch a discreet search. Once they discover us stranded, they'll transport us to shore."

"And there's nothing else we can do in the meantime? There is no other way ashore?"

"The Jews were very thorough. They scuttled the lifeboats and destroyed every mode of transportation. They obviously wanted to be very sure we didn't follow them."

The general finished his third drink and said, "That's the part that doesn't make sense to me. Why the lifeboats and the Sea-Doos and all the rest? It's not like we'd be able to give chase in those. It's almost as if they wanted to keep—"

The general reached into his pocket. Saad, too, felt a sudden vibration in his. He pulled out his phone and saw he was being notified with message after message.

"Well, that's good news," he said. But when he looked at the general, the man wasn't smiling. In fact, his look was quite the opposite.

Explosions sounded from the bow. The general grabbed Saad's arm and ran toward the stairs.

CHAPTER 64

23:48 / 11:48 P.M. IDT

The four quadcopter drones released their payloads of four flashbang missiles, each ten seconds after the one before. The projectiles plunged to the long bow of the yacht and detonated. Every time a new batch hit, the IRGC guards just starting to recover from the last barrage were once again thrown into confusion. Meanwhile, from out of the dark came four rigid-hulled inflatables—two to the bow, one to the stern, and one off the starboard quarter next to the garage.

Nir was in the boat off the port bow. When the boat was alongside, grappling hooks were shot up over the railing on the upper deck. The attached rope was threaded through a powered ascender, and he, Imri, and Dima were pulled up to the deck. Yaron and Doron were at the starboard quarter. After Lahav had shut down the scrambler, Nicole would restore power to that part of the boat and remotely open the garage.

The gunfire began first at the starboard while Nir was still climbing over the railing. Omer Azoulai was leading his team on that side of the boat. Imri took lead, followed by Nir, then

Dima. They moved forward toward the bridge.

Bullets whizzed past, and Nir could feel a tug on his pant leg by his calf. The three dropped to the deck. Imri and Dima opened fire. Since Nir didn't trust his aim, he'd agreed to shoot only if necessary.

"Clear," said Imri, indicating he'd dealt with the threat.

Nir didn't feel any new pain in his leg, so he stood, and the three began moving forward again. Upon reaching the stairs to the bridge, they squatted and ascended slowly. Gunfire continued from all around the upper deck, but none appeared directed toward them. When they reached the top step, Imri peeked above the window line. A shot rang out, and his helmet flew off his head. He fell backward into the handrail, and Nir grabbed him to keep him from flipping over. He was out cold.

Nir passed him down to Dima, who began assessing his injury. Meanwhile, Nir pulled the pins on a flashbang. Using a breaching tool, he smashed a window to his left. Gunfire erupted. Nir reached to the right, opened the door, and rolled in the grenade.

"Flashbang," he said to Dima. They both closed their eyes tightly and opened their mouths to help offset the percussive slam.

Whoomp!

Nir pushed through the door, saw an IRGC

soldier stumbling backward, and put him down. Two other men cowered on the bridge's floor. One was wearing a captain's uniform. The other was maybe a tech.

"Sitrep," came Azoulai's voice over the com.

"Upper aft cleared."

"Upper bow cleared."

"Garage cleared." Nir recognized Yaron's voice.

"Bridge cleared," he reported. Then he watched as Dima carried Imri in and laid him down on the floor. Dima turned and gave Nir a thumbs-up.

Thank You, God.

"How many down?"

"Three."

"Four."

"Nil," said Yaron.

"Two," Nir said.

"With the six before, that gives us fifteen. So we have at least five more guns out there."

Nir had a hunch. "Were all the dirties IRGC?"

All answered in the affirmative.

"I would bet the rest are with Ali Kamal. They're his boys." Turning toward the captain, he said, "Kamal's suite. Give me a number."

"It's 305," the man said with a shaky voice.

Nir pictured the schematic in his mind. "Third level. End of stern hall. Be careful. I'm guessing they're all there. And there's one more Quds guy around."

"*Root,*" said Azoulai, then gave orders for taking the hallway.

Nir turned to the man next to the captain and spoke in Arabic. "You know where all the staff on this boat are hiding, don't you?"

The man nodded quickly. Nir squatted and said, "Something very bad is about to happen on this yacht. I have boats to take you and the crew away from here before it does. I need you to gather them and take them to the garage. Do you understand me?"

Again, the man nodded.

"Listen, your instinct is to not trust me, but you know who I am, don't you? You know I'm the one they had locked in that room?"

"I know that."

"Good. One of you helped me. I'm here to give that help back. Do you understand?"

"I understand."

"Do you trust me?"

"I trust you."

Nir put his hand on the young man's shoulder. "Good. Now go save their lives."

He scrambled to his feet and hurried out the door.

"I can help," said the captain, standing.

"Sit down. I don't trust you as far as I can throw you, which isn't too far right now. You had to know all about what's been going on here.

479

You'll get out of this alive—but only if you play your cards right."

Nir heard a groan and saw Imri rolling onto his side. The young man threw up, then grimaced.

"Dude, you're polishing my boots," Dima said, stepping back from the mess.

"Hey, *achi*, you look worse than I do," Nir said with a smile.

"Impossible." A trickle of blood trailed sideways down Imri's forehead. "Israeli-made armor. I'm a fan."

"Good. Rest a minute, then we'll hopefully have a date in the salon."

A long burst of muffled gunfire erupted from somewhere down below. It was followed by an explosive blast, then a second. After that the gunfire grew more sporadic.

"Third deck cleared. All dirties are down."

Azoulai said, "We've got three in custody. We're ready for our mystery guest."

"On our way," Nir responded.

Dima helped Imri to his feet, and the three walked down the stairs to the salon. Only once did Dima make a comment about how pitiful the two of them were.

By the time they arrived at the door, Nir could hardly walk. He was exhausted and leaned heavily on the Russian. His shirt was soaked, and he smelled like sweat and blood.

"You good?" Imri asked.

"I'm good." Nir let go of Dima, stood to his full height.

Fake it until you make it.

He walked in.

CHAPTER 65

00:03 / 12:03 A.M. IDT

Saad Salim, General Arash Mousavi, and Ali Kamal all sat on separate chairs, hands and feet bound. Nir noticed the surprise register on each when they saw him come in.

Nir snapped his fingers and turned to Azoulai, who was standing by the bar. "That reminds me. One of the staff is dressed like a doctor and will probably say he's the ship's medic. He's not. I wouldn't mind having a word with him."

"*Root.*" Azoulai whispered something to one of his men, who hustled out the door.

"You boys look like you've seen a ghost," Nir said.

"Just kill us and die, Jew," said Mousavi.

Kamal's eyes widened even more.

"You don't look ready to be killed," Nir said to him.

"No. Please. I am so sorry for what I did. It was these two. They forced me to do it—to try to extract information from you."

"You know, that's what I was figuring, Ali. You're just caught up in this bad situation, right? Well, don't worry. I'm really here for the general. He's a very bad man."

482

Kamal nodded. "He is. If you only knew the things he's done. In fact, I can tell you all about them. Take me with you, and I'll tell you everything."

Mousavi was turning red with rage.

Maybe I should let Mousavi loose so he can kill Kamal. Cage match. That could be fun.

But that wasn't why he was here.

He slapped his forehead. "Wait a second. I'm sorry. I'm not really thinking straight. You know, concussion and all. I'm not here for Mousavi. I'm here for you, *habibi*."

Kamal's eyes grew big again, and now tears streamed down his face.

"That's right. I have a little message from your crown prince. He says . . . You know, I actually think your crown prince is kind of a jerk. So on second thought, I don't think I'll deliver his little speech." Turning to Azoulai, he said, "Let's go."

"That's all?"

"I don't have the energy for anything else."

Nir snapped his fingers again. Turning to Saad, he said, "You're the art lover. You've got those two original Marcos paintings, don't you?" Nir spotted them, each on a different wall. "There they are. Beautiful. I've got to know, are you a Marilyn or a fruit bowl?"

Saad did his best to look dignified, but his eyes were glassy. Nir wondered if he wasn't a little drunk.

"I prefer the fruit bowl."

Nir turned to Dima. "I totally had him pegged as a Marilyn." He whispered something to the Russian.

The big man walked over and picked up the chair Saad was sitting in, then carried it to where *Fruit Bowl* hung. He set the man down so he had a full view of the painting.

"I'll give your compliments to the artist."

There was a commotion at the door. The doctor came stumbling in, apparently pushed along by his *Shayetet* escort. He fell into a large decorative vase, which shattered beneath him. He landed sprawled out on the ground.

"Dr. Ghasemi, welcome to our little party," Nir said. He walked toward the man. "Yaron, would you kindly help him up?"

The Kidon operative hoisted the small man up by his zip-tied wrists. The doctor cried out.

Nir stood in front of the man and looked him up and down. He was whimpering and had turned his face so that he could only see Nir out of the corner of his eye.

"Look at me," Nir said. The man whimpered more.

"Look at me!" Nir took the man's face in his hand, squeezing hard into his cheeks. He twisted his head so they were face-to-face. "I've got one thing to say to you, you evil, little slug of a man."

Pulling his fist back, Nir punched forward. His fist stopped centimeters away from the man's face. Nir leaned forward and whispered in the man's ear, "Boom."

"Zip up his legs and put him with the others," Nir said as he strode away.

As soon as he cleared the door, he collapsed into a wall. Dima pushed past everyone and picked him up, then carried him.

"Put me down," Nir kept insisting, but the Russian ignored him.

When they got to the garage, it was packed with people being helped aboard the boats one by one.

Finally, Dima let Nir stand, although he was essentially holding him up.

"Bring me the captain," Nir said.

Doron found the man and brought him over. "I'm counting on you to get these people safely ashore. Do you understand? If you double-cross them or any harm comes to even one, I will find you, and I will kill you. Tell me *Yes, sir.*"

"Ye-yes, sir," the man stammered.

Nir held him with a hard stare, then said, "Go."

"Excuse me. Excuse me."

Nir turned and saw a young Filipino man. Although he couldn't recognize his face, his voice brought tears to Nir's eyes.

"Thank you. Thank you. Thank you," the young man said, shaking his hand.

Nir pulled him close and wrapped him in a hug. "Thank *you*."

As he held him, the Filipino whispered, "Jesus, friend. Jesus, friend."

Nir released him and said, "Yeah, you just might be right about that."

The rest of the staff and crew were loaded onto the boats, and they set off for shore. The *Shayetet 13* and Kidon teams left soon after, heading the opposite direction.

ARABIAN SEA, OFF MUMBAI, INDIA — AUGUST 24, 2021—00:43 / 12:43 A.M. IST

The two hadn't stopped arguing. Saad was doing his best to tune them out, as well as the incessant sniveling of the doctor, whom the Israelis had left hog-tied on the salon's floor. He wasn't quite sure how he was going to die, but he was positive he would—and soon. He didn't want to spend his final moments on this earth caught up in a blaming squabble. Ultimately, it really didn't matter whose fault it was. That would be for Allah to sort out.

His eyes focused on the ugly brown globe contained in the fruit bowl. He'd finally looked it up last night and discovered it was a jicama. A perusal of Wikipedia informed him that it was not a fruit but a root vegetable, like a turnip. That was so odd to him. Amidst all these colorful, exotic fruits, Marcos had painted a colorless edible root. Something about that was so profound. Was that representative of her? Was that how she felt in her life or in the art world?

If only I had her back on my boat. The questions I would ask her. There's so much I still don't—

CARL, MOSSAD HEADQUARTERS, TEL AVIV, ISRAEL— 22:45 / 10:45 P.M. IDT

The fireball was spectacular. It filled the large monitor on CARL's wall with light. When the concussive wave hit the drone, it briefly went off course but then soon reacquired its position.

All those months of work, thought Nicole. *It was all for this moment. Nir must be going out of his mind watching it from the water.*

Minutes later, she learned Nir had missed the fireball and the concussive wave and the wake that rocked the boat and the moment when the last of the yacht's bow submerged into the Arabian Sea. He hadn't experienced any of it. Instead, he was passed out on the floor of the inflatable.

SEPTEMBER 2021
[ONE WEEK LATER]

CHAPTER 66

ONE WEEK LATER
EILAT, ISRAEL—SEPTEMBER 1, 2021—
14:45 / 2:45 P.M. IST

I t is so stupid hot," Nir said. According to the forecast, they were in a cooling trend, which for Eilat in September meant the high was still 38 degrees Celsius. In just the short walk from the car onto the beach, he'd already sweated through his shirt.

"If you're going to bring me to the Red Sea," said Nicole, "I won't spend the whole day somewhere in air-conditioning. I'll be here, stupid hot or not." She was carrying both their beach chairs and a small cooler. Nir was on crutches.

"You know these things weren't made for sand," he said, trying to keep both balance and forward progress. The docs had said that it would only be another day or two before the swelling would be down enough for him to walk on his own.

"Want me to get some of those big hunky guys playing volleyball to carry you?" she asked with a wink.

He just growled.

She pointed to the left. "Look, there's an open one."

"Of course no one is using the umbrella. Everyone's inside in air-conditioning."

Nicole laughed and punched his arm. Then realizing what she'd just done, she said, "I'm sorry. You okay?"

"Oh, the abuse I endure."

They reached the large, thatched umbrella, and Nicole set up the beach chairs. Nir settled into his with a sigh and laid his crutches in the sand. She knelt next to the cooler and lifted the lid.

"Ah, finally, the mystery is about to be revealed," he said.

"Prepare to be amazed." She removed two tall glasses and set them on the lid. Then she opened a container of blueberries and dropped a handful into each glass. Next came some peach slices. This was followed by a bottle of Torani vanilla syrup, which Nicole tipped briefly. After placing the bottle back into the cooler, she took out a muddler and began mushing the ingredients together.

"Wait a second. Are you making *gazoz*? Who taught you to do that?"

Nicole had a big smile on her face. "Liora and Dafna. They had a CARL *gazoz* party a few days ago with the Kidon team. I think it was just an excuse for Liora to see Imri. But look at this. They even gave me a muddler."

Imri and Liora? That's interesting, he thought as he watched Nicole work. *Going to have to keep my eye on that.*

"You never cease to surprise me," he said.

Nicole beamed at the compliment.

Next came ice and sparkling water. Then she topped each glass with a sprig of mint and slid in a straw.

She passed both glasses to Nir, who held them as she stood, brushed sand off her knees, and took her seat. He passed one glass to her and said, *"L'Chaim."*

They clinked their glasses, and he drank deeply of the classic Israeli soda. It was perfect for a hot day. A breeze came up off the water and passed over his face. *Life couldn't get much better than this,* he thought. He reached out and took Nicole's hand, then closing his eyes, he soaked in the moment.

He woke as the glass slipped from his hand. It landed softly, its contents pouring into the sand.

"Oh, Nicole, I'm so sorry! I don't know what happened."

She smiled, but he saw concern in her eyes. She passed her glass to him. "It's okay. It's a little sweet for me anyway. How are you doing?"

"I'm fine. Just dozed. Between the sun and the breeze, it was just too nice."

"Good. Now, how are you really doing?"

Nir looked at that half-smile he loved. There

was wisdom, affection, and strength behind it. It was also her *Be honest with me* look.

"Physically, I'm getting better. I still can't believe it was two days before I woke up in Ichilov. Once I did, I had to get out of there— away from being hooked to all those wires and hoses. I hated that. Well, you saw me. Then they had me so drugged up. I was hearing voices and seeing shadows. I didn't like what those pain pills were doing to my mind."

"You were really out of it."

"I remember bits and pieces of the next couple of days, though. Like the *ramsad* coming by. One look at me, and I think his whole plan to rip me a new one for disobeying his order went out the window."

"No, he knew you weren't going to listen right from the beginning. I was sitting next to him when he told you not to go."

Nir laughed. "I didn't know that. Anyway, as soon as I could think clearly, I told them to get me off the drugs. Two days later I was released. I'm still pretty sore, but it's survivable. And now I'm here with you enjoying the beautiful scenery of the Red Sea. And speaking of beautiful scenery, how is Alicia?"

"That was the worst deflection ever, so don't think I'm letting you get away with it. But Alicia is great. Just talked to her a couple of days ago. She bought a house for her parents. Of course, she's still living in the same dive apartment, but that's just her. Oh, she's also building a school somewhere in Uganda west of Kampala. She's going there in November. Invited me to come along. She said you're invited, too, if you want to join us."

"I'll think about it. Glad she's able to do something good with all that gun money."

"I like to think it's the oil money that paid for the paintings. Helps me to sleep a little better at night. I'm also going to talk with her about ending our little partnership. I think we've gotten her to a good place. She doesn't need our help anymore."

"Good call."

She laid one hand on his arm. "Now, back to our pre-deflection conversation. How are you really doing?"

"Again, physically, I'm getting better. But the other stuff, the mental side, that's been a little harder to get over."

"What's going on?"

Nir hesitated. He wasn't big on being vulnerable with anyone. *But if I hope this relationship will keep growing, I need to trust Nicole even with things like this.*

"Honestly, I'm waking up two to three times a night. The dreams are so vivid, so clear. Sometimes I'm watching it take place, like I'm in an out-of-body situation. I can see on my face how the pain is breaking me down, but I can't step in to stop it. Sometimes I'm back where I was, feeling everything they're doing to me. Sometimes I'm even in both places, though I don't know how that works."

He gave a bitter chuckle. "But it's not even feeling it over and over physically. It's the help-lessness. Knowing someone has complete power over me and there's nothing I can do to stop it. That's what wakes me in a panic."

Nicole reached over and took hold of Nir's hand again. "You told me Jesus showed you He was there, but you didn't tell me how."

This was the part of his ordeal most confusing to him. He'd called out to Jesus for help, and it seemed like he'd received an answer. He didn't believe in coincidences, and the young Filipino man showing up when he did gave him exactly what he needed to push through until he was rescued. But was he Jesus? Obviously, he knew the man himself wasn't Jesus. But was his appearance Jesus showing He was there? Nir just didn't know. And for that reason, he'd decided to keep that encounter to himself. At least for now.

Still, he had thought a lot about Jesus in the hospital and been looking for the right time to tell Nicole about it. He was pretty excited to see her reaction.

"I can't really tell you how He showed

Himself," he said. "It just seemed like He made it clear He was there with me."

Nicole looked at him. She knew there was more, and he was grateful she didn't press the point.

Instead, she asked, "So what are you doing with that?"

"With the fact that Jesus showed Himself somehow? I thought a lot about that. I think now Jesus and I have kind of an understanding."

Nicole looked at him curiously. "What kind of understanding?"

"Well, first, I'm not denying He's real anymore. I mean, there's more to Him than just historical Jesus. So I figure that's a big step forward. But also, it's like He and I get each other now. He wants me to keep helping people, which I'm great with. And along the way, He'll step in when I need Him."

Nicole raised her eyebrows. "So this is what you've figured out? Jesus is like the Hutch to your Starsky? Did you talk to a chaplain or read some pamphlet?"

Nir was animated now. "No, it's just what makes sense to me. You know, as I've worked the whole thing through in my head."

"Got it. You know, I've got to give your logic process an *A*. Your conclusions? You better hope I grade on a curve. Who do you think Jesus really is?"

"I'm still figuring that out. You say He's God

Himself. I get that. But as a Jew, that sounds weird and maybe a little blasphemous. But who knows? You could be right. But maybe He's an angel. Like the ultimate archangel. Or maybe some other sort of spiritual being more powerful than angels but not quite God. I mean, we don't know all that's in the spiritual world, do we?"

"We don't."

"Or maybe He's like a Christian version of a *bodhisattva*."

Nicole shook her head and chuckled. "A Christian *bodhisattva*?"

"Yeah, like in Buddhism. I was reading about it in an in-flight magazine a while back. They're these guys who postpone *nirvana* so they can help people out."

"And to you, that makes more sense than 'In the beginning was the Word, and the Word was with God, and the Word was God'?"

Nir began to deflate a little. She wasn't taking this quite like he'd hoped. She wasn't upset or anything, but she also wasn't sharing the same excitement at his spiritual progress.

"I don't know. You may be right. He probably is God. Again, I promised you I would listen, and what you said makes more sense than ever. And, yes, there may come a day when I will, as you say, 'make Him my Lord and Savior.' "

"Please don't ever air quote again," Nicole said with mock seriousness.

Nir laughed. "My bad. But for now, that concept of Jesus as Savior still doesn't fully make sense to me. I know it's working for you. I see your peace and your hope and all the rest. But the free gift part still doesn't make sense to me. I'd much rather make a bargain. I'm just happy to know Jesus really does exist, and He doesn't seem to hate my guts even though according to all the people in the Crusades I was the one who nailed Him to the cross."

Nicole squeezed his hand. "You're right. He doesn't hate you. I've told you before, it's just the opposite."

"Right. That verse you asked me to memorize. God loved the world, so He sent Jesus, and anyone who believes in Him will have eternal life."

"Pretty close. I'm so glad you now realize Jesus is there for you in this life. But that verse also says He can be with you in your death, an event you've been flirting with a little too much lately."

"Speaking of flirting, how about you scoot— Shh," Nir said suddenly, putting a finger to his lips. "There they are."

Nicole looked at him with surprise. He kept his finger to his lips until he could see she heard them too.

It was just a low rumble, but it was rapidly increasing in volume. Then Nir could see the source, and he pointed to the west. Two jets whooshed overhead, followed by another two, then another two. Squadron after squadron of F-35s and F-16s roared by.

"Is that . . ."

"It is," Nir yelled so he could be heard. "The Lions of the South squadron. F-35s and F-16s out of Nevatim Air Base near Be'er Sheva. They've got to pass over us so they can skirt the southern tip of Jordan, then pass into Saudi Arabia and on to Iran."

It was an awe-inspiring sight, and Nir could feel the thunder in his chest. He said, "In *yeshiva*, when I was a kid, we learned the Torah says when someone was to be put to death, their accusers had to throw the first stones. We can't throw a stone, but I thought we needed to see this to bring closure."

He watched jet after jet pass over until the last was gone. Then he turned to Nicole and saw tears slipping down her cheeks. She was right to cry. What was about to happen was necessary but tragic. Sadly, when evil goes down, it takes innocent victims with it.

He reached over and took hold of her forearm. "Let's go."

Nir pushed himself up on his crutches and balanced himself as Nicole folded up the chairs. When she was done, he leaned over and kissed the side of her head. Then he began his journey back to the car.

AUTHORS' NOTE

Living day by day with a sword hanging over your head—that is the experience of the Jewish Israeli citizen. And while the attitudes of several neighboring states have upgraded from intense hatred to strong dislike due to the Abraham Accords, there are still plenty of countries who want nothing more than to see the State of Israel pushed into the sea. Chief amongst these enemies is Iran.

At some point, the radical Islamic regime in Iran made a truly brilliant tactical decision. Rather than face their enemies head-on, they invested heavily in the many terrorist militias in Syria, Iraq, and Yemen. Why invite direct military retaliation by Israel or Saudi Arabia by firing one of your own missiles when you can arm a small group of terrorists with a truck full of rockets or drones and let them bear the brunt of the payback?

Israel has been regularly dealing with these militias through surface-to-surface and air-to-ground strikes. Sadly, it has become routine. But what will elevate it all to the next level is if Iran is able to supply to several of these proxy militias dirty bombs or even small nuclear devices. Not only will there be the threat of a nuclear-tipped ballistic missile landing on a city, but there will be the very real danger of personally transportable devices being smuggled into a country that can kill thousands of people at a time. This is why Israel is so determined to ensure that Iran does not become a nuclear power.

It is this threat around which we have built this book. We recognize that it is quite possible that by the time this novel is published, Iran may have already joined the nuclear-armed club. However, we felt it was worth the literary risk in order to be able to communicate the wider danger that exists for Israel and other nations due to the lethal potential of Iran's proxy militias.

Our hope is that as the reader enjoys this book, there will be three elements that will come through.

First, we want the reader to understand the risk surrounding a nuclear-equipped Iranian regime. If Iran achieves nuclear weapons, they will eventually find a way to use them one way or another.

Second, we want to shine a light on the extent the State of Israel in general and the Mossad in particular have gone through to slow down Iran's nuclear progress. To that end we have written in a genre that mixes real and fictitious events. What you read about the two Natanz attacks and the one on the TESA factory in Karaj is accurate.

Both the vault heist and the assassination of Dr. Mohsen Fakhrizadeh occurred very much as written. We only went off script when it was necessary to include our characters in the operations or when we needed to fill in holes that exist due to secrecy or a lack of information. The Mossad does occasionally make visits in order to strongly encourage foreign nationals who work for Iran's nuclear program to upgrade their résumé and look for a new employer. The final operation is fictitious, but it is an example of what would be required should Israel determine that a great show of force was necessary in Iran.

Third, our desire is for the reader to witness the struggle and gradual transformation of a secular Jew from apathetic agnosticism to realizing that salvation is found through the true Messiah who has already come. Ultimately, the spiritual journey of Nir Tavor is similar to that of every person. We must recognize that all of us have sinned and that sin separates us from God. However, in His perfect love He sent His Son, Jesus the Messiah, to die on the cross to pay the penalty for our sins. Jesus then rose again, opening the door for our future resurrection to an eternity with Him. There is nothing we can do to earn that forgiveness and eternal life. Thankfully, salvation does not come through works but is a free gift that is received by believing in Jesus

Christ, inviting Him to become our Lord and Savior, and choosing to follow God with our lives. We trust that this truth will stand out above all others in this book.

Awaiting His return,
Amir Tsarfati
Steve Yohn

Center Point Large Print
600 Brooks Road / PO Box 1
Thorndike, ME 04986-0001 USA

(207) 568-3717

US & Canada:
1 800 929-9108
www.centerpointlargeprint.com